On Sunday something washed up on shore.

A mass of seaweed. Strands of golden brown kelp shrouding an elongated shape. As Jesse stood staring down at the shape, he felt...something. A dull knife-twist of...what? Not pain. Nor interest. More inevitability. Destiny.

He fell to his knees, the chill of the sodden sand seeping through his trousers as he tried to decide where to start. The strands of kelp were spongy and cold to the touch. Clinging thickly and stubbornly to—

To what?

He encountered a piece of fine-grained wood. Smoothed, planed, varnished. Part of a ship. A section of mast or bowsprit with rope lashed to it, the tarred ends trailing.

Stop, he told himself, already anticipating what he would find. The old horror, still raw after all these years, reared up inside him. But his hands kept digging and pulling at the slimy shroud, digging and pulling, finding more and more of the mast, the broken-off end, the—

A foot. Bare. Cold as ice...

Coming in June 1998
from Susan Wiggs and MIRA Books

THE DRIFTER

SUSAN WIGGS

THE LIGHTKEEPER

MIRA BOOKS

ISBN 1-55166-301-5

THE LIGHTKEEPER

Copyright © 1997 by Susan Wiggs.

All rights reserved. Except for use in any review, the reproduction or utilization of this work in whole or in part in any form by any electronic, mechanical or other means, now known or hereafter invented, including xerography, photocopying and recording, or in any information storage or retrieval system, is forbidden without the written permission of the publisher, MIRA Books, 225 Duncan Mill Road, Don Mills, Ontario, Canada M3B 3K9.

All characters in this book have no existence outside the imagination of the author and have no relation whatsoever to anyone bearing the same name or names. They are not even distantly inspired by any individual known or unknown to the author, and all incidents are pure invention.

MIRA and the star colophon are trademarks of MIRA Books.

Printed in U.S.A.

For Jay—again and always
You're with me wherever I go.

Special thanks to Barbara Dawson Smith,
Betty Gyenes, Christina Dodd and Joyce Bell for
performing feats of impossible electronic mail
contortions in order to read and critique
the manuscript.

Also, thanks to Kristin for having brainstorms when all
I had was a weak drizzle, Debbie for the neurotic
lunches, Suzanne for the most excellent advice and
Palina Magnusdottir for the
Icelandic translations.

Finally, thank you to Robert Gottlieb and
Helen Breitweiser of the William Morris Agency;
and to Dianne Moggy and Amy Moore of
MIRA Books.

And the sea gave up the dead...
—Revelation 20:13

One

On Sunday, something washed up on shore.

The morning had dawned like all the others—a chill haze with the feeble sun behind it, iron-colored swells gathering muscle far offshore, then hurling themselves against the huddled sharp rocks of Cape Disappointment. The rising sun looked like a wound trying to break through the clouds.

All this Jesse Morgan saw from the catwalk high on the lighthouse, where he had gone to extinguish the sperm-oil lamp and start the daily chore of trimming wicks and cleaning lenses.

But it caught him, the sight down on the strand.

He wasn't certain what made him pause, turn, stare. He supposed he had always looked but rarely paid attention. If he gazed too long at the gray-bearded waves slapping the fine brown sand or exploding against the rocks, there was a danger that he would remember what the sea had taken from him.

Most days, he didn't look. Didn't think. Didn't feel.

Today he felt a disturbance in the air, like the breath of an invisible stranger on the back of his neck. One moment he was getting out his linseed oil and polishing cloths; the next he was standing in the bitter wind. Watching.

He experienced a sensation so subtle he would never quite understand what made him go to the iron rail, hold tight with one hand and lean out over the edge to look past the jut of land, beyond the square-jawed cliffs, down onto the storm-swept beach.

A mass of seaweed. Strands of golden-brown kelp shrouding an elongated shape. For all he knew it could be no more than a tangle of weeds or perhaps a dead seal, an old one whose whiskers had whitened and whose teeth had dulled.

Animals, unlike people, knew better than to live too long.

As Jesse stood staring at the shape on the beach, he felt...something. A dull knife-twist of...what? Not pain. Nor interest.

Inevitability. Destiny.

Even as the foolish thought passed through his mind, his booted feet clattered down the iron spiral of stairs. He left the lighthouse and plunged along the flinty walkway.

He didn't have to watch his step as he followed the winding, rocky path to the desolate strand. He had made the short trek a thousand times and more.

What surprised him was that he was running.

Jesse Morgan had not been in a hurry for years.

Yet his body had never forgotten the feeling of pumping thighs and of lungs filling until the sharpness hovered between pain and pleasure. But once he reached the object on the strand, he halted. Stock-still and afraid.

Jesse Morgan had been afraid for a very long time, though no one ever would have guessed it.

To the people of Ilwaco, to the two thousand souls who

lived there year-round and the extra thousand or so who migrated to the shore for the summer, Jesse Morgan was as solid and rugged and uncompromising as the sea cliffs over which he brooded in his lighthouse.

People thought him strong, fearless. He had fooled them, though. Fooled them all.

He was only thirty-four, but he felt ancient.

Now he stood alone, and the fear scorched him. He did not understand why. Until he saw something familiar within the heap of seaweed in front of him.

Oh, God. Oh, sweet Jesus. He plunged to his knees, the chill of the sodden sand seeping through his trousers, his hands trying to decide, without consulting his head, where to start. He hesitated, awkward as a bridegroom on his wedding night, about to part the final veil that draped the sweet mystery of his bride.

The strands of kelp were spongy and cold to the touch. Clinging thick and stubborn to—

To what?

He encountered a piece of fine-grained wood. Smoothed, planed, varnished. Part of a ship. A section of mast or bowsprit with rope lashed to it, the tarred ends trailing.

Stop, he told himself, already anticipating what he would find. The old horror, still raw after all these years, reared up inside him.

Stop now. He could stand and turn his back this moment, could climb the path, wend his way through the woods and rouse Palina and Magnus. Send the assistant lightkeepers to investigate.

But his hands, still the eager, persistent hands of a bridegroom, kept digging and pulling at the slimy shroud, digging and pulling, finding more and more of the mast, the broken-off end, the—

A foot. Bare. Cold as ice. The toenails like tiny sea-shells.

He drew a harsh breath. His hands kept working, the movement frantic, a rhythm pumped by his own pounding heart.

A slim calf. No, skinny. Skinny and dotted with freckles, stark against the lifeless ivory skin.

Jesse was swearing through gritted teeth. Fluent phrases spat past a clenched jaw. He used to talk to God. Now he swore to no one in particular.

Each passing second stood apart in time, crystallized by the knowledge he had been fleeing for years. He had come to the very ends of the earth to escape the past.

He could not escape it. Couldn't help thinking of it. Of what the sea had stolen from him.

And of what the sea had brought him today. A woman, of course. That put the final twist of cruel irony on it.

He quickly moved upward, uncovered the face. And almost wished he hadn't, for when he saw her, he knew why he had felt so compelled to run.

An angel had died on his beach this morning. Never mind that her halo was fashioned of kelp and endless tangled strands of dark red hair. Never mind the constellation of freckles scattered across her cheeks and nose.

This face, this pale face with its lavender bow of lips, was the one sculpted by every artist who had ever tried to turn marble to poetry. The face envisioned by hopeful dreamers who believed in miracles.

But she was dead, back in the realm of angels where she belonged, where she never should have left in the first place.

Jesse didn't want to touch her, but his hands did. His idiot bridegroom's hands. They took her by the shoulder and tugged gently, at the same time rolling the mast to which she was still tied. He saw her fully now, head to toe.

She was pregnant.

Rage charged like a thunderbolt through him. It was not enough that a beautiful young woman had been taken. But the sweet, round swell of her stomach, that dark mystery, that whispered promise, had been claimed, too. Two lives had been snuffed out by the merciless breath of the wind, by the wall-size waves, by the uncaring sea.

This was the start, Jesse thought as he unbound the ropes and gathered her in his arms, of a journey he had no desire to undertake.

The corpse flopped forward like a rag doll. A cold hand clutched at Jesse's arm. He reared back, leaving her on the seeping brown sand.

She moaned and coughed out seawater.

Jesse Morgan, who rarely smiled, suddenly grinned from ear to ear. "I'll be damned," he said, ripping off his mackintosh. "You're alive."

He settled the plaid wool coat around her shoulders and picked her up in his arms.

"I'm...alive," she echoed in the faintest of whispers. "I suppose," she added, her head drooping forward, "that's something."

She spoke no more, but began to shiver violently, uncontrollably. She felt like a large fish in its death throes, and it was all Jesse could do to keep from dropping her.

Yet even as he bore his burden up the impossibly steep slope, running faster than he'd ever run in his life, he knew with stone-cold dread that this day had brought something new, something extraordinary, something endlessly fascinating and frightening, into his world.

Two

Panic rushed over him in huge, nauseating waves. Why him? Why now? He held her very life in his hands, yet saving a stranger and her unborn child was the last thing he was prepared to do.

At the same time, he knew he must rescue her. Twelve years ago, he had dedicated his life to watching over the shoals and keeping the light burning. He had taken an oath as head lightkeeper. He had no choice. No choice.

He ran swiftly, mounting the sinuous path toward the station, then racing down the other side of the promontory and into the woods where the lightkeeper's house was located. The dead weight of her dragged at him. He took the steps two at a time, pounded across the porch, shoved the door open with his shoulder.

Plunging into the dimness of the quiet house, he brought the woman to a room off the kitchen and deposited her on the bed. The mattress was musty with disuse, the ticking worn and yellowed. He plundered a tall cabinet, finding a few old quilts and a tattersall blanket that had seen better days.

He covered the woman. She didn't stir. He tried to get her to drink something—water, whiskey—but the liquid merely trickled over the sides of her mouth and down her neck. She was out cold.

He rushed to the porch to ring the big brass bell, summoning Magnus Jonsson and his wife Palina from their bungalow a quarter mile down the woodland path. He stirred the banked coals in the kitchen stove and filled a kettle with water, setting it on to boil. Then, bracing himself for the task ahead, he returned to the woman.

He had to get the wet dress off her. Had to touch her. Gingerly, he lifted the layers of blankets. His hand shook a little as he brushed aside a sodden strand of hair and found the top button of her dress.

The act of disrobing a woman felt alien to Jesse. Yet at the same time, it seemed unbearably familiar, as if he were that bridegroom once again.

He set his jaw and undid the row of buttons. She lay unconscious, oblivious to his clumsy manipulations as he peeled off one sleeve, then the other, rolling the flimsy wool garment over her arms and legs, dropping it on the floor.

Beneath it she wore a simple shift that had once been white. Her breasts and belly stood out in pale relief against the thin fabric. With his teeth tightly clenched, he forced himself to honor her modesty and cover her, working the shift off by touch alone. Yet he didn't need his eyes to detect her graceful curves, the smooth texture of her skin.

Her skin was dangerously cool.

In his blind haste, he tore the shift as he finished dragging it down the length of her. He added it to the pile on the floor, tucked the blankets more securely around her and stood up.

He was shaking from head to foot.

Back in the kitchen, he filled canteens and bottles with hot water and placed them around her, insulated by the blankets. That done, he leaned against the rough-timbered wall of the room and closed his eyes briefly. Finished. That phase, at least, was over. The difficult part lay ahead.

The lightkeeper's house was less a home than a refuge. The one-and-a-half-story dwelling, embraced by a towering forest, had been enough for Jesse, who needed little except to survive from one moment to the next. Yet now, with the light spilling through an east-facing window and slanting across the unmoving form on the bed, the house felt small, cramped. Dingy, even.

The birth-and-death room off the kitchen was designed with the idea that a patient lying abed should be close at hand, where the heart of the house beat the strongest. In all the years Jesse had lived here, no one had occupied this room, this bed.

Until now.

She lay unmoving beneath the blankets and quilts. Her face was pale and serene. Her dark red hair fanned out in untidy hanks, stiffened by salt. She held one perfect hand tucked beneath her chin. Her delicate eyelids were webbed with faint blue lines.

I'm alive. I suppose that's something.

The words she had uttered so quietly on the beach whispered through his mind. He had thought he detected an accent of sorts, a lilting inflection that was hard to place. She hadn't opened her eyes.

He caught himself wondering what color they were.

"Who are you?" he whispered, his voice harsh. "Who the hell are you?"

She was Sleeping Beauty from the fairy tale. Her bed should be a sunlit arbor entwined with roses, not a crude bedstead with a sagging mattress. She should awaken to Prince Charming, not to Jesse Kane Morgan.

He forced himself to turn away. It hurt to look at her, the way it hurt to look directly into the sun on a summer day. Better for all concerned if she were simply whisked away, still unconscious, never knowing who had pulled her from the sea.

Yet he had an urge to sink to his knees beside the woman, to grab her by the shoulders and plead with her to live, live.

He began to pace, wondering what was keeping the Jonssons. Trying to shove aside a jolt of urgency, Jesse observed his house through new eyes, trying to see it as a stranger would. Sturdy pine furniture, hand-hewn. A plain wag-on-the-wall clock, its long pendulum measuring the moments with unrelenting reliability. The shutters were open to the morning. Palina had offered to make curtains, but Jesse had no use for frills.

The longest wall in the keeping room was lined with books. Novels by Dumas, Flaubert, Dickens. Essays and stories by Emerson, Thoreau. When Jesse left the world behind, the only possessions he'd brought along were his books. He read constantly, voraciously, escaping into worlds of make-believe. In the early years, after the tragedy had first happened, he had clung to the books like a lifeline. The babbling voices of fictional characters had blocked out the howl of emptiness that screamed through his mind. The books kept him from going insane.

Lined up neatly on shelves in the kitchen, jars and cans and crocks were stacked by height so he always knew where his supplies were. The Acme Royal stove had been well maintained, blacked over and over again throughout the years he had been here.

The years he tried his best not to count.

Impatience drove him out to the porch to ring the bell again. He gave the rope pull a quick jerk, but he needn't have. He could hear Magnus and Palina coming.

Their voices took on a hushed quality in the strange green wilderness that surrounded the Cape Disappointment Lighthouse Station. The forest floor was paved with layers of brown needles, cushioning their footfalls. They spoke in their native Icelandic, animatedly, like old friends who had just met again after a long separation.

It never ceased to amaze Jesse, the way they found constant interest and delight in one another, even after some thirty years of marriage. They had a grown son, Erik, who was simple but beloved of his parents. Strong as a young bullock, Erik spent his days working in contented silence around the station.

The Jonssons appeared around a bend in the forest path. The morning sun, filtered through lofty boughs of the soaring cedar and Sitka spruce trees, was kind to their aging faces, giving them a soft glow as they smiled, lifted their hands in greeting and hurried toward him.

Magnus Jonsson had a fisherman's deep chest and broad shoulders, the result of decades spent hauling nets and cranking winches. He had retired after an injury had taken his left hand. When most men would have lain down in defeat and died, Magnus had willed himself to heal.

Beside her adored and adoring husband, Palina looked dainty, though she was as sturdy as any pioneer in the prime of life. She had bright eyes and prominent teeth, and in her face there was an unexpected depth that hinted at a keen, quiet intelligence and a vivid imagination.

"Good day, Jesse," she said, a light singsong in her voice. "And look at the fine morning *Odin* has given us." She encompassed the small clearing with a sweep of her arm, showing off her bright orange shawl. On the slope below, the horse pasture shone in the radiance of the sun.

"All the clouds chased off and the fog burned away by the breath of *Aegir*," Magnus added.

Jesse nodded a greeting. He had grown used to their constant references to the legends of the sea. And who was he to discount them? Many of the ancient tales they recounted held an almost eerie ring of truth.

"That's not all the morning brought," he said, motioning them up the steps to the porch. He pushed open the door and held it as they moved inside. They followed him through the keeping room and past the kitchen, into the birth-and-death room.

When the Jonssons spied the woman on the bed, they froze, clutching each other's hands.

"*Hamingjan góoa,*" Magnus said under his breath. "And what is this?"

"She washed up on the beach from a shipwreck." Feeling inexplicably awkward, Jesse was reminded of a moment in his boyhood, when he'd gotten a gift he hadn't wanted. What did one say?

Thank you.

But he wasn't thankful, not in that way.

"She's still alive," he said clumsily.

Palina was already bending toward the woman, clucking like a hen over a chick. Jesse moved closer. "Isn't she?" he asked.

"Yes, yes. Alive but nearly frozen, *litla greyid*, little one. Build up the fire in the stove, Magnus," she said over her shoulder. "Ah, you've got the wet dress off her." There was no censure in her tone; she was as familiar as he with warming chilled victims.

"She needs dry clothes, quickly." Palina took one of the woman's hands and gently cradled it between her own. "Ah, blessed, blessed day. Never have I known the gods of the sea to give a man such a gift."

A gift?

Foolishness. Superstition.

Now, where the hell was he to get clean, dry clothing for a woman? He possessed only two sets of clothes—winter and summer. Kentucky jeans, several shirts and standard-issue lightkeeper's livery. Those he wasn't wearing on his back were currently in the laundry kettle, ready to be boiled on the stove. Just this morning he had put his only nightshirt in to wash.

"You must have something at your house for her to wear, Palina," he said.

"Ah, no. She's half-frozen already. Just find something—anything!"

"There is noth—" Jesse cut himself off. Against his will, he glanced at the foot of the bed, where an old sea chest sat.

"There's nothing," he lied hoarsely, his throat raw. "Look, I can get to your house and back in ten min—"

"I need the dry clothing now." Palina fixed him with a gaze that dared him to defy her. "*She* needs them now."

Jesse clenched his fists. *No.* He recoiled at the idea of plundering his past. But then, with the reluctant movements of a condemned man, he did something he'd sworn he would never do.

He lifted the lid of the sea chest and removed the sectioned tray from the top.

A scent too rich and evocative to be borne wafted from the contents, and he almost reeled back. *Emily.* He plunged his hand into the stacks of folded clothes, found the thick, smooth texture of cotton flannel, yanked it out and flung it at Palina. *I'm sorry, Emily.* "Here," he said gruffly. "I'll help Magnus with the fire."

Feeling the burn of Palina's intense curiosity, he stalked out of the house and down to the side yard, grabbing his ax from the toolshed.

He upended a huge log and lifted the ax high in both hands, bringing it down to split the timber with a single blow. The heart of the wood appeared torn and shredded, a fresh kill. Jesse split it again and again with the grim, rhythmic violence that coursed through his body.

But mere expended energy couldn't keep the demons out. He had known that even before he'd opened the sea chest—a Pandora's box he had been trying to keep shut for most of his adult life.

Though he had barely looked at the flannel nightgown he'd handed Palina, he could see the fabric in its minutest detail—the little green leaves and blue flowers, the bits of white trim circling the neckline and wrists. Worst of all, the scent still clung to the garment.

His wife's scent. It was as haunting as a melody, bringing back wave after wave of unwanted memories. He could see her, could hear the sound of her laughter and smell the soaps and powders she stroked across her skin.

Even after all these years, he still bled inside when he thought of her. Of them. Of the hopes and dreams he had so thoughtlessly shattered.

He brought the ax down relentlessly, over and over, trying to purge himself of all feeling. His shoulders ached and sweat ran down his face, into his eyes and over his neck and chest. By the time Magnus came out, a huge supply of freshly cut wood lay massacred around Jesse.

Magnus stared at the wood. "You had best come in now," he said.

The house was warm, almost oppressively so. The woman's blue dress had been added to the laundry vat on the stove. Jesse hated the thought of the stranger's garment mingling with his own in the kettle.

Palina was bent over the bed, plumping pillows behind the woman and clucking, always clucking.

"You're a meddlesome old biddy, Palina," Jesse said. He was surprised. He sounded almost...normal.

"And proud of it," she retorted.

If Jesse had been the sort of man who smiled, he would have just then. He harbored genuine liking for Magnus and Palina, who knew when to keep their distance and when to lend a hand. At the moment, he needed their help.

"Well?" Palina prodded him. "Aren't you going to ask if your little visitor is all right?"

"Is she?"

Palina nodded, smoothing her hands down the front of her white apron. "With plenty of attention and care, she and the little one will be just fine."

He almost flinched at the mention of the baby, but he forced himself to remain stoic, emotionless. "We can use the flatbed cart to get her to your place," he said.

"No," said Palina.

"Then I'll carry her—"

"Not so fast, my friend." Magnus held up his good hand. "The woman is not coming with us."

"Of course she is. Where else—"

"Here," Palina said with brisk finality. "Right here, where she can heal and grow strong in the care of the man who found her. The man for whom the gift was intended."

"We must be practical," Magnus added. "You have plenty of space here. We have but two cramped rooms and a loft for Erik."

Jesse forced out a dry bark of laughter. "That's impossible. I don't even keep a dog, for chrissakes. I can't keep a—a—"

"Woman," Palina said. "A woman who is with child. Can you not even say it? Can you not even speak the truth when it is right here before you?"

Panic flickered to life inside Jesse. The Jonssons were serious. They actually expected him to keep this stranger. Not just keep her, but tend to her every need, nurture and heal her.

"She's not staying." He tried to keep the edge out of his voice. "If you won't tend her, I'll take her to town."

Magnus spoke in Icelandic to his wife, who nodded sagely and touched her neat kerchief. "Moving her would be a terrible risk after the shock she has suffered."

"But—" Jesse clamped his mouth shut until his jaw ached. He pinched the bridge of his nose hard as if trying to squeeze out a simple solution. If Palina was right, and something terrible befell the woman as a result of moving her, he would feel responsible.

Again. Always.

"It is the law of the sea," Magnus said, running his weathered right hand through his bushy hair. "God has given her to you."

They stood together on the tiled hearth in front of the massive black stove, Palina absently tugging at a thread on Magnus's empty white sleeve. Yet her gaze never left Jesse's, and he saw again a spark of faith, ancient and obstinate, in the depths of her eyes.

Faith.

"I don't believe in the old sea legends," he said. "Never have."

"It does not matter what you believe. It is still true," Magnus said.

Palina set her hands on her hips. "There are things that come to us from beyond eternity, things we have no right to question. This is one of them."

Every aching fiber that made up Jesse Morgan leaped and tensed in painful denial. He would not, could not, accept this stranger into his house, into his world.

"She can't stay." Fear turned his voice to a whiplash of anger. "I can't give her anything. Can't give her help or hope or healing. There's nothing *here* for her, don't you understand that? She'd stand a better chance in hell."

The words were out before he realized what he was saying. They came from the poisoned darkness inside him, and they rang with undeniable truth.

Magnus and Palina exchanged a glance and some low words. Then Palina tilted her head to one side. "You will do what you must for the sake of this woman. This child."

Her eyes sharpened with insight. "Twelve years ago, the sea took from you everything you held dear." Her words dropped heavily into the silence. "Now, perhaps, it has given something back."

The couple left the house. Jesse had no doubt that Palina was aware of what she had just done. She had breached the bounds of their association. In twelve years, no one— *no one*—had dared to speak to him of what had happened. That was the way he had coped—by not speaking of something that lived with him through each breath he took.

He stalked out to the porch. "Get back here, goddammit!" he yelled across the yard. He had never yelled at these people, never sworn at them. But their stubborn refusal to help him set off his temper. "Get the hell back here and help me with this—this—"

Palina turned to him as she reached the bend in the path. "*Woman* is the word you want, Jesse. A woman who is with child."

"Can you believe this, D'Artagnan?" Jesse asked in annoyance. He dismounted and tethered his horse to the hitch rail in front of the Ilwaco Mercantile. "The Jonssons think I have to keep that infernal woman because of some legend of the sea. I never heard of such a damned cockamamy thing. It's about as crazy as—"

"As talking to your horse?" asked someone on the boardwalk behind Jesse.

He turned, already feeling a scowl settle between his brows. "D'Artagnan gets skittish in town, Judson."

Judson Espy, the harbormaster, folded his arms across his chest, rocked back on his heels and nodded solemnly. "I'd be skittish, too, if you named me after some Frenchy."

"D'Artagnan is the hero of *The Three Musketeers*." Judson looked blank.

"It's a novel."

"Uh-huh. Well, if the poor nag is so damned nervous, you ought to let me take him off your hands."

"You've been trying to buy this horse for ten years."

"And you've been saying no for ten years."

"I'm surprised you haven't caught on yet." Jesse skimmed his hand across the gelding's muscular neck. D'Artagnan had come into his life at a low point, when he had just about decided to give up...on everything. A Chinook trader had sold him the half-wild yearling, and Jesse had raised it to be the best horse the territory had ever seen. Over the years, he'd added three more to the herd at the lighthouse station—Athos, Porthos and Aramis completed the cast of the Musketeers.

He joined Judson on the walkway. Their boots clumped as the two men passed the mercantile. As stately as a river barge, the widow Hestia Swann came out of the shop. Touching a bonnet that was more flower arrangement than hat, she lifted a gloved hand with a tiny wisp of handkerchief pinched between her thumb and forefinger.

"Hello, Mr. Espy. And Mr. Morgan. This *is* a surprise." She hung back, keeping a polite distance.

Jesse didn't take offense. He was a stranger to most of these people, even after twelve years. He didn't blame them for being wary of him.

"Mrs. Swann," he said, lifting his oiled-canvas hat.

A smile forced its way across her lips. Famous for her social pretensions, Mrs. Swann was unfailingly cordial to him—because of his family in Portland.

As if that mattered anymore.

"How do, ma'am?" Judson said. Jesse started to edge away.

She waved the handkerchief limply at her face. "Not so well, Mr. Espy, but bless you for asking. Ever since

Sherman was lost at sea, I've been suffering from melancholia. It's been two years, but it feels like an eternity.''

"Sorry to hear that, ma'am. You take care, now." Judson turned to Jesse as they started walking again. "What's this about you keeping a woman at your house?"

He'd raised his voice deliberately; Jesse was sure of it. Hestia Swann, who had been heading for her Studebaker buggy in the road, stopped and stiffened as if someone had rammed a broomstick up the back of her dress. With a loud creaking of whalebone corsets, she turned and bore down on them.

"What?" she demanded. "Mr. Morgan's got a woman at the lightkeeper's house?"

Judson nodded. Mischief gleamed in his eye. "Ay-uh. That's what he said. I just heard him telling his horse."

"Oh, for heaven's sake. Why would he be talking to his horse?"

"Because he's Jesse Morgan."

"And he's not deaf," Jesse said in irritation.

"You hush up," snapped Mrs. Swann. "This is serious business, keeping a woman—"

"I'm not keeping her—"

"Ah! So there *is* a woman!" Mrs. Swann exclaimed.

"What's that?" Abner Cobb came out of the mercantile, his apron clanking with its load of penny nails and brass tacks.

Jesse fought an urge to jump on D'Artagnan and head for the hills to the south of town.

"Jesse Morgan is keeping a woman at his house," Hestia Swann announced in her most tattle-sharp voice.

Grinning, Abner thumped Jesse on the back. "'Bout time, I'd say. You haven't had female company since we've known you."

"She's not company," Jesse said, but no one heard him. A babble of voices rose as others came out to the boardwalk to hear about this extraordinary development at the lighthouse station. Abner's wife joined them, closely followed by Bert Palais, editor of the *Ilwaco Journal.*

"Where'd she come from?" Bert asked, scribbling notes on a sheet of foolscap.

"I found her on—"

"Oh, I imagine the big city," Mrs. Swann proclaimed, her prominent bosom rising and falling with self-importance. "Isn't that right, Mr. Morgan?"

"Actually, she—"

"Perhaps she was someone he knew in Portland," the widow decided, then nodded in agreement with her own deduction while a few more people joined the group. "Yes, that's it. Jesse is one of the Morgans of Portland." She leaned over Bert's shoulder. "His family owns the Shoalwater Bay Company. They have connections well down into San Francisco, did you know that?"

"Of course I know that," the newspaper editor said. Not to be outdone, he added, "Mr. and Mrs. Horatio Morgan left in April for a grand tour of Europe."

"I remember reading about that big society wedding a few years back," Mrs. Cobb remarked. "Annabelle Morgan and Granger Clapp, was it?"

Hestia's chin bobbed like a wattle as she vigorously agreed. "Jesse's sister. It was the wedding of the decade, to hear people talk. Now, I wonder, is this woman a friend of Ann—"

Jesse didn't stay to hear more. He walked away, feeling like a carcass being picked clean by buzzards. Ordinarily, he did his business in town in a perfunctory fashion and got out, attracting as little attention as possible. No one except Judson, who hurried to catch up with him, seemed to notice that he had broken from the crowd.

"Much obliged," Jesse said through his teeth. He turned down an alleyway off Main Street.

"Where're you going?" Judson asked.

"To get Doc MacEwan."

"The woman needs a doctor?"

"Uh-huh."

"So, she sick or something?"

"Or something."

Judson scowled in frustration. "Well, what the hell is it, then?"

"She's pregnant."

Judson struck himself on the forehead and stumbled back. "Well, I'll be. You devil, you, Jesse—"

"And if you breathe a goddamned word of this," Jesse warned him, "I'll—"

He was too late. Judson was already running back around the corner. "Hey, everybody!" he bellowed to the crowd on the boardwalk. "Guess what?"

Jesse took hold of the brass handle on the door to the doctor's surgery. He stood for a moment, wondering what had happened to his quiet, isolated existence. Then he thumped his brow against the door once, twice, three times.

It didn't help.

Dr. MacEwan reveled in being a source of constant controversy. A proponent of radical medical ideas garnered from a fancy eastern college, the physician was aggressive, compassionate, outspoken and undeniably skilled.

Still, many in the close-knit community of Ilwaco regarded Dr. Fiona MacEwan with deep suspicion. Perhaps that was why Jesse felt a vaguely pleasant kinship with her.

He waited in his kitchen while Fiona examined the stranger from the sea. Despite a trying morning in town, Jesse let himself relax a little. By threatening the harbormaster with a large fist, he'd finally managed to get his point across. He told Judson to check his records for a ship that was due in the area. Before long, they would know the identity of the woman.

And now the doctor was here. In just a short time, Dr. MacEwan would take the stranger off his hands and his life would return to normal.

To normal. To its normal hellish loneliness.

Jesse gritted his teeth against feeling, because feeling had been his downfall. This lonely life, his exile, was his fate.

He looked out the broad front window of the house. The days were growing reasonably long, so he didn't have to worry about getting the light burning for several more hours.

Then the solitary vigil of night would begin.

Hearing a step behind him, he turned to see Dr. Mac-Ewan coming out of the birth-and-death room. Fiona had a broad face and hands that were as sturdy and work-worn as any farm wife's. She wore her thick, graying hair in a haphazard bun held in place by a pencil or a knitting needle or whatever happened to be at hand. Today it looked as if the object of choice was a crochet hook.

"Well?" Jesse asked.

"She's semiconscious."

"What does that mean?"

"Drifting in and out of sleep." Fiona removed her stethoscope, placing it in its black velvet pouch. "Did you notice she's wearing no wedding ring?"

"Not everyone wears one."

"It opens some interesting possibilities," she said. "She could be a widow—"

"Or a fallen woman." It was easier to think the worst of her.

"Why is it always the woman who falls?" Fiona mused. "And not the man?"

"For all we know, he's fallen into the sea, so she's better off than he is."

"True." Fiona lifted her immaculate white pinafore over her head and took her time folding it. "I got her to drink some water and use the necessary. But she's endured a terrible trauma and is still in danger."

"Is she...hurt in any way?" Jesse told himself he was asking because he wanted her well and out of his life. The sooner the better.

"I think her collarbone is bruised, so you'll have to be careful with that."

"*I'll* have to be careful?" A familiar dread crept like a spider across Jesse's chest.

"Yes. It seems tender there." Without asking permission, Fiona went to the larder and helped herself to a finger of brandy from his bottle on the shelf. "The right side."

"Seems to me you should be talking to the people she'll be staying with." Even as he spoke, Jesse felt a thump of suspicion in his gut.

Fiona tossed back the brandy, closing her eyes while a look of pleasure suffused her strong, handsome face. Then she opened her eyes. "She's staying right here. With you. Jesse, you saved her. She's your responsibility."

"No." He strode to the kitchen, slapped his hands on the table and leaned across it, glaring at the doctor. "Damn it, Fiona, I won't have—"

"*You* won't have," she mocked. "It's always about you, isn't it, Jesse Morgan? You see everything in terms of yourself."

"How else am I supposed to see it?"

"In terms of that poor creature in there, you great thick-headed lout!" Fiona sloshed more brandy into her glass. "I said she has no visible injuries other than minor bruises and abrasions. But that doesn't mean we can drag her from pillar to post, man. She's in a bad way, and don't fool yourself that she's not."

"You have to take her away." His voice was a low rasp in his throat.

"I'll do nothing of the sort."

"She can't stay."

"You kept that Mexican sailor for six weeks last year."

"That was different." Jesse had rescued the sailor from a lifeboat in the surf. "He slept in the barn, and he was able to send a telegraph for help."

"And he didn't speak English," Fiona said as if it were Jesse's fault. "So he didn't intrude on your solitude."

"Since when has it been a crime to want solitude?"

"It's a crime when you put someone in danger because you're afraid of having her under your roof."

The accusation chilled Jesse's blood. "That was a god-damned low blow, Fiona."

She sipped her brandy. "I know. I learned to fight dirty back in medical college. And I've never been beaten. Certainly not by such a creature as a *man*."

Jesse shoved himself back from the table. "What about her reputation? She's probably a decent, God-fearing person. Mrs. Swann's probably spreading lies about her all over town. It's not right for a woman to live under the same roof as a man she's not married to."

"Once I explain to everyone the condition she's in, only the smallest of minds will dare to think there's anything improper going on."

"You have enormous faith in your fellow man," Jesse said. "They'll flay her alive with their gossip."

"Since when does Jesse Morgan care about gossip?" Fiona asked, finishing her brandy and fastening the clasp on her large brown leather bag. "I'll stop in to see how she's doing. If she tries to talk, find out where her family is, how we can contact them."

Jesse followed her to the door. "Don't do this, Fiona. Don't leave her with me."

He could almost hear the snap as her patience broke. She glared at him, her eyes bright with outrage. "You'll keep this woman safe, Jesse Morgan, and you'll help her get well, I swear you will. She's pregnant, in case you hadn't noticed."

"I noticed."

"Pregnancy is always a risky proposition, even for a woman who hasn't suffered a major trauma. If she lost her family in the shipwreck, then the baby will be all she has left. It's only right that we do everything we can to make sure she carries the infant to term, which, unless I miss my guess will be four months from now."

After she was gone, Jesse stood for a long time listening to the wag-on-the-wall clock ticking away the moments. And in the room off the kitchen, the beautiful stranger slept on.

Three

Darkness. The rasp of her own breathing. Images and flashes of things that had come before. The face of a stranger. The feel of strong arms around her.

The ball of shame in her belly that she couldn't help loving.

It was the thought of the baby that brought her to full wakefulness. Beneath her, the bed was surprisingly soft, a welcome luxury after the cramped discomfort of the ship.

What've we here, then? A stowaway? I'll have to report this bit of baggage to the skipper.

Shuddering from the memory, she blinked slowly until she could make out vague, dark shapes in the room. The small square of a window with the shutters drawn. A washstand and sea chest. A tall piece of furniture, a cupboard of some sort.

A strong but pleasant smell hung in the air. Lye soap, perhaps. And coffee, though it had not been made recently.

Safe. She felt safe here. She had no idea where "here" was, but she sensed something vital in the atmosphere that protected and insulated her. Safe at last. Anywhere felt safe compared to the place she had fled.

As soon as the thought crossed her mind, she ducked

from it. She wasn't ready to think about that yet. She must not. Perhaps there was a way for her never to think about the past again.

Her hand curled over the gentle swell of her belly. No. There was no chance of forgetting.

"Hello?" she whispered into the darkness.

No answer. Just a low, constant growl of sound in the distance.

Gingerly she lifted the covers, wincing at a pain in her shoulder. She was wearing a gown of some fine stuff— thick cotton flannel such as she would have welcomed as a girl, shivering in her loft above the family cottage and wishing the peat fire gave off better heat.

Feeling the way with her hands, she moved along the wall toward the door, which was slightly ajar. A splinter of rough wood pierced her hand, but she barely flinched. After all she had been through, a splinter was hardly cause for notice.

In contrast to the door, the floor was worn smooth as if by years of pacing. She paused in the doorway, trying to get her bearings.

It was the sea she heard, the throaty basso call of waves on the shore. She had lived by the sea all of her life, and it was a good, strong sound to her ears. Even the ship-wreck had not soured that pleasure for her, the sense that, no matter what happened, the sea never ceased, the sound never died.

Faint heat emanated from a huge iron stove that dominated the kitchen. The room gave access to a larger area, a keeping room or parlor. She creaked open the door of the stove so the embers would give her some light. A warm orange glow painted the sturdy furnishings and a narrow stairway. She went up the flight of stairs and looked through an open door. Within the shadow shrouds,

she could make out a large tester bed, its four posters stark
and bony in the dimness.

The bed was empty.

What sort of place was this?

Though each movement caused a wave of dizziness, she
felt the need to press on, to answer the questions swirling
in her mind. Unsteady on her feet, she descended the
stairs, stepped outside and found herself standing on a veranda with a railing around the front.

The waves boomed as loud and rhythmic as a heartbeat.
High clouds glowed in the distance, and a strange light
silvered their underbellies so that they resembled fat
salmon swimming through the sky.

That light. She shook her head and grasped the porch
rail, feeling nauseous. Her injured shoulder throbbed. She
spied a small outhouse fronted by lilac bushes. The necessary room? Yes. She was glad to have found that. As
she stumbled across the lawn, the ground felt chill and
damp beneath her bare feet. When she finished and made
her way back, she noticed that the grass had been cropped
or scythed.

Again the silvery light drew her. Slowly, she made her
way up a slope covered by spongy grass to the top of the
yard. Beyond a thick stand of towering trees, a stately
silhouette stood out against the night sky. That was it,
then. A lighthouse.

A memory drifted back to her. The sickening lurch of
the ship's hull on the shoal. The groan and crash of boards
breaking apart. A seaman shouting raw-throated at her,
tossing her a rope. The solidity of a mast or yardarm bobbing free of the wreck, floating. She had used the rope to
secure herself. She recalled looking up, scanning the horizon.

As the sea swallowed the four-master—*Blind Chance,*
it was called—like a hungry serpent, making a great slurp-

ing sound, she had spied the light. She'd known it wasn't a star, for it lay too low on the horizon. She had followed the light, kicking toward it for hours, it seemed. The water, though cold, was bearable. With a rhythm as faithful as music, the rotating beacon had drawn her closer and closer: a long, thoughtful blink followed by a second or two of darkness.

When dawn tinged the sky, exhaustion had overcome her. The last image in her conscious mind had been that light. She remembered thinking that it was rather lovely for one's last vision on earth.

Now she stood amazed that she had survived.

But what of her rescuer?

She wondered if she should go and find him. She stood in the shadow of a huge tree, feeling the moist springy earth beneath her feet and trying to decide.

It was then that she saw him.

Her first impulse was to run and hide, but surely that wasn't necessary. Surely he couldn't see her.

He stood on the skeletal iron catwalk and faced out to sea. She could tell that his hair was long, for when the light rotated to the left it illuminated a dark, windblown tangle. There was something about the way he stood that caught at her. He kept his hands crammed in his pockets and his shoulders hunched as if it were cold.

But it wasn't cold. Cool, perhaps, but a lovely night.

There was a stillness about him. As if he were carved in stone, as immovable as the tower upon which he stood. It was eerie the way the light passed over him as it swung in one direction, then the other.

The light moved, but he didn't.

She watched for what seemed like a long time. But she, not the stranger, was the first to move. Fatigued, she returned slowly to the house and crawled back into bed. She barely made it; she was weaker than she thought.

In moments, she was falling asleep again. Falling asleep and, for the first time in too long, unafraid.

It was time to bid the night farewell.

Jesse always savored the endless moments between dark and dawn. The smells of damp earth and evergreen mingled in the air. The cormorants, nesting in the cliffs, released their distant, plaintive calls. It was a gray, nothing period of time when all the world fell still. Night was gone and a new day was coming. But for now he was alone.

That was what he treasured. The silence. The peace.

The new day held no promise. Just the sameness of the day that had gone before and the dull awareness that tomorrow would be no different, either.

This awareness was never more acute to Jesse than in these moments, when the horizon lightened like water spilled in a pool of black ink, and then colors of aching intensity tinged the sky from the east.

Yet today there was a difference, he thought, wrenching open the front door of the house, stepping inside, hurrying to the room off the kitchen. Because of *her.*

She had shifted position. He could see that immediately as he looked into the room where she slept.

In the gathering light, he observed the way she lay across the bed in comfortable abandonment, relaxed as a child, her sleep untroubled. One of the quilts had fallen in a heap on the floor.

His gaze darted around the room. The bowl and ewer on the washstand had not been disturbed. But the way the covers were twisted up looked suspicious. He bent forward for a closer study.

A small bare foot, so dainty it almost didn't look real, stuck out from beneath the sheets. A few damp pine needles clung to the sole of her foot.

Jesse straightened so quickly he smacked his head on a

low ceiling beam. He clenched his jaw, but a muttered curse escaped, anyway. It was damned eerie to think of this stranger walking around the house. His house. Seeing the things that made up his life. Invading the world he'd carved out for himself.

Looking at him. Judging him.

He tried to brush off the thought. The woman was ill. Why would she have any interest in him? She had probably stumbled around in a daze, perhaps seeking the husband she had lost in the shipwreck.

Yes, that was it. She'd have no interest in a lightkeeper, no reason to pry into his life. As soon as she recovered, she'd leave, rejoin her family.

As well she should.

Jesse lingered a few moments longer. The room lightened with the dawn. He told himself he should leave her be, but still he waited, caught up in a sort of horrified fascination.

Fiona had been so matter-of-fact about the whole situation. Couldn't she see how extraordinary this was? Couldn't she see that he had to stop this from happening, stop himself from knowing this woman?

The delicate beauty of the stranger was a blatant taunt. A test. To see if he was strong enough to resist an angel's face and a body as ripe as the sweetest fruit of the vine.

"Damn," he whispered to the empty air, "why couldn't you have the face of a lingcod?"

The odd thing was, he knew it wouldn't matter. If she'd come wearing a bridle or had three arms, he would feel no different. He would still be held in the thrall of her mystery. Her loveliness only added that extra twist of irony.

Daylight glowed brighter through the slats in the shutters. She sighed in her sleep and turned, her knees coming up and her arm sliding down to make a protective cradle for her belly.

She was five months along, or thereabouts, Fiona had pronounced. The baby had started showing. The mother would be able to feel its movements. Fiona had smiled as she told him this, as if he was supposed to welcome the news.

A long hank of hair fell over the stranger's face, and she sniffed as it tickled her nose. Jesse stared at the lock of hair. A shaft of newborn sunlight through the window touched it, turning the deep red to a blood-ruby hue. It was the color of dark fire. As the thought crossed his mind, he leaned down and gently lifted the lock away from her face. Its softness, the silky texture of it, were so acute and so unexpected that he almost yelped in surprise.

He stepped back quickly, horrified at himself. He had touched her. She was a stranger. Another man's wife. Or a widow. It didn't matter. Jesse Morgan had no right to touch her.

He left the room, closing the door to the merest crack, so he could hear her if she got up again. Then he made his way to his own room, kicked off his boots and collapsed with a rumbling sigh on the bed.

But he didn't sleep. He couldn't. Because he felt her presence in his house, the warm, alluring song of a siren's call. The taunt of a treasure he could not have.

"Good to see you, Mr. Jones," said the doorman with an obsequious smile.

Granger nodded a curt greeting. The shiny-faced doorman knew full well that Jones was an assumed name, and the man delighted in saying it with a wink and a nudge.

This was not a good day for winking and nudging. It was not a good day at all. He had arrived Monday morning at his San Francisco office only to learn that one of the company ships had failed to arrive in Portland. By Tuesday, company officials were preparing to call in the insurers, for it was likely the four-master had gone down. Wrecked at the Columbia bar. Wrecked like so many others.

He wondered what had happened. The skipper was one of the best, a longtime employee. Had fog hidden the shoals, even from that old salt? Had the lightkeeper been remiss in his duties? Granger certainly knew what a calamity *that* could cause. He had caused it himself years ago, exacting lethal revenge from his worst enemy—Jesse Kane Morgan. His best friend, his business partner, his rival, the man who had stolen everything from him.

Even now, all these years later, Granger still felt the sting of rejection as the woman he loved had turned him down, turned to Jesse, married Jesse. Emily and Jesse, the golden couple, the toast of Portland and San Francisco alike. The fact that Granger had destroyed it all didn't dull the sting. Perhaps he hadn't gone far enough. Perhaps there was still more to do.

He brushed past the doorman and strode across the tiled foyer of the Esperson Building. It was the best residence in San Francisco, and it was costing "Mr. Jones" a fortune.

Ah, but the rewards were sweet. As he climbed the brass-railed staircase, a bouquet of fresh flowers in his hand, he buried his nose in them and inhaled, thinking about the gentle stroke of her hand on his brow, the uncritical way she had of looking at him. She was his shelter from the storm, the place he came to when everyone else was against him. His nagging parents, his disappointing wife, his raging creditors—he left them all behind when he came here.

He'd be giving the place up soon, though. Now that he had what he wanted from the girl, he could move her into more modest digs. When he'd first met her—destitute, close to starving, yet maddeningly attractive all the same—he had needed to woo her. To feed her appetite for feeling safe and protected. He'd set her up in a luxurious apartment at the hallowed Esperson, visiting her whenever he found the time.

He found time often. And soon he would get his reward. A few months ago, she'd announced that she was pregnant. She'd looked at him with such hope in her eyes. "Now we must marry, so the wee babe has its papa's name," she'd said.

He shouldn't have laughed at her, but he couldn't help it. He did want her to have his baby—that was the whole point. The child would indeed bear his name, as soon as it was born and she surrendered it to him. But it had been a grave misjudgment on his part to tell her the plan. He should have kept it a secret until the very end. He'd underestimated her maternal instinct.

She'd been appalled, terrified, grabbing a hand mirror and preparing to hurl it at him. He'd tried to calm her down, crooning to her as he approached. "Don't be afraid. I don't want to have to hurt you..."

And in the weeks that followed, she did calm down, so much so that he began to hope she was coming to accept his point of view. She'd want her child to have all the advantages he could give the heir to his fortune—the best schools, the best doctors, the best society of San Francisco and Portland.

The flowers would please her, perhaps even coax a smile from her. He stood outside the door for a moment to catch his breath from climbing the stairs. The thought of the child seized him without warning, and he felt a yearning so powerful he nearly cried his need aloud. A son, an heir. Someone to bring along in the world, someone who'd watch him, worship him, learn at his knee. Someone to love as he himself had never, ever been loved.

With a twist of the crystal doorknob, he let himself in. His foot always managed to find the one floorboard that creaked, and now it squawked loudly in the silent apartment. "It's me," he called. "I've brought you something."

Silence. Perhaps she was sleeping. He'd heard women in her condition slept a lot. But the bed was empty. Made up as neatly as always.

A cold feeling of foreboding slithered over him, though he managed to keep control. Methodically, he went through every inch of the elegant apartment. Not a single thing was missing—not a silver fork nor a painted lamp chimney nor any of the clothes and jewels he'd given her. The only thing missing was the only thing that mattered: the woman.

He told himself to be calm, to wait. She'd gone out shopping or for a breath of air. Yes, that was it. But later, after questioning the doorman and learning that she'd left the week before and hadn't been seen since, he was forced to admit that she was gone.

With some surprise, he looked down at the bouquet of flowers he'd brought her. He hadn't even remembered he was carrying it. He'd mangled them beyond recognition, breaking and bruising every flower in the bunch.

Jesse stared at the rough-hewn ceiling beams, listening to the wag of the clock pendulum. Then, after a long time, he pulled his boots back on and went to tend the horses.

On his way to the barn, he encountered Erik Magnusson. Towering at least six and a half feet in height, the youth moved with a giant's ambling gait, unhurried and untroubled by the press of the world. The wind blew his straight, straw-colored hair across his brow.

"Morning, Captain," Erik called. Erik always called him by the head lightkeeper's title. "Did the lady from the sea wake up?"

"No."

"Father said we're going to tar the bottoms of the surf runners today." Erik's mind always flitted from one subject to the next like a hummingbird going from blossom to blossom. Jesse liked the big lad, but he never quite knew what to say to him.

"That's fine, Erik," he said. "It's good to keep the boats in proper order."

"You never take the boats out," Erik said, planting his hands on his hips. "Why do you never take the boats out?"

Because I'm a coward, Jesse thought.

"Why is that, Captain?" Erik persisted.

"The boats are for rescue and should never go past the surf," Jesse said, then started walking away. "I'm off to the barn."

He turned the four geldings out to the sloping pasture. Palina's rooster crowed, the sound insulated by distance and by the light, fine mist that hung in the morning air.

He ambled down the long, switchback trail to the beach. Twenty-four hours ago he had been on this same path, and in his arms he had held an extraordinary and unwanted burden. For years he had been successful in getting people to leave him alone, but the red-haired woman was different. He couldn't make her go away.

Why was he so reluctant to help her? He had come here to do just that—save victims from the sea, help boats navigate the perilous shoals at the mouth of the Columbia. It was the life he'd carved out for himself. It was his penance.

He negotiated the twisting path and walked across the damp, densely packed sand. His gaze automatically scanned the area, seeking more wreckage from the ship that had brought him the woman. But he saw only the endless expanse of the strand, littered here and there by seaweed or a chunk of driftwood. The morning breeze rustled through the dunes, rattling the reeds like dried bones.

A harsh barking sound came from Sand Island in the middle of the huge estuary. Sea lions. Sometimes they came to the cape, but Jesse shooed them off. Fishermen often shot the seals to keep them from preying on the salmon and steelhead.

As he walked, Jesse filled his lungs with heavy salt air and tried to empty his mind. But he couldn't stop thinking about her, the fairy-featured woman who had invaded his house, his life. Companionship was the last thing he wanted. No one seemed to understand that. The people of Ilwaco regarded her presence as a great adventure. Palina termed her a gift. Fiona called her a challenge.

He tried to tell himself she was no different from other women. He'd trained his mind well, punished himself effectively through sheer force of will. Women left no impression on him, sparked no desire, awakened no yearning.

Yet the stranger in his house was different in a way he couldn't explain. Though he didn't even know her name, some deeply suspicious part of himself knew she posed a threat to the life he was now living.

He turned his back on the sea and looked at his world, a lonely king surveying an empty realm. The lighthouse station was the quietest, most remote place on earth. Jesse had run here, thinking it was where he belonged, at the edge of the world.

But, as it turned out, he hadn't run far enough.

Jesse's movements were slow and deliberate as he got out a low stool and placed it squarely beneath the trapdoor to the attic crawlspace. It had been ages since he had needed anything from the storehouse above the ceiling.

But he needed something now. He hoped his equipment was in working order. Standing on the stool, he reached into the hole and groped around through cobwebs and sawdust. Eventually his questing hands found a bulky, oblong box and the three lengths of wood that went with it.

He set the box on the scrubbed kitchen table and stared at it for a long time. He had not used the camera in years, not since...not in a very long time. He wasn't even sure it still worked.

He flipped up the dual latches and lifted the lid. The odd device, with its mouth of brass, its glass plates and black silk shrouds, lay where he had flung them so long ago. The vials of chemicals had corroded at the caps. Red spots mottled the albumen papers.

Photography was a vexing business of washing the plate, coating it with gun cotton dissolved in alcohol, dipping it in silver nitrate. The exposure had to be enhanced by a flash in a pan, then the plate developed with acid and more chemicals. It was easy to make a mistake. He had found that out when—

He cut off the thought, cursing the memories that kept pounding at the edges of his awareness, wanting to be let in. He had come to the bluff in order to forget, and now the presence of that woman was making him remember another time, another life. Gritting his teeth, he assembled everything he needed; the chemicals and the plates, the tripod and the black silk shroud. Moving quietly, he went into the birth-and-death room.

She lay sleeping, her limbs loose, her breathing peaceful and even. Her hair streamed in a ruby and gold tangle across the pillow. Her body curved in on itself, protecting, always protecting the belly.

Jesse tried not to stare. Tried not to think. He made

himself concentrate on the task at hand. He wanted her
out of here. The best way to do that was to find her next
of kin. He needed to take a photograph and circulate it,
have it published.

Yes, that was the answer. Maybe the grateful family
would come for her before she woke. Before he learned
one blessed thing about her.

He positioned the tripod at the foot of the bed. Then he
placed the camera box on top of it, aiming the eye at the
woman.

And suddenly, the memories he had kept dammed up
inside him broke through, and the past stormed across his
mind. He felt it like a physical blow, heard the laughter
of a woman long dead and saw himself, a much younger
Jesse, laughing with her....

"Hold still, darling, I'll just be a minute."

"Oh, Jesse, you take forever." A dainty hand in a lacy
glove smoothed across his brow, pushing aside a persistent lock of hair from his eyes. Pink-tinged lips smiled up
at him. *"Just make the picture and let's eat."* The lacy
hand gestured at the lavish picnic spread out upon a
fringed blanket in the middle of a flower-studded meadow.
"Aren't you starved?"

*He had abandoned the camera then, reaching her in
three long strides, sweeping her into his arms. The picnic
and the photograph had been forgotten until much, much
later, when cool shadows slipped across the field.*

"There won't be enough light left for a picture, Jesse."

He ran his hand through the tousled silk of her hair.
"We have all the time in the world, sweetheart."

Stifling a ragged growl, he rid himself of the memory
almost violently, like a wounded man yanking out the
knife that had stabbed him.

Damn. It had started already. The stranger, with her serene face and air of mystery, was making him think, making him remember, making him feel.

The sooner he got rid of her, the better.

With grim determination he finished setting up the equipment. Then he looked at his subject. She lay like a rag doll, her hair covering part of her face and her arms and legs slack. No one would recognize her in this state.

He had to touch her. There was no other way. He stepped forward and took her by the shoulders, careful not to jar her injured collarbone. She made a sound, half sigh, half moan, and he froze. God, if she woke up now, he'd scare her out of her wits.

Almost as much as she scared him.

Her head flopped to one side, and she settled deeper into sleep. He still held her by the shoulders.

It was then that he noticed it. Her warmth. It seeped into him like rays of direct sunlight. The living radiance passed through his fingers and burrowed deep inside him. He was achingly aware of the soft, yielding flesh and the fragile bone structure beneath. The sensation of holding another human being was so overwhelming that he didn't quite know what to do.

She smelled of sea and wind and womanhood, and he closed his eyes for a moment, trying to get his bearings while his senses listed crazily.

The ordeal took endless minutes. He propped her against the pillow, centering her head just so. Then, not knowing what to do with her loose arms, he crossed them atop the quilt. But as soon as he got her hands in place, her head sagged to the side. He bolstered the pillow, making a trench. Then her hands sprang free as she stretched luxuriously.

Jesse swore quietly between his teeth. How did undertakers do this, anyway? At length he succeeded in arranging her so that her head was centered, the hair pushed away from her face, her hands demurely crossed.

"Stay," he whispered. "Just stay there a minute. I only need another minute."

He crept back to the tripod, treading lightly as if she were a house of cards that could collapse any moment. He put the silk over his head and bent to the camera. His other hand held the flash powder in a pan.

"One," he whispered through his teeth, "two, three..."

All at once, he exposed the plate. A boom and a flash of magnesium powder exploded in the room.

The woman sat forward like a ghost disturbed from eternal sleep. He expected her to scream, but instead, she grabbed the pitcher beside the bed and hurled it at him. At the same time, she spoke. *"Jesus Christ on a flaming crutch!"*

Four

She crouched against the headboard of the bed, the long nightgown bunched in a tangle, her hand reaching for the oil lamp on the table.

As soon as he realized her intent, Jesse blazed back to life. The damn-fool woman. She could hurt herself. Worse than that, she'd burn the house down.

"Don't touch it," he said between clenched teeth, striding across the room. His boots crunched on shards from the broken pitcher. Snatching the lamp, he placed it out of reach on a wall shelf and glared at her through the snaking yellow-gray smoke from the flash.

Color touched her cheeks, and her warm, hazel eyes shone—not with gratitude, but with anger. He was startled to realize that her fury matched his own. "You've done enough damage already," he grumbled.

"And what would a body expect, I ask you?" she demanded. "I wake up to find myself in the middle of a pitched battle and you think I'll simply surrender? You shoot at me, boyo, and I'll fire back, make no mistake."

Boyo? Jesse was reasonably certain no one had ever called him boyo. "I wasn't shooting at you," he said.

"There was an explosion. And I smell gunpowder."

She squinted through the smoke and wrinkled her nose, a perfect little nose sprinkled with freckles.

Jesse had no idea why he would make note of freckles. "You're Irish," he said stupidly, because it was the first thing that sprang to mind.

"And you've got some explaining to do." She leaned sideways to look past him. "What the devil sort of gun is that?"

"It's not a gun. It's a camera."

Her eyes widened. She pushed a hand through her tangled red hair. "A camera, is it?"

"Yes."

The color leaped up in her cheeks again, making stark crimson spots on her pallor. "And what in the name of Peter and Paul are you doing shooting off a camera in here?"

Jesse's already strained patience snapped. "Taking your picture, woman. What do you think?"

She made the sign of the cross and pressed back against the headboard, holding the covers to her chin. "Pervert!"

He gritted his teeth and clenched his fists at his sides to keep from doing something they'd both regret later. This was exactly why he lived here at the lighthouse, alone. He had no patience for other people, especially for mouthy Irishwomen who showed no gratitude for being rescued.

"Madam," he said, "it occurs to me that your mishap has addled your brain. You've been unconscious. I thought it best to find your next of kin, so I took your picture. I had intended to circulate it to the newspaper and telegraph offices so your friends and family would learn of your survival."

He strode to the door, the camera in one hand and tripod in the other. He paused and said, "I expect *someone* will be grateful that you're alive."

She moved quickly but clumsily, lurching from the bed.

When Jesse saw her bare feet heading for the broken pieces of pottery, he had no choice. He dropped the tripod and scooped her up in his arms.

She gave a little squeak of surprise and paddled her feet in the air. "Don't you do it, boyo."

He glared at her. The top of her head was even with his chin. He could feel the heat emanating from her body. The sensation was so unfamiliar that he almost dropped her. Instead, he set her on the bed and stepped back quickly, as if he'd approached a hot stove.

"I beg your pardon?" he asked.

"Granted." She gave a little bob of her head.

"I mean, I didn't follow you, madam. Are you asking me not to leave the room?"

"Aye, that I am."

"May I ask why?"

"Because I don't want pictures of me put in any newspapers."

Ah. So she was superstitious, then. Many immigrants brought their old-country beliefs with them; Palina and Magnus were proof of that. Quite a number thought it unlucky or even sacrilegious to produce graven images of themselves.

"Of course, now that you're awake, there's no need. You can simply tell me your name and destination. I'll report that to—" he broke off, frowning down at her "Miss—er, Madam? Is there something wrong?"

She had begun to sway back and forth, her eyes glazing over. "I...feel strange all of a sudden. Higher than Gilderoy's kite," she said, her voice low and harsh. "Could you—that is, I need..."

Her words trailed off and she slumped to one side. Jesse dropped the camera, wincing as the lens cracked. Without breaking the flow of his movement, he dashed over to the bed, catching her by the shoulders and supporting her.

"Ma'am?" he asked. "Are you…all right?"

She made no response. She'd fallen unconscious again.

Jesse heaved a sigh of frustration. After settling her upon the pillows, he hesitated. Against his will, something inside him seemed to be bending toward her, reaching for her. He could not believe the impact of feeling her warm body curled against his, the tickle of her hair brushing his face and the scent of her, evocative and forbidden.

"Damn," he swore between his teeth. She was everything he was trying to avoid.

As he tucked the quilts around the unconscious woman, his movements were slow, his hands gentle. He'd had no idea there was any tenderness left inside him.

The sooner he was rid of her, the better. He would send for Dr. MacEwan today to make certain this relapse wasn't serious.

Amazingly, the one photographic plate he had taken remained intact. After developing the image, he would have a picture of the stranger. The amber tones would fail to capture the vivid richness of her red hair and her cream-and-roses coloring, not to mention the freckles, yet it would be a decent likeness.

Sleeping Beauty, he thought.

The hell with her superstitions. If she wouldn't stay awake and tell him who she was, then he would publish her photograph and get the investigation started.

His boots crunched on earthenware shards from the shattered pitcher. In all the years Jesse had lived here, there had never been such a mess.

And she'd only been awake five minutes.

"Brass," Palina said, hurling the word like an invective. "It is the bane of my existence."

Jesse levered himself to the top of the ladder leading to the pinnacle of the lighthouse. In the lamp room, Palina and Magnus were well into the day's chores. Palina was polishing the brass of the central compressor and cursing it, as usual.

"Why do they have to make everything out of brass, anyway?" she muttered, her wadded cloth making tight, neat circles in the fittings behind the reflector.

Magnus, who had his good arm deep inside the mouth of one of the eagle-headed water spouts under the eaves, winked at her. "So you can see your beautiful face in it everywhere you turn."

"Humph," Palina said, but the brass she was polishing reflected a blush and a smile. She worked a few moments longer, pausing to wave at Erik, who strode across the bluff toward the horse pasture.

Life at the lighthouse station suited Palina and Magnus perfectly, because they enjoyed each other's company above all others. Erik fit easily into their world. They accepted their son's affliction with a God-given, abiding patience Jesse would never understand. And the boy—seventeen last year—seemed happy enough.

"'Morning," Jesse said to Palina and Magnus.

"'Morning, Jesse," said Palina. "How is our little guest today, eh?"

Jesse picked up a can of oil and held it to the light, checking the purity. The lampwicks consumed nearly two hundred gallons a month, and each ounce had to be pure. "Now that," he said, "depends."

"Is she awake?"

"She woke up," he said.

Both Magnus and Palina stopped what they were doing. "And?" Magnus prompted.

"Well, she cursed at me and then she threw a pitcher at my head."

Palina looked away quickly. "She must be confused, poor lamb."

"The woman's a menace."

"Well, what did she tell you about herself?"

"Hardly a thing. She accused me of shooting at her when all I did was take her photograph to publish in the newspaper."

"Ach, you frightened the little dear," Palina said. "Here she is in a strange place, all alone, having lost God-knows-what in the way of family, and she wakes up to picture taking."

"She didn't seem so defenseless to me."

"She was afraid," Magnus said, reaching into the lantern to trim the wicks. He shook his head, thick gray hair falling across his brow. The crystal facets of the huge Fresnel lens distorted his good arm, making it appear disjointed and huge. "She probably lost her husband in the wreck."

A knot of guilt formed in Jesse's throat. He should have been more patient with the woman. "I left word with the harbormaster to find out the name of the ship that went down. We should hear something today."

He hated this part of his job, hated it with a virulence that made him all the more determined to battle the sea for its victims. The waiting always got to him. He despised the course of events as it unfolded. The harbormaster would check all the schedules and manifests. Which ship was expected in the area? When was it due in port? Was it late? Then would come a list of the crew and passengers. And at each new stage of discovery, new grief would arise.

"She didn't tell you the name of her ship?" Magnus asked.

"She didn't even tell me *her* name." Jesse set down the bucket of oil and sat on the floor, his feet resting on a rung of the ladder leading down to the mezzanine. "We barely had a chance to exchange words. Then she—I guess she overexerted herself and she sort of got dizzy and had to go back to bed.''

Magnus peered at him through so many layers of glass that it was hard to tell where the real Magnus was. "Over-exerted? Now, what do you mean by that?"

The feeling of guilt sharpened. The sea—not a defense-less woman—was the enemy. He should be doing every-thing he could to help her. Instead, he'd let her presence stir up old, forgotten feelings inside him. None of this was her fault.

"She got upset," he said.

"And what upset her?" Palina asked.

"The picture flash must have startled her. She has a bad temper."

"Ah." The tone of Palina's voice spoke volumes.

"So you no longer hold the market on tempers," Mag-nus added.

"I don't have a goddamned temper," Jesse said.

Palina rolled her eyes.

"Palina," Jesse began.

She laughed. She was one of the few people who dared to laugh at him. "Captain Head Keeper, you would lose your temper if a leaf fell across your path. And this young woman is more than a leaf—"

"That's it," he said, getting up. "I'm moving her to your house today. You can take care of her. I clearly lack the proper temperament to minister to our delicate young guest."

"No," Magnus said. "*You* must keep her. When a man saves someone's life, he is bound to ensure her survival. Whatever she needs, you must give her. Whatever it takes to heal her, you must provide. To disregard this would be terrible for you both—"

"—for you *all*," Palina added.

"—in ways you cannot even imagine," Magnus finished.

"That's superstitious horseshit, and you know it," Jesse said.

"It is the law of the sea, and I'll not be the one to challenge it," Magnus insisted. "Will you? Will you take that chance, risk losing her? Just so you can have your life back the way you want it?"

"Maybe I will."

"Maybe you will not," Palina said, thrusting her chin out stubbornly and dipping her polishing cloth. She attacked the next panel with savage relish. "What if you move her and she dies, eh? Then how will you feel? This woman is a gift, Jesse Morgan. You know why she came. Do not look fate in the face and deny it."

A cold shaft of foreboding lanced through Jesse. He gazed out at the blue-gray horizon, then at the waves below the lighthouse. Foam creamed the rocks, seething in and out of the blackness.

A whistle sounded, startling him. It was Judson Espy, the harbormaster, riding up on a naggy-looking, dapple gray mare.

"The sea hasn't given me a goddamned thing," Jesse snarled. "Except a pain in the ass until we figure out who this woman is." He clattered down the iron helix of stairs. Perhaps Judson had the answers he sought.

Judson met him halfway across the yard between the lighthouse and the forest. He waved a sheaf of papers. "Interesting irony here."

"What's that?" Jesse hung back, wondering what ill tidings he would hear.

"There was a schooner-rigged four-master bound for Shoalwater Bay for a load of oysters. It left San Francisco with some trade cargo and was supposed to call at Portland. Never arrived."

Jesse crossed his arms, bracing himself for the news. He turned to look out at the sea, endless and infinite in its bounty—and in its power to destroy.

The story was all too common. The hungry maw of the Columbia River swallowed ships with great regularity, spitting out the remains like undigested skeletons along the beaches. "Do you have a list of passengers and crew?"

"Uh-huh." Judson handed him a list. "Came over the telegraph wire."

Jesse groped in his shirt pocket for his spectacles. Putting them on, he studied the list. Each time he did this, he was hurled back to the day he had stood on the river dock, frantically scanning a ship's manifest, hoping against hope that a mistake had been made, then feeling the world explode when he saw his wife's name.

"You all right?" Judson asked.

Jesse swallowed hard and glared through his spectacles. "All crew. No passengers?"

"Nope. That's the entire list."

He scanned the names, seeking something overtly Irish, like O'Malley or Flanagan. "You think she could be a seaman's wife and they just forgot—"

"They never forget. Look at the name of the ship. At the shipping company."

His gaze drifted to the bottom of the page. Jesse felt as if a noose were tightening around his throat. The noose of a past he wanted to forget. "It was the *Blind Chance.*"

"You remember it well, don't you?"

"The *Blind Chance* is a ship-of-the-line for the Shoalwater Bay Company."

"Your own company, Jesse. They never make mistakes on the ship's manifest."

"It's not my company," he said dully.

"Not anymore, I guess." Judson took the list from him.

"But it hasn't changed much since you left. That partner of yours keeps everything shipshape. What was his name again? Flapp?"

"Clapp. Granger Clapp." Jesse hadn't thought about Clapp in years. But then again, he hadn't thought about anything in years. Not Granger. Not his sister, who had married Clapp. Not his parents, away on a two-year grand tour of Europe. Not anyone.

Jesse wouldn't let himself care.

"So," Judson said, peering inquisitively at Jesse. "What do you think it means?"

"Either the woman was aboard unauthorized—"

"A stowaway!" Judson snapped his fingers. "Now we're getting somewhere."

"Or she wasn't on the *Blind Chance,* at all."

"She had to have been." Judson showed him another page. "Look. The keeper at Cape Meares recorded seeing the ship's stern lights at one-twenty in the morning on Sunday. She was logged in at Tillamook Light at four-forty. And you found the woman at what time, six? Seven?"

"Thereabouts."

"She was on that ship. On the *Blind Chance.* Had to be. As a stowaway." Judson shifted from one foot to the other. "Damn, this is a hell of a story."

Jesse put away his eyeglasses. "We ought to let the papers make the most of it, then. I took her picture. Have Bert Palais run it. And send it down on the next packets to Portland and San Francisco."

Don't you do it, boyo.

He heard her words in his mind, her voice trembling with superstition. She was out of her head, he told himself. Not rational, or she'd see the sense in publishing her likeness. Her family was probably frantic with worry, waiting for word.

Jesse knew what that was like.

Circulating the photograph was the best way to spread the word about this woman. He fished it out of his breast pocket where it had lain against his heart. His hand shook slightly as he handed it to Judson, but he pretended it was just the wind.

Judson stared at the photograph for a very long time. Then he let out a low whistle. "Damn, she looks like a princess out of that fairy tale. You know, where she pricks her finger—"

"I don't read fairy tales."

Judson put the photo plate in his pocket. "This is one amazing catch."

"You don't know," Jesse muttered, walking Judson back to his horse. "You don't know the half of it."

All that day, the new information and old memories haunted Jesse. Ordinarily, he kept the past in some dark corner of his heart, where he couldn't see it, couldn't feel it. But somehow, the arrival of the woman lit a candle in that shadowy place, shedding light on things he had kept hidden for years.

There was an almost eerie serendipity in the idea that the stranger had been borne into his life by the *Blind Chance*. In his mind's eye, he could see the schooner-rigged ship as it had been the day they'd christened it fourteen years before. Jesse hadn't known it at the time, but his future had been defined that day. He closed his eyes, letting the memories in....

The sleek hull of the ship gleamed with fresh paint, the brass fittings were polished to a sheen and the teakwood railings felt silky to the touch. The scent of ocean spray filled the air.

"Blind Chance," Emily had teased, tugging at his sleeve. "What sort of name is that for a ship?" She looked

as fresh and perfect as the ship, in lots of ruffles and lace, a bonnet shading her china-doll face. There was more to Emily than blond-and-pink prettiness, though. She had a streak of mischief in her that delighted, and a breezy charm Jesse knew he'd never tire of.

"Granger's idea. He insisted on being the one to name it, since I got to name the *Trident.*"

"Oh, now *there's* an original name." Her laughter made a bright counterpoint to the melody played by the brass band on the afterdeck. Everything about the day glittered with a diamond brilliance. The ship's rigging was hung with rows of ensign flags, each deck festooned with huge flower arrangements. Tables laden with sweets and hors d'oeuvres lined the pier.

Company officials and the crew and all their families had joined in the festivities. The ship, Jesse reflected, was a microcosm of his world—friends and family and business associates all united in commerce. He surveyed the scene around him with complete satisfaction.

"You're grinning like the Cheshire cat," Emily said, tapping her kid-booted foot in time to the music.

"And why shouldn't I? As the luckiest fellow in all creation, I think I have the right."

She leaned into him—discreet as always, for Emily was nothing if not a perfect lady—and said, "Do you think everyone will be surprised when we tell them our news?"

"I don't see how. It's been pretty obvious that I adore you, Miss Leighton."

"Oh, Jesse." A breeze off the bay caught her sigh. "It's going to be so perfect. We'll be so happy together." She gazed down at the midships deck, where ladies were milling about, twirling their fringed parasols. More than one shot a glance toward the rail where Jesse and Emily stood.

"Such a shame, though," Emily said.

"What's a shame?"

"After we make our announcement, that deck will be positively littered with broken hearts."

He grinned at her. "You exaggerate, darling."

"Oh, heavens, don't pretend you don't know. Half my class at Saint Albans sleeps with some token from you under their pillows."

"And what do you sleep with, Em?"

She winked. "Nothing but dreams, Jesse. Nothing but dreams."

They watched in companionable silence, waving as Emily's parents arrived. Gentlemen in seersucker suits joined the ladies, and the dancing began. "It's men's hearts that'll be in pieces, Em," said Jesse. He spotted Granger in the high bow of the ship. Together, he and Granger would take over the helm, leading the Shoalwater Bay Company into the future.

At the moment, Granger sat on an upended crate with his fair head bent, a thick rope in his hands as he demonstrated sailors' knots to a rapt group of boys.

"No matter what else you think about Granger, he does love children," Emily said, noticing where Jesse's attention had wandered. "I always thought he would be the first of us to marry."

A few moments later, Granger left the boys practicing their half hitches and went to the deck. Jesse's younger sister, Annabelle, was there, looking coltish and shy as she clung to her mother's hand and greeted the guests.

Granger made an elaborate bow before the ten-year-old, then led her into a dance. Even from a distance, Jesse could see her blush with pride and pleasure.

A blast from the ship's horn interrupted the dancing. Jesse's father waved to him and Emily, gesturing them down to the pier. Thomas Clapp, Granger's father, announced through a bullhorn that it was time for the christening. The crowd surged along the dock and gathered there, buzzing with excitement.

Photographers with their cameras mounted on tripods jockeyed for position during the brief speeches from Morgan and Clapp. Granger leaned over and gallantly kissed Emily's hand, whispering, "I hope you saved me a dance."

She blushed, but before she could reply, the speeches ended. Both Jesse and Granger were handed bottles of Dom Perignon, tethered by scarlet ribbons to the prow of the ship.

"Lord have mercy," Granger complained good-naturedly. "What a waste of fine champagne." He pressed his lips to the bottle in a passionate kiss, and the crowd roared. His grin was slightly hard-edged—chiseled, Jesse knew, by the constant, strident demands of his parents. "Ready, old pal?" Granger asked.

"Not quite." Jesse's heart filled with anticipation. What a perfect time, what a perfect day, to share his news. He made a great show of stepping back to hand Emily the bottle. "This is an honor that belongs to Emily Leighton, my bride-to-be."

For just a heartbeat, there was stunned silence, broken only by the shivering of lines against the masts and the lapping of the water at the hull. In that heartbeat, Jesse took it all in—Emily's glowing smile, his mother's wordless gasp followed by a gush of tears, his father's hand lifting to slap him on the back, Mr. and Mrs. Clapp exchanging a cold glare before pasting on their smiles. But most of all, Jesse saw Granger. More clearly than he'd ever seen him. It only took a moment, but he saw something in Granger's eyes ignite and then die. Granger, too, had been in love with Emily.

"Congratulations, son," his father declared, and the

hearty applause that followed chased away the frozen moment Jesse had sensed when he'd looked at Granger.

"All the best to you," Thomas Clapp said expansively. He thumped his own son on the back a bit harder than good nature dictated. "How about that, eh? Your partner beat you out again. Looks like you'd better find yourself a bride and give me some grandkids to spoil."

Granger went red to the tips of his ears. "All in good time, Father," he muttered.

Something had changed that day. Though Jesse hadn't realized it at the time, there was a subtle shift in the dynamics of the three friends, as if the world had tilted on its axis, never to right itself again. Jesse and Granger and Emily. They'd always been the merry trio, together at parties and holidays; going to the opera where Emily sat enraptured while Granger and Jesse drank secretly from a shared flask and tried not to guffaw at the posturing on stage; practicing the newfangled game of baseball while Emily pretended to understand it.

But after that day, a frost hung in the air. Granger became more and more distant. He spent Friday evenings at Madame Fanshaw's Mansion of Sin rather than in the company of Jesse and Emily. The three of them would never be easy together again.

Emily had recovered first from Thomas Clapp's insensitive remark. She laughed, cloaking the moment with humor, then said, "If we don't do this right now, I'm going to uncork this bottle and drink it all myself!"

The last thing Jesse remembered about that day, that glittering day that had changed the course of his life, was the sight of two green bottles swinging through the air, pausing ever so slightly at the top of the arc where the sun shone through the green glass, then shattering against the hull and exploding into a million sun-sparkled bits of emerald.

* * *

She was trapped in the dream, and she could not find her way out. It was as if some drug had been fed to her, holding her limbs and head immobile while she was forced to watch and feel things against her will.

The door. An ordinary door of four wood panels and a crystal knob. She sat in a chair opposite the door, watching, waiting.

The door opened. Slowly. She heard the tread of a footstep and the creak of a floorboard, always the same board, always the same tone. Her days had taken on a sameness that was almost comforting in its uneventful boredom.

But today was different. Today she had something to tell him. Something that would make him so happy. He would sweep her up in his arms and whirl her around, and she'd forget all the past slights, all the little unknowing cruelties he'd committed. She would be important to him now. She had something he wanted. Desperately.

A bar of light slanted through the open door. A tall, broad male form came toward her. She waited to see the handsome face, the neatly combed hair held in place with just a little coating of wax, the smile that set her heart to fluttering.

She found herself looking at a stranger. Taller, broader even, than *him*. And infinitely more frightening.

The light shone from behind, so she only saw his shape, but it was enough to send chills through her. Big shoulders and powerful arms revealed by rolled-up sleeves. Hair that was too long, too wild, flowing like a mane that stirred with the slightest movement.

It was the man who had shot at her earlier. Defying the throbbing pain in the region of her right shoulder, she made the sign of the cross. "Mother Mary and Joseph, help me."

She heard the rasp of a Lucifer, then an oil lamp on the wall shelf flared to life. Just for a moment, her captor's face was bathed in radiant gold, and she saw it in fine, exquisite detail, as if she were looking at a painting in church.

A painting of the Dark Angel. There was an icy purity in the blue eyes that made her blood run cold. A high, noble brow and heavy eyebrows. The shape of his mouth was so flawless that she felt the urge to trace it with her finger.

Then the Dark Angel turned and spoke. "Are you awake?"

She burrowed deeper into the covers, holding them to her chin. "And who's doing the asking?"

He stared at her as if she had sprouted antlers. "Are you afraid of me?"

The words sent her hurtling back in time, back to a place she had risked her life to escape. *Don't be afraid. I don't want to have to hurt you....*

Whimpering, she dived under the blankets and drew her knees up to her chest. It was warm here, and she shouldn't be shivering, but she couldn't stop. What a turn she had come to. What an awful, awful turn. She had gotten to a place in her life where she wanted only one thing—to feel safe.

"Ma'am?" The stranger's voice was low, tentative. Edged with annoyance.

No one had ever called her "ma'am," as if she were a lady of consequence. The blethering fool, she thought, letting her mind drift like a bit of wood bobbing on the waves. Didn't he know better?

Feeling like an idiot, Jesse stood with the lamp in one hand, the other hand stretched out toward the shivering mound on the bed. Confound the woman. Couldn't she make up her mind whether to be awake or asleep?

Tonight, Erik was tending the light. The lad was steady,

grinding the gears every four hours as Jesse had trained him to do. But he only allowed Erik to sit watch if the weather held no threat.

Early in the evening, Jesse had gone out to the edge of the promontory and stood for a long time, feeling the wind and tasting the air, watching the rush of clouds across the lowering glow of the sun.

People said his foreknowledge of bad weather was a mystical gift, but he knew it was simply a skill born of long practice. He had learned to read the mood of the sea and the clouds. The first tenet of warfare was to know one's adversary. He had made a study of it. In the room at the bottom of the lighthouse he had an array of instruments any university scientist would envy—astrolabes and quadrants, barometers and gauges for all manner of measurement.

He was diligent in keeping his log, earning special commendations from the district lighthouse inspector for his attention to detail. Of course, he didn't do any of this in order to earn commendations.

In the beginning, he'd done it to earn salvation. But after twelve years, he'd given up hoping for that. Now he just did it to survive.

Quietly he replaced the lamp on the wall shelf and stood looking at the hump of quilts and blankets. This was his night to sleep, and here he stood, wakeful and agitated, staring in resentment at the woman from the sea.

Earlier, Palina had brought up a fresh quilt and a jar of strong broth. He had heated some of the broth and set the bowl on the bedside table. "Ma'am?" he said softly. "You should try to eat."

No response. Setting his jaw, Jesse awkwardly pulled back the blankets to reveal a tangle of hair and a flushed cheek. "Ma'am?" he said again, his voice tighter now, more impatient.

She moaned and shivered again, then turned her head away without opening her eyes. She had slipped back into that state of half sleep.

"Fool woman," Jesse muttered. "You're never going to get better if you don't eat something." He unfurled the quilt Palina had brought and settled the colorful blanket over the woman.

She stirred, and a small foot emerged from beneath the covers. When Jesse bent to tuck it back in, he was struck by the fine texture of her skin.

In a dark corner of his heart, part of him wondered if she was going to die like everything else he touched.

She released a contented sigh and settled deeper into sleep. The quilt seemed to have a calming effect on her. Ever whimsical, Palina had depicted on the fabric some favored Icelandic myth. This one showed a beautiful mermaid rising out of the sea, borne along on the crest of the boiling surf.

Palina and her myths. She used them to explain everything. She used them instead of simple common sense.

Jesse frowned. Common sense wasn't working here. In truth, it was all too easy to see the Irishwoman as a creature of myth. She had appeared alone from the sea. She was shrouded in mystery. No one had come searching for her. She wore no wedding ring, yet she was pregnant. The foreign lilt in her voice only added to the mystique that hung around her like the golden glow of a lamp.

She took a deep, shuddering breath that startled Jesse. He hated being startled. He hoped to God that word of her would get out quickly. Bert Palais had promised to circulate the photograph and description as far as his newspaper contacts would reach.

Hurry, Jesse thought, turning down the lamp and walking quietly out of the room. Hurry and get her away from here.

He thought of a time years before when he'd been out yachting with friends. That had been in the early years, the oblivious years, before the darkness and the fear. By accident, a belaying pin had stabbed through the fleshy part of his hand. He'd stood frozen for a moment, staring at the vicious steel shaft protruding from his hand. Then he'd grabbed a bottle of whiskey and sucked it dry. And he'd told his friends on the yacht the same thing.

Hurry. Hurry and take it out of me. Before I feel the pain.

The sooner he found her, the better.

He stood in a parlor that reeked of furniture polish and expensive tobacco and wealth and privilege. Outside, the traffic of Portland creaked and rumbled past with a familiar and welcome cacophony. On the desk in front of him lay the morning journals.

The item that had seized his attention was on the bottom of the back page, tucked amid advertisements for Hiram's Glory Water and Do-Right Farm Tools. A grainy photograph and a small block of text:

Ilwaco, W.T.—The head lightkeeper at Cape Disappointment rescued a single shipwreck survivor on Sunday last. Captain Jesse Kane Morgan, formerly of Portland, pulled from the surf a young lady of unknown family and origin.

According to Harbormaster Judson Espy, the only commercial vessel known to be missing at this time is the oysterman *Blind Chance*, of the Shoalwater Bay Company.

Anyone knowing the identity of the young lady is advised to address himself to the lighthouse station....

A strong hand, the fingernails manicured and buffed to a sheen, reached for the newspaper and snatched it up, crushing the page in a fist gone suddenly hard with fury.

Could it be...? He must find out. He would have to be discreet, of course. But he had to find out. He had to learn something else as well—what a man's rights were to a child he'd fathered.

It was insult enough that the wench had gotten away. That an illiterate Irishwoman with dirt beneath her nails had outsmarted him. But—irony of ironies—she had been rescued by Jesse Morgan.

"Granger?" A feminine voice, tentative and respectful and cultured the way he liked, called from the doorway.

"Yes, Annabelle?"

"I...I was just going out. To call on the Gibsons."

He eyed her across the room. His perfect wife. Every gilded curl in place. The folds and tucks of her morning gown precisely aligned. The parasol and reticule made to match. Ah, she was a credit to him.

He smiled and crossed the room toward her. She didn't flinch as he bent and kissed her cheek gently, tenderly. Lovingly. "Have a fine day, Annabelle, dear."

"I shall, Granger." She took one step back toward the door, then another. What a vision she was, arrayed to take Portland by storm with her beauty and her charm. Yes, he was the envy of his peers.

Standing at the window, he watched her go. Only after a footman helped her into the drop-front phaeton outside did he look down at what he held in his hand. The crushed newspaper. He hurled the ball of paper into a small bin in the kneehole of the desk. When he looked up again, the phaeton was rounding the corner of Lassiter Way. Pedestrians craned their necks to peer at the beautiful Mrs. Annabelle Clapp.

His perfect wife. In all ways but one.

She was barren.

Five

~~~~~~~~~~

She awoke to sunlight and pain and the disconcerting notion that she had been dreaming of the baby. Formless and vague, the wraithlike images followed her into wakefulness. Light had pervaded the dream. And the rainbow colors of hope and joy shot through the light.

She lay still, listening, wondering about the dull ache in her shoulder. How had she hurt herself? Something to do with the shipwreck. She had a blurry recollection of holding a rail, feeling the wood twist and hearing the snap of timbers being wrenched apart. The screams of the seamen and the roar of the ocean echoed in her ears.

The memory of violence and black night and churning waters should have plunged her into a panic. Yet instead, she thought of the lighthouse. The beacon, flashing a message of hope to her as she washed ashore.

Pressing her good arm behind her, she sat up, unable to move again until a wave of dizziness passed. Mother of God, but she was ill. A squeak of alarm came from her throat, and she laid a hand on her stomach.

"Are you still there, baby? Have you survived all this with me?" she whispered. She felt the small, hard knot and breathed easier. Still there. Still a part of her. She'd failed at every last, blessed thing she'd ever attempted, and she didn't want to fail at motherhood.

For a while, she held herself motionless, waiting. Finally, the baby moved. She'd first felt it a week earlier—the fluttering of fairy wings. A small, precious miracle grew inside her.

Grasping the sturdy bed frame, she got up. She went outside to the necessary, seeing no one along the way, hearing only the morning birds of early summer and the whispery sighs of the wind through the trees.

On the way back, she stopped in the yard. The trees were the grandest, tallest things she had ever seen, and they looked enchanted, all clad in lichen and draped in long, green beards of moss. Their tops swayed in the breeze as if dancing to music only they could hear. Surely the majestic forest could speak if only she knew how to listen. It could tell her what sort of place this was, what she could expect here, if she was safe with that moody, dark stranger.

Her gaze traveled down the broad lawn to a meadow where horses grazed. She saw a barn and, in a sunny corner, a vegetable garden fenced off from rabbits and deer. The entire place had an impersonal air of order, as if no one actually lived here.

But someone did, of course.

A very puzzling someone.

High on the distant bluff to the west was the lighthouse. The stony sentinel, painted white with three bands of red, stood proud and impervious to the wind and the sun. The flashing beacon had been her guiding star after the wreck. She could hardly look at it without feeling the harsh sting of thankful tears in her throat.

Weakness plagued her. Dizzy, she made her way back to the house. A railed veranda faced west. Green shutters and lime-washed siding, the chimney made of smooth, round stones. At one time, flower beds must have graced the front, for along the gravel walkway, she spied some bald rose hips struggling up through wild fern and weed. Hidden close to the ground were runners of alyssum and larkspur, defiantly blooming in anticipation of the coming summer.

A pity about the flowers, she thought. Blooming flowers would liven up the place considerably.

Stepping inside, she held the back of a chair and let her eyes adjust to the dimness. Books everywhere, stacked on tables and shelves. The interior of the house was excruciatingly neat, from the bin of wood beside the stove, to the supplies precisely aligned, like little tin soldiers, on the shelves in the kitchen pantry.

Mum would have liked that, she thought, letting in a warm wave of fond memories. Mum liked a tidy kitchen.

The memories departed like the tide before an onrush of impulse far stronger and more urgent. She was starving. At the sideboard, she found a pitcher of fresh milk with the cream still on top. Drinking straight from the pitcher, she sated her thirst. Her weakened hands held the pitcher clumsily, spilling a little down her front and onto the floor. Like Goldilocks in the nursery story, she helped herself to what food she could find—hard-tack biscuits from a tin, and a jar of spiced apples so delicious they made her teeth ache.

"Is that better, baby?" She stroked her stomach and, for the first time since she had washed up on shore, she smiled. Ah, there. It felt so fine to smile.

Brushing the crumbs from the splendid gown she wore, she made her way back to the snug little bedroom adjacent to the kitchen. Sunlight streamed in through the square panes of the window and played across the floor, flowing like a river of gold. Surely it wasn't just the trees that were enchanted. This whole place, this house, this strange and wild jut of land—all of it lay under a soft green enchantment.

And to think she had almost stopped believing in magic.

How foolish. Mum always said that magic happens when a body needs it the most. And so it had. She had needed a miracle in the most desperate of ways, and here she was in a distant place, feeling unaccountably protected. Though she had barely survived, bringing nothing with her save the babe in her belly, she felt a surge of hope.

She picked up one of the quilts on the bed. Lovely, it was, with a mermaid and a sapphire sea. Now that she felt better, she wanted to explore. She wanted to make certain she and her baby were really and truly safe at last. But she couldn't very well go about in a flannel nightgown. Perhaps there was a dress or robe somewhere.

In the tall cupboard, she found a few bits of linen and gingham and cotton muslin. Some pieces had been cut but not stitched, as if the dressmaker had gotten interrupted long ago. Beneath the dry goods, she found a pile of inexpressibles—as Mum would call them—creased sharply along folds that clearly had been undisturbed for years. She selected a pair of sheer bloomers. Swiss dimity, they were, more dear than a season's catch of herring.

She burrowed deeper into the cupboard, and way at the back, she found a dress hanging on a hook. She let out a long, heartfelt sigh. How fine it was, a sprigged muslin of rich green and gold, with leg-of-mutton sleeves puffed at the shoulder and tapered down the arms. A beautiful, wide sash was looped around the waist. Behind the dress hung a long white shift. More Swiss dimity.

Was he married? Whose clothes were these?

The garments weren't new, and judging by what she'd seen in San Francisco, the gown was quite out of fashion, too full in the skirts for current style. But the fabric smelled of lavender sachets, and she felt better having real clothing on. It hurt her shoulder to reach for the buttons in the back, so she simply tied the sash. She didn't have much in the way of a waistline these days, but the dress, cut to accommodate an outmoded crinoline, fit reasonably around her middle.

Putting a hand to her hair, she scowled at the feel of the tangled mess and went in search of a brush. This she found in another part of the house, the gentleman's tiny dressing room adjacent to his chamber on the upper story. The smell of shaving soap spiced the air. She peeked into the bedroom at the massive bedstead. Though the headboard was intricately carved, only a single meager-looking pillow was visible. A blanket of rough olive-colored wool, frayed at the edges, draped the mattress. There was no coverlet.

A little thrill of apprehension chased down her back as she pictured the man with the wintry eyes who had taken her photograph. This was where he lived. Where he slept. Where he dreamed his dreams.

She knew nothing about him except that he had saved her life. That was enough for her to believe she was safe with him.

Except for the photograph.

Her brush strokes became agitated. She must remember to tell him that circulating a photograph was absolutely forbidden. Fear, which had been her constant companion since she'd made her escape, crept like a spider along her spine. She had to decide how much to tell her host, but she would make up her mind about that later. It would probably be wise to lie.

By standing on tiptoe, she could see herself in a small, round shaving mirror affixed to the wall above the washstand. She looked like death eating a soda biscuit, as Mum would say. But she was alive, sweet Jesus, she was alive, and the baby was alive, and she wanted to crow with the sheer wonder of the miracle.

The ecstasy of feeling safe, safe at last.

"What the hell are you doing in here?" demanded a gruff voice.

She whirled too quickly, and for a moment, she saw stars. They swirled like a halo around the head of her dark angel. He stood at the top of the stairway, one huge hand resting on the newel.

When she saw the menace in his face, the fear came roaring back at her, and a thousand times she called herself a fool for thinking she could ever be safe.

"Well?" he said.

Ah, that voice. Like the bellow of a windstorm, it was.

But she had weathered a greater tempest and lived to tell the tale, so she squared her shoulders and blinked until the stars flickered and died. This was the man who had saved her. Why would he harm her now, after giving back her life?

"I was brushing my hair," she said.

Carefully, deliberately, she set the brush on the shelf where she had found it and stepped out of the cramped dressing room. She walked past him and descended the stairs.

He followed her and stood in the middle of the keeping room, right where an oval rug would have added a perfect touch of warmth. But there was no warmth here.

The man seemed to fill the entire space, so tall and broad was he. He glared at her, his eyes blue flames behind a layer of ice. "Where the hell did you get that dress?"

She touched the gown, lifting the skirt a few inches and admiring the fine print on the green and gold fabric. "Why, you left it in my room, so I supposed it was meant—"

"I didn't leave it," he said. "No one left it."

Though he hadn't raised his voice, she could feel his rage crackling like a brush of heat lightning in the air. What had sparked his fury? Wasn't he pleased with her recovery?

In the past weeks, she had grown adept at hiding her fear. She faced him squarely. "I helped myself to a few things from the tall cupboard."

A red curl fell across her face, and she tucked it out of the way. "You wouldn't be needing the gown for anything, would you?" Her hand went to her throat as an unsettling thought struck her. "Blessed saints. Would these be belonging to your wife, then?"

The icebound flames in his eyes seemed to burn colder. Every inch of this man radiated a threatening strength. The sheer contempt in his face should have alarmed her, but instead, she looked at him and felt curiosity edging out her fear.

"I don't have a wife," he said.

A simple enough statement, but she sensed turbulence beneath the rocklike surface. What would she find deep inside this man, if she dared to peel back the layers?

"Then who do these clothes belong to?" she asked.

"No one," he replied. "Not anymore."

The tone of his voice made her wary of pursuing the issue. She simply stood there, showing no response save polite expectancy.

He put both hands to his head and combed them through his long hair. "You'd better sit down." Ungraciously, he added, "I don't want you having another fainting spell on me."

She lowered herself to a wooden settle that faced the small fireplace. The fieldstone hearth had been swept clean. Not a speck of ash touched her bare feet as she swung them against the planks of the floor. "Faith, I don't plan to swoon again. It was the hunger, I suspect. I helped myself to something to eat."

"I noticed."

Guiltily, she glanced through the open doorway to the kitchen. The apple jar was gone. The milk pitcher had been washed and put up, the biscuit crumbs cleared from the table. Hoping to improve his mood, she smiled. "Those were the most delicious apples I ever tasted."

He sat on a stool across from her. His face might have been carved in marble, so expressionless did he hold himself. "It's from last year's harvest. There're a few apple trees at the station."

What a strange man he was, calling his home "the station."

She took a deep breath. "There's something I need to tell—"

"—something I need to ask—" He broke off.

They stared at each other for an awkward moment. She laughed. "We both spoke at once."

"I need to know your name," he said, not only unamused but looking baffled by her laughter. "So we can set about contacting your family."

Mirth died a swift death. She sat very straight upon the settle and forced herself to look him in the eye. "My name is Mary Dare, and I have no family."

Ah, but it hurt to say it. He would never know how much. No family. It was like admitting one had no heart, no soul.

"Mary Dare." He leaned forward in a sort of grudging bow. Interesting to note that he had a small, miserly store of manners. "Your real name?" he inquired.

Anger—and guilt—chased off her maudlin feelings. "And you are?" she asked defensively.

"Jesse Kane Morgan. Captain of the lighthouse station."

"'Tis an honor to meet you, Captain. But I confess, you have the advantage of me. Where, can I ask you, is this 'station'?"

"Cape Disappointment."

"Sure and that's a terrible name for such a lovely place," she said.

"Blue-water men trying to get their ships over the bar don't think it's lovely. We're at the mouth of the Columbia, in the Washington Territory."

Washington Territory. Fancy that. She had traveled to a whole new region and hadn't even known it until now.

"Were you on the *Blind Chance?*" he asked. "As near as I can figure, it's the only ship lost in the area on Sunday."

Sunday. It occurred to Mary that she didn't even know what day it was. Nor did she know what manner of man he was, this cold stranger, or what the future held.

All the information coming at her began to swirl like a fever through her mind. Sunday…Washington Territory…the *Blind Chance*… And through it all, the lighthouse beacon had guided her. With a harsh little cry, she launched herself from the settle and landed on her knees before him, clutching his hands. Her pose was that of a supplicant before a savior. "Captain Morgan, I've forgotten my manners. You saved my life. Our lives. Mine and the baby's. That is what I should be telling you. How can I ever thank you?"

He wrenched his hands away and stood. She heard an oath barely hidden in the harshness of his breathing.

"I'm sorry," she said. "I didn't mean to startle you."

"I don't like being touched." Each word sounded measured, as if doled out from a meager supply. He walked away from her.

"Sure and if that isn't the saddest thing I ever heard."

She followed him to the large front window, where he stood looking out at the distant bluff, his back to her.

"Never mind that," he said brusquely. "I need to know several things about you, Mrs. Dare."

"The first thing you should know is that—" she took a deep breath "—it's not Mrs. Dare." There. She'd said it. All along, she'd planned to lie to him and pretend she'd been a married lady and then widowed. Yet out popped the truth.

He didn't move, didn't react. "Miss Dare, then, is it?"

"Mary. Just Mary."

"Did you have friends or family on the *Blind Chance?*"

"No." The corners of her mouth curved up in an ironic smile. "I didn't even have a ticket."

He turned then, eyeing her suspiciously. Lord, but he was fine to look at, and he had no notion at all of his appeal. In fact, he was put together and clothed like a man who didn't care for his appearance in the least. He just *was*. She itched to comb his hair for him, to trim it.

"I figured you were a stowaway."

The thought of the ordeal she had endured sapped her strength. Her bad shoulder began to throb, and she touched it gingerly.

"Dr. MacEwan thinks you've hurt your collarbone."

"A doctor's been to see me?"

"Yes. You don't remember?"

"I'm...afraid not." She tried to stifle a yawn, but wasn't quick enough. The dizziness spun upward through her. She felt her eyes roll back, her eyelids flutter.

"You should lie down and rest," he said.

She nodded. His voice had a different quality now. She still heard that undertone of impatience, but the edges sounded smoother, somehow. "Thank you. I think I will." She reached for his hand, then stopped herself.

I don't like being touched.

Aye, it was the saddest thing she'd heard.

"Thank you again, Captain Morgan."

"Jesse."

"What?"

"Call me Jesse." He strode across the room toward the door. "Now, go and rest."

It was all Jesse could do to keep from running when he left the house. And that, perhaps, was what he resented most about this whole impossible situation. That the presence of this strange woman, this Mary Dare—imagine, her bearing the name of a shipwreck—could drive him from his own house, from his refuge against the outside world.

He walked across the clearing, heading for the barn. Whistling sharply, three short blasts, he didn't even look to see if D'Artagnan obeyed. The horse came when summoned. It was the first lesson Jesse had taught him.

Within minutes, he had saddled up and was headed along the sinuous path to the beach. The horse was always game for a run, and as soon as they reached the flat expanse of brown sand, Jesse gave the gelding his head.

For a while, he felt something akin to exhilaration. The wind streamed through his hair and caught at his shirt, plastering the fabric to his chest and causing the sleeves to billow around his shoulders. The horse's hooves kicked up wet sand and saltwater. Man and horse were like the skimmer birds, buzzing along the surf, heading nowhere as fast as they could.

From the corner of his eye, Jesse could see Sand Island, then the vast blue nothingness beyond the giant estuary. This was his world, his life. It was where he belonged. Alone. Eternally. He needed to be rid of Mary Dare, and quickly.

Because, somehow, her presence reminded him that his world was unbearably vast and empty.

God. The sight of her in that dress had nearly sent him
to his knees. The memory had cut into him like a dagger:
as if it were only yesterday, he'd seen Emily twirling beneath the chandelier in the foyer of their Portland mansion,
laughing as the skirt belled out across the parquet floor....

"I put it on just for you, Jesse. Just for you."

"Oh, Em. I'd rather have you take it off for me."

*She giggled and blushed. "That, my love, will come. We
have plenty of time for that later."*

Jesse dug in his heels and rode harder.

He brought the horse up short at the boathouse tucked
into a protected cove at the foot of Scarborough Hill. The
rickety structure housed a pilot boat. Now that tugboats
were common, the boat wasn't used much to guide big
ships out to sea, but Jesse kept the craft in perfect condition, varnishing the wood and caulking the seams, keeping
oil in the lamps and the sails in good repair.

It was a sickness with him, taking care of this boat. For
after Emily's accident, Jesse had never gone to sea again.
He never would. He was too afraid.

Disgusted with himself, he headed back to the lighthouse station. What a majestic sight it was, the lime-
washed tower standing proud on the overlook of the cliff.
And yet how small it looked, dwarfed by the huge trees
beyond and the waves curling over the black rocks almost
to its base.

When he reached the top of the trail, he heard a musical
"Halloo!"

He smacked D'Artagnan into a trot and went to greet
his visitor.

Lifting her navy blue skirts high above practical brogans, Dr. Fiona MacEwan alit from her buggy. "Good
day, Jesse. I stopped in to check on our patient."

He dismounted and led his horse to the crosstics in the
barn. "She woke up," he said tonelessly.

"Is that so?" Fiona beamed, reaching to secure one of the wooden knitting needles that held her hair in place. "And is she all right? Did you learn her name?"

He put up the saddle and tack and cleaned the sand from his horse's hooves and coat. "She says her name is Mary Dare and that she has no family." He decided to conceal the fact that Mary had been a stowaway. He needed to learn more about the situation before he went trumpeting that about. For all he knew, he had given shelter to a thief or a murderess.

Or a hapless woman on the run from something she would not name.

"It'll be hard for her, then, to be alone in the world," Fiona said.

He turned D'Artagnan out to pasture. "Will it?"

"You don't think so?"

"Come on, Fiona."

Her gaze skated over him from head to toe. "Some people prefer human companionship. Crave it, even. I suppose you can't understand that." Showing nothing in the way of sympathy, Fiona patted him briskly on the cheek. "Did anyone ever tell you you're the best-looking man in the Territory, Jesse Morgan?"

"No." He scowled furiously.

Fiona smiled. "That sort of thing matters to some women."

"But not to you."

She sent him a mischievous wink. "Hardly."

That was one of the reasons Jesse tolerated her. There was nothing Fiona wanted from him.

They walked together toward the house. "She claims she has no family. I assume that means no husband?" the doctor asked.

"That's what she said."

"Mmm." Fiona's voice held no judgmental tone. Jesse liked her for that. "That'll be harder still, then."

"Now that she can get around, you'll be taking her into town. Get her settled and—"

"We mustn't be hasty." She preceded him into the house and set her bag on the kitchen table. Together, they went into the little bedroom.

Jesse's breath caught, air hooking painfully into his chest. Mary Dare slept in the sunlight atop Palina's quilts. She still wore the green-and-yellow dress.

Later, Jesse. I'll take it off for you later. We have plenty of time.... His dead wife's voice whispered in his ear, and he shook his head, forcing himself to look at Mary Dare.

The light caught at her hair and limned the porcelain delicacy of her skin. Beneath her eyes, circles of fatigue bruised the fragile skin. Despite the meal to which she'd helped herself, she looked gaunt and frail.

"She's weak as a kitten," Fiona whispered. "I'll not be dragging her down the bluff to town in this condition."

Jesse cleared his throat. "But—"

"She's staying." Fiona clamped her hands at her hips and jutted her chin up at him. "Do you have a problem with that?"

"Yes."

"Then get over it, Jesse. For once in your life, think of someone besides yourself!"

Mary Dare flinched in her sleep.

"Sorry," Fiona muttered. "You're a vexing man, Jesse Morgan."

"I'll look after her until week's end," he said. The words tasted sour on his tongue. "And not a minute longer."

Stung by Fiona's triumphant smile, he stalked out of the room.

* * *

"How are you feeling this morning?" Jesse asked. Even to his own ears, his voice sounded rusty, like a hinge on an unused gate.

Mary Dare's smile made the sun seem dim. "Hungry," she confessed, stepping into the kitchen. The green dress was wrinkled in the back and her hair was sleep-tousled, heavy waves draping her shoulders.

"There's bacon." He pointed. "And Palina's cardamom bread. Coffee?"

"I'll have a glass of milk, if there is any."

"There's always milk. The Jonssons keep a cow."

"That's lovely. And when shall I be meeting the Jonssons?"

"Soon. They're on duty at the lighthouse."

"What are they doing there? I don't see a speck of fog."

"Cleaning the equipment. They'll be done soon." He watched her eat and drink. Though not gluttonous, she consumed the bacon and bread with efficiency and relish. Expectant mothers needed plenty of good, fresh food. Fiona had told him so. But, of course, that wasn't the first time he'd heard that advice.

"Jesse, darling, I have the most marvelous news!" Emily had breezed into his study, a vision of frothy white against the walnut-and-leather backdrop of his library shelves. "I've just been to the doctor, and he confirmed it. You're going to be a papa!"

He shook off the memory and waited patiently for Mary to finish. She looked better today. Better every moment, in fact. Her pallor seemed less alarmingly pasty. Her eyes were bright, almost eager, and the dark circles were fading.

Excellent, he thought. Get her well enough to make the trip to town, and he could be rid of her. Free. Alone. That was all he wanted.

"Can I make you some tea?" he asked. "Dr. MacEwan left an infusion that's supposed to aid in digestion."

"I believe my digestion's fine," she remarked with a wink.

That smile. It was brutal in its simple, dazzling beauty. It hammered at him like a fist.

When she finished her breakfast, he whisked away the dishes and washed them in the sink. Over his shoulder, he said, "Do you need to go to your room and rest?"

"I'd like to take a walk."

"You'll tire yourself."

"Just a little walk, mind. The fresh air will do me good, don't you think?"

Jesse seized on the idea. Anything to get her to feeling better. Anything to get her away from him. She had no idea how each moment he spent in her presence drilled at him, disturbed him in ways he didn't want to be disturbed.

"We'll go to the strand." He turned toward her. "There's a way down that's not too steep."

Her smile lanced through him again, warm sunbeams thawing frozen flesh until it ached. "I'd like that, Jesse," she said.

This was for her, he told himself as he put one of Palina's knitted shawls around her shoulders, awkwardly tying it in the front. Mary stood like a docile child, watching him. Trusting him.

The fresh air was going to help her feel better, and when she felt better, she could leave. That was why he was doing this.

When they were halfway down the rock-strewn track, she called his name. He stopped and turned. "Is it too much for you?" he asked, feeling a touch of dread. What if he had to carry her again? To hold her close and feel her warmth and the beating of her heart? "Do you need to go back?"

"No. It's not that. Jesse?"

"What is it?"

"You've been more than kind to me, and sure I'm the last person to criticize, but could I just be pointing out one small thing?"

"What?"

"It occurs to me that you're not accustomed to walking with a companion."

He snorted. "Of all the—"

"It's true. You march along like a parade marshal. When two people walk together, they generally go side by side."

"We're not together," he said. "You said you wanted a walk, so we're walking."

She blew out an exasperated breath and came toward him, her feet clumsy in the oversize India-rubber boots he'd lent her. "A walk isn't just *walking*," she said with a magnificent lack of logic. "It's talking and sharing."

"I don't do things like that." He turned and trudged down the hill.

They crossed the grassy dunes and came to a long strand of sandy beach. He turned and watched her, walking backward. "Look, I'm sorry you're alone. But if you expect companionship from me, you're bound to be disappointed."

"It would take a lot more than that to disappoint me," she said.

Her statement piqued his curiosity, but he thrust it aside. He didn't want to know what had disappointed her in the past. He didn't want to know what she dreamed about for the future.

"I live alone by choice," he said gruffly. "I don't want a companion."

Her eyes widened, but she nodded. "You didn't ask to

save me. No doubt if you'd had a choice, you never would have come down on the beach and found me that day."

Damn it. Was wishing her out of his life the same as wishing he'd never found her? "Mary—"

She held up a hand. "I understand. Now, let us have our walk." She tossed back her head and let the wind blow through her hair. "It's cold here."

"Take my coat."

She shook her head. "The shawl's enough. I'll be rid of these boots, though. I love the feel of the sand beneath my feet." Before he could protest, she kicked off the boots.

"Put those back on," Jesse said. "Your feet will freeze, and then I'll be stuck with you even longer."

"A fate worse than death, I'm sure." Her dainty feet barely made an impression on the hard-packed sand as she walked.

And for no reason he cared to examine, Jesse found himself walking beside her. Stubborn female. She should be eager to get away from him. In the past, his growling and snarling had effectively kept other women at a distance. This one had no respect for the iron in his soul.

"This place is truly the edge of the world," said Mary. With an easy movement, she slipped her arm through his.

The shock of the contact jolted him like a physical blow. His muscles turned to stone. Perhaps she felt some measure of the intensity, for her cheeks flushed with color. "Is something the matter?"

He glared at her hand. "Don't—"

"I forgot." She extracted her arm. "You don't like being touched." She headed northward on the beach with her face into the sea breeze. The wind sheared down from the towering forested cliffs, causing tears to gather in the corners of her eyes.

He thought of offering her a handkerchief, but stopped

himself. She glanced sideways at him, her glorious red hair swirling on the wind. Chagrined that she had caught him studying her, he hunched his shoulders and pulled his hat over his brow.

She stopped when she came to a huge, twisted piece of driftwood. She studied it for a moment, observing the whorls in the grain, the deep gashes and cracks, the holes bored into it by worms. Without saying a word, she wandered on. A few feet from the log lay a scattering of shells, all broken and crushed, some with slimy green weed clinging to them. He saw her shudder, and she quickened her pace.

Jesse wondered what she was thinking. Was she remembering the shipwreck? The father of her baby? He had so many questions to ask her. Yet he didn't want to. He didn't want to know the hopes and dreams that filled the head of Mary Dare.

Because the more he knew about her, the more real she became to him. All he wanted to know was how soon he could get her to a better place than his house.

She halted again when she came to the remains of a dead seagull. It had been picked clean; the bones resembled a chicken carcass. The wings, still intact, lay spread far apart as if the bird had been tortured.

Mary turned and looked out to sea, at the long white lines of waves marching relentlessly toward the shore. Jesse kept watching her, wondering what was going on behind her haunted eyes. He wasn't certain how to speak to her. It had been so long since he had spoken at length to anyone.

The silence spun out, growing more and more uncomfortable.

Jesse cleared his throat.

Finally she spoke. "Everything that washes up on the shore is damaged."

The statement hit him like a sucker punch—hard, unexpected. For a few moments he had no idea what to say, how to react. He stared at her. She was so damned pretty with her hair flowing behind her and her face pushing into the wind, those large eyes seeming to see everything.

"The sea is rough on things," he said tersely, yanking his gaze from her.

"Yes."

She sounded so bleak and hopeless, so un-Mary-like. Her mood should not be a matter of concern to him, but it was. He couldn't help it. "Sometimes treasures wash up on the beach." His words sounded awkward, inept.

She blew out a breath and started walking again. "I've never seen any."

He studied her as she moved away from him. "I have."

She seemed not to hear. He could tell by the set of her shoulders that she was filled with doubts and regrets and other things he had no right to share. And that she didn't believe him. That was what bothered him the most.

He picked up a piece of wood and turned it over in his hands, then lengthened his strides to catch up with her. To walk beside her. Exactly as she wanted.

"Sometimes the damaged things are treasures in their own way," he said, sounding unbelievably stupid but unable to stop himself. "A piece of driftwood has its own kind of beauty. A broken shell becomes a piece of jewelry. A dead fish feeds the scavengers."

She tossed her head. He could tell she was having none of it. And he could tell their conversation was not about driftwood and dead fish, but about Mary Dare, who had washed up on the beach. Who believed herself damaged.

He drew back his arm and hurled the piece of driftwood as far as he could, not looking to see where it landed.

"I suppose some things are best left to feed the scavengers," she said.

Six

"Faith, I've never slept so much in my life," Mary mumbled as she pushed aside the covers and got out of bed. She squinted at the window. Great pink fronds of light spread down through the trees and across the far-off horizon as the sun began to set. "I've slept the day away."

She shuffled over to the washstand to splash water on her face. Then, smoothing the wrinkles from her borrowed dress, she went into the kitchen. Jesse Morgan was there, fixing supper.

She stood in the doorway and watched him for a moment. He moved with the unhurried deliberation of an old man, yet he wasn't old at all. He was young and vigorous. What made him seem ancient?

I don't like being touched.

She was filled with questions about her reluctant host. And she knew he would not willingly answer them. Not yet, anyway.

She cleared her throat. He paused in the midst of lifting the lid from a cast-iron pot on the stove. He replaced it and turned to face her. "Supper's ready."

"It smells delicious." She walked to the table. "Where is the jar of wildflowers I picked?"

He scowled. "I set it out on the porch."

Without another word, she walked out and found the jar on the stoop. The bursts of daisies made her feel as if she held sunshine in her hands. The spicy perfume warmed her senses. Almost defiantly, she set the jar in the middle of the table. A light yellow powder settled on the surface.

"They make a mess," Jesse said.

"I'll wipe the table clean after."

"They'll be dead in a few days."

"I'll pick more."

He looked at the ceiling for a moment, then shook his head as if to clear it. "Did you sleep well?"

"Aye, too well at that. The walk must've taken more out of me than I thought." She hesitated, thinking of their conversation on the beach that afternoon.

Sometimes the damaged things are treasures in their own way, Jesse had said. She wondered what he meant by that. Was he softening toward her? Was he starting to care?

She almost laughed at herself. He had clearly spent years teaching himself not to care. A few days with her was not going to change that. And she was a fool for wanting to change it.

Oh, but she did want to.

"Shall I slice the bread, then?" she asked.

He hesitated, then nodded.

While he spooned up stew into two speckled enamelware bowls, she randomly selected a knife at the sideboard and attacked the loaf.

"That knife's for filleting fish," he said.

"Is it, now?" She set the sliced bread on a cloth napkin and carried it to the table.

He poured a mug of beer from a corked bottle.

She looked longingly at the tin-lined icebox in the corner. "These days I find I have a craving for milk," she said.

His ears reddened as he poured her a glass. She couldn't help smiling. Mum always said men didn't know how to behave around a woman who was expecting. It was as if they would admit no connection whatever between the sex act and the appearance of the baby in a woman's belly.

She sat down at the table. He picked up his spoon. Making the sign of the cross, she bowed her head, murmuring a prayer of thanks. When she looked up, she saw him regarding her oddly.

"Habit," she admitted. "And faith. You don't give thanks, Captain Morgan?"

"For what?"

"For the fruit of the earth and the sea. For life and health."

"No."

Mum would have a calico cat if she knew her globe-wandering daughter had crossed paths with a heathen like Jesse Morgan.

"I'm thankful to you as well," Mary said, sampling the stew. "'Tis because of you entirely that I'm here at all, eating this delicious meal and—" she struggled to keep a straight face "—sharing your sparkling company."

His brow darkened like a thundercloud. "I'm pleased you survived the wreck—don't think I'm not," he said grudgingly. "But I live alone by choice. I'm not used to sharing my home."

"I had no idea," she murmured. Then, contrite, she added, "The stew is delicious. And I had the loveliest day today." It was true; she realized that as soon as the words were out. Not long ago, she had been certain that a beautiful day spent in the company of a friend was a dream that would never again come true for her. Jesse Morgan was not exactly a friend, mind, but she had enjoyed being with him. Enjoyed the day. There was something timeless and wonderful about a shoreline where the earth and sea meet. She had always felt it, back in Ireland and now here at this remote spot.

"You're getting stronger every hour," he remarked.

She wanted to throw her arms around him in gratitude. "Thanks to you."

"I'll take you to town where you can recuperate properly," he said. "Tomorrow—"

"I'm recuperating just fine right here," she retorted, stung. So that was why he was so all-fired eager to feed her and pamper her. Not because he cared, but because he was fattening her up in order to send her out into the world.

"You can't stay here." He grabbed his beer mug and took a long drink.

Her appetite gone, she set down her spoon and pushed her dish away. "Faith, and who would want to? I ask you that. I've been made to feel the intruder ever since I woke up in that room."

Mary caught her breath and clapped a hand over her mouth. Ah, this temper of hers. Mum always used to say it would get her in trouble. She took her hand away from her mouth. "I'm sorry. That was uncalled for. You saved my life. What right have I to expect anything more from you?"

He clenched and unclenched his jaw. Why, she wondered—not for the first time—would nature favor a man with such extraordinary handsomeness, then make him want to hide away from the world?

"Ilwaco has a good hotel and several boardinghouses," he said. "You'll be closer to the doctor in town."

How could she explain? Could she tell him that she was running? Running. She had reached the very edge of the world, and now he wanted to send her back...to what? A wave of nausea struck her. Willfully she fought it, tamped it down, conquered it. She'd come too far to give in to terror now.

Trying not to tremble, she traced her finger around a knot in the scrubbed pine table. "Do you know what it's like, Jesse Morgan, to be stripped of everything, right down to the clothes on your back?"

He regarded her without expression. "No."

"It's extraordinary. Liberating, if you will. And completely frightening."

"I can help with the money until you find some acceptable situation."

"Ah. And is there such a position in this town called Ilwaco? Will they accept an unmarried Irishwoman with a babe in her belly?"

"Why wouldn't they?" he said.

She stared at him, stunned to hear such naiveté from a man who clearly knew the dark side of human nature. "People have small minds and cold, tight little hearts."

"That's not my problem," he grumbled.

"God forbid that it should be," she retorted. "God forbid that you should have to cope with another person." Surprised at herself, she got up from the table and walked away from him. What was it about the man? she wondered. He brought out the worst in her.

He got up, too, and followed her across the keeping room. "I didn't ask you to come washing up on my beach."

She whirled to face him, surprised to find him standing so close she could feel his body heat. "Then I apologize profusely for doing so."

They glared at one another, chins jutting, each silently defying the other to speak. Mary felt a stirring in her chest, her throat. And then, all in a rush, came the mirth. Untimely as Indian summer, it came bubbling up through her, and no amount of glaring and posturing could stop it. She laughed until the tears came, then used her sleeve to dab at her eyes.

Jesse Morgan looked thoroughly annoyed. "You're getting hysterical. You should go and rest."

"I've been resting all day. I've been resting since Sunday. And I wasn't laughing at you but...but...I don't know. At the entire situation. There's not a reason in the world I should have survived, but I did."

"There's a reason—" He cut himself off and turned away, going to the front door and pressing his fist to the lintel while he looked out.

"What do you mean?" she asked softly, looking at him, always looking, studying him from behind. Why did he fascinate her so? Why did he draw her toward him, make her eager to brave his temper and his insults?

"Nothing. What I really need to know is why you claim to have no kin, no friends, no one in the world."

She swallowed hard. "Because it's true."

"Everybody has someone."

"Even you, Jesse? Do you have someone?"

He turned back to look at her. "My parents, but they're on an extended trip abroad. And a sister," he said tersely. "I haven't seen her in a long time."

"What is her name?"

"Annabelle," he said. "And she—" He broke off and braced his arm on the door frame. "We're speaking of you, not me. I want to send a letter or a wire. Surely there's someone—"

"There is no one, damn your eyes!" she burst out. "No one! No one!" She knew what was coming next—he was going to ask her who put the baby in her belly.

Without giving him a chance to speak, she pushed past him and slammed out of the house. Blinded by tears, she stumbled across the yard to the path leading to the lighthouse. The lamp was not yet lit for the night, and the tower stood in stark silhouette against the fiery sky: a beacon of hope, a sentinel of loneliness.

She heard his tread like a muffled thump on the path behind her, and she turned to look at him. Angrily wiping at her wet cheeks, she said, "When you found me, I was running. I wanted to run away so fast and so far that I didn't care if I reached the very ends of the earth and fell off. Can you understand that?"

He looked solemn. "Oddly enough, I can."

"Then you must know how I feel." She studied the outline of the lighthouse high on the bluff. "People don't generally run toward things, but away from them. It's no accident that I wound up here. At the edge."

"A lot of people do," he said. "We have more ship-wrecks here at the Columbia bar than anywhere else on the coast."

"I wasn't talking about shipwrecks." She reached out and, before he could pull away, she grasped his hand in hers. "Don't do this, Jesse. Don't turn me in now."

"Turn you...?" He stared down at their clasped hands. She expected him to pull away, but he didn't. He took a step closer. "Tell me what sort of trouble you're in. Did you steal something? Murder someone?"

"Certainly not. And you know that. In your heart, you know I'm no criminal."

She took a risk, a huge leap, knowing in advance it was the wrong move but unable to stop herself. She pressed the palm of his hand over her stomach, where the child grew. "Isn't my trouble rather obvious?"

He reared back as if she were a flaming brand. "Jesus Christ, woman!"

"What? All I wanted—"

"And all *I* want is to be left alone. Stay away from me,

Mary. Just…stay away." He strode up the hill toward the lighthouse.

She watched him go, his long body and longer shadow flowing along the sunlit pathway. She wouldn't see him again until morning, for he would be all night tending the lamp.

What a strange and mournful existence it must be for him, keeping the beacon lit through the night, watching the ships pass by. Did he ever wonder who they were, where they were going? Did he ever think of leaving this place?

He was a man of deep secrets. He was hiding something in his past that made him turn his back on the present. She ran her hand down the dress she was wearing, the fine sprigged muslin that smelled of lavender sachets.

None of her affair, she told herself, and yet she knew she had to try to know this man. The world had given up on Jesse Morgan. The world kept its distance.

There's a reason…

She had been spared from death when everyone else on the *Blind Chance* had drowned. Jesse would not tell her why he thought that was so, but Mary stared at the lighthouse and watched the lamp flare to life inside as he lit the wicks for the night. In an unguarded moment, he had said, "There's a reason…"

She knew why.

She had followed his light after the shipwreck. His light had helped her survive. The man who had kept it lit for her could not know it, but he was the reason for her survival.

He claimed to want nothing to do with her. But it didn't matter. She could help him. Maybe they could help each other. Just as he had pulled her from the angry surf, she knew she must draw him into her own light and awaken the man behind the glacial blue eyes.

She wasn't even certain she wanted to do this. All she knew was that she needed to. Though shaken and hurt and angry, she had no other choice, no other place to go.

She felt the bluster of a freshening wind coming up from the sea. Clouds gathered on the horizon. A storm was brewing.

"You're a fool, girleen," she said aloud. "The man's a foul-tempered beast. He clearly can't stand the sight of you." Her hand stole to her midsection. "You should know better than to trust a man with a handsome face."

As the dawn crept past huge gray thunderheads, Jesse kept one eye on the incoming storm and the other on the station log. As head keeper, he was required to write a journal of the daily activities at the station. His reports were terse and dry: "Heavy seas and a wind from the southwest. Squalls attended with showers of rain."

Sunday's entry followed suit. "Recovered one survivor, a female, from the wreck of the oysterman *Blind Chance*."

He would never write down the fact that she was as beautiful as an angel and as lost as a lamb. Nor that she was with child. Those things would force him to regard her as a person, not merely a duty. He wasn't ready to do that. He would never be ready.

He finished the current entry and wiped the nib of his pen. The storm would break with the dawn, and he must get ready. He felt the pull of an almost mystical connection with the sea and the sky. Long before most men saw a storm coming, Jesse felt it in his bones. It was not a pleasant feeling; it was more like a queasy, vague sickness.

Right now, the sensation was acute. He drank a tepid cup of tea. He washed his face and trimmed the wicks in the great lantern, then stood and looked out at the leaden sky and the boiling sea.

The iron gray of the water clashed with the coal-tinged

storm clouds. Sea spouts whipped up out of the water, set
in motion by the seething tempest. For now, though, the
horizon was swept clean of anything but the jagged line
of the crashing distant combers and swells.

He stood in the beacon house and watched and listened.
A quickening wind slapped at the glass panes of the pulpit
and whistled insidiously through the cracks. Behind the
lighthouse, the great trees bowed their heads in deference
to the power of the coming storm. The grasses on the
dunes of Sand Island lay flat as if ducking for cover. A
flock of seagulls huddled together with their heads tucked
under their wings, each with one foot drawn up.

Jesse checked the time. He was nearly at the end of his
watch. Before long, Magnus would come to relieve him
and begin the daytime duties. Jesse went out on the catwalk and greeted the storm. Unlike the birds and the trees
and the world around him, he took no pains to retreat. He
shoved his face into the wind and let the slanting sheets
of rain slap at him with punishing, needle-like sharpness.

He stood gripping the rail like the captain of a great
ship that was going nowhere.

And then he saw it. First a flicker on the incoming surf.
A flash no bigger than a wavering candle. Then the sight
of a hull climbing a swell. The instant it appeared, another
swell surged up to swallow it.

Someone was out there, trying to get to shore.

Jesse pushed away from the rail and went inside. He set
the fog bell to ringing and hurried down the winding stairs.

He raced for the barn, mounting D'Artagnan bareback
to save time, and urging the horse with reckless haste
along the path to the beach. *Hang on hang on hang on.*
The rhythm of the command was pumped from his heart
to every limb of his body.

The boat was still out there, still being thrashed in the
surf, drawing closer and closer to the jagged black rocks

that lay tumbled below the cape. Jesse couldn't tell if there were any people in the small craft. He'd find out soon enough.

He galloped a hundred yards to the north, where the dunes descended gently to the sandy beach. Then, with a firm tug on the reins, he steered the horse out into the surf.

He had spent years teaching the horses this maneuver, and D'Artagnan obeyed without balking.

The snarling waves lunged at Jesse. He bent low over the horse's neck and rode straight at them. The gelding's hooves kicked into the bared teeth of the sea.

The battle began.

For Jesse, this was the essence of life. It was the only thing that made him feel alive. Raw energy flared through him. The fight against the sea had a rhythm all its own, pushing and pulling, neither force ever letting go.

He would never go to sea—the horror of the past had ensured that—but in the surf, where land and water met and clashed, he was in his element. The horse half surged, half swam toward the small, floundering boat.

It was a ship's boat. He could see its rounded hull through the lashing rain. A swell the size of a house built up, blocking his path to the small craft. His legs clung to the sides of the horse as D'Artagnan reared. Water washed over man and horse in a huge, drowning cascade that seemed to have no end.

Time stopped. Silver bubbles rushed past his open eyes. No, not bubbles. Stars. He saw stars. His lungs were ready to explode. In a moment it would all be over.

He and the horse shot out of the bottom of the swell and burst forth as if the sea itself had given birth to them. And there, only a few feet away, wallowed the distressed boat.

He made out a row of Cyrillic characters in the chipped

paint on the hull. The Russians had evidently wrecked somewhere and abandoned ship.

A couple of men hauled ineffectually at the oars. A sailor in the bow spotted Jesse and screamed in fear. Jesse's lips peeled back in a grimace. No doubt they thought he was a horseman of the apocalypse, come to lead their souls to hell.

Another man hurled the tarred end of a rope in Jesse's direction. Ah, yes, that fellow had much more sense than his companions. Better to throw the devil a line than to trust in God.

Covered from head to toe in borrowed oilskins, Mary stood on the beach with Palina and watched the drama play itself out in the surf.

When the fog bell had awakened her, she'd seen Erik and Magnus race past on horseback, heading down the hill toward the beach. She had gotten to the strand just in time to see Jesse and his horse being swallowed up by the biggest wave in the sea. Her soul had begun to burn to ashes; Jesse was underwater for a long time. And then, when it seemed time to abandon all hope, he and the horse had burst free of the gray-metal waters as if the sea had spat them out.

Jesse had tied the line from the boat to his horse. The horse was now plunging through the surf toward land. The wind blew so hard that Mary and Palina clung to each other to stay on their feet.

Magnus and Erik met Jesse as the boat grounded itself in the sand. Shouting incoherently, the sailors—six in all—clung to the men and horses and ropes, whatever they could get their hands on, and let themselves be dragged to safety.

"Come, we must help with the injured," Palina said, taking Mary's hand.

Mary hurried to the waterline, where the sea bit at the sand. As she reached with both hands for one of the victims who was staggering toward her, she happened to glance at Jesse. She expected to see in his face the grim determination of a man battling the elements for dear life. Instead, what she saw shocked her.

What she saw was a pure, raw joy, frightening in its intensity.

Seven

❧

"**Y**ou'll catch your very death," Mary said, standing in the doorway of the barn and watching Jesse with the horses. "You haven't stopped to rest or dry off or eat since it happened."

"If I fell sick every time I got wet, I'd be long dead," he said, not looking at her. He brushed D'Artagnan and murmured something to him.

"Do you talk to your horse often?" Mary asked.

"He doesn't sass back at me."

She bristled. Jesse had been perfectly solemn as he spoke the words, so it took a minute for her to realize that this was his idea of a jest.

"Very funny," she said, stalking into the barn. Her Goodyear's rubber boots, too large by far, clomped on the straw-strewn floor. "What can I do?"

He didn't look up from his grooming. "Give them each a scoop of sweetened oats."

While she found the barrel and the scoop, she spoke over her shoulder. "What will the sailors do?"

"Since none of them were injured, they can go right to the telegraph office in town. They'll have to wire their shipping company and then wait for a boat bound for Russia.''

''Do they ever stay, people who survive the shipwrecks?''

He didn't stop working, but his hand faltered as he curried the horse's withers. ''No. They never stay.''

Mary didn't believe him. As she poured oats into each horse's feeding trough, she kept her eyes on Jesse. He was soaked to the skin, his Kentucky jeans hugging his hips and thighs, his boots squishing as he moved. A plaid shirt clung to his shoulders and chest, outlining his form in a way she should not have noticed, but did.

''Something wrong?'' he asked.

She flushed. ''Palina said lightkeepers are always supposed to be in uniform when they're on duty.''

''I'll make note of that.'' Again he had that deadly solemn expression, but his lips twisted wryly.

This time she laughed. ''You are a caution, Jesse Morgan.''

''Aren't I just?''

She leaned against a stall door. What a strange and fascinating man he was, one moment dour and unpleasant, the next moment dour and incongruously amusing. She wished he would smile at her, just once.

''Do you ever laugh, Jesse?''

He scowled, working at a tangle in the horse's mane. ''What the hell sort of question is that?''

''A perfectly reasonable question. I find myself wondering what you find funny.''

''Very little. Particularly after I've been on duty all night and battling the waves all morning.''

''You loved battling the waves.''

This time he stopped what he was doing and stared at her. ''That's not true.''

"No need to get your dander up. It was just an observation."

"A mistaken one." He unhitched D'Artagnan, led the horse to its stall and took off the bridle. The gelding immediately plunged his muzzle into the feeding crib and started crunching the oats. "Get up to the house and into some dry things."

"You're dismissing me, then?"

"If I were to make myself any clearer, you would see straight through me."

She made a huffy sound and turned, marching out of the barn. On the slope leading across the meadow to the house, she turned back once, to see if he was looking at her. She kept thinking that surely he was watching her go, watching and wondering and thinking that perhaps he had been rude.

But no. He continued to work as if she had never been there. While she watched, he bent and picked something up from the floor. Then he stripped off his shirt and wrung it out. Mary lost all sense of time as she observed him in the gray misty light of the rainy day. His chest was broad and deep, more thickly muscled than she had imagined.

He sluiced water from the bucket over himself and draped a blanket over his shoulders. Then he closed the door to his horse's stall. And did the most extraordinary thing.

He slid one arm around the beast's neck and clung there, looking suddenly so drained and exhausted that Mary almost ran to him. There was such tenderness in the way he stroked the animal, leaned his forehead against the horse's head, and finally let go, backing away.

Mary had a lump in her throat as she made her way to the house.

Jesse took a long nap in the barn. Never before had he stumbled to the hayrick and spread out the old buffalo blanket and slept there. It was oddly comforting, being in the company of the beasts in a place that smelled of straw and horse and molasses-sweetened oats.

But when he awakened, he felt out of sorts. *She* was keeping him from his own house.

Muttering under his breath, he put on his damp shirt. He swore as the clammy fabric clung to his back and chest. It was all that woman's fault. She had disrupted his life and made him miserable.

It was time for her to go. She was well enough now. Hadn't she spent the entire morning helping the shivering Russian sailors up to the Jonssons' house, drying their clothes and feeding them as if she'd been at the job for years?

Hadn't she given the youngest sailor a smile so brilliant that the lad clutched at his heart and collapsed in the sand, pantomiming a direct hit of Cupid's arrow?

The woman was trouble, and no mistake.

He would tell her to leave. He would tell her now.

He went to the house, yanked open the door and froze where he stood.

For several seconds, neither he nor Mary moved. A moist warmth from the hot bath hung in the air, and the scent of soap filled the room. Jesse's eyes drank in the scene as if they had been dying of thirst and the sight of Mary in the kitchen was a drink of purest water.

At first, finding her in this state was so unexpected that for a surreal, disoriented moment, he didn't quite grasp what he was seeing. Then he grasped it far too well.

Mary Dare stood in the battered old zinc bathtub in front of the stove, caught in the act of reaching for a washing cloth. Warmed by the glow of the lamp on the table, her skin looked creamy and pure, her dark red hair forming damp squiggles down her back. His gaze followed the swirls plastered to her skin, down to the roundest, most perfect backside he had ever beheld. It was all he could do to stifle a moan of pure animal lust.

She gasped and lunged for the towel draped over a chair. Even in the midst of that swift movement he could see the curve of her breast, so sweet it made him ache. The shape was softly echoed by the swell of her belly.

It was then that he returned to his senses.

So did Mary. She covered herself with the towel and squeaked out his name. "Jesse. I didn't expect you to be up so soon," she said. Her cheeks were scarlet.

His thoughts were scarlet. Cloaking himself in indignation and emitting a long string of curses, Jesse whirled and stomped out the door.

He stood on the porch in the glaring slant of the sunset after the storm, threw back his head and gritted his teeth. He wanted to howl. Very slowly, he counted to ten. And then to twenty. But it didn't help. His entire body was on fire. In every cell, he felt the heat of passion.

"Damn it," he said through his clenched teeth. "Goddammit. Goddammit." He had forgotten how powerful lust was. Or perhaps he had never known. It had been so long since he'd allowed himself to feel it. He'd never wanted to feel it again. And here she was flaunting herself in front of him, peeling back the hard shell of his self-denial and making him remember what he had been trying for years to forget—that he was a man with a man's desires.

Within a few moments, the screen-mesh door creaked open. "Jesse?" her soft voice called to him. "I'm sorry. I didn't mean—that is, I thought—ah, listen to me. You've got me flustered now. Come inside. Supper is ready."

He kept his back to her.

"Jesse?" She sounded shaken, yet always in her voice there was that damnable undercurrent of good humor.

"I'm...coming," he forced out. If it were not so painful, he would have been furiously amused at his choice of words.

"All right. Don't be long." The door tapped gently against its frame.

Feeling like a fool for avoiding his own house, he went in. Without looking left or right, he strode to his room and yanked on a set of dry clothes, then returned to the kitchen. He couldn't help but notice Mary had dressed hastily; a couple of the buttons down the back were left undone.

For a moment, he considered telling her, helping her. He pictured himself lifting the damp strands of hair away from the nape of her neck. She would smell of soap and lavender there, and her skin would feel warm and moist to the touch.... He banished the notion with a cold wave of self-loathing.

Oblivious to his thoughts, she lifted the lid from a great pot. Steam, redolent of cabbage and bacon, filled the air. "Colcannon," she said. "My mother's recipe. Sit down, Jesse."

He wasn't used to this. Wasn't used to another person moving around his house, fixing his meals. With an ungracious nod, he jerked out a chair and sat down. Mary served him a large helping of the colcannon. He had never heard of the dish and wanted to refuse it, but he was starving. The concoction of potatoes and onions, cabbage and bacon and butter was too damned tempting. He dug in, shoveling away several mouthfuls before pausing to take a long drink of beer.

Mary watched him from across the table. "Do you like it, then?"

"I was hungry. It's been a long day." He glanced out the window. "Day's nearly gone. Someone should've gotten me up."

Ignoring his gruffness, she ate daintily and sipped her

milk. "I went down to the barn to see what was keeping you. When I saw how soundly you were sleeping, I covered you and just tiptoed back out."

"Wasted day," he muttered. But the food and the beer were mellowing him, and his mortification at finding her at her bath had begun to fade.

"Wasted?" She lifted an eyebrow. "Faith, and who else today has saved six lives?"

He shrugged and hunched over his meal. "It's no more than my job. When I signed on as head keeper, I took an oath saying I'd do no less."

"Why do you love it so, Jesse?"

He paused with his fork in midair and glared at her. "I don't love it. I just do it."

"No, I watched you. When the danger was greatest, that's when you seemed most joyful. The swell that washed up over you and your horse might've crushed you, killed you. And you enjoyed it."

"That's about the most damn-fool notion I've ever heard. A boatload of men was about to go cracking against the rocks. I had to stop that from happening. It wasn't a matter of enjoying anything."

"Have it your way, then." She took a bite and chewed slowly. Just as he was starting to savor a companionable silence, she broke it. "How do you get your horse to do that?" she asked. "To ride through the raging waves?"

"Training." He scraped his plate clean.

Without asking if he wanted it, she got up to get him a second helping. "Did you train the horse yourself, then?"

"Yes."

She sat back down and toyed with her food. She was clearly waiting for him to elaborate on his training techniques. Grimly, he attacked the second helping of colcannon and said nothing.

"Well." Mary smiled brilliantly. "I feel quite grand,

eating a simple meal with silver-plate forks. Where did this come from?'' Her small thumb traced the shell design. ''Whose initials are these?''

Jesse tried to contain his exasperation. She seemed determined to force him to talk. ''I don't know. It's from a ship that wrecked at the bar nine years ago. There were no survivors, but a lot of salvage washed up on the beach. I found a box of silver tableware.''

''Strange,'' she said with a dreamy sigh.

He grunted a reply.

''Aye, to think of people long dead, and here we sit using their things.'' Just when he thought she was going to get maudlin, she smiled. ''It's a lovely thought, isn't it? That you salvaged something from a great tragedy and here we are, sharing a good meal and friendship and using their silver.''

Damned if she wasn't the oddest woman he'd ever met. He shoveled in the rest of his meal and rose to wash up before she could do it herself. While he worked, she went to the door and looked out. ''We should go to the Jonssons and check on the sailors.''

''If there was a problem, they would have told us.''

''I'm not speaking of a problem,'' she said fussily, taking down a mackintosh from a peg near the door. ''If you don't want to go, I'll go by myself.''

''It's too dark out,'' Jesse called over his shoulder. ''You'll—''

The door slammed.

''Fool woman,'' he muttered, yanking on his coat and jamming his cap onto his head. He grabbed a lantern and followed her out. ''You'll lose your way in the dark.''

''Not if you light my way,'' she called defiantly.

Damn her, she was pushing him, pushing him out into the world, and he didn't want to go. He didn't like being pushed. But he knew he had to follow her. Before he did, though, he glanced up at the bluff to see that all was in order at the lighthouse. It was Erik's turn at watch.

Holding the lantern to the side, Jesse could make out a shadow slipping along the path down the hill. He hurried toward her. "I must say," he said dryly, "your swift recovery pleases me."

"It pleases me, too," Mary said.

The glow from the lantern outlined her features, and in spite of himself Jesse was struck. He supposed that somewhere in the world there was a more beautiful face, but he certainly hadn't seen its like.

Until lately, he had not considered himself to be a man who dwelled upon a woman's looks, but there was something about Mary, a quality that was ancient and wise, giving depth and meaning to her beauty.

It frightened him to think this way about a woman. It was even more dangerous than lusting after her. And Jesse was guilty of both.

"I'm pleased because your recovery means you can leave," he stated. "Have you decided where you'll go?"

She trod heavily on the path, snapping a twig. "Have you decided that you care?"

He wanted to say no and mean it. But to his eternal surprise, he couldn't. "It's a matter of concern to me."

"Ah, aren't we grand in our speech tonight?" she said teasingly. She lifted her face to the night sky. Between the slender, lofty branches of the giant evergreens, the stars were beginning to wink. In just a few hours, the moon would push into view. Without warning, she slipped her hand into Jesse's. "There's no shame in caring."

He snatched his hand away. "There's no point in it, either."

With a huff of indignation, she marched along the path, covering the quarter mile to the Jonssons' with admirable stamina. Before long, lighted windowpanes shone through the darkening woods. Mary stopped at the front gate.

"Is something the matter?" Jesse asked.

"Listen. Just listen."

The sounds that came from the snug wood-frame house were as warm and inviting as the lamp glow in the windows. Jesse heard male laughter and then Palina's voice, singing. Someone was playing the mouth organ, and feet thumped upon the plank floor.

Mary smiled up at Jesse. "How lovely it must be for them, to know they're safe."

He didn't know what to say. With Mary, he rarely did. She pushed open the gate and went up on the porch. Erik's spaniel dog, Thorvald, lifted his head and barked a greeting. Magnus came out, a mug in his good hand. "Welcome! Welcome!" he called jovially. "We have just opened a bottle of Palina's marionberry cordial."

Mary positively beamed as she stepped inside. It struck Jesse that here was a person who thrived in the company of others. She seemed to need it the way a plant needed the sun. It was just as well that she was leaving, then, for company was the last thing Jesse could give her.

She greeted the Russians in turn, laughing as her tongue stumbled over their names. She took the hand of each one, squeezing tenderly.

"Faith, it's a blessing entirely that you're here, and safe, all of you," she said. To Jesse's amazement, tears sparkled in her eyes, but she blinked them away.

One of the men stood and grabbed Jesse by the shoulders. He was stocky, his face weather-burned and creased into a grin to reveal tobacco-yellowed teeth. "I am Dmitri Spartak," he stated, his accent rich and rumbling, "of the fishing schooner *Natalya*. Thanks be to you for saving us."

The Russian pulled Jesse forward and kissed him, a loud smack on each cheek.

"*Nostrovia!*" the others toasted, lifting glasses and mugs in Jesse's direction.

There had to be something in the irony that Jesse's first kiss in twelve years came from a man with stained teeth and several days' growth of beard. He tightened his lips self-consciously, almost grinning. The man with the mouth organ struck up a lively tune, pounding the floor with his foot. The others leaped up and started dancing around. Mary and the Jonssons joined in, laughing with the pure joy of being alive.

Jesse looked on, watching them all, their faces flushed and heads thrown back in abandon. He heard the odd cacophony of Russian, Icelandic, and Irish brogue, and suddenly felt a genuine smile start inside him.

It had been so long since he had smiled that at first he didn't recognize the warmth in his throat, the feel of his mouth turning up. Mary stopped dancing and walked to his side. "You look so bonny when you smile, Jesse Morgan."

He closed his face into its customary scowl.

The dancing and drinking went on until the marionberry cordial and the events of the day took their toll. One of the Russians—the one who kept making calf eyes at Mary—curled on the floor with a blanket over him. The others sat around the table, their ballads slowing in tempo, their speech slurring.

Jesse noticed that Mary looked tired, her cheeks pale beneath the freckles, her small hand held up to stifle a yawn. Damn. The last thing he wanted was for her to have a setback.

"We'd best be going," he said, taking his keeper's hat from a peg by the door.

Her feet shuffling, Mary fetched her coat and joined

him. Dmitri lifted his glass a final time. "You are the most blessed of men, Jess-Morgan," he said. "Such a wife you have! She is as beautiful as the moon." He winked. "And baby. Certain you will have strong boy-child for family honor."

Jesse took a step toward the door. He felt his ears catch fire. "I'm not...that is, she's not...we—"

"Good night to you all," Mary said, grabbing the lantern and pushing Jesse out onto the porch. "Best of luck and high blessings upon you."

"Good night!" they called, and the sound of their voices subsided as Mary and Jesse started toward home.

"Now, don't you go lighting into me," Mary said as he glared at her. "It was just easier to let them think us man and wife."

"Humph." She was right, but he'd never admit it.

They walked in silence for a time, listening to the shush of the sea in the distance and the wind soughing through the trees. The green scent of budding leaves filled the air. Mary walked clumsily in her borrowed boots, and when she stumbled, Jesse grabbed her.

She leaned against his chest for a moment. "Thank you."

"I didn't want you to drop the lantern," he said grudgingly. But he kept one arm firmly around her for longer than her stumble warranted. He told himself this was probably a trick of hers, acting helpless. But he didn't care. He took a deep breath, inhaling the scent of her hair and feeling her closeness, the warmth of her, the giving softness pressed against him. God, it felt good. Too damned good.

Keeping hold of the lantern, he put her away from him. "Be careful," he said. "There are a lot of rocks in the path."

"I'll be careful." Her hand tucked itself inside her coat,

and he imagined her touching the little round swell of her baby. Not just her baby. It took two to make a child.

A cold shaft of suspicion pierced through Jesse. Had she been a sawdust girl, selling her body to strangers? Or had someone forced himself on her, held her down and—

He closed his mind to that image. "Why don't you ever speak of the father of your child?"

She walked on as if she hadn't heard. She remained silent until they reached the porch of his house. He set down the lantern, and she leaned her hands on the railing, watching the sky. Every five seconds, the Cape Disappointment light swept the area like a sudden moonbeam.

"He is nothing to me," she said at last. "Nothing but a foolish, foolish mistake."

Jesse could hear the lie in her voice. She still held feelings for the mysterious man. An image of Mary, standing in her bath, flashed through his mind. He recalled the memory with painful starkness. Having seen her like that forced him to view her not just as a shipwreck victim but as a woman, one who could inspire passion and lust and perhaps even love.

No, there was no perhaps about it. Mary Dare was made to be loved. Of that he had no doubt. But if she was looking for love here, she had come to the wrong place.

In his imagination, he saw her with another man. A young and handsome buck with a ready smile and readier wit. The idea of a man holding Mary, stroking the glorious naked body Jesse had seen, filled him with fury. He had no right to feel proprietary toward her, but he did. Against all logic, he did.

"I hardly think of him anymore," she declared.

"How can that be?" His tone was brusque. "You have a daily reminder."

She took in a sharp breath. He saw her knuckles go

white as she clutched the railing harder. "You're cruel, Jesse Morgan. Where did you learn to be so cruel?"

He caught her chin on the edge of his hand and turned her face up to his, so that she would have to look at him and see for herself that there was nothing here for her to redeem.

"Haven't you guessed?" he asked ruthlessly. "I learned it from a woman."

Eight

~~~❧❦❧~~~

Mary worked at the kitchen table, deftly snipping and fitting and hemming a pile of odd cuts of fabric she'd found in the tall blue cupboard. The work took her back, reminding her of more pleasant times in Ireland when she and her mother had worked side by side.

But the present kept intruding on her remembrances. Try as she might, Mary could not stop reliving the moment Jesse had walked into the house and seen her at her bath.

Even now, the memory had the power to make her hands tremble and her heart pound. She felt a proper mortification, of course, but there was something else, too. A feeling she was too honest to discount. In that terrible, wonderful, drawn-out moment when he had stared at her while she stood frozen, electricity had passed between them.

Desire. Recognition. Need. All three, and more. For the first time, Jesse had looked at her and seen a woman, not a nuisance or a duty.

The acknowledgment had only lasted a second, of course. Long enough to convince Mary that she was not boarding with a dressmaker's dummy, but with a flesh-and-blood man.

The idea was both frightening and exhilarating.

After all she had endured, she should know better than to look at a man with anything other than contempt and distrust, but Jesse Morgan was different. He was a singular man, one who defied all the warnings that rang through her head. One who contradicted everything the past had taught her.

She was thankful for the solitude of the empty house today, for it gave her time to debate the matter in her mind. Jesse Morgan was a jackass of the first order. He didn't give a tinker's damn about what others thought of him. She should be glad that they had reached an accord at last.

They disliked each other intensely. It was the one thing they didn't argue about. And that, she realized, was a great pity indeed, for she had made a momentous decision.

She was going to stay here with him.

She had to. It was the only place she felt safe. The lighthouse station was remote, protected, hidden. The perfect home for her and her child. She knew what Jesse's reaction would be: horror and denial. He would order her immediately out of his house, out of his life.

And then they would quarrel again.

Mary disliked quarreling, so she decided not to inform him of her plan. Soon enough, he would realize she wasn't going anywhere.

"Good morning," called a voice from the doorway.

Mary smiled at Palina. "Come in! There's coffee on the stove."

The older lady helped herself to a cup and brought it to the table. "You are making curtains, yes?"

"I am." Mary held up a length of pretty yellow gingham she'd found in the cupboard. "This house begs for a touch of color."

"More than you know, little mermaid," Palina said.

"More than you know. This house needs color and laughter and many other things in it."

"Unfortunately, all I can provide is the color." Mary stabbed her needle through a pinch of fabric, pleating the curtain. She wondered what Palina would think of her decision to stay here in defiance of Jesse's wishes. "Now that I'm feeling better," she said tentatively, "Jesse will make me leave."

"You must not let him."

Mary smiled. Perhaps the idea was not so far-fetched, after all. Still, she needed reassurance, and so she said, "It's not proper for me to be here. A woman with child and an unmarried man. The village down the hill won't tolerate that."

"Jesse Morgan is not a man to cling to what is proper and what is not. Nor does he put great store in the opinions of others," Palina said. "You must stay. It is the law of the sea."

Bemused, Mary cocked her head. "I'm not sure what you mean, Palina."

"You are here due to the will of a power far greater than us. Jesse found you as he was meant to. If you go away now, the circle will never be complete."

A chilly shiver touched the base of her spine. "What do you mean, he was meant to find me?"

Palina finished her coffee. She picked up a chintz pillow cover Mary had made and fitted it over a drab, musty pillow on the settle. "You must let him tell you himself."

"He tells me nothing." Mary slid a slender wooden stick through the pocket of the curtain she had just fashioned. Together, she and Palina put it up over the front window.

"He will explain it in his own time. In his own way. I can tell you only that the sea took something very precious from him." Palina cradled Mary's chin in her hand. The touch felt so familiar and motherly that Mary thought of her own mum and suddenly wanted to weep. "Now the sea has given you to him. It would be extreme bad luck to dishonor that covenant."

Feeling weary, Mary rubbed the small of her back.

"Are you uncomfortable?" Palina asked. "Is it the baby?"

Mary smiled tiredly. "I get twinges and sometimes my stomach itches. Is that...normal?"

"Of course." Palina hugged her. "I will bring you an ointment for the itch. All will be well, you'll see." She stepped back, smiling as she inspected the new curtains. "Simply charming. Thank you for the coffee."

After Palina left, Mary was filled with nervous energy. She worked fast and furiously on the house, trimming the windows with curtains, making fresh slips for the pillows on the furniture and runners for the tables. Almost defiantly, she festooned the rooms with jars of wildflowers, setting them on tables, on windowsills, on the mantel, and finally on the shelves of the ornate headboard over Jesse's bed.

She lingered in his room, looking around and trying to find some clue to this mysterious past Palina had hinted at. Except for the grand bedstead, it was as spare as a monk's cell. Above the washstand hung a small oval mirror. A razor strop was laid over the rack on the stand. A comb lay next to a shaving cup and brush. From hooks on the back of the door hung three changes of clothes and a lighthouse-station uniform—blazer and cap with the beacon insignia.

Mary touched the thick woollen sleeve of the coat, then leaned her cheek against it. The fabric smelled of the sea and of Jesse. She closed her eyes and thought of him, of the dark, moody splendor of his company and the unspoken matters that haunted him.

"A problem shared is a problem solved, Mum would say," she murmured. Palina's talk of a covenant with the sea had underscored Mary's decision to stay. It was right. It felt like the only choice she had.

But by the time the sun touched the horizon, sitting there like a great egg yolk before sinking behind the line of the sea, Mary began to have second thoughts. He had never stayed gone so long. Had she pushed him too hard, driven him away?

Sighing, she went to the porch and sat on a low wooden bench. Along the ridge of the bluff, Magnus plodded to the lighthouse to take the watch for the night. Mary lifted her hand to wave at him, but he was too far away to see.

She sat humming an old Irish tune, idly rubbing her collarbone. After all the work today, it ached a little. But it was a pleasant pain. She had earned it with hard work well done, and she knew the bruise was healing.

"Ah, what's to become of us?" she asked, touching her stomach. "I've run until there is no place left to hide, and now I don't know where to turn."

"Then perhaps," said a voice from the shadows, "you'll tell me what you're running from."

Mary gasped and jumped up. "Jesse! You startled me."

He emerged from a break in the trees at the edge of the yard. At first she could only make out the shape of his blowing hair and broad shoulders. Then he reached the porch, and she saw that he was carrying something in both hands.

"Where've you been?" she asked, feeling wary and embarrassed. She had not meant for him to hear her despair.

Ignoring her question, he set down his parcel and went around the side of the house. She heard the whine of the pump, then he returned with a bucket and scrubbing brush.

He stopped beneath the kitchen window and inhaled. "Good Lord, woman, what have you made tonight?"

"Roasted salmon and potatoes."

"Where did you learn to cook like that?"

"I'm a fisherman's daughter," she said. There was much more she could have told him. She could have told him of Da's twinkling eyes and the way he used to hide seashells in his pockets for her to find. She could have told him about her boisterous brothers, and her mum's tidy kitchen, and the cottage in County Kerry, and so many other things. But she'd save all that for another time.

"Atlantic salmon is not so very different from the Pacific variety." She eyed the sack at his feet. "What did you find?"

"This washed up on the beach." He bent over the burlap sack and took out a mass of slime.

Mary sat on the porch steps and draped her arms around her drawn-up knees. Using his pocketknife, Jesse worked at the mass. The rope was old and waterlogged, a net of some sort, shrouding a round, hard object.

He set aside the webbed net and put his find in the bucket, scrubbing with the brush. Mary watched in silence. She liked watching him. There was a strength in his arms and shoulders that gave her a warm feeling of safety.

"And are you going to tell me what that is?" she asked when she could stand it no more.

"Yes." At length he drew it out of the bucket.

Mary gasped in wonder. It was a perfect orb made of aqua-colored glass. The size of a large head of cabbage, it glowed blue-green in the fading sunlight. Like a church window it was, so rich with color that she was certain it was a priceless jewel.

"A fishing float," said Jesse. "They sometimes drift across the ocean from Japan."

She smoothed her hand down the curve of the glass

globe. Tiny air bubbles dwelt within the glass, frozen in place for eternity. "You spent all day looking for it."

He upended the bucket and set the float on it so that she could see the sun winking through the aquamarine glass and casting rainbow sprites of pigment on the wall of the house.

"It's for you," he said.

He had spoken so quietly that she was certain she'd misheard. "For me? A gift?"

"I said it was for you." His voice turned gruff.

She rose slowly and stood on the bottom step so that she was eye level with Jesse, watching him, wondering what in the world had possessed him to search all day to bring her a gift.

"It's only a bit of flotsam," he said, clearly regretting the gesture already.

A feeling started inside her. It was like a wave gathering strength miles offshore, rolling outward from the very center of her and taking her completely unawares. She had never thought to feel such a simple, pure joy. The last person she expected to inspire it was Jesse Morgan.

The wave of happiness unfurled on her face; she could feel it, could feel the smile forming, could feel the sparkle in her eyes as she looked at him. "It's the most beautiful thing I've ever seen."

One side of his mouth lifted. For a single, breath-held moment, she thought he was going to smile, too. Then he stunned her by touching her, just with one finger, running it along her cheekbone. His face was completely solemn. "Not everything that washes up on the beach is damaged."

The exuberance inside her was simply too bright and shining to contain. She wound her arms around his neck and kissed him long and hard on the mouth.

He made a startled sound in his throat. Her assault threw

him slightly off balance; she felt him take a stumbling step away. He put his hands on her waist to steady himself. His surprised mouth was softer than it looked, softer than she had ever imagined it to be. He tasted of the salt air.

It was the sweetest kiss Mary Dare had ever known. And he wasn't even returning her kiss.

He recovered with disappointing speed and set her away from him. A dazed look gentled his features, but just for a moment. "Jesus Christ," he said, and the glacial chill returned to his eyes.

"I only wanted to thank you," she whispered.

He muttered something incoherent and pushed past her into the house, slamming the door behind him.

"Someday, Jesse Morgan," she called after him with defiance in her voice, "you'll kiss me back."

She heard him take exactly two steps; then he must have noticed the colorful changes she had made in the house.

The next thing he said was perfectly coherent, and so foul that Mary flinched just to hear it.

Jesse stood in the middle of the keeping room with his hands on his hips, biting his tongue to keep from saying something even worse. What the hell did the woman think she was doing?

She had kissed him. *Kissed* him. Brazen as a Seattle sawdust girl, she had thrown her arms around him and kissed him smack on the mouth. No one kissed Jesse Morgan. It was a thing that did not happen to him.

Didn't the fool woman realize that?

Someday, Jesse Morgan, you'll kiss me back.

Not in this lifetime, dear girl.

The kiss meant nothing. He should simply forget about it just as he'd forgotten the mosquito that had bitten him that morning.

Ah, but his idiot traitor body remembered every move

she had made, every nuance in her face, the taste and smell and sinful softness of her.

He'd spent the day being haunted by the memory of her in the bath, the steam rising upward in lyrical wisps, the stunning lushness of her body. Everything in him tried to deny the desire he felt. It was ridiculous, lusting after a woman pregnant with another man's child.

Someday, Jesse Morgan, you'll kiss me back.

The words taunted him, a seductive, persistent whisper. Shaking his head, batting at the invisible demons like a great bear beset by wasps, Jesse willfully banished the kiss from his memory. He forced himself to confront the next issue—what *she* had done to his house.

It didn't even feel like his house anymore.

His gaze skipped contemptuously from the low fire burning cheerfully in the hearth, to the vats of flowers in colors so bright they hurt the eye, to the abomination of chintz curtains and fringed pillows and lacy table runners everywhere he looked.

No, it didn't feel like his house at all. It felt like a *home*. Jesse hated that.

He whirled around to confront her as she walked in the door. She cradled the float as if it were infinitely precious.

He snarled in self-contempt. He had combed miles of beach in order to find her something without flaw, just to prove his point. Just to show her she carried no permanent scar from her ordeal. And all the while she'd been here, in his house where she didn't belong, rearranging his life without even a by-your-leave.

"I worked all day," she said softly. The glass ball, held delicately in front of her, glowed with a life of its own. The sunset through the door behind her burnished every hair on her head.

"Do you like it?" she asked.

"No," he bit out, ignoring the way she seemed to draw

in on herself. If his harshness hurt her, that was her problem, not his.

"I preferred things the way they were." He strode across the room, ruthlessly grabbed the frilly valance over the big window and tore the fabric down with a great rending sound. "If I'd wanted lace hanging about my windows, I'd have put it there years ago."

She bit her lip. For one horrible moment, he thought she was going to start crying. Lord save him from a weeping woman. But Mary Dare didn't weep. She set the glass ball carefully on the mantelpiece, stalked over to Jesse and stood with her hands on her hips, glaring up at him.

His errant gaze was drawn to her mouth. Only moments ago, she had kissed him. No matter how angry he got, he couldn't stop thinking about that. The floor had seemed to give way beneath him, listing like the deck of a ship in a storm.

Twelve years. It had been twelve long years since he'd kissed a woman....

"Kiss me goodbye, Emily. Kiss me now, and we'll be together again before you know it."

"Oh, Jesse, I don't want to go."

"You have to, my love. Your stepmother's expecting you." Jesse hooded his eyes from her direct gaze. Did Emily know? Could she look at him and see how he'd betrayed her?

"Faith, this is a miserable, cold place," Mary said. "It could do with some cheering up."

"I don't want cheering up."

"And that," she said, stabbing a finger at his chest, "is precisely your problem, Jesse Morgan. You live—no, you *exist*—like a condemned man. Nothing is real to you except the stories in those books you're always reading." She shook her fist at the crammed bookshelves.

"Those stories happen to be interesting to me."

"Because they happen to other people, and you only have to watch," she retorted. "You wear your solitude like a shield. The moment someone comes along and scratches a little window in that shield, you start storming around and swearing and ripping the draperies and trying to run me off. I won't stand for it, do you hear me? I won't."

"Fine. Then leave. All I want is my own life back. You can find some other place to start anew."

"What's wrong with starting here, I ask you that?"

"What?" he sputtered. "I'll tell you what. I didn't ask you."

"Well!" She turned in a swirl of skirts and indignation. "Supper's ready."

Despite his anger at having his house rearranged, Jesse was starving. Grimly he removed the jar of wildflowers from the table and whipped off the frilly table runner. He and Mary glared at each other.

"Put it back," she said between her teeth.

"No," he said simply.

She glared at him for another moment, then sniffed as if he wasn't worth the trouble. "Have it your way, then, *bodach*."

"What's *bodach*?" he asked, stumbling over the foreign phrase.

She sniffed again. "'Tis the Gaelic version of what you called me when you first saw the curtains."

Feeling curiously and inexplicably better, he washed up while she set out plates of salmon and potatoes and baked apples. There was an awkward pause while Mary gave thanks, then Jesse dug in ravenously.

"I appreciate the supper," he said after inhaling half the salmon. By way of apology, he added, "It's delicious."

She studied him as she took a few bites of her meal.

"Palina came to visit this morning. She said my leaving would be a mistake. Said it was the law of the sea that I should stay."

"Palina's full of more sh—nonsense than a bull moose."

"You don't believe in the legends of the sea?" A speculative gleam came into her eye. "You don't believe in destiny?"

"I don't believe in anything at all."

"Ah, Jesse." She smothered her baked apple with cream. "What happened to you? What made you like this?"

Her question was a painful fist of intrusion. Damn the woman. "Palina probably gossiped enough for you to know."

"She said the sea took something away from you. That you'd have to tell me yourself. Was it someone you loved, Jesse? Did you lose someone in a boating accident? Or a—"

"It's none of your goddamned business." His throat felt suddenly raw, and he slaked his thirst with a long pull from his mug of beer. "Tomorrow, Magnus will take you to town and see about finding a proper place to stay."

As if she hadn't heard him, she gazed at the glass fishing float on the mantel. Tiny flames from the grate reflected on its underside. Mary smiled wanly. "You know, that's surely the most extraordinary gift anyone's ever given me."

"It was just to prove a point," he said ungraciously.

"Even so, thank you." She pushed back from the table and carried her dishes to the sink. "I feel tired all of a sudden. I think I'll go to bed."

She hadn't really agreed with him about going to town, Jesse noticed uncomfortably. He watched her shuffle out of the kitchen and close the door to her bedroom. In the crack beneath the door, he could see her bare feet. He heard a soft thump as she leaned back against the door. He imagined he could hear her even softer sigh as she let out a long breath. He pictured her pressing against the door, her eyes closed, weariness pulling at her dainty Irish features.

Well, why wouldn't she be weary, after spending the day disrupting twelve years of solitude? And why in the world should he regret making her feel small and intrusive and useless?

He should have felt a deep satisfaction in getting her to see reason at last. Instead, he felt as if he had just stepped on a puppy.

"What the hell are you still doing here?" Jesse said the next evening.

Mary stood at the top of the yard where the path led to the lighthouse station. She had gone there to wait for him to finish his chores. He was on watch tonight and would have just a short time for his supper.

"Yes. Still here," she said, thrusting aside a feeling of guilt. She *had* to stay. He wouldn't understand, but she had to.

"Magnus was supposed to take you to Ilwaco," Jesse said.

She searched his face, trying to read what he was thinking. His eyes were sapphires encased in ice; his mouth was set. For the life of her, she couldn't tell what was going on in the man's head.

"The road is blocked. We were on our way down in the buckboard, but we had to turn back. A great tree has fallen across the road."

And may the Lord God forgive me entirely, she thought. She herself had come across the storm-damaged tree that morning, had seen it leaning precariously. It had been a sin for certain to ask Erik to give it a few extra heaves until it fell across the roadway. But she couldn't go to town. She couldn't leave this place where she was safe and hidden.

"Magnus said it was caused by the storm," she explained, though she strongly suspected Magnus, too, was in on her deception. "The Russians were able to climb over and walk to the village, but Magnus wouldn't hear of me doing so in my condition. He couldn't get the buckboard or even the horses around the tree. It was an act of God, surely."

"I see." Jesse started toward the house. "And did he spend the day clearing the road?"

She followed him, taking two steps to each of his one. Lord, but the man had long legs. "Not exactly. He said you'd have to get some sawyers from town to cut the tree—that huge, it is. A Douglas fir."

Jesse stopped walking. "All right. Just tell me. What exactly were you and Magnus up to all day?"

The sharp suspicion in his voice sounded ominous. "What makes you think we were up to anything?" she fired back.

For the second time in as many days, she thought he was about to smile. But his lips merely tightened, and he reached out and ran a finger with surgical precision down her cheek. "Because, dear heart, your thoughts are as clear as a Japanese fishing float."

His touch was curiously compelling, though she was certain it wasn't meant to be. "That transparent, am I?"

"That transparent."

She grabbed his hand, holding it tightly so he couldn't snatch it away. "You've found me out. Come, then. I'll show you."

"I can hardly wait," he grumbled.

Sunlight made a dazzling display on the lawn as she

drew him along the path. She could feel the tense reluctance in him, the way he leaned back and barely refrained from wrenching his hand out of hers. If he dug in his heels, she wouldn't be surprised.

"Someday I must tell you about Mulligan," she said over her shoulder.

"Who is Mulligan?"

"The mule we had back in Kerry. So contrary Da used to threaten to use him for crab bait." She gave Jesse's arm a firm tug. "I just happened to think of him."

He walked next to her at a less recalcitrant pace. "I see."

She squeezed his hand. "I thought so."

A brisk wind swept the area. The budding leaves in the trees chimed like wild bells. Mary inhaled deeply of the air, redolent of the new, green season and the ever-present sea. "How lovely it is here," she said. "Most especially now."

"Why now?"

She brought him around a bend in the path, into the yard of the keeper's house. "That's why."

"Shit." He stood there and stared at the front of the dwelling.

"Perhaps you could be a little more stinting in your praise, Captain Morgan," she said, trying not to feel the sting of his displeasure.

"You planted flowers."

"Aye, that I did."

"Everywhere."

"Pretty much."

"I don't like them. Take them out."

"No. Flowers are beautiful. Does it mean anything at all to you to have beauty in your life?"

"No," he said starkly.

She flinched. "Then I feel sorry for you." She was

tempted to launch into a tirade, but she stopped herself. A fit of temper would be no more than he expected. "I had a good day, Jesse. A lovely, magical day. Going out and getting the flowers from Palina's place. The larkspur is so rich and blue, and the primroses look just like smiling faces. And I found the roses."

"Roses?" he choked out. He strode across the lawn and glared at a trim bush of tender, pink buds. "How the hell—"

"They were here all along, but you never noticed. Never knew you had them. Someone must have planted them years ago, and then they were neglected." She bent and patted the soft bark loam she had used to mulch the main flower bed. "Even neglected roses will struggle to survive, Jesse. These have been struggling for years in spite of your neglect."

She gazed thoughtfully at the colorful garden. Her hand caressed her growing stomach. "A rose belongs to the one who tends it. Not to the person who planted it and left long ago."

She heard his breath hitch as if he had taken a blow. For a moment, a heartbeat, the blink of an eye, a sharp and unexpected yearning suffused his face. She had found it at last. A chink in the armor.

"I wonder why the roses kept struggling even though they were ignored," she said. "It seems so much simpler to dry up and die." She strolled between the beds Magnus had patiently dug, bending now and then to touch a shy blossom or tamp the dirt around the roots. "Roses tended with care will flourish—you watch. By the autumn, they'll be rioting here."

"In the autumn," he said softly, "they'll be neglected again, because you won't be here to tend them."

Nine

❧

Jesse wondered if Mary had guessed how close she had come to breaking him. Through the first hours of his night watch, he tried not to think, not to feel. But no matter how hard he worked to take his mind off Mary, the explosion of newly stirred emotion wouldn't leave him alone.

As she wouldn't leave him alone.

Devil take her. Devil take her and her infernal meddling. What was it about the woman? Why did she feel she had to dedicate herself personally to the wholesale disruption of his life? How much clearer could he be with her? How could he make her understand that there was no life for her here?

He was an empty shell of a man. A hermit hiding out, and he wanted it that way. He had nothing to offer a woman like Mary Dare.

Moving with the automatic precision of long habit, he went to the mezzanine level of the lighthouse and gave the equipment a grind. Every four hours, this had to be done. The machinery drove the movement of the light. With a pattern as regular as a heartbeat, the beam swung from horizon to horizon, all night long, every night.

Often the light was the only thing that stood between

ships at the bar and total disaster. The number of hulks and sunken vessels attested to its imperfections, but the treacherous shoals had caused fewer accidents since the lighthouse had been installed some twenty years earlier.

Jesse was manic about keeping the beacon lit. Not once in his tenure had the lamp gone out or even blinked. Before he had taken over this post, the light had indeed gone out. Twelve years earlier, as the ship carrying Emily had attempted to cross the Columbia bar, the beacon had been extinguished. The loss of the light had caused the ship to run aground.

There had been an investigation, of course. The lightkeeper in charge had been devastated, claiming a gentleman from Portland had given him too much to drink and challenged him to a friendly game of cards. Caught up in the whiskey and the gaming, the keeper had grown careless.

The tragic consequences of that failure had driven Jesse to the remote bluff, where he served out a life sentence, determined never to waver in his duty. He imagined himself doing this for the rest of his days. Growing old and dying right here in these cramped quarters—but only after his turn at the watch was up.

Moving like the ancient man he felt he was, he made his way to the tiny clerk's desk in a cubbyhole of the mezzanine and turned up the flame of his lantern. He opened the station log, selected a pen from the shallow drawer of the desk and unscrewed the cap on the bottle of ink.

As he opened the book, a stray breeze, sneaking in through a window, ruffled the pages. For a moment they all flipped past him, a bleak record of his days here, rustling like dead leaves tumbling along the ground.

For some reason, the thought depressed Jesse more than he cared to admit. He had a fleeting urge to go out along the bluff for a walk, but he decided to stay in the tower. It was his last sanctuary since Mary had arrived. She had disordered every other aspect of his life. At least the light-house had been spared from her intrusion.

"Yoo-hoo!"

Jesse jumped so abruptly that ink sloshed out of the bottle, splashing over his hand in rivulets like black blood. "Damn, damn, damn," he said between clenched teeth.

"Are you there, Jesse?" a voice called brightly from the bottom of the stairs.

"No."

Her laughter wafted up the tower like a stray wind. Then he heard the strange musical *bong* of her footsteps on the iron grille of the stairs. While the sound of her approach crescendoed, he muttered a string of curses under his breath, soaked a rag with linseed oil and scrubbed the ink from his hands.

And from the surface of the desk.

And from the planks that covered the floor.

He didn't even attempt to get the stain out of his pant leg.

By the time her bright moppet's head of curls appeared in the doorway to the mezzanine—the next to last room before the beacon room—he had stored up several choice invectives to hurl at her. But she smiled at him, and he forgot everything in the world. Everything except a promise she had made to him the day before.

Someday, Jesse Morgan, you'll kiss me back.

Would today be the day? he wondered.

"Hello, there," she said. In the light of the lantern on the desk, she shone like a new copper penny. She set down a tin pail. "I brought you some refreshments."

Tired, that's what Jesse was. Tired of fending off her relentless, cheerful, unapologetic intrusions. He decided, just for tonight, to surrender. It was less taxing than setting up a resistance.

"Fine," he said in quiet resignation.

She froze in the act of taking out the teapot. "What did you say?"

He took the can from her and set it on a small round table in the middle of the room. "I said, fine. Thank you. It's quite…thoughtful of you." The polite phrases tasted foreign on his tongue, like exotic fruit.

She leaned very close to him. His instincts warned him to step away before she kissed him again, but she didn't kiss him. She sniffed the air delicately.

"What are you doing?" he asked.

"I wanted to see if you've been drinking."

"I don't drink when I'm on watch. Why would you think I'd been drinking?"

"Because you were nice to me. Polite. It's simply not like you."

"Madam, you don't know me well enough to know what I'm like."

She unwrapped a linen napkin to reveal still-warm slices of some sort of bread. A subtle smile curved her mouth. "Ah, but I do. I find 'madam' rather grand and to my taste, thank you very much. This is Irish soda bread. Have you ever tried it?"

"No."

"It's delicious with tea." She fussed around the table, setting out the bread and pouring the tea. He simply sat back and let her. His impulse had been right. It took less energy to let her have her way. Resisting her was wearing him out. An unexpected feeling of contentment filled him as he sipped from his mug of tea. It was delicious—warm, undeniably strong and just a little sweet.

Like Mary.

He frowned into his mug, trying to rein in his thoughts,

hoping she didn't read him as well as he read her. She strolled around the tiny, octagonal room, inspecting the weather instruments. "What is this one?" she inquired.

"A self-registering patent thermometer. The temperature is fifty-two degrees Fahrenheit," he said.

"How does it know?"

"The relative temperature of the air creates a pressure that pushes the liquid mercury up the glass tube." He couldn't help the patronizing note that crept into his voice. Surely weather and astronomical instruments lay far out of her range of knowledge.

She touched her finger to the reservoir bulb in the bottom of the tube and watched as the line of mercury nudged upward. "Well, I think it's magic."

"It's science."

"Ah," she said with a sage nod. "And is it science, too, that explains why the North Star isn't perfectly north at all?" She pointed an old-fashioned sextant out the window and sighted Polaris. "Your compass gives one reading for north, but the star gives the other."

Chastened, he helped himself to a slice of soda bread. "The compass is drawn magnetically to a point that is not true north."

"A magnet, is it?"

"A magnet, not magic." He watched her put away the sextant. "Most people don't even know there's a difference."

"I think you'd be amazed at what I know, Captain Morgan." She went up the ladder to the beacon room and stood with her nose pressed to the glass, looking out with a wonder expressed by every fiber of her being, from her eager palms on the window to the tense set of her shoulders.

"It's wonderful," she said, her breath fogging the glass.

"How can you stand to look at a sight so wonderful without bursting?"

"I try to restrain myself," he said.

"See the way the beam swings, like a bird made of light, with shadows chasing in its wake."

"I suppose so."

She touched the door latch. "May I?"

Since the wind was low and the night perfectly clear, he nodded. "Just hang on to the rail. It's a long way down."

Eagerly she went outside, and again he went with her, telling himself he needed to keep a sharp eye and a restraining hand on her. She held the rail and looked out at black eternity. The breeze lifted her hair from her neck, and when the beam swung past, he could see how pale the skin was there, how delicate.

Jesse felt a hunger that hadn't plagued him in ages. A hunger to taste the just-bathed skin of a beautiful woman. This was no fleeting need, but a forest aflame inside him, raging ever hotter, further and further beyond his control. He couldn't stop himself from wanting her. From imagining the way she would feel, her velvety skin next to his. From wondering if there was any taste sweeter than Mary's willing lips.

He wrenched his gaze away from her. "Like it?" he asked tensely.

"Oh, aye. Such a lovely sight. So many stars. Plentiful as snowflakes, they are, and just in that band there, they all blend together like a great white mist."

"The Milky Way," he told her.

"A spiral galaxy. In the old days they called it an island of stars."

Jesse stared at her.

She stared back.

"You surprise me," he said.

A smile bowed her lips. "Do I, then?"

"The things you know...they're just—" He broke off, feeling awkward. It was hard to imagine that there had been a time when he'd been easy in any social situation, a sought-after conversationalist, a favorite of the most discerning hosts in Portland and San Francisco. Years of living alone had stolen that ability, as so much else had been stolen from him. "It's just..."

"Just the sort of thing you don't expect an ignorant Irish lass to know," she finished for him. "No need to be polite about it. Lord knows, I've encountered more than my share of prejudice against Irish. It was the worst in New York City." She screwed up her face. "Lots of fat immigration officials and harbormen blaring, 'No Dogs or Irish.'"

Jesse had told himself he wasn't interested in her past, yet now his curiosity was piqued. "You've been to New York City?"

"I didn't stay but a week before setting out for San Francisco." She turned back to the horizon. "It's why I love being here so, at the edge of nowhere. You've not judged me, Jesse Morgan. Well, not too much, anyhow. You never said, 'No Dogs or Irish.' Have I remembered to thank you for that?"

With the first kiss I've had from a woman in twelve years, he thought.

"It means a lot, that you've not sat in judgment of me."

"I'm the last person to sit in judgment of anyone," he said, more sourly than he meant to sound.

"Ah, that'll want explaining," she said.

"You're a nosy female, Mary Dare."

Her laughter flowed like a river of light through the air. With a whimsy that was foreign to him, he imagined he could see her mirth illuminating a path through the darkness like the beam from the lighthouse. Then she sobered a little, her gaze following the arc of the beam.

"This was my guiding star," she said, her voice quiet. "Did you know that? When I was lost, after the ship completely broke apart, this was the light that I saw. If not for the beacon, I would've drowned with the rest of them."

I'm glad you didn't drown. He couldn't speak the words, but his heart said them for him. Not with joy, but with a firm conviction he hadn't felt in years.

Unaware of the upheaval inside him, Mary looked again out at the ocean, her face bright with fascination and acceptance. She didn't see what he saw. He saw a hated enemy. He saw the thing that had turned his life into a bleak, endless string of gray days.

She—who had been its victim—loved the sea.

He had convinced himself that he didn't want to know this woman. The less he knew about her, the safer he was from her intrusions. But there were things he had to ask her. Things he had to know.

For official reasons, he told himself.

"Can you speak of it now?" he asked. "Can you tell me of the shipwreck?"

Her gaze stayed riveted on the crystal facets of the huge lens through the window. "I don't mean to be secretive."

"I'm aware of that."

"I know you must think me an unforgivable thief." She seemed mesmerized by the slow revolutions of the lens. The lilt in her voice was subdued. "It wasn't until the ship got in trouble that they found me. A fire in the galley brought me out, and a good thing it was, too. I confess the men were a wee bit surprised."

That was surely an understatement, Jesse thought.

"Before they could decide what to do with me, the weather kicked up."

"They?"

"The ship's cook and his worthless helper. He was trying to put out a grease fire in the galley and I simply had to step forward to help him. He should have known better than to use beef fat for frying potatoes. I mean, honestly." The lilt came back into her voice as she grew indignant. "The great lout had been feeding the seamen poorly, anyway. It was all I could do not to take over and set him to rights."

He could picture it. She was bossy and brazen enough to want to have things her way.

"I was a better cook than he would ever be," she said. "It's how I earned my fare to San Francisco."

"Cooking?"

She grinned. "I was a ship's cook. That's how I came to sail 'round the cape from New York."

"Cape Horn. You sailed around Cape Horn."

"It was a ship out of Buenos Aires. You sound amazed, Captain Morgan."

He was more than amazed, but he couldn't tell her that, couldn't tell her about the feeling that squeezed his chest. The idea of such an adventure seized him with a yearning so sharp it pained him in a place he thought long dulled to pain. How exhilarating it must have been to sail the horse latitudes and the roaring forties around the cape, through the icebound gateway between the two greatest oceans of the world.

It was an exhilaration Jesse Morgan would never, ever know.

Yet hearing her speak of it made him want to go there, to feel the roll of a pitching deck beneath his feet and the sharp cold wind in his face.

Impossible.

In the early days after Emily's death, he had tried to make himself put out to sea. He had no fear of the surf, which reason told him was more treacherous by far than open water, but the terror in his mind didn't listen to reason. The moment he set foot on board a ship, horror seized him, without fail, slashing at him with great talons of accusation, driving him back, back to the place where earth and sea meet, where he was destined to stay forever.

"...had read the law but never took up the practice," Mary was saying.

Her sprightly voice snatched at him, drew him back to the present. "What?" he asked with an impatient shake of his head. "I didn't hear what you were saying."

"I was telling you about Mr. Stevenson. A fine gentleman, for all that he's a Scot and has some strange ways. Malcolm, he insisted I call him. He was on the ship that brought me 'round the cape. Headed for a place in the South Seas, he was. Sandwich Islands, but he called it by its native name—Hawaii. Quite ill, poor soul, though he never complained. Consumptive, I think. Yet for all that, he simply adored adventure."

"And this Mr. Stevenson was your...friend." Jesse couldn't help himself. His gaze strayed to her stomach.

"Don't you dare." Her voice lashed out with more fury than he thought her capable of. "Malcolm Stevenson is a man of honor with a lovely wife. Don't you dare think for one moment that Malcolm...that I...we—"

Jesse cleared his throat. "If you came here expecting civility, you came to the wrong place."

She buried her face in her hands. Her shoulders shook. She looked so small and lost that Jesse had a strange urge—the impulse to touch her.

He resisted it.

When she raised her face to look at him again, her cheeks were pale in the eerie beacon light, but she seemed quite composed. "Malcolm was my friend and a great teacher. He's the one who taught me about the weather and the stars. There is so much in this world I don't know." She sighed, a lifetime of regrets whispering on a single breath.

Her hand rested on her stomach. "It's odd when I think about it sometimes. They say the voyage 'round Cape Horn is the most treacherous in the world. Yet the greatest danger I encountered was right here."

The wind picked up, pressing the fabric of her dress against her legs, outlining a form Jesse didn't want to see but couldn't help gawking at. He opened the glass pane and stood to one side. "Let's go in. The tea will be getting cold."

Without even thinking, he put out his hand to help her. She glanced at him, eyes wide with surprise. Then a smile curved her mouth, and she put her hand in his. Her fingers were cool and slightly damp from the sea air. He tried not to feel the strange energy that passed between him and Mary as they crossed the threshold from the catwalk into the beacon room. He wondered if she felt it, too.

"Thank you," she said.

They went to the small chamber below, where the tea waited. Their silence was comfortable—and unexpected, given Mary's verbal proclivities. The sound of the wind and the sea only made the inside feel more cozy. Her gaze was wistful as she moved to the desk and idly thumbed through the station log. "He was going to teach me to read and write," she said.

"Who?"

"Malcolm. He knew how badly I wanted to learn. But after the ship made port in San Francisco, I...decided that it was best to stay there."

He heard a disturbing inflection in her voice when she mentioned San Francisco.

"What is in this book?" she asked.

"Reports. It's much like a ship's log. All lighthouse keepers must record a summary of activity each day."

Her face lit up. "You mean this is a record of your days? Every single day?"

"Ever since I came here." He pointed out the volumes stacked under the desk. "These are from the keepers before me."

"Every single day," she said slowly. "Sure and it's a rare thing, to have such a record." She plunked the log-book onto the table in front of him. "Read me the entry about the day you saved me."

Jesse was annoyed to feel his ears redden. He flipped back a page and put his finger on Sunday's date. She bounced up and down excitedly. "Read me what it says, Jesse. I daresay no one has ever written a word about me before."

He cleared his throat. "Sunday, second of June, 1876. Six-oh-two of the morning. Recovered one survivor, a female, from the wreck of the oysterman *Blind Chance*."

He closed the book.

Mary stared at him. The wonder shining in her eyes had a curious effect on him. He wasn't used to adulation from anyone. Particularly from someone like her. She gazed at him as if he had just presented her with the moon on a platter. How she must admire him for writing about her in the log.

"You call that a story?" she said at last.

He blinked. "No. I call it a log entry."

He realized then that her wide-eyed wonder wasn't wonder at all, but profound displeasure and disbelief. "What did you expect?" he asked, slightly annoyed. "*Robinson Crusoe?*"

"Who?"

"Never mind."

She stood and pressed her palms to the surface of the table, leaning toward him and looking a bit like a fierce pixie. "'One survivor, a female.' Is that all you can say?"

"It is precisely what happened—"

"I had no idea that an event that has altered the course of my life could be reduced to such a terse, stingy recollection."

He glared back at her. "This is not some penny melodrama. It's an official log."

"Who said official has to mean idiotically boring?"

That put him at a loss.

She dragged out a volume at random from beneath the desk. Her face lit up as she spied masses of spidery text scrawled with copious flourishes. "Is this in the same style as your entry?"

Jesse scanned the page. The keeper before him had been far more indulgent with his pen. He had written a saga of tempest-tossed weather and dire supplications to God. "It goes into a little more detail."

"Fine," she said, putting the musty old log away. "Then we must rewrite your entry."

"We?"

"I just told you I don't read or write. So I'll dictate and you write down what I say."

A protest leaped to Jesse's lips. He hesitated, weighing his options. He could refuse, and she would stay here all night arguing with him. Or he could agree and write some abomination in the logbook. The lighthouse inspector almost never came to Cape Disappointment, and even when he did, he rarely checked the log closely.

With grim resignation, Jesse dipped his pen and turned to a fresh page. "Very well. What would you have me write?"

She closed her eyes, concentrating deeply for a few moments. "Now then. Are you ready?"

The ink was drying on the tip of his fountain pen. "Ready."

She folded her hands, pressing them dramatically to her

chest. "Strong blew the wind that night, howling like the great banshee of Dunglow, snatching at the cold shivering souls of unborn children. And deep in the darkest part of the night, when the blackest of storms swept in, and not a mother's son on board the ship could know what lay ahead... Have you got all that, then?"

Jesse was writing furiously, trying to keep up with her ridiculous narrative. He nodded.

"...it was then that the tempest rose. Bless our eyes to the heights of heaven, the poor benighted *Blind Chance*—bobbing, it was, like a cork in a bucket—did ride upon the most lethal shoal in the sea. *Crash!*"

Jesse flinched as she punctuated the sound by slapping her hands on the table.

"By the hand on me," she went on, her voice rising, "I swear the ship broke apart with a great rending of timbers that sounded like all the horrors of hell."

She closed her eyes and clutched at her chest, clearly transformed by the magnificence of her own story.

"And then, like the very arm of Cuchulain the Giant, a great wave scooped our brave heroine into its cold, wet clutches and hurled her down the decks." She stood and thrashed from side to side, pantomiming the action. "Like a ball she was, rolling at ninepins." She paused. "I say, that is a rather nice turn of phrase, isn't it?"

Jesse felt his shoulders begin to shake. His eyes smarted with tears. He felt something in his throat, but he was so unaccustomed to it that he didn't realize it was laughter until a rusty bark came out.

Fortunately, she didn't recognize it as laughter, either. "I know, dear Jesse," she said in a soothing voice, "it was quite harrowing and you may well weep for me, but as you can see, I'm all right, so don't be distressed."

"I'll try to control myself," he managed to say, his penmanship deteriorating as she dictated.

"She knew her everlasting fate lay in the hands of the Almighty Himself. Frantically, she lashed herself to the mast as it floated by. In minutes the great sucking maw of the sea had swallowed up the *Blind Chance* and all it contained, including—and may God rest their blessed souls—every last man aboard. Only our intrepid heroine lived to tell the tale...."

She went on, caught up in her story as if it were Melville's *Moby Dick*. Jesse's handwriting covered page after page of the logbook. Through it all, he barely managed to hold his laughter in check. She was so unguarded and earnest as she dictated, absolutely convinced that her fanciful version of the adventure belonged in the records for posterity.

"...and down to the beach he ran, like a great, fearless hero of legend. Dark, he was, with hair of raven silk and eyes of sapphire. He swept the poor woman up into his brawny arms and placed the most magical, the sweetest of kisses on her cherry lips—"

"Now wait just a minute." He paused in his writing. "Who are we speaking of here?"

She regarded him in utter innocence. "Why, you, of course. The moment you found me. Dip your pen again, there you are... All right, where was I? Read that last bit back to me."

He tried. He honestly and truly tried to keep his face solemn and dramatic. "He swept the poor woman up into his brawny...arms and placed the most magical...the sweetest of kisses on her cherry lips..."

By the time he finished reading, Jesse was completely incoherent. Unable to continue, he put down his pen, planted his elbows on the table, covered his face with his hands and shook.

A moment later, he felt her touch on his shoulders.

"There now," she whispered. "I know it's a moving account, but try to hold in your tears—"

Jesse, who had not been moved to mirth in twelve years, threw back his head and loosed the loudest, longest stream of laughter of his life. It felt like a celebration going on inside him. He struggled to regain control, then finally dared to look at Mary. She had been pacing and gesticulating the whole time she spoke, but she'd stopped and was staring at him as if he were a lunatic.

"Ah, Mary," he said. "I shouldn't have laughed but—" His gaze strayed to the phrase "brawny arms" and laughter threatened to erupt again. "I...apologize." He tried to will himself to sober up, but he was like a drunk who knew he had no hope of conquering his intoxication.

Her lips twitched, and suddenly she was smiling, too, her face as bright as the rising sun. "'Tis lucky you are, boyo, that I happen to have a sense of humor." She touched his hand. "Jesse."

He looked up at her. "Yes?"

"I've never seen you like this before tonight. I've never heard you laugh."

He placed his free hand on top of hers. "It's not something I often do, Mary Dare."

"You should. Mum used to say laughter is a song without words." Mary turned away. The corner of her shawl knocked the pen to the floor. As one, they stooped to pick it up, both reaching out at the same time. Slowly they rose, facing each other, gazes locked, the pen between them forgotten.

"Mary." Her name twisted from his throat on a pained whisper. "My God—" He spoke no more, but dropped the pen and threaded his hand through the abundant soft hair at the nape of her neck. A hunger reared within him. He could no more control the urge than he could subdue his mirth earlier.

He crushed his mouth down onto hers. The searing intimacy of their embrace consumed him. He delved into her, savoring her warmth and feeling a new awareness inside him unfurl with a painful awakening. The moment took on a vividness, an intense sharp-edged reality. Everything alive and vital he had been trying to avoid for years was suddenly barreling back at him, full force.

He could not tell how long the embrace lasted. The entire world turned upon this kiss. He heard the roar and swish of his own heartbeat and that of the ocean; he heard Mary's short, breathless gasps as she clung to him. Her small fists buried themselves in the fabric of his flannel shirt.

He had the uncanny sense that kissing Mary was the only way to get from one side of the moment to the next. It was a notion more suited to Mary, who believed in magic and who had no compunction about pouring her soul out onto a public document. But he needed this, needed to engulf himself in the taste and soul and texture of her. He wanted to disappear inside her, to fill himself with her, to remember what it was like to feel again.

She was saving a part of him he didn't realize needed saving. Just as he had pulled her from the chilly surf, she pulled him toward her own lively radiance. The warmth built higher and higher inside him, a furnace being stoked.

Only when he heard the metallic grind of the machinery did he return to the world. He wrenched away from her. Christ, he had forgotten everything, drowned everything in the honeyed oblivion of kissing her.

"The equipment," he muttered, stepping back.

"I don't understand."

He was already clattering down the stairs to give the gears a turn. He discharged his duty quickly. When he turned, she was standing there with her hair mussed and her lips full and shining—*cherry lips*—stung by his kiss and her willing acceptance of it.

Someday, she had told him, *you'll kiss me back.*

How had she known?

"The—uh—the gears need turning every four hours. In all the time I've been here, I've never missed a turn."

"You're very devoted, then."

"It's my duty, no more, no less." How formal he sounded. The realization that he had nearly forgotten years of training for a moment of lust in a strange woman's arms had disrupted his routine.

She was pregnant, he reminded himself coldly. She refused to speak of how she had come to be that way or why she was alone. He needed to keep his distance from her. She was none of his affair. As soon as the loggers cleared the road to town, he would be free of her. Free.

"It's late," he said after the gears were wound far tighter than they needed to be. "You should go to bed."

She gazed at him for a long moment, a moment measured in heartbeats and unspoken longing. "I'll go, then." She went to the stairs, her hand on the rail. "Jesse?"

"What?"

A sweet-sad smile softened her face. "I wasn't finished with my story."

"Perhaps...we could finish it another time."

"Perhaps." She took two steps down, then looked back at him. How heartbreakingly pretty she was. And how wasted that beauty was on a man like him.

"But Jesse?" she persisted.

"Yes?"

"I don't know how it ends."

Ten

When Mary awoke late in the morning, a blurry dreaminess lingered. She lay abed for a few moments, squinting at the bright sunshine coming through the slats of the shutters. She smiled, thinking that the clear, luminous warmth of the sun was exactly what she felt in her heart.

Because of Jesse.

Something had happened last night. Something magical and extraordinary, something Malcolm Stevenson would call destiny.

In the darker moments, when she had been recovering from her ordeal, she had wondered—quite sincerely—why she had been spared from drowning when every other soul on the *Blind Chance* had been sucked into eternity. She thought perhaps it was because of the baby, but now she knew it was something more.

She had survived because Jesse needed her. She knew it for certain.

It was not for her to question such things, of course. Who was she to guess at the workings of the higher powers of the universe? Whether it was Palina's legends of the sea or the luck of the Irish or the very hand of God, it did not matter. She was here for Jesse.

She washed and dressed, then brushed her hair until the long red curls crackled with the friction of her vigorous strokes. She slipped out to the privy, stopping on the way back to pluck a just-opening rose. When she walked into the kitchen, Jesse was there, reaching for the enamelware coffeepot on the stove.

"Top of the morning!" she called.

He seized the handle of the pot. "Ouch!" he yelled, jumping back and shaking his hand. "Goddammit, ouch!"

She dropped the rose and rushed forward, grabbing him by the wrist and plunging the burned hand into the bucket of fresh water in the sink. "Faith, and what did you go and do that for?" she demanded.

"I didn't do it on purpose." He lifted his hand and scowled at the blister forming on his fingertip. His hair, sleep-tousled and rich brown in the morning sunlight, tumbled over his brow. "Didn't sleep well last night," he grumbled.

Mary ducked her head to hide a smile. "Well, I certainly did. What a lot of work it is, keeping yourself up on watch at the lighthouse."

He covered his hand with a dish towel and picked up the coffeepot, pouring the steaming liquid into a thick china mug. Then he carried the mug to the table.

Mary cleared her throat.

He looked at the cup, then held it out to her. "Coffee?"

"Thank you," she said, taking it. "I don't mind if I do." She was going to teach this man to live with another person if it drove her—drove them both—round the bend. Putting aside her coffee, she retrieved the rose, set it in a jar of water and placed it on the table.

Jesse poured coffee into a second mug and sat down. He scowled at the rose and moved the jar to the far corner of the table.

Without saying a word, Mary moved it back.

He reached for the jar again. She caught his eye, letting her sharpest glare stab at him. "Don't even think about it, boyo," she said. Though she spoke softly, there was no mistaking the command in her voice. Mum had taught her that.

He said nothing, but thereafter ignored the fresh rose on the table. Mary admired the perfect blossom, filled with all the colors of the dawn. The petals embraced one another timidly, still hiding. By tomorrow they would be unfurled. An open-faced, rosy smile would greet her in the morning.

She considered sharing her whimsical thoughts with Jesse, but he looked as forbidding as a bear sitting across from her, his beard dark and bristly on his cheeks and chin, his glacial eyes glaring out the window.

"Soft day," she said.

"What's that?"

"The day. In Ireland we'd call it soft. It means there's a light mist in the air with the sun coming through. A rainbow day. Sometimes we call it that, as well."

He rewarded her with a noncommittal grunt.

She managed to catch his eye. "Jesse—"

"Mary—"

They both spoke at once.

Mary burst out laughing. "How awkward we are with each other this morning. What is it you wanted to say?"

He cleared his throat and took a sip of his coffee. "I'm sorry about last evening..."

"Yes?" She was not going to make this easy for him. "I'm afraid you'll have to be a little more specific. 'Tis a great thick head I have, you see."

He studied her for a moment. His mouth softened, thrilling her, for she thought he might smile again. Oh, do, she silently urged him. What a miracle it had been last night, at the dead of midnight when his laughter had filled the lonely outpost of Cape Disappointment, as unexpected as the sun in winter. She hadn't meant to make him laugh, but the fact that she had filled her with hope.

This morning, his face had returned to its customary grimness. She knew then what a rare gift his smile had been. "So it's begging pardon you are, Captain Morgan," she said lightly. "And I've a mind to accept it, but first I should know what infraction you've committed."

"I should not have taken liberties with..." His voice trailed off. The tips of his ears were suspiciously red.

With a look of wide-eyed innocence, she stirred a spoonful of sugar into her mug and watched him expectantly.

He sucked in a harsh breath, expelled it and said, "It was ungentlemanly to...mishandle you."

"It was?"

"A man cannot simply force himself on a woman."

"I don't remember any forcing last night," she said with quiet candor.

"Then we were both wrong."

"Were we? How so?" Her indulgence was melting quickly, like chocolate left too long in the sun. He was the most vexing man she had ever met. She tried to keep careful rein on her temper, though she could feel the resentment roiling in the back of her mind. Anger had begun to wash in like the tide.

"Was there any harm done by it?" she asked. "Any damage caused by two lonely people reaching out to each other? Tell me that, Jesse Morgan. Did it hurt either of us?"

"No!" he burst out. "But it shouldn't have happened." He shot up from the table and practically flung his empty coffee mug into the sink. He pressed his hands on the counter and bent his head. She watched him trying to wrestle his temper into submission, visibly calming himself. When he turned to her, his face was expressionless.

He stood beside her, reached down and stroked a finger delicately along the side of her throat. "It's best forgotten, because it can only mean trouble," he said. "That's all I wanted to say."

Without another word, he stomped out to do chores in the barn. She sat for a long time, sipping her coffee and watching the beams of morning sun that poured in through the window she had cleaned—was it only yesterday? Aye, there was the perfect glass globe he had brought her. A gift. An offering that contradicted every cold thing he said to her.

As admissions of heartfelt sentiment went, "It's best forgotten" did not rank terribly high, but to Mary's ears, the words offered a promise she needed to hear.

Absently she rubbed her stomach, where the baby grew. She had seen a fine-looking man sink onto bended knee, had heard him claim undying devotion and she'd been stupid enough to believe the pretty words. She had willed herself to trust a man who offered her pearl earrings and midnight carriage rides. Learning wisdom from the most painful of lessons, she knew better than to put stock in flowery phrases and insincere pledges.

A simple look in Jesse Morgan's eyes meant more than a thousand false declarations from a handsome man with a waxed mustache and a fancy carriage.

"We're going to be all right," she whispered to the baby. It was the first time she had truly believed that since she had packed up her meager belongings and her mortified shame in San Francisco and stolen aboard the *Blind Chance.*

And because she had new hope for the baby, she started to picture it. A boy, for everyone knew the firstborn should be a boy. Her own family had boasted three strapping lads—Riordan, Alois and Padriac.

She sighed. Rory, Ali and Paddy were long gone now, though it took little effort to conjure an image of the trio of fiery redheads bending over the nets with Da, making the repairs for the next day's fishing off the coast of Ballinskelligs. Her baby would look like them, she decided with certainty, born of equal measures of hope and denial.

Aye, a great thick shock of Kerry red hair and a fine spray of freckles across the nose. Angel kisses, Mum had told her when Mary had come home crying from church because the Costello twins had poked fun at her freckles.

Her own little lad would wear those angel kisses with pride, because he would know they were a legacy from a proud Irish family.

A family that was no more.

A terrible wave of grief threatened to swamp her. She stiffened her spine, refusing to dwell on the past. What would she name the child? As she washed up after breakfast, she pondered the beautiful Irish names she knew, but all the time, she kept thinking, *Jesse.*

Jesse. In the Good Book, the story of Jesse was an extraordinary tale of faith. And the Biblical Jesse had named his son David.

Mary smiled, hanging the mugs on cup hooks and placing the lid on the jar of coffee beans. David was the most beautiful name she could imagine.

She spent the first part of the morning putting to rights the valance Jesse had torn in his rage. He wanted so badly to be a bear, full of anger and lashing out at everything. He might not realize it yet, but he had met his match.

He had been alone too long. The uncaring world had left him alone. Palina and Magnus and Erik were pleasant enough, but they had one another and were far too respectful of Jesse's insistence on privacy.

Mary had no such respect. She would fill his days like the sunshine flooding this lonely house on the hill, and before he knew it, he would be smiling and laughing again.

It was the least she could do for the man who had saved her. The man who had been moved to laughter by the words she'd spun. The man who had taken her in his arms and kissed her as if his very life depended on it.

A dark remembrance clouded her mind. She suddenly recalled another man's arms, another man's kisses. Would she ever be free of the past?

Thrusting aside the worrisome thought, she decided to give the entire house a good tidying. Aye, she had devoted the previous day to digging in the garden. Today she would take the cleaning of the house in hand. She sang as she worked, using strong lye soap and great buckets of water from the artesian well in the yard to scrub floors and walls and windows. She went over every inch of the kitchen. The place wasn't precisely dirty; in fact, it was painstakingly neat. But there was a neglected feel to it.

As if the house had no soul.

She worked her way to the stairs and went up to Jesse's room. Another place with no soul. It might have been a room in a boardinghouse, belonging to no one in particular.

She shuddered. Her residence in San Francisco had been more opulent, with rich red draperies dangling with golden tassels, but it had felt the same as Jesse's room.

The abode of a stranger who was taking care to leave no mark. The difference was, Jesse had been here twelve years and had still not made it his own.

She cheered up the window with a bright swag of yellow gingham left over from her efforts downstairs. The bed was made military-style, with its drab blanket of rough wool, the pillow lying flat and lifeless. She fetched one of

Palina's quilts from her own bed and spread it carefully over Jesse's.

The intimacy of the gesture gave her a deep, secret thrill. She had chosen the quilt with the mermaid on it. Although not depicted in detail, the figure was naked from her waist up. Aye, let him sleep beneath that each night and see if he could keep his thoughts pure.

As she bent to plump the pillow, she frowned at the meagerness of it. Surely she could find another pillow somewhere. She opened a tall pine cupboard and peered inside. She found a rifle and a supply of bullets. A long knife such as a tanner might use.

She spied another pillow high on a shelf. Standing on tiptoe, she pulled the corner toward her, yanking hard when the ticking caught on something.

There was a scraping sound, and the pillow sprang free. In its wake came a polished box, falling first upon her foot, then to the floor with a loud crash. "Ouch," she cried, grabbing her foot. She bent to pick up the box.

Low and flat, the coffer had brass fittings. The pain in her foot forgotten, Mary studied it for a moment. A deep-colored, fine-grained wood, like walnut or cherry—maybe even rosewood—shone with the patina of age. In the center of the lid was an oval plaque. Three letters were stamped in the brass. Mary traced her fingers over them, remembering her alphabet. "E...L...M," she said aloud.

Someone's initials, she decided. Not Jesse's, though. She knew the shape of the J, and there was no J here.

She lifted the box to replace it in the cupboard. A spring gave way with a soft, tinny *ping*, and the latch flew up. With a gasp, she fastened the catch. But it refused to stay. The hinged latch kept flipping up, again and again.

Frowning, she set the coffer on the floor, its lid hanging askew. The first thing that struck her was the stale, musty scent of old perfume—not an unpleasant smell, just an old one.

She knew she was looking into the past. Jesse's past.

The top layer of the box contained thin, crinkled sheets of paper. Carefully lifting the tissue, Mary discovered a lovely white chemise of the finest batiste she'd ever felt. A pair of lace gloves with buttons so dainty they surely had to be secured with a crochet hook. An ancient dried rose, crumbling between folds of tissue. A fan with ivory ribs and forget-me-nots painted on the silk.

She sat on the floor and stared at her discovery. A woman's prized possessions. Things of surpassing fineness, too. Surely they had belonged to a lady of quality. Jesse's mother, perhaps?

Mary drew her knees up and rested her chin on them, feeling an unaccustomed tightness where the baby grew. Something told her these things had nothing to do with Jesse Morgan's mother. At length she picked up a tooled-leather picture frame. The two halves were hinged and closed like a book. Slowly she opened it.

And she saw there, cradled delicately in the palms of her hands, the secret Jesse had kept hidden from her.

Jesse entered the house, something close to a smile on his face and a perfectly formed sand dollar nestled in the palm of his hand. He had thought of Mary when he'd found it on the beach below the great bluff. This find wasn't as impressive as the glass globe, but the sand dollar had no flaw.

Well, it was dead, but that didn't count. It was still perfect in shape and symmetry.

The house smelled different. Cleaner. The light seemed altered, too. Although the day had grown overcast, the keeping room looked brighter. He ran a hand over the back of the settle. The wood frame had been scrubbed, along with the floors and windows and everything else he could see. Mary had been hard at work today.

The knowledge meant only one thing to Jesse. She was well enough to leave him. She would be gone as soon as the road was cleared.

This was exactly what he had expected right from the start. He should be grateful. The whole ordeal would soon be over. He'd have his life back. Just the way he wanted it.

Except he wasn't sure he wanted it anymore.

The sense of impending loss struck him like a blow. Swearing under his breath, he yanked off his hat and shoved his fingers through his hair.

Mary was not supposed to happen to a man like him.

And yet she had. Though he had come here to hide from the world, she had washed up on his beach, practically into his arms, this stranger who had the power to move him. To make him forget his vow to turn away from the world. To challenge him to start dreaming again.

There are things that come to us from beyond eternity, things we have no right to question, Palina had said that first day. *Twelve years ago, the sea took from you everything you held dear. Now, perhaps, it has given something back.*

Jesse Morgan had lost the desire to believe in anything, and yet, since Mary had come, some part of him that hadn't died was slowly awakening. He told himself he didn't want that. He couldn't take that risk. He was here to grieve and to atone, not to heal. Not to learn joy again.

Mary seemed to have other ideas. She was a woman alone who had lost everything except the babe she carried. Who was he to cast her out into the cold?

"Mary!" he called. "Are you there?"

A chill crept through him.

"Mary?"

The wall clock ticked mockingly into the silence.

He strode to the kitchen, wrenched the cork off his whiskey bottle and took a large swig. Grimacing at the roughness of the liquor, he closed his eyes. So she'd left, after all. It was what he'd wanted, wasn't it? Wasn't it?

Then he heard it—the creak of a floorboard.

Setting down the bottle, he dashed up the stairs. He wasn't sure what he expected to see—that she had fallen, hurt herself, God forbid that a problem had arisen with the baby. If anything happened to her or the baby, he'd never survive the loss. He went into his bedroom, gripping the lintel over the door.

"Mary?" Her name rasped from a throat gone dry.

She sat on the floor with her back against the wall below the single dormer window. Her face was ashen, her eyes large and somehow bruised-looking, as if she had been injured. He took a step toward her.

And then he saw what lay on the floor in front of her.

The word that exploded from him was one he had never said to a woman, but even the foul expletive was not strong enough to express his rage.

She didn't flinch, only blinked up at him. Then she said, "You should have told me, Jesse. You should not have kept this from me."

In two strides he was across the room, flinging things back into the teakwood box. He tried not to see, tried not to remember, but each treasured possession set off an explosion of memories.

"You should never have come here," he said in a low, deadly voice. "This has nothing to do with you. You had no right to open that box, to—"

"The box fell. I didn't open it on purpose," she said, unmoved by his rage. "Tell me."

He reached for the hinged leather picture frame. Mary got to it first. For a moment, their hands touched. She snatched the photograph away, holding it so that the past was staring him in the face. "I want to know, Jesse."

"Damn it, *why?*"

"Because I care."

"Don't—"

"It's too late, Jesse. I do care, and you can't stop me."

He remembered the night before, when she had borne down on him like a locomotive. It had been easier to take a ride with her than to fight her. Stopping her from caring was like stopping a river from flowing. Even if he built a wall, her caring flowed up and over the barrier.

She simply didn't belong here. In his house. In his life. Looking into his past. Perhaps the best way to convince her of that was to tell her everything.

He forced himself to study the framed photograph. And suddenly he was back in time, back in a place he could never recapture and would always regret. "I was twenty years old in that picture," he said.

"You were so handsome. Comely as a prince in a fairy tale." She set the frame on the floor between them. "Thank heaven you got over that."

"What?"

"Looking like an illustration in one of Malcolm's books. Every hair patted down, every fold of your clothing smoothed. Now you look human, as if there is something besides air behind that face of yours. Much better."

He forced himself to look at the picture in the other half of the frame. If ever nature had fashioned a face and body without flaw, here it was. Decked in bridal lace, she stared demurely at the viewer, a soft smile on her lips, her hair in shining ringlets beneath the veil. He remembered getting dizzy simply looking at her, dizzy with love and with the idea that she would be his. Forever.

Forever turned out to be less than two years.

"Go on," Mary whispered.

"Her name was Emily Leighton. We were married fourteen years ago." He made himself speak as if the event had happened to someone else. In a way, it had. He was a different person than the self-assured, baby-faced bridegroom in the photograph.

"And these—" Mary gestured at the box "—were Emily's things."

He took the frame and closed it, fastening the tiny clasp. The photograph of him and the one of Emily would be facing each other in the dark. Forever. He didn't have to look at it to remember his joy that day, or the joy that followed. They had been the fairy-tale couple of Portland, the match of the decade. The daughter of the Leighton timber barons had wed the heir to the Morgan shipping fortune. It was as close to a royal wedding as Portland had ever seen. Business associates and family members had come from as far off as Seattle and San Francisco to wish them happiness.

And their life had gone well—too well. So well that Jesse should have known better than to think it could last. But at the age of twenty, he didn't understand that life was brutal, that love was painful, that joy was a fleeting illusion.

"How long were you married?" a soft voice asked.

Mary. He had almost forgotten she sat there, so lost was he in his memories. "Almost two years," he said. "And then she…" He looked out the window above Mary and was sucked into the darkest remembrance of them all.

It had been a sunny day at the harbor in Astoria. Deceptively sunny. Back then, he had lacked an understanding of coastal weather. The azure sky and calm seas had fooled him into thinking conditions were fine for sailing.

From the distant past, he heard their shouts pounding in his head. It had been the only quarrel of their marriage….

"How dare you?" Emily had railed at him. "How dare you pack me off as if I'm a child?"

Vividly he remembered the softness of her shoulders as he held her, his grip becoming firm when she tried to pull away. "Emily, please listen. It's only for a few days. I'll be joining you in San Francisco before you know it. You won't miss me at all, darling."

She shuddered and took a lace-edged handkerchief from her little reticule. "You know I hate being without you."

"Nonsense, you did so quite cheerfully last summer. You and your stepmother had a fabulous time going to the opera and spending all my hard-earned money." Though he felt sick with guilt, a teasing tone lightened his voice. "You're a lady of fashion, dearest. An annual trip to the big city is _de rigueur_. You're simply going earlier than usual this year."

"This year is different." She looked down, staring pointedly at her stomach, where the baby grew. His baby.

When she had first told him, fireworks and pinwheels of joy had detonated in his head. His _whoop_ of gladness had rung through the huge house they shared. But long weeks later, the joy had mellowed to anticipation—and Emily had barred him from her bed.

Careless and spoiled, Jesse had drifted almost casually into the arms of Lucy, who had a brassy laugh and a physical sensuality that had woven a spell around him, fed his sense that nothing could taint his charmed world and fooled him into thinking he was invincible.

Until she'd started making demands and he'd come to his senses. He'd woken up one day, seen the harsh morning sun on his lover's face and realized how perilously close he'd come to destroying everything he had. He knew then that he had to tell Lucy it was over, and he wanted Emily far away when he did so.

"This year _is_ different." His voice thickened, and he

had to clear his throat. He gathered her to him, knocking her elaborate hat askew and not caring. "I swear, everything will be different once we're together again." He gestured at the matronly woman in a gray pinafore, standing with the steamer trunks. "Mrs. Ferris will be with you every moment. You won't even miss me."

Emily's chin trembled. "I will. You know I will. Come with me, Jesse."

"I can't, Em." He raked a hand through his hair. "Granger set up a meeting of the board of directors for next Wednesday. I can't miss it."

"Granger Clapp is always interfering with us. Every chance he gets."

Jesse suspected it was true. He and Granger had both courted Emily, and when she had chosen Jesse, his rival—and friend—had not lost gracefully.

"Let me wait with you," Emily said. "I'll sail with you next week."

"No. It's all arranged." He had kissed her cheek, tasting her tears and hardening his heart against her pleas. He happened to look up at the sky just then, and he'd seen a thin line of dark clouds like a frown on the western horizon. It was nothing, he told himself. This packet sailed each week without incident.

"Kiss me goodbye, Emily. Kiss me now, and we'll be together again before you know it."

"Oh, Jesse, I don't want to go."

"You have to, my love. Your stepmother's expecting you." Jesse hooded his eyes from her direct gaze. Did Emily know? Could she look at him and see how he'd betrayed her?

"I love you, Em," he'd told her. "I love you so." Poison words. They'd sent her to her death. Jesse had vowed never to speak them again. Never to *feel* them again.

As the tug began hauling the ship to the mouth of the

Columbia, Emily stood at the rail. His Emily. His beautiful, perfect wife, pregnant with his child. She had waved a handkerchief—he remembered it looked like a little white bird—and Jesse had felt the strangest darkness come over him, like a cloud obscuring the sun.

Years later, he knew exactly what was wrong, what had happened that day. The truth and the memories roared like an unchained beast inside his head.

"How did she die?" Mary whispered. She had been waiting patiently through the long, black moments while he remembered.

He kept thinking of that white handkerchief, fluttering at him. A bird. No, something purer, cleaner. Something weightless and formless. A soul, ascending to heaven.

Condemning him to hell.

He looked Mary Dare square in the eye. How calm and sane she appeared, though pale and slightly apprehensive. As well she should be. Who the hell was he to think he could let her into his life? She had lulled him into a false sense that he could be a man again. And that was wrong. He could never be. Not now. Not ever.

And so he told Mary the truest thing he knew about that day at Astoria harbor.

"What happened to Emily?" His voice was brutal. "I killed her."

Eleven

—❧∞∞∞❧—

Mary left Cape Disappointment the same way she had arrived—with no more than the clothes on her back. Only this time, they were dry clothes. A good dress of sprigged muslin and a fringed shawl.

The garments had once belonged to Emily Leighton Morgan. *E.L.M.* Jesse's wife. His love. The woman he said he'd killed.

As she slipped out of the house unnoticed, Mary wondered what memories had passed through his mind when she'd helped herself to the nightgowns and chemises and dresses in the cupboard. She ought to be thankful he didn't go mad, mistake her for the hapless Emily and do away with her, as well.

Terrible thoughts dogged Mary's footsteps as she hurried along a twisting path through the emerald forest. She had always thought this was a magical place, but she hadn't realized the enchantment was a dark one. The inky greenness that clung to each giant tree, furring the trunks and draping the branches, now seemed ominous to her. On the path, a hideous large banana slug slimed its way across a broad leaf. The ferns, their tender fronds rolling out like slender tongues from secretive centers, suddenly looked sinister.

This was a place of darkness, of fear, of suspicion. A place for lost souls that prefer not to be found.

Like me.

She had deemed Cape Disappointment the perfect spot to stay in safety and obscurity, but she had been wrong. What a muddle she'd made of everything. He would be glad when he discovered her gone.

The image of Jesse Morgan hovered in her mind like the epiphytes clinging to the trees, haunting the shadowy secret places in the forest. She knew there was much he held back from her, but he'd made one thing abundantly clear: she shouldn't expect anything from him. He was not interested in anything she had to offer him. He would never love her, never marry her. He had all but admitted that she'd been the first person to make him laugh in years, but it would take more than laughter to light the dark corners of his soul.

It wasn't the first time she'd misjudged a man.

After he had accused himself of murder, she had stared at him in horror. He'd seemed to relish her shock. Like a trench dug by a desperate warrior, he'd made a barrier between them. He had been trying to do that all along, trying to drive her away. But until he had made his ghastly claim, Mary hadn't realized how intent he was on getting rid of her.

He was right. She didn't belong with him.

She would never forget him. He resembled the sculpture of the Archangel Gabriel in Saint Michael's chapel back in Ballinskelligs. And etched in every line of his face was an age-old hurt that Mary Dare, who'd never been able to mind her own business, had convinced herself she could heal.

She scowled at the loamy forest path and concentrated

on her journey. A feeling of fear shot through her. Foolish. She had faced more dire straits than this, for certain. After Da and the boys had died, and Mum had quickly followed, she'd been completely alone. In debt, she was forced to sell everything the family owned for the dubious prize of a ticket to America.

And America, for all the folk back home canonized its virtues, had hardly proved to be paradise. What had she gotten from coming here besides a broken heart and a babe in her belly? A sob—half anger, half despair—tore from her. She forced down the knot of panic in her throat and plunged onward. She hadn't even found a proper home for her baby, and in just four short months, she'd be holding the poor wee thing in her arms and wondering how they'd both survive.

The daylight was fading, and she knew only vaguely where she was going. Keeping the sun to the left, she headed northward through the shadow-laden forest. The town called Ilwaco lay to the north. Somewhere, there was a road.

Ah, yes. The road that had been cut off by a huge dead-fall. She had encouraged Erik to hack away at the stump, causing the tree to topple, making the road impassable.

She had *wanted* to stay.

After what had happened to her, she wasn't ready to face the world. And with each passing day, she had grown more and more fascinated with the lightkeeper who lived cut off from the world in the beautiful house by the sea.

Again his image flashed in her mind. Dark hair, glacial eyes, unsmiling mouth, large and competent hands. Ah, Jesse. He had so much to give. She wasn't certain how she knew it, but she did, with a knowledge as strong as faith itself.

She stopped walking for a moment to catch her breath. "No one but me really sees him," she said aloud. And the certainty hit her again. For some reason, she was seized by the conviction that she alone could save Jesse Morgan from whatever strange invisible bonds held him in a past too dark to contemplate.

"And why would I be wanting to do a thing like that?" she asked herself, stepping over another slug and continuing down a muddy slope. If he lived alone, like a beast in a cave, that was surely no concern of hers.

Was it?

She loosed a long, disgusted sigh. Aye, it was, like it or not. Her destiny was inextricably bound up with that of Jesse Morgan. Hadn't he lit her way to shore after the shipwreck? Hadn't he pulled her from the sea and made her warm and dry and safe? Hadn't he sat tirelessly at her bedside when she had lain senseless?

Aye, he'd done all of that, but mostly, he had given her a place in his life when his every instinct told him to get rid of her.

Her thoughts rambling, she trudged on through the increasing darkness. The sun had dropped low in the sky, and a damp chill pervaded the air. She came to a slippery patch of mud, and her feet flew out from beneath her. She grasped at a mass of tangled vines and managed to keep herself from falling.

Feeling foolish, she righted herself and sat down on a low, flat rock, moist from the constantly dripping trees. Her body needed to rest. Just for a few minutes. She picked up a stick and started idly drawing in the needle-laden mud at her feet.

She could neither read nor write, but there was one phrase she knew by heart, because it was the first thing she had learned upon coming to America.

She formed the letters in the mud with the stick: N-O I-R-I-S-H. *No Irish.* The lesson had been drummed into her the moment she'd set foot in New York City and later

San Francisco. She had seen the *No Irish* sign in every shop front and back entry of every home and business she'd visited. America did not want poor Irish girls with no family and no money. That fact had driven her to desperate measures. It had driven her to make the most terrible mistake of her life.

She had found only one place that did not have the sign—the lightkeeper's house right here, at Cape Disappointment.

That, she knew, was because Jesse Morgan did not discriminate. He hated everyone equally.

Did the people of Ilwaco town hate the Irish? Or would they welcome a penniless, unwed, pregnant woman? That thought drew a bark of bitter laughter from her throat. The world was a hard place. She had best simply accept it and forge ahead. Laboriously, she rose and started along the path.

As if to mock her new sense of resolve, a rain shower started. The fine droplets hissed through the tree branches and spattered on the large, broad leaves with a rhythm like the bodhran drums of the old country. The cold rain needled her face.

Mary lifted her shawl to cover her head. She wouldn't have minded the rain so much except that it brought darkness with it. "Perfect," she muttered under her breath as the path became increasingly obscure and slippery. "Wet, cold and dark. My, but I've had a day!"

Very few things had frightened Mary Dare since she had left Ireland nearly a year ago. But as the green halls of moss and ferns grew black with the wet and the cold, she felt a frisson of unease. It was like a raindrop, chilling and unexpected, rolling down the length of her bare back.

She could die here. No matter that she had survived the worst the sea could dish out. Here on solid earth she could die, and the child could die, and it would make no difference to anyone in the world.

The sky—what she could see of it between the arching branches of the impossibly tall trees—had turned from gray to black. It was a true black, unrelieved by the sparkle of a distant star or the moon.

She leaned against a tree and slid down its trunk, too exhausted to do anything but stare dully into nothingness. She'd ventured too far from the lighthouse to see its beam. She had no idea where she was. She could only sit and wonder what would find her first—the dawn, or a marauding bear.

The bear came first.

She heard the thud of its tread on the path somewhere close by. Too close for comfort. Paralyzed by fear, she stayed where she was. But deep inside her, stubborn determination unfurled. She had not voyaged halfway around the world to surrender her life and that of her unborn child to a bear, of all things.

Her hand closed around a large, sharp rock, slick with moss. She shot to her feet and stood motionless, awaiting her chance. Nearer and nearer it came, and the hairs on the back of her neck felt as if they were standing on end.

Then she saw it. The flash of its horrid, malevolent eyes. How bright they were, illuminating the rise of the path she had recently slid down.

"You'll not find me an easy meal, you great horrid beast," she shouted. With all her might, she hurled the rock. It hit its mark with the sound of a stone striking a bag of wet sand.

A terrible squeal tore apart the silence. Mary stumbled, her heel catching a tree root and sending her sprawling backward onto a bed of creeping vine. The footsteps, muffled by layers of dead leaves, sounded uneven, out of control.

The squeal rose once more, and Mary saw the flash of light again. And all in a rush, the complete stupidity of what she had done hit her. It was no bear she had struck with the rock, but a different animal. A horse.

D'Artagnan. Jesse's horse.

A lantern—not the glowing eyes of a wild beast—illuminated the shiny sinews of the underside of the horse's chest as it reared in panic. And high on the gelding's back, with his oilskin cloak flapping in the wind and his hair flying out in wild disarray, was Jesse Morgan.

Why had he come for her? He wanted to get rid of her.

Frozen by shock, Mary pressed her knuckles to her teeth. She could not speak, could barely breathe as Jesse wrestled the horse back to calmness.

After what seemed like a long time, D'Artagnan lowered his front hooves and hung his head in submission. Jesse spoke to the horse quietly as he dismounted. Holding the lantern in one hand, he skidded down the slope to where Mary cowered in wet, limp shock in the thick ivy ground creepers.

"For chrissakes," he said, setting the lantern aside. "Were you trying to kill my damned horse?"

Still she couldn't speak. All she could think of were his last words to her: *What happened to Emily? I killed her.* Yet all she could feel was the tenderness in his big hands as he drew her to her feet. All she could see was the suppressed panic and sweet relief flooding his eyes as his gaze coursed over her and found her none the worse for the wear.

"I'm fine," she said faintly, but she swayed against him. Ah, he was so warm and strong and dry as he opened the front of his oilskins and brought her inside. She found herself thinking of the stories of the selkies—the seal people of Ireland. He was letting her under his skin, placing her next to his heart.

Surely it meant something.

"Ah, Mary, Mary," he said in an aching, weary whisper. "What the hell am I going to do with you?"

Mary looked as small and defenseless as a child as she sat in her dry nightgown, a blanket draped around her shoulders and her bare feet submerged into a basin of hot water. A mass of dark red hair hung in damp tendrils over her shoulders and down her back. She was shivering uncontrollably.

Jesse eyed her with exasperation. What an infuriating bit of baggage she was. It was hard to believe that someone so small and fragile-looking could turn his entire life inside out.

He had thought it would be a relief to be rid of her. When she'd stormed out of the house, he had wanted to feel satisfied. He had wanted to go back to what he was before. Instead, visions of Mary, struggling through the forest, had haunted him. The voice of the wind, growing stronger by the moment, had forced him out into the night to bring her back.

If he had let her go, he wouldn't be able to live with himself. Now that she had returned, he knew he couldn't live with her, either.

She took a sip of tea from the cup he had given her. Her hand shook as she set it down and took up a hairbrush. She made a few ineffectual tries at getting the tangles out of her hair, but her hand was shaking, and she seemed too weak and exhausted to do even this simple task.

Deep inside Jesse, compassion twisted painfully. It was such a womanly thing, to want one's hair just so, even though it was the middle of the night and there was no one about to notice whether her hair was combed or not.

Yet it mattered to her.

He did not know what made him cross the room and

take up the brush. It must have been the utter exhaustion and need in her huge eyes. The frightening pallor in her cheeks. And the endearing sense of vanity that persisted, even now.

She drew back, questioning him with her eyes.

"Just hold still," he told her softly. "Just sit, and let me do this."

He shouldn't have, of course. He knew that. Knew that brushing a woman's hair was quite possibly one of the most intimate acts outside the marriage bed. There was a forbidden familiarity in lifting the heavy, damp mass, inhaling the fragrance of rain and woman, and drawing his fingers, then the brush through the long waves. Her hair held every silken hue of autumn, from fire-tinged gold to deepest russet.

She sighed and leaned back, turning her face up to the light. Her eyes drifted shut, and the lines of weariness around her mouth eased.

Jesse's gaze stole over the curve of her throat, tracing into the shadow of her neckline. His hand was in her hair; it would take no more than a minor slip to trail his fingers down her neck, to caress her breasts...

Like a dreamer shaking himself awake, he cast off the desire. He should hurry. He should dispense with the intimate task. Instead, he found himself lingering. And waiting. To see if she would speak at last. Uncharacteristically, she had said almost nothing since he had found her.

He brushed her hair until it was dry and shining. Until he was half-crazy with wanting her. Then, slowly, he set aside the brush. For a moment he stood like an artisan admiring his handiwork, pleased with what he saw—as if he'd had more than the slightest bit to do with it. Finally, he went down on one knee before her so that his face was level with hers. He wasn't quite sure what to do with his hands, so he laid them on top of hers in her lap.

He teetered like a cliff jumper in the dark, uncertain what awaited him if he leaped. Silence was all he had ever wanted from Mary, silence and peace. Yet now that she was quiet, her silence discomfited him. She regarded him with large, haunted eyes, her lips saying nothing, her gaze saying everything.

"Mary." His voice sounded rusty and brusque. "I shouldn't have let you go—"

"And why not?" she asked, her brogue edged with annoyance. "Isn't that what you've been wanting since the moment I arrived—to be rid of me?"

He fought the urge to look away. He wished he were blind to her beauty, but he couldn't be. "I prefer to live alone," he said. "I've never pretended otherwise. It's just...I've no room in my life for another person."

"Then why did you come after me?"

"I didn't want you to come to harm."

She glanced down at their hands, but didn't remove hers. "It was not fair for me to foist myself upon you. I'll be gone as soon as I can do so properly."

A chill seized him. When confronted with a choice, he chose for her to stay. When had that happened? he wondered. When had he begun to think in terms of her staying? He tried to back away from the thought, but it was too late. The idea had embedded itself in his mind. In his heart.

"The road's too damned dangerous," he said, unable to keep the irritation from his tone. "If I hadn't found you tonight, you might have died, or caught a chill and fallen sick again." He felt the blood drain from his face. "If I'd lost you, too—" He stopped, appalled at what he'd almost admitted.

She sat for a long time, staring at him. He felt sick with what he had revealed. He knelt before her naked, as it were, and she seemed to have nothing to say.

Finally she spoke. "If you'd lost me, too."

"I beg your pardon?"

"You said 'too.' As in 'also.'"

He felt color surge into his face, searing him to the tips of his ears. "I didn't mean—"

"On the contrary, Jesse Morgan." She took his hands and turned them up in her lap, studying the creases in his palms. "I think, when you're not keeping yourself under rigid control, you speak the truth. At other times, you speak only guarded words not worth hearing. I want to know what really happened to your wife. We can't go on from here until you tell me that."

He shot to his feet and pivoted away. "You're assuming I want to 'go on,' whatever that means."

"It means we're coming to know each other. Whether this is a good thing or not is not for us to say. Not yet."

"Why bother?" He glared at the blackness outside the window.

"Faith, I don't know that, either. All I know is that I was the only survivor of a deadly shipwreck. You saved my life."

"That's my job. It's what I *do*."

"Everything happens for a reason. We may not know these reasons, but that doesn't mean they don't exist." Sloshing the water as she stepped out of the basin, she paced the plank floor behind him. "Tell me what happened to Emily. Just telling me can't hurt anything. Why did you say you killed her? Was it just to frighten me, or—"

"Yes, goddammit!" He spun around and glared at her. She flinched, hitching up one shoulder and turning her head to the side. The defensive gesture infuriated him even as it broke his heart. He'd made her afraid of him.

He held his hands determinedly at his sides, even though he had the vague and incomprehensible urge to touch her. "I drove them out of my life and to their deaths," he said. "I didn't actually wield the knife, but they died because of me."

"They," she whispered.

She'd caught him out again. She'd gotten him to say more than he'd intended. The woman had an uncanny knack for such things.

Just telling me can't hurt anything.

"Emily drowned in a shipwreck. I made her go, even when she was begging to stay." Each word broke from him as if forced out by a hammer blow to the chest. "She was...with child when it happened."

It was a wonder he remained standing when he finished. Yet he was. Standing. Facing Mary. Looking into her beautiful eyes and seeing compassion there.

"The drowning's not your fault," she said softly.

"I didn't tell you," he said tightly, "in order to gain your pity."

"I know that. But if I felt no pity for a man who lost his young wife at sea, then I'd be a hard woman indeed, would I not?"

"You could never be hard, Mary Dare. Not in that way. Hardheaded, perhaps," he suggested.

One corner of her mouth quirked up. "Hardheaded for certain, but that's nothing new to me."

Jesse could not believe he had survived the moment of saying aloud what had happened to Emily. Even after twelve years, the memory still scalded him. Speaking of it did not lessen his pain.

But it didn't make the pain worse, either.

Mary turned and went to the kitchen. He heard the clink of a bottle, then she returned to the keeping room with two glass jars half filled with amber liquid.

"Palina's corn liquor," he said.

"I'm not much for spirits, but tonight I need just a tiny sip or two."

They sat on the settle and looked at the fire Jesse had built in the hearth. For a while they simply watched the flames and listened to the sparks crackle into the silence. She sipped her drink while he downed his in a few easy swallows. Smiling slightly, she handed him her glass. He finished hers, as well.

"You're corrupting my moral fiber, Mary Dare," he said. The whiskey had a relaxing effect on him.

"I'm certain you did that on your own long ago," she said. "All I want is for you to talk to me. Tell me about Emily. You say you drove her out of your life. Why did you do that?"

"Because I was a fool." He might as well tell her. She'd be as disgusted as he was with himself. "I had let myself stray to another woman. She was nothing to me. Just a diversion."

"Oh, God."

"Now do you see? Now do you understand?"

"I understand you were young. Probably very spoiled, if you're like most young husbands. Not that you're excused, mind. And I assume you planned to say goodbye entirely to the other woman, yes?"

"Yes. Then she started to make demands...threats. I had to end the affair, and I wanted Emily to be away when it happened. So I put her on a ship bound for San Francisco."

At the mention of San Francisco, Mary looked away. "And the ship wrecked," she said.

"At the Columbia bar. The tug had just cast off its lines, and she'd set sail. Then a storm rolled in, and the boat got in trouble on the shoals and broke apart during the squall." He watched the flames, letting the tongues of orange and yellow mesmerize him. "No one survived."

"And you've spent each day since then blaming yourself."

"I made her go," he said. "Even when she begged to stay, I made her go. Because I was out whoring, Emily took ship. Because she took ship, she died. A horrible death."

The clock pendulum thundered in the silence. The fire crackled, punctuating the long, desperate moments.

"You have to find the end of your grief, Jesse." She regarded him with a purity of purpose in her eyes that he could not escape.

"There *is* no end, don't you see?" he said.

"You're wrong," she said. "There is an end. You've just never bothered to find it. You've been so wrapped up in trying to punish yourself that you've given up hope. I won't let you, Jesse. I won't let you anymore."

He heard the promise in her voice. Part of him stood aloof, fascinated by this small, vehement creature who had entered his life like a half-drowned madonna and who was now settling deeper and deeper into his world, against his will, against all common sense. She had a verve for life he didn't think he'd ever possessed, even with Emily. Even when he'd had everything a man could possibly desire.

His chest ached. He knew why. Though his head was muddled by the whiskey, he understood what was happening. Life hurt. She was thawing his heart, and the sudden warming was pure agony.

"When your pain is your own," she said, "you're being selfish. Share it and see what happens."

As if watching someone else govern his body, Jesse saw himself draw back his arm, hurl the empty jar at the fire. It exploded in a fount of shattering glass. "I don't need this," he roared, leaping to his feet. "Christ, I don't need *you*."

She said nothing, but he felt her stare as he strode to the front door and wrenched it open. His intent was to stalk out, to relieve Magnus early from his watch and spend the rest of the night trying to escape all the feelings Mary dredged up in him.

But he stopped when he reached the door. Without turning, he knew she was still patiently watching him, letting him take the lead now that she had poured salt on the raw wounds of his grief. Damn her to hell.

"After Emily's death," he heard himself say, "I thought time would heal the sadness. Isn't that the way it works? A man is widowed. He grieves, then his life goes on." He turned to find her looking at him, as he had known she would be. "After twelve years, I have my doubts."

He glowered at the hearth, now littered with shards of glass. "When Emily was with me, I lived as if I had all the time in the world. I left things undone, things unsaid. Now I *do* have all the time in the world, and I spend it alone. Thinking of all I should have done." He plowed a hand through his hair. "I just needed her one last time," he finished. "Damn it, why couldn't I have had just one moment of warning?"

"Do you really think that would have made a difference?" She rose from the settle and crossed the room. She was going to touch him. He knew it, and he knew better than to allow it. Yet when her hand came up, brushed at his hair, then settled in cool comfort on his cheek, he didn't pull away. "What you said or failed to say could never change anything. You can heal if you'll let yourself feel again."

"Why should I believe you?"

"Because what you believe isn't helping."

"You're assuming that healing is something I want."

"It is something you *need,* Jesse Morgan, for without it, you're a dead man."

"Exactly," he said coldly. He closed his hand around her wrist and moved it away from him.

"Turning your back on the world is wrong. And I can show you how wrong it is. But you've got to trust me."

"You're tired," he said, unwilling to let her probe deeper, to get closer to his wounds with the acid of her observations. It occurred to him that he had lived more and felt more in the past hour than he had in the past twelve years. "Go to bed," he said in his most dismissive tone. "I'll clean up here."

He took a long time sweeping up the broken glass. She stood watching him, not moving. Was she wondering whether or not to fight him on this front, as well? For some reason, his gaze strayed southward to the slight mound of her belly, where the baby grew.

A terrible longing rose inside him. Until tonight, he'd had no idea that he had the capacity to feel the things Mary made him feel. He thought all those feelings had died with Emily. Yet here they were again, born like a bonfire in his heart, making him hurt, making him hope.

Scaring the hell out of him.

Twelve

The next morning, Mary lay abed. She stared at the ceiling, noting the pattern in the plastered beams and listening to the skylarks and water thrushes outside. The birds started each day with an argument, calling across the yard to each other. Soon, when the hawks and eagles began to circle on the hunt, the songbirds would fall silent.

She closed her eyes and wondered where the songbirds went when they weren't singing. A moment later she left off birds and started thinking of Jesse. Again. And always. Everything had changed between them last night, of that she was certain.

A pleasant fluttering stirred inside her, and she smiled. The babe was growing larger and more active by the day. Before long, she'd be as big as a house. Her smile faltered. She remembered how Jesse had looked at her just before he'd said good-night. His gaze shifted downward, had taken in the swell formed by the growing baby. In his eyes, she had seen...what? Anticipation? Dread? Curiosity? She could not be sure.

She knew it was asking a lot, expecting Jesse to accept a stranger's child. But that was exactly the way it must be. It was what she dreamed of.

She sat up straight, her eyes open, her heart pounding. She had her answer. The desire and need she had hidden— even from herself—had finally made themselves known.

At last she was able to admit the truth. All her lofty thoughts about fulfilling her destiny, helping Jesse to heal from his age-old grief—all of that was only so much blather. An excuse to hide what she really yearned for. She wanted to stay here forever with Jesse Morgan. She wanted to raise her child here. She wanted to love Jesse. And sweet saints, with an ache so sharp that she winced, she wanted him to love her.

"Foolish baggage," she muttered under her breath as she rose and washed and cleaned her teeth. "He's a rude beast who lives alone, licking his wounds. What in heaven's name does he need with the likes of you? And remember, you gave your heart to the *last* man who saved you, and see how that ended."

She brushed out her hair in quick, vicious strokes that gradually slowed as she lost herself in remembrances of the night before. Jesse had brushed her hair. She thought about the sensual, lingering strokes, the intimacy of his hand touching her head, trailing the length of her hair. She remembered the sensation of his gaze caressing her so frankly that she felt as if he'd actually touched her. Perhaps there was hope for them if only Jesse could let go of the past. He had to learn to believe that loving did not always mean pain and loss.

Mary had come out of nowhere, a woman the age Emily had been when he'd lost her. Emily had been pregnant when he'd lost her. Mary had been pregnant when he'd found her. No wonder he saw her as a threat.

She wanted him to see her as a promise.

After helping herself to breakfast, she tugged on a shawl and went outside to see her garden. Purple lobelia rioted over the verges of the path, and the roses raised sunny faces skyward. The beauty of the landscape caught at her. It was a high miracle indeed that she'd found such a place as this, a place where the greens were so green it made her eyes smart, where the shape of the land meeting the sea created an odd, painful ecstasy in her chest.

She hurried across the yard, heading for the lighthouse. Jesse was working outside, filing the worn edge of a metal flywheel. A carelessly twisted leather strap held back his long, dark hair, and his hands wielded the file rhythmically, almost hypnotically. How faithful he was to his duty. How unrelenting.

After what he had told her about his wife, Mary was beginning to understand. He lived alone by choice, deeply afraid of the sea, yet determined to do battle with it. Each time he safely guided a ship to harbor, it represented a small triumph. Each time he pulled a victim to safety, it gave him revenge against the gray widow-maker.

Driven by his loss, he was manic in his compulsion to keep the lighthouse burning. Yet not even his daring rescues had healed his grieving heart. She suspected he clung to his grief because it was familiar; it was all that he knew. Her intrusion into his world had disrupted that pattern.

Risking his life at the edge of the sea would not make him whole again. There was only one thing that could accomplish that. He might not know it, but that one thing was love.

She hurried up the path toward him. "Soft day," she remarked, speaking to his back as he bent over his clamps and vises.

"Is it?" he asked. How fine he looked, with his shirt stretched across his broad, strong shoulders and the sunlight glinting in his hair.

"Oh, aye. A bit of mist in the air might bring the selkies out to play. The selkies are seal people, you know."

He stopped working and glanced up at her. She tried to

read his face. Sun sparkled in his eyes like a flame reflecting off blue ice, but beyond that he wore no expression she could discern.

"Uh-huh," he said, then went back to work.

Mary smiled at him, though he was no longer looking at her. As heartfelt declarations went, "uh-huh" fell a bit low on the scale, but it was more than he would have said to her a week ago, and less than he would say next week.

A shiver coursed through her at the thought of a future here. With him. People would think she'd run mad, wanting to stay with a lonely, solitary man at the edge of the world, but it felt right. She was happy here. She hadn't been happy with—

He swore and she jumped.

He glared down at his bleeding hand.

"Jesse!" She took his wrist and studied the angry gash across the palm. "Dear God, your hand!"

"Never mind that." He yanked a handkerchief out of his pocket and wrapped his hand. "The gear is broken. I'll have to go to town and have it forged at the smith's."

"And we'll get someone to look after your hand. Dr. MacEwan, is it?"

"We?" he asked, lifting one eyebrow. His face was a shade pale, and she suspected the injury hurt worse than he admitted. Already the handkerchief had turned crimson.

"I'll go with you."

His eyes narrowed. "Fine. You can take a room at the Palace Hotel—"

"That is not what I meant!" She felt cold with panic. "I intend to stay with you, Jesse, and you'd be mean and horrid entirely to cast me out. I'll go to the town with you. But I'm coming back here."

"It's too dangerous for you to ride in your—" He interrupted himself and suddenly seemed to find great fascination in the soaked handkerchief around his hand. He would not even speak of her pregnancy, would not even acknowledge it. But the present moment was hardly the time to confront him about that. "We'll take the buggy," she said.

"The sawyers haven't finished moving the tree from across the road."

"We'll go by boat. Wc'll take the pilot sloop you keep in the boathouse."

He fell still as if a sudden frost had turned his entire being to ice. The only thing alive was his eyes, and they burned hot and bright with pure fury. "No," he said.

Baffled, she cocked her head. "Sure and the sloop's as seaworthy as a tarred barrel. 'Tis an innocent enough suggestion. Why are you acting this way?"

"We'll not take the boat." He flung aside the metal file. Like a knife, it stuck into the soft ground, the shaft vibrating with the force of his action. He struck out down the path, heading straight for the barn.

But just for a moment, she had seen it. The emotion had flickered so quickly across his face that she fancied she had imagined it, but Mary knew she had guessed the truth.

Jesse was afraid to go to sea.

An odd thought, that, since he was so fearless when it came to riding into the surf to rescue people. But the very mention of setting sail in a boat had terrified him.

Ah, Jesse, what thoughts have haunted you all these twelve years?

She wanted to ask him, but given his present mood, she thought better of it. In the barn, he was already busy hitching the two-wheeled buggy to Aramis, the smallest of the four horses. He worked with brisk, economical movements. Without turning to look at her, he said, "If the road's not clear, I'll bring you back."

"And if the sawyers have finished?"

"You can come."

She stayed in the shadows of the barn with a secret smile playing about her mouth. Bit by bit, she was coming to know Jesse's world, to learn its rhythms and nuances, to see the different facets of it. And bit by bit, she was coming to love it here. The trip to town would simply make her even more a part of his life.

He should never have let her come along.

In the buggy, Jesse glanced sideways at his relentlessly perky companion and stifled a sigh. He had no force of will where she was concerned. Now, why was that? In twelve years, no one had penetrated his indifference. No one had convinced him to do anything he didn't feel like doing. And now, in a matter of days, Mary Dare had taken over his life. He didn't like it.

But perhaps bringing her to Ilwaco was the best choice he could make. She'd see the advantage to living in town. For someone who talked as much as she did, she ought to get along just fine in the village.

She sat with her head thrown back, letting the wind pluck strands of red hair from her thick braid. The woman was a beauty; no mistaking that. She was part of his trial by fire, he decided. Part of his punishment.

He thought for a moment about Palina and Magnus and the tale they had told. If he let Mary go, disaster would follow. He was a rational man. He refused to believe in portents. And if Mary freely chose to stay in town, he was surely released of his obligation.

"It's so lovely here," she said, her gaze sweeping the open, marshy area and the cluster of brightly painted houses in the distance. "Truly, this is a magical place."

He gave the landscape a cursory glance. The road had been cleared; the sawyers had gotten through the huge trunk of the fir that had fallen across the road. The smell of fresh-cut wood hung sharp and pleasant in the air.

"Prettier than Ireland?" he asked idly.

"Oh, I don't know. Ireland will take your breath away, with all the smooth green hills and sheer cliffs and the leaping sea. Ballinskelligs is a bit like this, only without the trees." She put her hand on his sleeve. "I like it better here."

He pretended to adjust the reins so he could pull away. He flexed his wounded hand, hoping the bleeding had stopped. Damn the woman, she was always *touching* him as if it were her right.

He liked her touch.

The thought barreled into him, swift and unexpected. Instantly he closed his mind, choking off the idea. She was unwanted baggage in his life. The sooner he got rid of her, the better.

"Jesse, look!" Mary practically stood up in the buggy, pointing off to the right where the great marshes spread out. In the strong light of a high noonday sun, the great bogs glowed bloodred. "Who are those people?"

"The Siwash," he said, watching the distant figures bent over in the wild bogs. "They're working in the cranberry bogs."

She gripped the black enameled rail of the buggy and stared. "Indians? Wild Indians?"

Jesse almost smiled. "If you're expecting an attack by bloodthirsty savages with hatchets, these folks won't fit the mold. Whoa." He drew back and stopped the buggy at the side of the bog. One of the workers spied him and waved an arm. Picking his way through the knee-deep water, he revealed bare feet that seemed impervious to the chilly bog water.

"Jesse Morgan!" he called, then in Chinook, said, "You are too much of a stranger. Many greetings."

"Greetings to you, too, Abel Sky," Jesse said in the same language. He had learned enough Chinook to converse lightly with the natives and to trade with them. Abel Sky was a man of middle years, with a fit body, a lively mind and several plump wives.

He grinned up at Jesse, revealing gaps where teeth were missing and a mischievous gleam in his eyes. He wore a felt hat sideways; it was the only way to fit over his broad forehead, which had been flattened in infancy by a papoose board.

His leather apron and beaded bark vest made a stark contrast with his natty hat and tattered tail coat. "I thought you would never get around to taking a woman, Boston," Abel Sky said, switching to English. He called all white men "Boston."

"I haven't taken—"

"How do you do?" Mary broke in, her face nearly as red as the stems and tiny leaves of the berry plants. "My name is Mary Dare."

"Mary Dare." He took off his hat and bowed as grandly as any gentleman. "Abel Sky likes this hair of flame." Without warning, he reached up and grabbed her braid.

She gave a little squeak of fear.

Jesse suppressed a chuckle. Abel Sky was a big tease and always had been.

"If I were to trade for this Boston's scalp," Abel Sky said, "I could buy much tick-tocks and jewelry."

Moving with surprising speed, Mary grabbed his wrist and twisted it until he let go of her hair. "Just you try it, boyo."

Abel Sky cradled his wrist in mock agony. "She is a devil woman! Where did you find such a dev—" At that moment, he noticed Mary's ripe shape. His wrist and offense forgotten, he grinned wider than ever. "Hey, Boston, you are a sneaking dog in the night! You—"

"We'd best be going," Jesse said. Good God. They hadn't even gotten to the edge of town, and already the awkwardness was starting, the speculation. He was an idiot to think there could be anything easy about having Mary Dare in his life.

Both she and Abel Sky seemed oblivious to his discomfiture. They were laughing together, and Abel Sky handed her a small pouch of dried and sweetened cranberries. She eyed him inquisitively, though not with the fearful distrust most white settlers showed the Siwash. Before Jesse was able to pry her away, Abel Sky had invited her to the tribe's settlement, promising her a taste of alder-smoked salmon and oysters. She asked him about his wives and children, listening intently as he described his eldest son's prowess at handling a high-nosed, seagoing canoe. In one conversation, Mary Dare learned more about the diminutive Siwash than Jesse had in twelve years of knowing him.

They finally took their leave and soon came to First Street, paved with planking and dominated by the Ilwaco Mill and Lumber Company. Huge floating logs, denuded of bark and branches, filled the waterfront and the area around the piers.

Mary spotted the side-wheeler *T. J. Potter* at anchor awaiting the tide. "I've never been on a steamer," she remarked. As much as she talked, Mary Dare said very little about herself. Jesse supposed he should be grateful. The less he learned, the less it would matter when she left.

Her eyes were bright and hungry as she looked around the town. Along with the side-wheeler, fishing vessels and lumber barges crowded the harbor. Businesses lined the street; shoppers and tradesmen hurried along the boardwalks. A businessman in a dove-gray suit stood on the walkway. As the buggy rolled past, the bespectacled man smoothed his hand over his thinning hair. Then he took a pocket watch from his waistcoat pocket and flipped it open and shut, open and shut, a nervous habit. A strolling couple, pristine and resplendent in tennis whites, came out of the Palace Hotel.

In the next few weeks, Jesse reflected, more tourists would arrive, wealthy people from Portland and Seattle who came to summer at the seashore.

Years ago, Jesse had been one of them.

He headed for the smithy at the end of Spruce Street. Smoke streamed from the conical forge chimney, beckoning like a long, wavering finger.

"Hello!" a singsong voice called from the crowded boardwalk. "Hello, Mr. Morgan!"

Jesse tried not to cringe too visibly. After debating for a moment whether or not he could ignore the summons, he pulled back smoothly and stopped the buggy.

With her bosom puffing like a set of bellows, Hestia Swann bore down on them. Feathers dyed improbable colors nodded above the broad brim of her hat. When she looked up at Mary, there was a smile on her face, but her eyes glinted with sharp darts of curiosity.

"This must be your guest," Hestia crowed. "My, just look at the poor thing! How pale she is, and thin, for all that she's expecting a child. Just look at her. Has she a name, Mr. Mor—"

"Mary Dare," said Mary, mirth barely suppressed in her voice. "And I might be thin and pale, but I'm not deaf. Nor am I an ee-jit."

Mrs. Hestia Swann drew herself up and regarded Mary fiercely. "Impertinent, perhaps."

"Oh, aye, my mum always used to say so." Mary inclined her head. "How do you do, Mrs...."

"Swann," Jesse broke in, thinking that he'd lost his mind, bringing Mary to town in broad daylight. "This is Mrs. Hestia Swann."

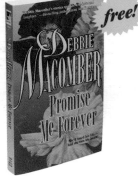

BOOKS FREE!

THE BEST OF THE BEST™: HERE'S HOW IT WORKS—

Accepting free books places you under no obligation to buy anything. You may keep the books and gift and return the shipping statement marked "cancel." If you do not cancel, about a month later we will send you 3 additional novels and bill you just $3.99 each, plus 25¢ delivery per book and applicable sales tax, if any.* That's the complete price, and—compared to cover prices of $5.50 each—quite a bargain! You may cancel at any time, but if you choose to continue, every month we'll send you 3 more books, which you may either purchase at the discount price...or return to us and cancel your subscription.

*Terms and prices subject to change without notice. Sales tax applicable in N.Y.

"'Tis a pleasure to meet you, Mrs. Swann."

Hestia's mouth pursed into a perfect, tight "O." "An Irish girl?"

"I am," Mary said. "From County Kerry."

Jesse saw her straighten. The pallor left her cheeks, crowded out by spots of color. He managed to catch Hestia's eye. He didn't have to say a word. With one freezing look, he stopped her from saying anything insulting or prejudicial against Mary or the Irish in general.

"I'm certain you're welcome in Ilwaco," Hestia said quickly, her gaze fleeing Jesse's. "And it's surely a miracle you survived a shipwreck."

"Aye, it's a miracle indeed," Mary said. "I've Captain Morgan to thank for that."

Jesse allowed himself to relax a little. By not using his given name, Mary deflected Hestia's suspicion about exactly what had been going on since she'd washed up on the beach. He was trying to figure out a way to bid Mrs. Swann good day when another woman joined them.

"Well, here's our patient, looking the very picture of health!" Fiona MacEwan declared, contradicting everything Hestia had said. She rocked back on her heels, revealing her brogans and clutching a shopping bag under one arm. Without waiting for Jesse to introduce them, she grinned up at Mary. "I'm Dr. Fiona MacEwan. It's good to see you looking so well." She winked at Jesse. "We feared you'd never wake up except by means of a kiss from a true prince."

Hestia gasped, but Mary only laughed. "If that was what it took, I'd still be sleeping like the dead. Are you truly a doctor, then?"

"That I am. A graduate of the Women's College of Medicine in Philadelphia. That's back East."

"Then you'll be the one to have a look at Captain Morgan's poor hand." Mary indicated the bloody bandage.

"Indeed I shall," Fiona said briskly.

"I've got business at the smithy," Jesse said. "I'll stop in later."

"We're so pleased you're here, Mrs. Dare," Hestia said, clearly having decided to hold out the olive branch. "Now, what about the centennial celebration? Will you be there, Captain? And will you be bringing your guest?"

Jesse almost laughed at the absurdity of it. He never, ever attended social events, and Hestia knew it.

"Centennial?" Mary asked.

"Our nation was born a hundred years ago—July 4, 1776. There's to be a regatta and a dance social in Oysterville. And you'd stay at the Pacific House Hotel, of course."

Mary's face lit up. "I should like that very much, indeed I should."

"We're not going," said Jesse.

"I think it would be an excellent tonic for my patient," Fiona declared, clearly planning to ignore him. "Come along now, and we'll show you the town while Jesse is off at the blacksmith's."

Within moments, they had helped Mary out of the buggy and were leading her toward the mercantile. There were, Hestia explained airily, certain things a woman needed if she was going to attend a social.

Feeling twitchy and irritated, Jesse watched them disappear. Damn. This was precisely what he wanted to avoid. People. Friendships. Laughter and fun.

Mary seemed to be dragging him into it against his will.

"No doubt about it, Mr. Clapp," said the nervous solicitor. "She's the woman you're looking for."

Granger studied the antique globe beside his desk. He felt no surprise; Stoner's discreet investigation only confirmed what he'd suspected all along. "And?" he prompted.

"She calls herself Mary Dare, it seems, and looks none the worse for having survived a shipwreck." Stoner idly took out his pocket watch. One-handed, he flipped the cover open, then closed it, and repeated the gesture as if it soothed him.

Granger spun the globe, his finger stopping its orbit at his favorite spot—the Sandwich Islands. No one knew it yet, but those lush, tropical isles in the middle of the Pacific were his ultimate destination.

But he couldn't go there yet. He still had work to do. He still needed a son, an heir. His parents were quite fond of pointing out that a male heir had been born to every generation of Clapps since the *Mayflower* had landed. He was duty-bound to honor the tradition.

"Her condition?" He arched an eyebrow at Stoner.

The man paled. His ivory-white hand dived into his pocket, taking the watch with it. "As I said, sir, she seems none the worse—"

"I'm speaking of the baby, and you damned well know it," Granger said.

Stoner smoothed his hand over his sparse hair. "Sir, I'm not qualified to—"

"Then I'll find someone who is." Granger slapped his palm down on the desk.

Stoner flinched. His bony Adam's apple lurched as he swallowed. "She is most definitely with child, sir. Judging by the mother's good health, I would venture to say the child is healthy, as well."

A sense of pride such as Granger rarely felt came over him. He had made a child. After all these years, he had finally managed to get a child in a woman's belly. The fact that she was a low-class, deceitful Irishwoman caused

Granger only minor worry. The fact that she seemed to be in the care of Jesse Morgan enraged him.

"Have you done the research I instructed you to do?" Granger asked. "What are my rights as the father of that child?"

"Well, sir, I'm afraid the law's a bit vague on that point, especially since she's in Washington Territory. But—"

"For Christ's sake, tell me." Granger shot to his feet and started to pace. "And don't lie to me."

"The truth of the matter is, sir, that the law does not necessarily favor the father in a case like this." Yet possibility glinted in Stoner's eyes; Granger could see it, could almost taste it in the air.

"I hired you to find a way to make this work," Granger said. "My wife has yearned for a child of her own."

Stoner nodded, smoothing his hands down the lapels of his dove-gray business suit. He looked around the study. Granger took note of the admiring way the solicitor regarded the Remington painting over the mantel, the Tiffany window, the electric-powered globes illuminating the library shelves. "I have the ear of the territorial governor. Though you might have to be patient—and a bit free with, ah, donations—you'll get what you're looking for, Mr. Clapp. Never worry about that."

"I wasn't worried," Granger declared. "Wasn't worried in the least."

Thirteen

━━━⟲⟳⟲━━━

As she got ready to go to the centennial celebration, Mary eyed the boots Jesse had thrust into her hands. "Here," he'd said gruffly. "See if these fit."

Fit for a princess, they were, and they put her in mind of the first pair of shoes she'd ever worn. It was the day of her confirmation, ten years earlier. At the proud age of thirteen, she had formally joined the Church after taking catechism each night by the light of a tallow candle, with her Da reciting the Latin prayers while she and her brothers memorized them.

Her father was a fisherman, and the family lived too far from the village to attend church regularly, especially after Mulligan the mule died and the wheels rotted off the cart. Father Farrell, who came four times a year to supper— Mum always scrubbed the cottage for days beforehand— had hinted that it might not be such a bad idea for Mary to honor the occasion of her confirmation by wearing shoes. So out they came, Mum's skinny leather button boots. Mary thought they were the grandest thing a body had ever seen.

Until she got to the church. And realized that thirty years earlier they might have been called grand, but now they were hopelessly outmoded, shamefully old-fashioned compared to the shiny patent-leather shoes that clad the proud-stepping feet of the Costello twins and the Mahoney daughters.

Blushing at the memory, Mary saw herself as she had been at that tender age, all gawky arms and legs, with her cheeks on fire beneath a galaxy of freckles. Pointing fingers and girlish giggles had driven her feet as far under the pew as she could tuck them. The ragged hem of her dress had brushed the perfectly clean stone floor of the church. She had ducked her head and prayed to the Lord God of Heaven to be rich.

Now, years later, on the other side of the world, she stared into the cheval-glass mirror Jesse had brought down from the attic and made a different wish.

"I want my mother," she whispered. "Ah, Mum, I'd give anything to have you touch me now." She lifted her hand to her just-washed hair and stroked it back along her temple. "Here, like you used to, Mum. Ah, it hurts, it does, to think you'll never touch me again."

She closed her burning eyes. "I need you, Mum. I always knew I'd be a mother one day, but in my dreams, you were there helping me, holding my hand and telling me all will be well. I'm scared, I am, and I'm trying my best to hide it, but I need you."

The softness of memories showered her. She remembered the way her mother smelled of laundry and cooking. She remembered the sound of Shannon Dare O'Donnell's laughter as her big fisherman husband whirled her around the tiny keeping room of the cottage, dancing to the tune Rory played on his pipes.

Mary forced her eyes open and dragged herself back to the present. She rushed to the basin and sluiced cold water over her face. Don't cry, she told herself. Don't cry now. If you start now, you'll never stop.

She turned again to her reflection in the cheval glass. Dr. MacEwan and Mrs. Swann had bought more ribbons and laces than she'd ever seen in her life. The addition of a Hamburg lace collar on the plain poplin dress made her feel grand indeed. Streamers of green satin beribboned her hair. Mum would be proud, she thought.

"Here I am almost a mother on my own, getting weepy like a little girl," she muttered, pulling on an old-fashioned basque jacket. "What would you say to me, Mum, if you could talk? Would you tell me it's going to be all right? Ah, please say it. Tell me everything's going to be just fine."

"Mary?" Jesse called.

She jumped with a guilty start. "I'm coming, Jesse. Just a moment."

She picked up the boots and wished the Mahoney girls could see them. The leather was so soft it must have been cured by butter. Endless rows of gleaming buttons fastened up the sides.

Emily Leighton Morgan had been a grand lady indeed. She must have been rich. All of her clothes were of the best, the dearest materials. But if she had been rich, then why was Jesse here, living like a monk in poverty and simplicity at the lighthouse? Had he abandoned it all in his grief?

Frowning, she straightened the silk stockings Hestia Swann had bought her and pulled on first one boot, then the other. The buttons were lovely round bits of faceted black onyx.

But after five minutes of trying to force the first button through its tiny loop, she began to understand why only wealthy ladies wore such frippery. Who could possibly fasten them without help?

After more long moments of trying, she blew out her

breath in defeat and clomped out to the keeping room.
"Jesse—"

He turned with impatient abruptness. "Mary—"

They interrupted each other, then fell silent, awkwardly
staring.

He looked like a bridegroom out of a young girl's most
cherished dream. A snowy white boiled shirt and cravat
adorned his strong throat. Black trousers, with a waistcoat
and frock coat to match, gave his appearance a formality
she had never seen before.

"You look so handsome," she said at last.

He didn't acknowledge the compliment but said, "And
you look...nice."

He wasn't exactly in paroxysms of ecstasy, but coming
from him, it was lavish praise.

"Thank you," she said. A blush stung her cheeks.
Reaching down with a tentative hand, she lifted the hem
of her dress. "I'm afraid I've no talent for getting these
boots buttoned." Forcing herself past the awkwardness,
she sat down and stuck out one foot. "Can you help?"

"No," he said swiftly. Now it was his turn to be flustered. He lifted his shoulders stiffly and glared at her, his
discomfort visibly hardening to anger. "Just do up a couple of buttons so the boots don't fall off."

"I can't even get one of them done."

"Then wear the rubber beacon gaiters."

She tossed her head in disdain at the very idea. "That
would be attractive. Do you really want to be seen in the
company of a woman wearing bogtrotters?"

She forced herself to hold his gaze, even as she was
tempted to bury her face in her hands. Couldn't he see
how important this day was to her? She was going to a
social. She would meet people who would look at her,
judge her, decide whether or not they wanted her for a
friend. Couldn't he understand what was at stake?

As their gazes stayed locked, she felt an inner curl of insight. Of course he couldn't understand. Shut away out here at the lighthouse, determinedly shunning the world, Jesse Morgan had no understanding of why a body would want to be with people. To know them and be their friend. To be a part of their lives.

"I wanted to look nice today," she said, breaking the strained silence.

"You always look nice," he replied gruffly. "Didn't I just say so?"

A smile pulled at her lips. "I almost fainted when you did." She thumped her heel on the floor. "I'm trying to explain this. You speak little of your past, but I've been able to guess that you've never wanted for anything. You're educated. You can read and write and you speak like a gentleman. By now you've surely guessed that isn't the case with me."

He nodded, narrowing his eyes. "Go on."

She was encouraged by his interest. Usually he shied from learning things about her, as if he could protect himself from her by showing no concern for her past.

"Until I was thirteen years old," she said, "I never wore a shoe in my life."

She watched the comprehension dawn on his face like the morning sun. He, who had grown up in a world of unspeakable bounty, had probably never envisioned what her life in Ireland had been like—until this moment.

"Wait here," he said through clenched teeth. He strode away. She heard him rummaging around in a drawer in the kitchen. He returned with a small buttonhook. "Put out your foot," he ordered.

She hiked back her skirts and petticoats. A few inches of her calf showed, and she rather liked the way it looked with the thin stocking stretched over it.

Jesse cleared his throat and gingerly pulled together the

first button and eye. He seemed to be trying to do everything within his power to avoid touching her. At first.
When it became clear he needed to brace one hand around
her ankle in order to wield the buttonhook, he did so dog-
gedly.

It was a simple thing, that touch, his left hand curved
around the back of her calf. Mary felt her eyelids drift to
half mast. There was something curiously evocative in the
sight of the hook being inserted into the eye, then drawing
the button through. For no apparent reason, she remembered the night in the lighthouse. The night he had kissed
her.

The night she had wanted so much more than kissing.

He moved on to the next button. "See how it's done?
I'll let you try it—"

"Oh, I'm certain I couldn't," she said quickly, watching the juxtaposition of his big hand with the tiny buttons,
his tanned skin and her pale, stocking-clad leg. "It's hard
for me to lean over. You'd be all day waiting for me."

He lifted one skeptical brow. "No doubt."

She smiled. "I never imagined wearing shoes that had
to be fastened by someone else. I was born dirt poor and
never knew it."

He paused in midmotion and glanced up at her. "What
do you mean, you never knew it?"

Despite a sudden thickness in her throat, she laughed.
"Faith, and how does a fish know it lives in water, or a
bird in the air?"

He started working again, the buttonhook moving stead-
ily up the front of her shin while his other hand cradled
the calf of her leg. Up and up... Ah, she was hungry for
his touch.

"Good question," he observed, clearly oblivious to her
burgeoning desires.

"How can a girl know such a thing when she lives in the very center of the world?" she went on.

He applied himself to the other boot. "Ireland, you mean."

"Aye, County Kerry, just at the coast, with the wild blue Atlantic clawing at the cliffs and the great green hills rising up beyond, the stone terraces reaching toward the heights as if to touch the very face of heaven. I tell you, it came as a huge surprise to me to learn I was poor."

He rewarded her with a grin. "And who told you so?"

She had to swallow several times before she could find her voice. "Just a few of the gossips in church."

She looked away, but he saw it anyway, she knew he had. His hands went still. A moment later, ever so gently, he put a finger under her chin and drew her gaze back to his. "Teased you, did they?"

"Oh, aye." She blinked fast. "It was so long ago, I've no idea why it would come back to me now."

He said nothing. He neither moved nor took his hand away. She felt the warmth of it under her chin, against her neck, and she realized that for her, a human touch was like air and water. Necessary. Vital.

He was quiet for so long that she finally said, "What?"

"You...startle me," he admitted with roughness in his voice. "There is something enchanting about a girl who has to be told that she's poor. And something brutal about the moment it happens."

She shrugged, discomfited by his interest and regard. If that was Jesse Morgan's idea of brutality, he was a more tender man than she had thought. "I had three braw brothers who took care of people with smart mouths," she said.

He took his hand away. "Had...?"

"They're gone now. Dead. All of them."

"Jesus Christ." He shot to his feet. His abruptness frightened her.

"What's the matter?"

He spun around to glare at her. "You lost your entire family."

"I've already told you that."

"I assumed you were speaking of your parents. When were you going to get around to telling me you had three brothers? And what the hell else are you keeping from me?"

"What else do you want to know?" she shot back.

He drew a deep breath; she could see him struggling to be patient. "What happened to your family?" he asked.

Family. For a moment, she could see them in her mind's eye, shimmering like heat shadows on the horizon. Mum and Da with their arms around each other's waists, Rory with his ever-present pipes, Ali and Paddy scuffling playfully on the grassy bawn.

"Last year, it was. One day, Da and the boys went out fishing and never came back. Then Mum...she stood out on the cliffs all that day in the rain, waiting and waiting. I tried to get her to come in, but she just stood there, soaked, staring out to sea, for hours and hours." Mary remembered the look on her mother's face when she finally turned away from the sea. Her eyes were dead. "A few days later she took to her bed with a fever. Her lungs filled up, and then she was gone."

"Jesus Christ," Jesse said again. "And you're only now getting around to telling me."

"I didn't think you'd be interested." The lump in her throat was back. She was a bundle of emotion these days.

"How do you stand it?" he asked raggedly.

"It's not a question of standing it," she said. "The fact that they're gone just *is*. The same as a rose's petals drift to the ground in the autumn. The same as the sun sets and the moon rises. I can't change it. Can't make it stop, can't make it go away.'' She lifted her hand to her chest. "And so they live here now. Here in my heart.''

Jesse was staring at her with a stunned expression. Mary couldn't help herself. She smiled. It felt good to smile. Healing and warm.

"After losing them all,'' Jesse said, "how can you still smile?''

"They wouldn't have it any other way. They'd not want me to be miserable for the rest of my life. They'd want me to remember the love and the joy, not the sadness and the emptiness.''

"You presume to know a lot about what they would want.''

"I do know,'' she said. "And you'd know it, too, if you'd let yourself.''

"Save your platitudes,'' he said. "They won't work on me.''

"Because you're so superior? So educated and literate?''

"Because I don't live with my head in the stars.''

She placed her foot back in his hand, so he could finish buttoning her boot. "You ought to try it, then.''

Jesse had never thought much of the drive up the twenty-mile length of the Long Beach Peninsula. Clustered settlements, dunes, wheeling birds, gorse-topped salt meadows, cranberry bogs—they were all just *there*. Sights and sounds brushed him like a passing breeze, leaving no impression.

Yet this drive—like everything else—was different in the company of Mary Dare. She regarded life as a series of small wonders. A house, clad in worn and greening shingles, was cause for her to lean out of the buggy, to wave at children playing in the yard. A bear poking through the shellfish in a mudflat elicited a gasp of fearful

delight. When she spied a bush of watery orange salm-
onberries, she insisted on sampling them and picking a
hatful for Palina, since they'd stayed behind to man the
lighthouse.

So much for the fancy hat Hestia had bought her in
town.

The sight of a bald eagle swooping down to catch a fish
with talons outstretched nearly moved Mary to tears, so
taken was she with the primal beauty of the moment. She
was even fascinated with Nahcotta, a busy town surrounded by reeking oyster middens.

Her eyes danced as she gazed out across the blue-gray
expanse of Shoalwater Bay. "Look at all the schooners,"
she exclaimed.

"Oystermen," Jesse said. The fleet was draped in pen-
nons of red, white and blue for the occasion. He felt a
twist of yearning. The two-masted vessels were fast and
fine, their sails spread out like wings. In the far reaches
of memory, he recalled a time when he used to set sail on
his yacht without a backward glance. Sailing without a
care in the world used to give him the sensation of flying.
Of course, all that had changed after Emily. All that was
gone now.

"Oystermen," Mary said, breaking in on his thoughts.
"They carry nothing else, then?"

"Nothing beyond their crews. They'll be taking their
harvest down to San Francisco."

"So many of them." She shuddered delicately. "What
is it about oysters that people crave so madly?"

Jesse scanned the meadow ahead for a place to leave
the horse and buggy. Already the outskirts of town were
crowded with buckboards and gigs and carts, anchored like
odd boats in a sea of salt grass. As conspicuous as a giant
frigate, the Ilwaco/Oysterville stagecoach dominated the
clearing beside a stream.

"They say the miners and railroad workers in California crave oysters. I imagine after months in a muddy trench in the hills, a man would welcome the fresh taste of an oyster." He angled the buggy into a spot beneath a huge willow tree. The branches drooped all the way to the ground, some of them trailing in the river, making an umbrella-shaped shady area.

"Da used to bring home oysters every once in a while," Mary said. "I was never fond of them."

He heard a fleeting wistfulness in her voice. *They're gone now. All of them.*

The one thing Jesse could understand was grief. Yet while he walked with the darkness each day of his life, Mary seemed fine. Strong. Holding the memories in her heart but not clinging to them like a drowning sailor grasping at flotsam and jetsam in a turbulent sea.

How do you do it, Mary? How do you stand it?

It amazed him that there was another way to cope with loss. Her way, he thought with resentment. Perhaps it worked for her; after all, she hadn't been faithless to someone she was supposed to love. She hadn't sent her family to their deaths.

After tying up beneath the sheltering willow, he jumped out of the buggy and reached for her. An impersonal helping hand. That's all he had any right to offer her.

But when it came to Mary, everything was different. Most women would grip his hand and step down, then move gracefully away. Mary fit herself between his hands so that he was holding her under the arms, his thumbs dangerously close to her breasts. God...her breasts. How long had it been since he had felt the softness of a woman's breast in his hand?

The contact brushed him with fire. And the heat didn't end there. Oh, no. She had to smile into his face, her eyes impossibly bright and her lips as soft as ripe cherries. With her small hands, she cupped his shoulders, bracing herself for the ride.

He found himself handling her gently, as if she were a fragile snowflake. He lifted her up out of the seat and then drifted her down, down, ever mindful of the precious burden she carried.

Almost immediately, he yanked his thoughts away from Mary's child. At some point—he wasn't sure when—they had made a tacit agreement to avoid speaking of the baby and who had fathered it, and why Mary refused to name the man.

Yet Jesse recognized the feeling that always gripped him when he sensed a coming storm. There was an inevitability to the impending disaster. They would have to confront the issue as surely as the people of the Washington coast had to confront a storm. It would bring destruction in its wake, would turn lives inside out and rip them to shreds. Nothing they could do would ever stop it.

And that was how he felt about Mary's child. He ought to tell her so. That would get her to leave without hesitation.

But when he set her on the ground, she looked up at him and gave him such a dazzling smile that he caught his breath.

Damn.

If she stayed, he was going to break her heart. But if he let her go now, he would never know if she was right about him. Until Mary, he had thought his life wouldn't change. He had thought he didn't want it to change. But she had opened his mind and his heart to possibility.

A possibility that would die if he lost her.

Jesse used his hands to part the willow boughs like a curtain. As they passed beneath the dragging branches of the tree, the long, narrow leaves seemed to nod and whisper.

"The centennial of Independence Day," Mary said, shading her eyes and twisting to look at the streamers strung across the top of the Pacific House Hotel. "Independence from Mother England is a thing the Irish have been craving for centuries. A cause to celebrate, to be sure."

She took his hand and pulled him toward the gathering crowds of people. "What is that building there?" she asked, pointing at a crude log structure on Front Street. Flags waved from wooden turrets in each corner.

"That's the old fort. Years ago, during the Indian Wars, the townsfolk built it." In spite of himself, Jesse grinned briefly. "The Siwash always thought it was a big joke. The wars never bothered people out here. They all got along. The settlers laughed at it, too, and never did get around to putting a roof on it."

A few Siwash men and women were circulating through the crowd, looking exotic in their bark-leather garb and elaborate shell jewelry. Yet at the same time, they fit in, somehow, the men smoking and gossiping in small groups, the women pausing at the various booths to sample the wares.

Jesse tried to remember the last time he had seen so many people and so much activity in one place. Not since...before. Not since Emily.

The centerpiece of the town was a whitewashed courthouse, looking like a sugar cube upon a broad lawn. Inside, the Honorable Hiram Palmer presided. He was known as a man who would grant any petition—for the right price.

The tinny sounds of a band rose from the grandstand. The melody of "Little Brown Jug," accompanied by clapping and stomping, clattered across the courthouse lawn. Swags of red, white and blue bunting draped the rotunda atop the main building.

A dance floor had been erected in the midst of everything. At the periphery of the yard, sawhorses groaned under the weight of boards laden with food—mounds of oysters and fried chicken and berry pies and huge kegs of beer and lemonade.

There had been a time in Jesse's life when the act of walking into the midst of a crowd had been as natural and uneventful as breathing. Refinement had been bred into him by the finest schools money could buy. Huge gatherings of dignitaries in Portland, company meetings in San Francisco, soirées at the opera had all been as familiar to him then as Cape Disappointment was now. His grandfather had built an empire. His father had gold-leafed it with his own Midas touch. Jesse had shown every sign of gilding the lily of what the Morgans had built.

Then one day, it was all gone.

And nothing mattered. Nothing at all. Not even taking the next breath of air.

Yet now Mary was willfully dragging him back into a world he had shunned for years. True, these were not the Portland upper crust, posturing and making business deals and debating high-flown ideas. There were summer folk among them, but in general the people here were locals.

Mary squeezed his hand, then tugged him toward the bustling town. "It's a grandstand, boyo. Not a gallows."

He scowled at her. "What?"

"You have the look of a condemned man on the way to his own hanging. I just wanted to reassure you that it's a grandstand."

"I'm not much for being pleasant in company," he muttered.

She started walking, pulling him again. He was briefly reminded of himself, pulling a victim in from the biting surf. Sometimes the victims resisted—but afterward they were always grateful.

He hoped to slide unobtrusively into the crowd, to stand amid the foot-stomping men and the laughing women, but Mary clearly had other ideas.

Before he could object, she lifted her hand and waved it vigorously in the air. "Halloo!" she called. "Yoo-hoo, Mrs. Swann! We're here!"

Several dozen pairs of eyes turned in their direction. Jesse felt splayed out in front of them, as naked as a plucked chicken. This was hell, he decided. Hell on earth.

Fourteen

If the pearly gates of heaven had opened wide before Mary, she would not have been more excited than she was at this moment. Everything about this day, this place, was new and thrilling.

This was the second chance she had hoped for. Prayed for. It was the second chance that explained why she alone had survived the shipwreck. This town rolled out before her like a newly tilled field. She could plant it with anything she wanted.

No one ever need know she had been a whore to a rich man.

"Jesse," she said, hurrying to the fringe of the crowd. "Thank you for bringing me here today."

With long strides, he kept pace with her. "You owe me no thanks," he said in a low voice, and she almost laughed at the sound of it. With every fiber of his being, he was resisting. The fact that she'd wheedled him into coming even this far was amazing.

"It will be a fine thing, you'll see." She spied Mrs. Swann chugging toward them, parting the crowd with her progress. The widow's petticoats were so wide that she left a wake wherever she walked. Her hat was a wonder of engineering. The broad straw brim bore more bunting than the grandstand. Carnations in red, white and blue sprouted in all directions like a display of fireworks. Rising proudly from the center was a small American flag.

"There you are, the two of you," Hestia Swann exclaimed, angling a red and blue parasol at them.

At a pause in the music, a man in a top hat and narrow beard shouted through a bullhorn, greeting everyone and wishing them a happy Independence Day. Cheers rose.

Mrs. Swann held out her arms, the parasol dangling from one wrist. "And just look at you, Mary Dare. What a picture you make."

"Thanks to you and Dr. MacEwan."

"Oh, pshaw. We didn't put those roses in your cheeks." The woman peeked from beneath the brim of her massive hat and winked at Jesse. "I for one can guess who's responsible for that."

"I won't take credit," Jesse said. "Mary's healing has nothing to do with me."

"Ah, but it does." Mrs. Swann plucked a handkerchief from her sleeve and dabbed at her eyes. "It's so romantic I can hardly bear it. You brought this young woman back from the very brink of eternity, Jesse Morgan."

Mary squeezed his hand. "Aye, that you did. For better or worse."

For better or worse. She knew Jesse heard an echo of the past in the words. He probably wished he had never come.

"Oh, look!" Mrs. Swann exclaimed. "It's Reverend and Mrs. Hapgood. And their dear little boy." Filled with self-importance, she made the introductions. The Hapgoods were soft-spoken and seemed shy to Mary. The little boy had white-blond hair, apple cheeks and eyes full of mischief. Mary didn't doubt the child was a handful.

After exchanging pleasantries, the Hapgoods moved on,

greeting new acquaintances. The older woman dabbed at her eyes again. "Such a blessing, that family. See how they dote on their son."

"He's adorable," Mary said.

"And more precious to them than any of us can imagine." She dropped her voice to a whisper. "She lost her first, you see."

Mary's heart gave a leap of panic. "I'm so sorry to hear that."

"We'd best be going," Jesse said, his voice gruff.

"What happened?" Mary asked, morbidly curious. "How did the child die?"

"Oh, he didn't die," the woman said. "That's what's so sad about it. He was taken by—"

"That's enough, Mrs. Swann," Jesse said.

She fanned herself vigorously with her handkerchief. "How unforgivably insensitive of me," she said, flushing crimson. "I'm not ordinarily such a gossip. Can you forgive me?"

Mary couldn't help smiling. There was something dear about the woman. She sensed a sad loneliness in Hestia Swann.

"How are you feeling, dear?" asked Fiona MacEwan, joining them as they walked toward the tables draped with checkered tablecloths.

"Very well, thank you. I do get tired—"

"She's fine," Jesse said tautly. "She's well enough to move out—"

"Oh, look!" Mary interrupted him before he could take the thought further. "Lovely oysters." She hurried toward the table. "I'm told Shoalwater Bay oysters are the best in the world."

She stood before a vast array of raw shellfish. On the opposite side of the table, men were shucking them and setting them out with lemon wedges in a huge basin of chipped ice.

"You just said you hated oysters," Jesse pointed out.

"I said I'd never liked oysters," she corrected him, smiling sweetly at the man opposite them at the table. From the corner of her eye, she saw Mrs. Swann step forward, but the doctor took the widow's arm and led her away. They were matchmaking, bless them, and Mary loved them for it. "That probably means I've just never had good ones."

"You came to the right place." One of the men shucking oysters grinned and stuck out his arm. In the palm of his rubber-gloved hand he held a large opened oyster. "It's a taste of heaven on the half shell."

She stared at it. The pale moon-colored flesh glistened in the sunlight.

Jesse placed his hand in the small of her back and urged her forward. "Taste it. You traveled all morning to get here."

She was trapped by her own big mouth. She never did know when to button her lip, Mum always said. Gingerly she took the rough-edged shell and lifted it to her lips. All around her, people were sucking down the oysters. She tried not to think about the fact that the creature was alive, sitting there innocently, unaware that it was about to be swallowed.

She closed her eyes and gulped the thing, grimacing as it slid through her mouth and down her throat. It tasted of the sea and of some vague muskiness she was better off not thinking of. She opened her eyes and dropped the shell on the growing pile on the ground.

"Wonderful," she exclaimed, her voice only a little faint. "Thank you." Clutching Jesse's arm, she moved down the table. "Do you think I could have a glass of lemonade? Right away?"

He laughed, and she got over her horror long enough to laugh back. After that, Jesse seemed to relax a little, exchanging greetings with people he passed. Many of them knew him by sight, though he confessed he had no idea who they were.

A whole beef was roasting in a large pit on a bed of hot coals, and they gave it a wide berth as they passed, feeling the heat from several feet away. Mary looked around her in a state of wonder. "I feel as if I'm in the middle of a lovely dream," she said, taking Jesse's arm.

"Is that so?" His muscles tightened, but he didn't pull away.

"It *is* like a dream—the ladies in white, the music, the children dressed in their finest, the fleet out in the harbor. Everything's so beautiful. How blessed you are to live in such a place, among such people."

"I suppose," he said reluctantly. But he was in one of his more agreeable moods today. When he was agreeable, he seemed to let her have her way rather than struggle and clash with her.

"In Ireland, it was lovely," she said, "but we lived so far from everyone else, and the village rarely had cause to celebrate. We've not yet convinced the English of our independence." She inhaled the smells of cooking and the sea and the human smell of the crowd.

A loud thunking sound drew her attention. She hurried ahead to see an area roped off at the side of the courthouse. On a great flat rock, men were setting up logs and splitting them.

"Try your hand at this for the lady?" called a man in a straw hat, his sleeves held back by bands.

"It's a log-splitting contest," she said over her shoulder.

"You don't say."

"Oh, Jesse." She laughed.

"Three tries a penny," the hawker coaxed. "The prize is a patriotic eagle brooch for your wife."

Mary felt a chilly wave sweep over her. The dream-world took on the cold, hard edges of reality. *Wife*. She chanced a look at Jesse. His face was unreadable as he stalked past the rope barrier and wrenched a long-handled ax out of a stump.

The crier grinned. "Three tries a pen—"

"I don't need three tries." Jesse slapped a coin into the man's upturned palm. He peeled off his frock coat and shoved back the sleeves of his white shirt, baring his sun-browned forearms. He stood in front of a fresh upended log, bracing his feet apart in the trampled ground. Bystanders gathered at the fringes of the yard to watch. Mary heard curious murmurs: "Who is he?" "The lightkeeper of Cape Disappointment." "Rescued more folks than any other keeper on the coast." "I've heard he's a strange one...."

She moved away from the whispering voices. Let them talk. There was nothing strange about Jesse, except that for twelve years, everyone had believed he wanted to be alone. In all that time, she was the only one who saw he was hurting inside. She was the only one who believed he could heal.

The puzzle was to get *him* to believe it.

He loosened his cravat, letting the ends trail down his chest. Then he regarded the upended log with total absorption, as if the rest of the world didn't exist. What a gift it was, to have that concentration. All around him lay hacked-up logs, strewn there by men who had failed.

It never occurred to Mary that Jesse would fail. There was an almost mystical connection between him and the blade of the ax. His motion was as smooth as the gliding wind as he swung the ax up over his head, then brought it down in the middle of the wood, right at its vulnerable core. A smell of fresh evergreen wafted up. The log split apart in two perfect halves.

A smattering of applause rippled through the crowd. The hawker grinned good-naturedly. "Nobody warned me Paul Bunyan would be here today," he said, handing over the prize.

Jesse rejoined Mary. She moved close as the crowd jostled them, and she felt the damp warmth emanating from deep within the muscles of his arms and shoulders. A thrill shot through her.

He pushed the brooch into her hand. "I don't have much use for this," he said.

"Thank you." She was about to make some tart reply about his graciousness, but the remark earlier about her being his wife had unsettled them both. A day, which had started out soft and buoyant and full of carefree feelings, had suddenly, with a single word, turned dark and ominous.

And she didn't know how to fix it.

She pinned the brooch to her bodice and carried Jesse's coat draped over her forearm. He seemed to have forgotten the coat and certainly didn't need it; his back and shoulders were damp with sweat.

"Good God, do my eyes deceive me?" asked a clipped male voice.

Jesse and Mary stopped walking. A man in a straw bowler hat, dressed all in white, strode toward them. On his arm was a lady, also clad in white from head to toe.

Mary had only to look at them to see that they embodied wealth and privilege. The whites were too crisp to be anything but brand-new. The smooth leather shoes on the man and the alabaster kid slippers on the woman barely seemed to skim the grass, so light and airy was their step.

The man was fair of hair and eyes. His open grin was both cultured and guileless. "It can't be," he exclaimed, "but by God, I think it is." He stuck out his hand. "Jesse Kane Morgan. Hell's bells, man, don't you remember me? Elliot Webber, of the Portland Webbers!"

"Of course I remember." Jesse shook the man's hand.

Elliot frowned, taking back his hand, trying to be surreptitious as he wiped it with a white handkerchief.

Jesse cleared his throat. "Sorry. I was just trying my hand at splitting logs."

"I know," said the woman. "I saw."

In those few seconds, Mary understood. The woman had seen Jesse wield the ax, had seen the sun glinting in his hair, had seen the rippling breadth of his shoulders and back as he cleaved the log in two.

Mary glared at the woman, but she hadn't taken her eyes off Jesse. Elliot said, "This is my wife, Sarah."

Jesse bowed from the waist. "Mrs. Webber."

Mary had never seen him bow before. She hadn't yet decided how she felt about that, when Jesse indicated her with a slight tilt of his head. "This is Mary. Mary Dare."

She felt, with a wave of gratitude, Elliot's gaze heat with appreciation as it coasted over her hair and face. Mum had cautioned her about being vain, but she indulged herself for a moment. "How do you do?" he asked.

"Quite well, thank you," she said.

He took off his hat and regarded her through narrowed eyes. "Have we met before, Miss Dare?"

"Why, no. Surely not."

"You look familiar." Elliot shrugged. "Jesse and I were school fellows," he explained to his wife. "He was captain of the cricket team, and I was his deputy." Elliot winked. "Always top dog, weren't you, Jesse? And that Shoalwater Bay Company! You built it into quite the enterprise. Everyone was shocked when you bowed out after—ah, sorry, old chap. Listen to me, babbling on about the past."

"What brings you to the area?" Jesse asked stiffly.

"We summer here every year," Sarah said.

She spoke oddly, Mary thought. "Yee-ah" for "year." Silly affectation.

"Today I aim to trounce the local oystermen in the regatta," Elliott said, hooking his thumbs into his white gallowses. He had the arrogance of a man to whom everything—from a wife to money to victory in a regatta—came easily. "Had a bit of trouble yesterday—one of my crewmen drank too much and he's under the weather." Elliot snapped his fingers. "Say! How would you like to take his place, Jesse? You used to be a fine sailor back in our school days. Remember when I crewed for you in the Willamette regatta? You'd have a high time. After the first cannon fire, we sail out into the bay, and—"

"Sorry, Elliot, but no."

Only Mary heard the tautness underlying his voice. Only she understood. She slipped her free arm through his.

"But it would be just perfect," Sarah interjected. "The two of you would make the ideal team against these unwashed locals. You could put them in their place once and for all."

Mary felt the tenseness in Jesse's arm muscles. He, who was so strong and so fearless in all things, feared going to sea.

"You must go." Sarah pouted appealingly. "It's simply beyond anything to think that the silver cup will be won by some common fisherman, maybe even a foreigner. One of those strange Norwegians or dirty Irish or—"

"No." Jesse's voice cut like a knife. "In fact, we've got to go somewhere right now."

But he hadn't spoken soon enough. Mary felt as if someone had set fire to her. Shame and rage and frustration burned inside her, not just for Jesse but for herself.

"And God forbid," she burst out, proudly rolling the

brogue over her tongue, "that a dahr-ty Irish should take the prize." With a dramatic flourish, she swung Jesse's frock coat around her shoulders.

And realized her mistake.

She could feel both their gazes drifting down to her middle. She could see the small, tight workings of their minds, assessing the situation. Their conclusions crackled invisibly in the air like heat lightning. Sarah spoke at last. "Well!" With a huff of breath and a brush of her skirts, she swept away.

Elliot gave Jesse a lame grin and went after her.

Mary was at a loss. She couldn't believe how hot her throat burned. How deep the ache bit into her chest. The fragile contentment, the dreamlike happiness of the day, had vanished. In the space of just a few minutes, she had been called wife and then regarded as a whore.

Both of them dug at her, taunted her with what she wanted and all she could never have. Blinded by sudden, shameful tears, she started quickly toward the edge of town.

Somewhere in the distant meadow, a horse whinnied and the wheels of a buggy rattled. In front of her, tall heaps of oyster middens framed a view of Shoalwater Bay, the fleet lying at anchor, the sun a dazzling strip of liquid amber on the water. It was as if someone had melted a pot of gold and spilled it across the surface.

Mary clung to the image, trying to do everything at once. To tamp down her rage. Shrug off her shame. Blink away her tears. She was failing miserably at all three.

"Mary." Jesse's hand touched her shoulder.

She spun away from him and stepped back. One step. Two steps. "Don't touch me. Not now. Don't touch me...unless you mean it."

"Oh, for Christ's sake—"

"Help!" A frantic voice screeched across the fairgrounds. "Oh, someone, please help—"

"I have to go," Jesse said, already running in answer to the call.

Mary leaned against the fence as he raced off to investigate. Part of her went weak with relief. She was coming so close to loving him. It was starting to hurt too much that he wouldn't let her. She needed to collect her thoughts and harden herself against the callous judgment Sarah Webber had made.

But nothing would change what she was. An unmarried woman, pregnant, boarding with a reclusive man.

"Help!" the woman shrieked again. "My baby!"

It was Mrs. Hapgood, the reverend's wife. Suddenly, Mary's troubles shrank to small, petty annoyances.

Bone-weary, Jesse trudged back to the courthouse yard. In his arms he carried a precious burden. The little Hapgood boy clung to Jesse's neck.

"That was quite a ride you took," Jesse remarked. "I'll bet you weren't expecting the horse to take off like that."

"I was scared, mister. Real scared." The boy clung tighter.

Jesse was struck by the smell and the feel of the child. There was something unique and impossibly sweet in the smell of a little boy. It evoked images of innocence and laughter and the joy of endless possibility.

Jesse thought of the careening buggy the lad had set off, and the image hammered home just how fleeting life was. How a single moment could snatch it all away.

He caught himself doing something impulsive and unexpected just then. He lifted the boy higher and pressed a kiss to the top of his head. The brush of his lips across the silk-fine hair raised an ache in Jesse's chest.

He had little time to ponder it. Portly as a bowling ball,

Mrs. Hapgood came barreling down the road. Her husband raced along in her wake. "My baby," she shrieked. "My baby! My baby!"

The boy twisted in Jesse's grip. "Mama! Papa!" There was such utter relief in the shrill call that Jesse shivered. Gladly, he relinquished the child. The Hapgoods made a sandwich around the boy, pressing him between them and covering his face with kisses. From the father's eye squeezed a single tear. He looked up and mouthed the words "thank you" to Jesse.

But the glint of the sunlight on that single tear was all the thanks Jesse needed. He nodded and went in search of Mary.

He didn't have far to look. And it didn't take long for him to remember their quarrel.

Elliot and Sarah Webber. Damn them. Damn them to bloody hell. The look on Mary's face when Sarah had said "dirty Irish" had been, to Jesse, a glimpse of hell. He knew it wasn't the first time Mary had endured this sort of slight. And suddenly he wanted to make sure it was the last.

He wanted to protect her. If only she were like the Hapgood boy, in a runaway cart, shrieking for help. All he'd have to do was stop the buggy, and she would be safe.

She hadn't moved from her spot at the edge of the lawn. Her gaze was turned out to sea, her profile a stark statement of everything wrong between them.

The child. Her belly displayed it proudly now. That silent threat. That taunt.

Jesse's arms still remembered holding the boy. The preciousness of life. He could never feel that tenderness for the baby Mary carried. He didn't even want to try. The very thought made him recoil. He couldn't imagine acting the father to a child he had made, let alone a stranger's bastard.

But Mary wasn't a stranger, his conscience argued.

Feeling torn, he approached her. Never had her eyes looked so large, so soft, so deep with despair. Where was the joy? Why wasn't it there? No matter what happened, Mary always took joy.

"You're quite the hero again," she said quietly. "That family is lucky you were here today, Jesse Morgan. Aye, you're a lucky man to have around."

The irony of her words bit at him. Like a storm cloud, the encounter with the Webbers shadowed the rest of the day. He could feel her effort to keep up a brave front as they strolled through the crowd and cringed as cannon fire signaled the start of the regatta.

She perked up a little when an oyster boat manned by a local Finnish crew won the race, rounding the buoy and surging into the bay well ahead of the fancy rigs of visiting folk from Portland and Astoria. As the sun slipped down past the peninsula and summer color gilded the sky, Jesse looked at Mary and realized that it had been forever since the happiness of another person had mattered so much to him.

Perhaps it had never mattered so much. He had loved Emily, yes, but with a young man's brash confidence and carelessness. Now he was older, and he knew tomorrow was only a promise, not a guarantee.

"What are you looking at, boyo?" Mary asked.

He cleared his throat. "You. I hope you don't think I give a rat's ass what Elliot Webber and his wife said."

She tossed her head. "Certainly not."

"Let's get something to eat at the banquet."

She hesitated, then nodded, holding her chin high as they took their place at a long table set up on sawhorses at the edge of the courthouse lawn.

People congratulated Jesse, thumping him on the back, remarking about his heroism, and he never once believed it. Didn't like the attention, either. The Hapgood boy had been in trouble. Jesse had moved quickly and unthinkingly to get him out of it. That was all there was to it.

After supper, Mary fell to chatting with the young couple next to them. They were full of gossip and giggling, and Jesse was pleased to see Mary coming back to herself, smiling more readily and relaxing. He could feel her foot under the table, tapping in time to the music.

Jesse wasn't prepared when she turned to him and said, "Tell me what happened to Mrs. Hapgood's child. The first one."

"I have no idea—"

"Yes, you do. Now, either you can tell me, or I'll go ask Mrs. Swann."

Jesse took a deep breath. He didn't want to speak of this, didn't want to see Mary's face when she heard it. But the words came forth, relentless as the sea itself. "She had a baby out of wedlock. The child's father—he'd been her employer—claimed the baby once it was born. She's never seen it since."

Mary fell completely silent, completely still. Jesse couldn't tell if it was the gathering darkness or his own imagination, but she had never looked so small and defenseless.

"Would you like to dance?" someone asked. Jesse was shocked to realize it was his own voice.

She turned to him, her face soft and wistful in the torchlight. "I do love a dance," she admitted. "But not here. I'd feel too conspicuous." She glanced down at her stomach.

Yet he heard the yearning in her voice, heard the need calling to him. He took her hand and drew her to her feet. "Come on."

She followed him, not resisting, but clearly baffled. "Where are we going?"

"You'll see."

Beyond the circle of torchlight, darkness reigned. But the blue glow from the rising moon enabled him to see where he was going. On the east side of the courthouse, far from the crowd of people, stood a gazebo clad in white lattice. Summer roses twined along the sides. He led Mary up three steps to the platform. A riot of flowers obscured the night sky.

Feeling awkward, yet curiously liberated, Jesse bowed formally before her. "May I have this dance?"

He expected her to play along, to bat her eyes and let him sweep her into his arms. Instead, she burst into tears.

"Christ," he muttered, straightening.

"I'm sorry." She sniffed into her sleeve. "It's just that all I've wanted this evening was to dance, and now you're making my wish come true. How did you know?"

"Know what?"

"That I wanted so badly to dance?"

"You don't exactly hide your feelings. Now, do you want to dance or not?"

"Yes," she said, and her tears evaporated on a brilliant smile. "Yes, I want to dance with you."

No matter how much time had passed, he still remembered how to dance. He recalled the steps and the rhythm and the posture. What he hadn't remembered was the sweetness of holding a woman in his arms. Or perhaps it was a sweetness he had never really savored until this moment.

Mary gave her all to him—the grace of her dainty footsteps on the planks of the private gazebo. The warmth of her fingers cradled in his. The intimate inward curve of her back where he rested his hand. The satiny texture of her hair, drifting against his chin as they moved together.

Adoration shone in her eyes when she looked at him

and said, "Thank you, Jesse. Thank you for dancing with me."

Then he was kissing her, and he had no idea how it had started or if he should or whose fault it was. All he knew was that he was kissing her, his hands sliding down her back, cupping her intimately against him while his mouth explored hers. Exploration turned to seduction. His tongue traced the seam of her lips until she opened for him, letting him in, letting him taste her, letting his tongue make love to her with a rhythm echoed by the movements of their bodies against each other.

Without loosing his hold on her, he brought her to one of the benches at the periphery of the gazebo, and together they sank down, holding each other, hungry and desperate. She tasted of an earthy essence, elemental, vital. His hands slid over her, finding her breasts full and soft. She wore no stays or busked corset. Only a thin layer of fabric lay between his hand and her breasts.

It was the most searing sensation he had experienced in a long time. Years it was since he had cupped a woman's breast in the palm of his hand, years since he'd understood the fragile eroticism that held him in its thrall.

"Ah, Mary, Mary, you feel so damned good," he murmured. Her head fell back, and he ran his lips along the column of her neck, loving the smooth texture of her, imagining the way she would feel against him. "I need to be closer to you," he said, lust and not reason talking. "Closer, yes, as close as we can be."

He drew her onto his lap, and the pressure of her weight stirred the wildness inside him. The pulse in his ears roared like the sea, and he had never wanted, never needed a woman as he needed Mary now. He sensed the answering need in her. She was all woman in her desire. Her hands were frankly suggestive as they glided up his chest, parting his shirt.

Yet even as everything inside him strained for her, he felt the pain. Love hurt. He had learned that years ago. The lesson had been scored into his heart by a wrenching loss.

He held her closer, closer, and wondered how he had survived the last twelve years without this blessed ache. He'd had no idea it was possible for him to feel like this...until Mary.

This was it, then. This was the night he was going to cross the invisible boundary between them and make her his. He would hold her close and—

Something thudded into his midsection. It felt as if she were shoving him with a small fist. Half-dazed from kissing her, he lifted his mouth from hers. "Do you want me to stop?" he asked in a harsh whisper.

"Lord, no," she whispered back. "And why would you be thinking I wanted that?"

"You were pushing—" He stopped, feeling the sensation again.

Mary giggled. "It wasn't me, but the babe. He's moving around, and you must've felt him."

He nearly pushed her off his lap. He caught himself in time and settled for placing his hands firmly on her shoulders and moving her to sit beside him. A sudden frost descended on the gazebo. "I'm sorry," he said, feeling his insides turn to stone. "I've been disrespectful. I'll see it doesn't happen again."

"But Jesse—"

He shot to his feet and took her by the elbow, helping her up and steering her out of the gazebo and across the lawn. He felt dizzy, as if he had nearly leaped over a precipice but had jumped back at the last second.

"What's wrong?" she asked as they crossed the courthouse lawn. "It's perfectly natural for the baby to move. There's nothing in the least wrong with it."

"I didn't say there was."

"Then why did you suddenly stop?"

"Did you really want me to give you a tumble right here and now?" he demanded acidly. "Because that's where we were headed. Another few minutes and I'd have had your skirts tossed up over your head. Is that what you wanted, Mary?"

"I—"

"Is it?" Cruelty honed a knife edge on his words. "It's a simple question. Is that what you wanted from me?"

"No. Damn you, Jesse Morgan. You know it wasn't."

He turned away from her and strode toward the hotel.

Fifteen

~~~❧⚭❧~~~

The next morning, Mary stood in the parlor lobby of the Pacific House Hotel, observing the people bustling about, most of them leaving after the holiday. Porters rushed back and forth with steamer trunks and valises. Near the front door stood a businessman, nervously opening and closing the lid of his pocket watch as if the motion could make time pass more quickly.

What a grand place this was, as grand as some of the places she had seen in San Francisco. She put aside the memory. That chapter of her life was over. It had to be over. It did no good at all to think about it, for if she did, the fear would conquer her.

She smiled a greeting to Mrs. Hapgood, who hurried past with her little boy in tow. Mary pictured a much younger Mrs. Hapgood, frightened and alone, having her baby ripped from her arms.

The image chilled Mary to the bone. Was it true, then? Could a rich man lay claim to a child he had sired?

The very moment the thought crossed her mind, she saw him. He sat high in a thronelike leather chair across the room, his boot propped on a stool while a shoeshine boy buffed it. The pressure of panic built in her throat, higher and higher, until she was certain it would come out as a scream. Her gaze stayed on him as she tried to edge toward the lobby door. He was holding up a newspaper, oblivious to her. Perhaps she had a chance.

She took another step toward the door. Before she reached it, he lowered the newspaper and stared directly at her.

Mary nearly melted into a puddle of relief. It wasn't him. Her mind was playing tricks on her. She managed to smile wanly at Mr. and Mrs. Cobb from the Ilwaco Mercantile as they passed her. She told herself to stop being silly. She had gotten away, had survived a shipwreck, for mercy's sake. Surely she had not endured all that only to lose her freedom now.

San Francisco was many miles away.

But he had a residence in Portland. He lived just across the river...with his wife. With his childless wife.

Her teeth started to chatter. Where was Jesse?

Nervously, she fingered the fronds of a potted palm and watched the people in the lobby. Coming here had been a mistake. She had thought that moving out among society was what Jesse needed. He had to stop hiding at the lighthouse.

She hadn't paused to consider herself. Jesse and the lighthouse made her feel so incredibly safe that she had forgotten that she had a powerful man after her, a man determined to have a child.

Her child.

She swallowed convulsively and noticed that she'd mangled the palm leaf. She rubbed her hands in the folds of her dress.

"You know, I just realized where I've seen you before," someone said.

Mary looked around, startled. Her face went stiff with

dislike when she recognized Elliot and Sarah Webber from the previous day. "I'm certain we never met," she stated.

"He was awake half the night trying to place you." Sarah's eyes were narrow and hard. "And finally he remembered."

"We saw your picture in the paper some weeks ago," Elliot said triumphantly. "You're that shipwreck victim."

"It couldn't have been my picture," Mary said, her voice steady but her insides quaking. "There's been no picture of me."

"There certainly has," Sarah said. "It was in the *Daily Journal*. So Jesse rescued you, and he's looking after you out of the kindness of his heart." She sounded relieved. Clearly she hadn't wanted to believe Jesse could actually care for a dirty Irishwoman by choice.

"You're wrong," Mary said. "There's been no picture." She invoked all the hauteur she could summon as she swept past them and strode out of the hotel.

She heard Jesse calling her name, but she didn't stop, didn't slow down. She went straight to the livery. The stableyard swarmed with boys rushing to and fro, getting the rigs ready for departing guests.

Jesse grabbed her arm, stopped her. "Didn't you hear me calling to you?"

"I heard."

He peered into her face. "You're white as a ghost. Are you ill? Should I send for Dr. Mac—"

"You sent my photograph to the newspapers." She waited for him to deny it. She didn't want to know he had betrayed her.

"Of course I did."

She flinched as if he had struck her. "I asked you not to. I begged you not to."

"At the time, I knew nothing about you. Your family could have been frantic to find you." His face darkened as if he had stepped into shadow. "I know what that's like. The waiting. The wondering."

"Did it ever occur to you that I might have a very good reason for not wanting my face plastered all over newspapers from coast to coast?"

"Then you should have told me the reason."

"You never gave me the chance." Her voice rose, and several people in the stableyard turned to stare at her.

Jesse took her by the elbow and steered her toward the willow tree by the stream. "Tell me, then," he said.

She hesitated. Why had he betrayed her? Why, after she had told him not to take her photograph, had he sent it out for anyone to see?

I know what it's like. The waiting. The wondering.

This man, this angry, wounded man had suffered while waiting for news of his wife.

Mary blinked away tears. "I told you from the start that I wanted nothing to do with the man who fathered my baby. I said he was...a mistake. The worst kind of mistake."

Jesse leaned against the trunk of the tree. He folded his arms across his chest. She could see the wall going up, could see it happen before her eyes. Just as it had last night. The recognition of pain, the withdrawal. The moment he'd felt the baby move inside her, he had drawn away.

"I'm afraid of what would happen if he found me. He...can be a very determined man."

"Why the hell would you get involved with someone like that?" Jesse asked.

"He can also be very charming." She could not meet his eyes. "When I arrived in San Francisco, I had nothing. A small bag of coins that were my wages as a ship's cook, but that was soon gone. There are not many choices for a penniless Irishwoman. A woman who had lost everyone dear in her life. I tried to go into service, but no one would have me. Then I met Mr. Jones, and he was so charming to me, so caring." She clenched her fists into the fabric of her gown. "He gave me a home, visited me, brought me flowers and sweets." She closed her eyes, remembering the long dark nights when she had escaped into a world of sensual abandonment, knowing it was a sin, knowing it was for all the wrong reasons, but needing the closeness of another human being as she needed air to breathe.

That was the worst of it, perhaps. Grieving over her family, she had gone knowingly and wantonly into a forbidden relationship. She had fooled herself into thinking they loved each other, just to make it all right. She had given up the most precious, private part of herself just so she wouldn't feel so alone.

She should have known there would be a price.

Jesse said nothing. The long, slender fronds of the willow tree hung between them, obscuring him from full view. Yet somehow that obscurity made him easier to talk to, like a priest in confession, behind his shield of carved rosewood with the scent of frankincense heavy in the air and the old whispers of the church eddying through the silence.

"I never knew he was married," she went on, "until it was too late. You see, when I told him...about the baby...he was so happy. I thought he'd want to marry me then, to give the child his name." She studied the shifting pattern of the morning light through the willow branches. "As it turned out, he wanted the baby." She took a long breath and swallowed hard. "But he didn't want me."

Jesse didn't stir. She heard the soft hiss of his indrawn breath, as if he'd burned himself.

She wiped her cheeks, feeling the heat of mortification emanating from her skin, from her very soul. "He used me as a broodmare, and after the birth he would have taken the baby from me if I hadn't managed to sneak away like a thief in the night.''

She felt exhausted after unburdening herself, and she slumped against the trunk of the tree. She wished Jesse would do something, say something. She wished he would touch her. He merely stood in silence, the brim of his hat pulled over his eyes, the whispering leaves stirring in the breeze.

"Being here, among all these people," Mary said, "reminded me that I'm not out of danger. Particularly since you sent out my picture. The story of Mrs. Hapgood giving up her first baby frightened me, Jesse. I'm nobody. I have nothing. The same thing could happen to me. What if he sees that photograph?''

More silence. More soughing of the wind. And then at last, Jesse spoke. "He told you his name was Jones.''

"You don't think it was?''

He snorted skeptically and walked away. Mary could only stare after him. He was a hard man, she knew that; more than once she'd tasted the bitterness of his callous personality. But surely he should have at least a word of commiseration for her.

He didn't even look over his shoulder to see if she was following. Which, of course, she was. "I don't believe you, Jesse Morgan," she scolded. "I'm in trouble because of something *you* did and you think you can simply walk away.'' In the stableyard, Mrs. Hestia Swann stood awaiting her rig. She was staring at Mary with a stunned expression.

Mary could just imagine what the older woman was thinking. But Mary was furious. She had spent all of last night in misery, all of this morning in fear, and she was tired of it. Jesse deserved a piece of her mind, and by crikey, she was going to give it to him.

"I told you my most private fears," she said, walking

quickly to match his long strides, "and you have nothing to say about it. Nothing at all. Honestly, I sometimes wonder if your head is made of wood. Your heart of stone. Not once did you tell me it would be all right, that you would look after me, that you'd keep me safe."

He was leading her across the courthouse lawn. She was too angry to wonder where he was going.

"Faith, this is your fault entirely. You were the one who made my photograph. You were the one who sent it out for all the world to see."

Her words echoed with a hollow sound as they entered the courthouse. Cool dimness surrounded them, and their footfalls rang on the tiled floor.

"Have you nothing to say?" she cried. "By the hand on me, I should hope you would, or—"

She broke off as he wrenched open a door and stepped into a large, high-ceilinged room where a small man worked at a desk littered with papers. He looked up, frowned, then smiled politely.

"Jesse Morgan," Jesse said curtly. "I'm the lightkeeper at Cape Disappointment."

"Yes, I know of you. How do you do?"

"This is Mary Dare." Jesse barely turned to her, saying, "Judge Hiram Palmer."

She blinked in utter confusion, but managed to dip a slight curtsy.

"What's the fee for marrying folks?" Jesse asked.

"Why, eighty cents for the filing fee, but—"

"Fine." Jesse dug in his pocket, then slapped two silver dollars on the desk. He added a double eagle to the others. "And that's for doing it now."

"Now?" the judge asked.

"Now."

"*What?*" Mary demanded, her mind starting to go numb with shock.

The judge scurried to a side door and murmured to someone. A clerk came in, bobbing his head in greeting. He retrieved a form and started filling it out in spidery script.

Mary heard the roar and swish of blood in her ears, felt Jesse push an ink pen into her hand, watched herself write her name where he indicated, then watched Jesse sign.

Trying to gather her wits, she clutched at his arm. "What in the name of all that's holy are you doing?"

"Marrying you."

"Why?"

"It's what you want, isn't it? For the baby to have a legitimate father, so no other will have a claim on it."

She stared at him, this hard, embattled man who wanted only to be left alone, and terror and gratitude welled up inside her. "Yes, but—"

"Then hush up and marry me."

The next day at dawn, Jesse stood alone at the lighthouse. He had been married for nearly twenty-four hours, but he didn't feel like a bridegroom.

He wasn't even certain what he was supposed to feel. The day seemed like all the others he had trudged through during his time at the station. After his turn at the watch, he stood on the promontory and looked out to sea, studying the sky, reading the weather. He glared at the iron-colored swells and saw in them the enemy he would spend his life battling, the enemy he could never vanquish.

Yesterday he had found new depths to the meaning of awkwardness. His impulsive decision to marry the woman he had pulled from the sea had been so enormous that he had a headache all the way home.

There had been no speaking of it on the long ride, because Abner Cobb and his wife, as well as Dr. Fiona Mac-Ewan, had begged a lift from them. Mrs. Cobb and Mary had chatted like old cronies. Fiona had plenty to say, as well, taking delight in reading aloud to Mary every single word and clause in the ornate printed broadsheet of the marriage certificate. Abner had dozed and Jesse had driven in silence.

Upon arriving home, Jesse had spent a long time putting up the team and buggy; then it was time to start watch at the lighthouse. He had passed the lonely hours of the night thinking about her.

Mary. His wife.

Sweet Jesus, he had a wife.

The rays of early-morning sunlight were hard in their intensity as he entered the main yard of the house. The changes Mary had made slapped him in the face. Daisies and petunias rioting along the verges. Geraniums and lark-spur exploding from hanging baskets around the porch.

And everywhere, the roses. For years they had lain dormant, refusing to die, refusing to go away. With a little attention, she had coaxed them into lush fruition. Everything, he thought grumpily, *everything* seemed to come to life beneath her touch.

Feeling weary and out of sorts, he trudged up the steps and went inside. The house smelled of freshly brewed coffee. He thought how welcome that was, and for a moment he was grateful. To come home to warmth. To something as simple and as comforting as a pot of fresh coffee.

Yet his gratitude was fleeting. Taking pleasure in the things Mary offered had never been part of his plan. He must not grow to expect these things, to crave them. He'd married her only to ease her mind about the safety and legitimacy of her child.

Liar, whispered a voice in his mind. *Liar, liar, liar.*

"Good morning," she said from the kitchen. Wearing a soft, tentative smile that seared his heart with its brilliance, she poured coffee into a cup and sweetened it—a single spoonful, on the scant side. Exactly how he liked it. She must have been watching him, memorizing his habits and his preferences. It astonished him that anyone would care how Jesse Morgan preferred his coffee.

"Thank you." His voice sounded gravelly, ungracious. Well, what did she expect? A total transformation brought about by a few dollars and a large sheet of paper?

They sat at the kitchen table, nibbling on soda bread and drinking their coffee. He forced himself not to look at her, for each time he did, his body grew hot and restless with desire. She was ripe and lush. Forbidden fruit.

She cupped her chin in the palm of her hand. "You married me." She sounded slightly dazed.

"Yes."

"I can't believe you married me."

"Uh-huh."

"Is that all you have to say?"

"Is there something else I should say?"

"I suppose…not right now." She paused. "I've been up for hours," she said, still regarding him with wonder in her eyes. "Thinking and thinking and thinking. Sure a body could never sleep with all that's happened."

He, too, had been up for hours. He, too, had been thinking. But he said nothing.

"I have a confession to make," she said. "Quite soon after I got here, I made a vow. I vowed that I would stay no matter what. Even if it meant deceiving you. Even if it meant getting Erik to fell a tree across the road to town. I would've done anything to stay. This is where I feel safe. This is where I want to bring my child into the world."

He sipped his coffee. The ruse with the tree didn't surprise him in the least.

"The fact of the matter is," she said, "that I was wrong. Not about wanting to stay here, but about my reasons for wanting that. For you see, if I had simply wanted to stay, then marrying you yesterday assured that. But I made a discovery. Living here was only part of what I truly want."

He had the distinct feeling he wasn't going to like what she was leading up to. He said nothing, but drank his coffee and waited, trying not to notice how full and moist her lips were, how clean her hair smelled.

"What I really want," she said in a soft, lilting voice, "is for you to love me."

"Christ." He slammed his mug down and shot up from the table, stalking to the window to glare out at the dawning day.

"I knew you'd be cross," she said. "But I have trouble hiding my feelings from you, and so I thought it best to simply tell you."

"You expect the impossible," he said.

"How can you say that? We've never even tried—"

"And we never will." He spun around to face her. "I married you so you wouldn't have to worry about Jones or whoever the hell he is coming after you. That's all."

"You refuse to let yourself have feelings." Her voice was quiet yet firm. "I've watched you, I know there's something left inside you—a tenderness, a need. But you keep your true heart walled off." She looked him square in the eyes. "Resurrection is what the living need to do. Not the dead."

Her words tore him open, left him exposed. At the same time, they challenged him. Challenged him to fall in love again. But he couldn't do that. Love was fleeting; the pain of loss lasted forever.

Fury roared through him. He stood frozen, reeling inwardly with the temptation to believe her, to take her into his arms and accept her invitation. Finally he found his voice. "I don't need you to tell me what is inside me."

"I shouldn't have told you that. Shouldn't have admitted that I wanted your love." Her voice turned thin with regret. "But you see, I've grown used to telling you everything that's in my heart. And you know me, I can't stifle myself." She turned and started clearing the breakfast dishes. "I'm your wife now. You made it so. I have to try to discover what that means."

Jesse would never know what spurred him to cross the room so quickly, to take her in his arms. Perhaps it was the way a shaft of light streamed in through the kitchen window and struck dazzling threads of gold into her hair. Perhaps it was the way she moved about the kitchen, unhurried yet efficient, as if she had always been there. Or perhaps it was the sweet-sad yearning that haunted her face.

Not pausing to answer his own questions, he found himself holding her, furrowing his fingers through her hair and hearing the *ping* as her hairpins came loose and sprinkled the floor. He brought his mouth down onto hers, hard and swiftly, devouring those moist, mobile lips, struck anew by the softness of her.

He wanted her badly enough to ignore all the reasons he couldn't have her. He started making love to her right then and there, standing up and pressing her against the counter, his hands and mouth questing, feeling and tasting her skin and her curves and pulling at her clothes. He understood that this would change everything, but he no longer cared, for his soul was lit by the dark fire of need.

He took her by the hand and led her up the stairs to the bed he had shared only with his own shattered dreams.

Sixteen

⤙⟨⟨**⟩⟩⤚

Mary was uncharacteristically quiet as she untied the yellow curtain at the window and let it drape over the panes. The light in the room turned to liquid gold, richer by far than ordinary daylight and not in the least concealing. She turned away from the window and faced him, a tentative half smile on her face. "I suppose," she said, "we'll have to adjust to a lightkeeper's schedule."

He stood with his hands loose at his sides, his heart knocking in his chest and the passion inside him climbing higher by the minute.

"Look," he said to Mary, giving her one last chance to back out. "You don't have to—"

"Hush," she interrupted. "I *want* to."

With her gaze fastened to his, she stepped out of her pantaloons, reached around behind her and loosened her sash, then unbuttoned her dress and let it drop to the floor. The shift she wore beneath was made of translucent white fabric, and with the window glowing behind her, she might have been a church icon, so clean and pure were the lines of her shoulders, her face and neck. Then his gaze traveled downward to the frank swell of her belly and he corrected himself. No church icon this, but a pagan goddess, ripe and full.

Up until this moment, he hadn't been certain how he would feel upon seeing the evidence of another man's touch. He expected to feel resentment, jealousy. Regret, perhaps, and curiosity. But he never would have guessed he would feel desire. The sight of her, looking so splendid and glowing, torched his blood.

She took hold of the ribbon that tied the top of the shift and gave it a long, slow pull. The shift gaped open. She wore nothing beneath. She'd grown bigger, more lushly beautiful than the day he had stumbled upon her in her bath.

A sound came out of his throat. It resembled the noise an animal in a trap might make—low and tortured. He took her in his arms, forgetting to breathe, forgetting everything except his need to touch her. They kissed briefly, fiercely; then Mary stepped back.

He removed his shirt and boots. As Mary shrugged out of her shift, he peeled off his Kentucky jeans and yanked back the covers on the bed. They lay together facing one another, and his hands and mouth wanted to be everywhere at once. He explored the silkiness of her hair with his fingers while his tongue traced the shape of her lips. His hand curved along her shoulder to her breast, cradling its fullness while he brought his lips down over it. In that instant, he knew a yearning so sharp that it pierced through twelve long years of self-denial.

He slipped his palm along her side to find the small of her back and the rise of her hip. A light sigh escaped from her, and she whispered, "Jesse, love, it's so good to have you touch me."

The feel of her breath in his ear nearly made him explode. He explored her inner thighs, and she moved rhythmically against his hand. Then her fingers closed around him, and he nearly leaped out of his skin, loosing a ragged cry.

"Easy, there," he growled. "Twelve years without a woman is hell on a man's self-discipline."

"Fie on discipline," she whispered, her small tongue swirling across his bare chest. "I want to feel you inside me, Jesse. I want it now."

Of all the things she had ever asked of him, this last captured his soul. He parted her legs with his own and slid into her, struck by the sheer ecstasy that closed around him, welled inside him and turned his passion to a white-hot, impossible heat.

"God—" He broke off to take a ragged breath. "Don't move," he ground out between his teeth. "Mary—"

"Don't be ridiculous." She undulated her hips and he responded with a roar of sensation that rolled out along his limbs, culminating in a cry of half protest, half exultation. The surge of his climax seemed to go on forever, lifting him, winging him away, until nothing beyond the moment and the woman in his arms existed. There was only Mary and the moment she had given him, and her quiet, contented murmurings in his ear.

His temples were damp with sweat when at last he moved off her slowly, gently. Immediately she curled against him, pressing her hands to his chest and propping her chin on them to gaze at his face.

He saw everything in her eyes—his own reflection and the depths of all she felt. She was a remarkable creature. She had changed his life. He didn't want that, but she was like the tides. Inevitable. Making her way slowly, deliberately, into the very center of him.

"I was...too quick," he heard himself grumble. "Damn, it's been too—"

"Hush. Stop your growling." She placed a finger or

his lips, then traced the shape of them. "I'll not hear a word against what we did. Not ever."

"But—"

"I said not ever. Why can't you just take joy when it comes to you? Why do you have to find a reason that it shouldn't be good?"

He didn't answer. Couldn't answer. For her hand had trailed down his chest and lower, having a remarkable effect on him. Within moments, he was ready again. She smiled softly and moved atop him.

His fevered imaginings in all the long, lonely nights on watch had conjured up such a scenario. Only this was better. This was real. When she joined with him, he was filled with such a sense of wonder that it was as close to happiness as he had come in years, perhaps ever.

There was a forbidden eroticism in having her atop him like this, her breasts swaying enticingly, inviting the caress of his hands and his mouth, the yellow light gilding her and surrounding her with a blurry softness that made her seem as illusory and as fleeting as a dream.

But unlike a dream, she was something he could touch and hold. Something he could believe in. Something that could destroy him with a single stroke of fate.

Mary awoke in the late afternoon. At first she felt disoriented, for she didn't recognize the sloping ceiling and the four slender bedposts that surrounded her. Then she smiled as a quiet joy radiated through her.

She lay abed with Jesse. Her husband.

The marriage had happened so swiftly, she still could scarcely believe it. Of course, she'd had her doubts when they had returned to the station and he'd disappeared for the night. She'd suffered through all sorts of awful imaginings—he was regretting his mistake. He would never come to her. He would never put away the past and let himself love her.

But this morning had changed all that. This morning, he had made love to her. She curled against him and let warm shivers of remembrance ripple over her. He had been fierce, not gentle, but that had only added to her excitement. He'd said little, but he always said little.

She lifted her head to gaze at his sleeping face—strong lines softened by a day's growth of beard and by the filtered light from the window—and admitted to herself that he was a long way from loving her. But he was a lot closer now than he had been a few weeks ago.

She supposed she shouldn't have admitted that she wanted his love, not just his acceptance. He was such a contrary man that he was bound to resist anything she openly wanted.

But it was true. She felt as if his love would answer all the secret needs and aches inside her. She felt as if his love was the reward that waited at the end of a long journey.

"Ah, Jesse." She bent her head and pressed her lips to his bare chest. "Don't be afraid to love again."

"Mmm?" He stretched and scooped his arm around her, burying his face in her hair. "Did you say something?"

She reveled in the sensation of their flesh sliding together, creating a delicious friction. "I always have something to say."

When he opened his eyes, she saw the darkness there, the doubt. She refused to let it cast its shadow on her. Not now. Not when the bed was so soft and warm and the room glowed with the filtered light of the afternoon sun. Not when her body craved his touch more than food.

"Halloo!" A faint call sounded from the yard.

"Shit." Jesse glared at the ceiling. "It's Fiona."

Grabbing her shift and dragging it on as quickly as she could, Mary hurried to the window. She lifted the corner of the curtain to look out. "Well, yes," she said over her shoulder. "Fiona...and a few others."

"Shit," he said again.

By the time they had dressed and hastily combed their hair, a large, boisterous party was coming up the walk. Dr. Fiona MacEwan and Mrs. Hestia Swann led a contingent of people from town along with the Jonssons.

Mary hastened to let them all in, blushing and laughing through their congratulations.

"I simply had to come and see if it was true," Mrs. Swann announced. "I can't say I approve of the courtship, but I certainly approve of the marriage." Her straw hat, still festooned with ribbons of red, white and blue, bobbed madly as she looked Mary up and down.

Bert Palais slapped Jesse on the back. "Welcome to the world of being a husband and papa," he said. "Things'll never be the same."

Jesse set the beer jug on the kitchen table and started passing around mugs. He moved through the crowd of well-wishers with a sort of awkward dignity that struck at Mary's heart. This was all so sudden for him, she realized. Twelve years of being alone had not prepared him for this.

"I knew it would happen," Palina said, tears of joy running unchecked down her face. "It was destiny. You saved him, Mary. You and the baby saved him from a desperate loneliness."

"I'm not certain he wants saving." Mary watched him from across the room. Even from a distance, she could see that his shoulders were tight, his movements jerky with tension. He reminded her of a wild animal, cornered and not certain where to turn.

"If you ask him, he'll say he wanted things to stay as

they were," Palina said. "So don't ask. Just love him,
Mary."

She smiled. "I think I can manage that."

But she could tell Jesse didn't like being the center of
attention, the object of toasts and best wishes. A tragedy
in the past had taught him that love was merely a preamble
to pain and loss. It would take more than a mere celebration to convince him otherwise.

Mrs. Swann sat heavily on the settle and gazed for a
long time at Mary. "How lovely you look, my dear. How
very, very lovely." And then Hestia Swann, the iron-
willed matron of Ilwaco society, burst into tears.

Mary rushed to her side. "Mrs. Swann! What's the matter?"

The older woman selected one of a half-dozen hand-
kerchiefs from her reticule and dabbed at her nose and
eyes. "Forgive me. I was just overcome by memories of
Captain Swann and the children. But Sherman's gone on
to his reward and the children, bless them, have gone off
to California. I feel so very much alone."

"Ah, 'tis sorry I am, Mrs. Swann."

"Thank you, Mrs. Morgan. I try not to despair, but
sometimes I feel my life is without meaning or purpose. I
might as well lie down and die."

Mary cast an urgent look at Fiona MacEwan, but the
doctor was busy inviting a thin-faced woman into the
house. On the porch, dutifully lined up like soldiers on
parade, were five of the thinnest, palest children Mary had
ever seen.

"There, there," she soothed Mrs. Swann, taking the
lady's hand.

"I just rattle around in that huge house Sherman built.
It's so big, I've shut off most of the rooms because it's
simply too hard to see them empty."

In a way only Mary could see, Hestia Swann and Jesse

Morgan both suffered from the same problem. They had lost all they held dear. And neither knew how to cope.

"Look at me," Mrs. Swann sobbed, "drowning this joyous occasion with my own bitter tears."

"Don't you worry about that," Mary said. "My mum used to say each tear you cry quenches an angel's thirst." She felt Jesse's eyes on her. Flushing, she looked up and shrugged. She expected him to be disgusted with the sentimental notion, but instead he looked intrigued. Even touched.

Seeking a distraction for her friend, she took her arm and whispered, "Who is that woman who just came in?"

Hestia Swann sniffed and blinked her eyes. "That's Melissa Clune. Her man was the cooper on poor Sherman's ship. They perished together, our husbands did. But a cooper doesn't command the same income as the skipper, and she's got at least five little ones. I don't know how she's getting by."

Mrs. Clune approached Jesse, her thin hand clutching a tattered shawl as she greeted him. "I came to wish you well, Captain," she said. "And to say thank you for all you've done."

"All he's done?" Mary whispered.

"He paid her room and board through the season."

"Jesse?"

"Yes. Tried to keep it quiet, but word got out. Your husband has a soft heart under that prickly exterior," Mrs. Swann explained.

Jesse stared at the cooper's widow as if horrified by her display. Sweat broke out on his forehead. "It was nothing, Mrs. Clune. Surely the least I could do, and in no way a compensation for your terrible loss."

"I wanted to stop in and say goodbye," she said. "I can't expect you to pay my keep forever, especially now that you've got a family of your own."

"It's my privilege to help—"

She held up a small, shaking hand, exhibiting a pride not apparent at first glance. "I have to find a way to survive on my own." She laid her gift—a small crocheted bundle—on the table, then backed away toward the door. "Goodbye, Captain. My best to you and your bride."

"Wait," Mary called to her. She got up, taking Hestia Swann by the hand. She herded all of them out onto the porch. "Mrs. Swann, just how many empty rooms do you have in that house of yours?"

The older woman looked startled by the question. Then, as comprehension dawned, a keen gleam came into her eye. "Why, exactly enough." Her assessing gaze swept over the quiet children. "Just exactly enough."

Later, Mary stood with Jesse on the porch while the guests headed for home. Erik would take the watch tonight, and Mary shivered deliciously, anticipating her first full night as a married woman.

She leaned her head against Jesse's solid shoulder. "Thank you for this day."

"You're thanking me?"

"Of course. You've made me so hap—"

"I've done nothing of the sort," he said, jerking away so abruptly that she swayed. Shoving his hand through his hair, he paced the length of the porch. "Look, don't make this into something it isn't. Our getting married isn't going to change the world."

A subtle chill of doubt slithered through her. She couldn't help wondering if Jesse *had* married her only out of charity, seeing as how he'd supported Mrs. Clune. No. She pushed the thought aside. Even Jesse wasn't so extreme.

She regarded him solemnly, knowing her heart was in

her eyes. Not caring that she showed him. "You've changed my world, Jesse. I love y—"

"Damn it." His fist thudded on the rail. She felt its reverberation down the length of the porch. "Don't do this, Mary. Don't build this into some sort of melodramatic claptrap. You're always doing that."

"But people can heal from their grief. They can go on. Look at Mrs. Swann and Mrs. Clune—"

"So you threw them together under one roof," he said. "But it's not going to help those children when they wake up at night crying for their papa. It's not going to help Hestia when she needs her husband to hold her."

"I cannot believe you can be so bitter," she said.

"I can't believe you're so naive," he returned.

"Naive about what?"

"About love."

Her mouth dropped open. "What?"

"You pretend you know what love is. But if you ever truly loved, deeply, with your whole heart, then you'd know it's not something you just snap out of because it's over."

"You make it sound like a disease."

"Maybe it is. A disease that has no cure." He strode to the door. "You're fine company, Mary," he said. "Too fine for me. When we were…together today, it was good. Better than good. That's enough for me. If it's not enough for you, then you should have spoken up in the judge's chambers." He went inside, and the door tapped shut behind him.

Mary stood glaring out at the evening, watching the pink swirls of clouds on the western horizon. She didn't dare go in, not yet. If she went in now, she would be obliged to give him a piece of her mind, or perhaps to flounce away as she had that other time, making a fool of herself.

She forced herself to be calm, to absorb the pain and get used to the hurt. Maybe he didn't love her. Maybe he didn't want her in the way she hoped, but staying with him was the only choice for her. Without Jesse, she and the baby would be homeless, penniless.

There were worse things, she decided, than being married to a man who loved a ghost, who hadn't decided to start loving a flesh-and-blood woman.

Yet.

"You're quite certain?" Granger Clapp asked his solicitor.

Mr. Stoner pushed a folded newspaper across the desk. "There's an announcement in the *Journal,* and I checked the courthouse records myself. She married Jesse Morgan the lightkeeper."

Although Granger didn't move a muscle, he felt an arctic blast of rage blow through him. "How does this affect the suit to claim my child?"

Stoner cleared his throat. He took out his pocket watch, flipped it open and shut without looking at it. "We really haven't a legal leg to stand on, sir. I'm afraid—"

"Yes, you are, aren't you?" Granger said. "Afraid to do what truly must be done."

"I don't understand, sir."

"Never mind. You are dismissed." With narrowed eyes, Granger watched the man scurry out. The chilled fury inside him hardened to a core of resolution. It was happening all over again. Once more, Jesse Kane Morgan was stealing the future, taking what should have been Granger's, and Granger's alone.

Granger would make him pay, just as he'd done twelve years before.

Within a matter of weeks, reports came from town about the transformation of Swann House. Not only did Mr

Clune and her brood find a home there; Hestia made it a project to seek out the families of other crewmen who had perished with her husband. She offered a room to Mrs. Selkirk, the aging mother of the fifth mate, and one to Rheingold, the ailing son of the ship's chandler. The young man had been in agony, worried that he would end his days in a charity asylum. Now he occupied a sunny room on the second story of the busy house, served by the Clune girls and often Hestia herself.

Mary and Palina took to visiting once a week, bringing eggs and butter, reveling in the boisterous atmosphere of a thriving household.

"You cannot believe the change," Mary told Jesse one night at supper. "It does a body good just to see them." She took a sip of the mulligatawny soup she'd made for dinner. "You should pay a visit."

"I'm not much for visits."

"You could come with me, since Palina and Magnus have gone away."

"With the Jonssons in Astoria for a fortnight, I've got more work than ever here at the station." Each autumn, the Jonssons took a holiday to Oregon, and this year was no exception.

Mary fell silent as they ate. Although he never said so, he loved her cooking. The creamy soup was another of her mother's specialties, redolent of carrots and celery with two secret ingredients—a tart apple and a pinch of curry powder.

"It's lovely there," she said at last. "Melissa Clune is manic about cleaning. Every window and surface sparkles. Rheingold—he's the one who was so ill—is resting comfortably, although Fiona says there is no cure for his fistula. He and old Mrs. Selkirk are quite the pair. Hestia is giving lessons to all the children. She swears young Edward—he's the eldest—will be the first Clune to go to university.'' She cocked her head. "What is that like?"

"What?"

"University. It all sounds so grand, but I haven't the faintest idea what it's like."

"Picture a lot of overprivileged young men who think they know everything and fight like cocks to outdo their fellow students. They debate high-flown ideas as if such things as justice and social morality can actually be resolved by talking over drinks. And they create rivalries that sometimes last a lifetime."

"It doesn't sound like such a grand place after all. Do you think it will help Edward to go to such a place? To learn such things?"

His lips thinned in a slight smile. "I suppose. But to be honest, the hardest lessons I learned were taught to me right here at the station. My teachers were the storms and the tides and the waves. Somehow, a dry lecture in an echoing hall at university doesn't compare."

"Yet you went. I try to picture what your life was like before you came here, and I can only think of huge houses and fancy parties. It's so hard to put you into that picture."

"I left all that behind," he said. "By choice."

"I think you left too soon," she said quietly.

"What the hell is that supposed to mean?"

She knew she was about to push his temper over the edge, but she didn't care. There were some things that simply had to be said. The two of them had been getting along during the early weeks of their marriage, but that was because she had stayed away from his heart.

Aye, she shared his bed but not his heart. The truth was she felt no closer to him now than she had the day she married him. She had been treating him as if he were about to explode. That had to stop.

"You should have stayed with that life long enough to accept Emily's death," Mary said at last.

She could see the fury forming on his face like a sudden frost. She forced herself to go on. "What you have is a broken circle. You didn't stay long enough to complete it."

He cut the air with a sharp movement of his hand. "You're talking horseshit, and it's none of your damned business."

"Losing her made you afraid to cherish anything else," she forged on, ignoring his crudeness.

"You don't know what it means to cherish anyone," he growled.

She shot up from her chair. "Don't I? Don't I? What of my family? Every last one—Da and the boys lost at sea, and Mum dying in my very arms. How can you say I never loved them?"

"Because you can still be happy after losing them!" he roared.

She sank into her chair, feeling an odd twinge low in her back. "Ah. So that's it, then. You think I never loved them because I'm not tormented by losing them. You think you're the only one who knows how to love. You loved Emily so much that you've made yourself miserable for twelve years proving it. I'm impressed."

"I never asked you to come meddling into my life. I told you I'd hurt you—"

"Keep trying, Jesse. But you can't hurt me. Because I know you don't mean any of it." In fact, she knew nothing of the sort, but she had to say so or she would fall to pieces. "I loved my family," she said fiercely. "I loved them so much that I would never dare to dishonor them by being miserable over their deaths."

She got up from the table again and walked to Jesse's side. She closed her hand over his. "Each time I smile, it's a small celebration of the love I felt for my family. Each time I laugh, it reminds me of the joy we shared. And each time I touch you, Jesse, I thank God for the family who taught me that touching and loving are the very essence of life.''

She brought his hand to her cheek, then to her lips. "If I dared to pretend otherwise, it would be a denial of all my family meant to me.''

For several moments, he sat as still as a statue. Then he rose and took both her hands in his. "I was wrong to say you didn't love them,'' he admitted. "But your way doesn't work for me. It'll never work for me.''

"You should try it. Try letting go of the past. Try loving again.''

He dropped her hands. "That,'' he said, "is impossible.''

It was the speed with which he'd dropped her hands that convinced her. He would love her one day. It would take a lot of hard work on her part, but he would.

Wouldn't he?

He went to the door and looked out. Autumn was sweeping in, the days growing shorter. The swish of falling leaves accompanied every sigh of the breeze. Tonight, Erik was sitting watch.

Mary bent and added a driftwood log to the hearth fire. She caught her breath as the twinge in her back struck her again.

"Is something the matter?'' Jesse asked without turning.

"No.'' She straightened, rubbing the small of her back and went to the long bookshelves that covered the far wall. "Will you read to me tonight? The poem you read about King Arthur was that grand. I was hoping to hear more.'' She took down a newer-looking volume. The leather on the spine was still shiny. "So many books. What is this one?''

He crossed the room and took it from her. "This was a gift from my sister. It's a book of essays by Emerson." From between the pages, a folded sheet of paper drifted to the floor.

Mary stooped to pick it up. "A letter?"

"Annabelle used to write to me. She gave up because I never answered her letters."

"Will you read me this one?"

He shrugged and went to the settle. Mary plumped the pillows behind her to cushion her back. He was about to share something from the past—surely that was progress.

He opened the letter, handing her an amber-toned photograph. "That's Annabelle and her husband on their wedding day."

Mary took the small, stiff photograph and glanced down at it. A chill seized her heart, and she gave it a keener look.

Then her world flipped over. Somehow she managed to sit still, to hold the photograph by its corners and to stare benignly at the smiling couple in the picture. But inside, everything turned black. She felt the darkness. The coldness. And the sheer horror.

Jesse was reading something—the letter? An essay? Mary didn't listen, couldn't listen. She could only stare at the photograph. Annabelle was as beautiful as her name sounded, resembling Jesse, with the same clean facial lines and a dignity of bearing that must be bred in the bone of these two.

But Annabelle's husband... The image was seared into Mary's heart. Even with her eyes closed, she could see his sharply handsome face, the perfectly trimmed mustache and the sleek, sandy-colored hair. The smiling, lying lips. The eyes that seemed to twinkle with mirth, but actually were a mask for malice.

Sickness pushed up into her throat. She swallowed hard, conquered it. Took a deep, shuddering breath.

"Jesse?" Her voice was faint. Quavering.

He stopped reading. "What?"

"I have something to tell you."

"Now?"

"Yes. I—it can't wait."

He folded the letter and set it aside. She handed him the photograph. "Your sister is very beautiful."

"I know. When I last saw her, she was only twelve years old. It's hard to picture her all grown up. I suppose I should've gone to her wedding, but I didn't want to leave the station."

"And her husband?"

"Granger Clapp. We were schoolmates, then business partners." His voice was flat. She could not tell what he was thinking.

"Granger Clapp." She repeated the name, tasted the bitterness of it. She forced herself to look Jesse in the eye. "I knew him," she said.

He frowned. "You knew Granger?"

Her every instinct screamed at her to lie, to deny it, but this was Jesse, and she had to tell Jesse the truth. She forced the words past the shame and mortification clogging her throat. "He told me his name was Jones. Granger Jones. He's the father of my baby."

Seventeen

~~~oGQo~~~

Once, while Jesse was training his horses for sea rescue, a wave had sucked him under. He recalled the moment with brilliant clarity. The wave had possessed an otherworldly, malevolent force. Its curved hollow had felt like the inside of a clenching fist as it snatched him off the panicked horse, swept him under. Drew him down to the gray depths and held him there.

The wave had tumbled him round and round in a rolling motion so that he had no idea which end was up. The universe had pulled the world out from under him. He remembered the chest-squeezing panic, the sense that everything was spinning out of control.

He felt the same way now.

Only this time, it was not a force of nature that tilted his world almost beyond recognition. It was Mary, his wife, and the secret she had just revealed to him.

He was a dying man in those first few moments. Chill numbness seethed over him until he felt as if his skin had hardened to an impenetrable shell. Then, only then, did he trust himself to move. He got up and went out onto the porch.

The autumn night had settled over the cape. A swirl of

stars lit the sky and, at regular intervals, the beacon light swept past, touching the tops of the trees with silver. The sea boomed hollowly against the rocks. Drying leaves and old roses spiced the air with a faint, evocative scent.

He heard Mary come outside, and he forced himself to look at her. To look at her lovely, fragile face, the eyes wide with fear, the generous curve of her breasts above the huge, prominent belly. Mocking him. Taunting him.

"Jesse," she said, her voice as sweet as a lullaby, "I wish you would say something."

"What the hell is there to say? That it doesn't matter? That I'm not surprised you were Granger's lover? That I'm going to lay a father's claim to my niece or nephew?"

She flinched, caught her breath.

Yes, he was hurting her. Lashing her with his words. A part of him understood perfectly that he should not blame her. But he did. Goddammit, he did blame her.

She had offered him his dreams back, only to snatch them away just when he started to believe they lay within reach. She had made him dare to hope again, had made him think it might be possible to love her, and then she had told him this.

Mary's revelation proved he'd been right all along. Love meant nothing but pain and loss. The absence of love, the numbness of indifference and isolation, were preferable to living with someone who held it within her power to slay his heart.

Though he had made her wince, she recovered quickly. She faced him without fear, without apology. "I never thought *Blind Chance* to be a prophetic name for a ship, but as it turns out, it is." She planted herself in front of him, on the top step of the porch. "We have to talk about this. We have to decide what to do."

"Exactly what choices do you think we have?" His fist

thumped against a pillar support of the porch, and his voice rang loudly through the yard.

"This comes as a great shock to me, too," she said. "So don't go raging around like an injured bear. I certainly didn't plan for the ship to wreck and for you to find me." She took a deep breath, visibly calming herself. "Bert printed the news of our marriage in the *Journal*, didn't he?"

"Yes."

"Do you think Granger reads that paper?"

"I imagine he does." From their school days onward, Granger had always taken an inordinate interest in the affairs of Jesse Morgan. At first, Granger had been motivated by pure envy. Jesse never planned to best him in sports and in studies; it just happened. Jesse never flaunted his loving parents in Granger's face, but there was no hiding the fact that on mail day at school, Jesse always received a wealth of letters and parcels while Granger got nothing. Jesse never planned to vie with Granger for the hand of Emily Leighton; they simply both fell in love with her.

Yes, Jesse supposed Granger would show a keen interest in the news of his rival's second marriage—especially since it was to the woman he had used so deliberately.

"Did he know you by your real name?" Jesse asked her.

"My name?"

"Did he know you as Mary Dare?"

She smiled up at him. He wished she wouldn't smile, for it made her so beautiful, but she did. She could always find a smile for him. "You're the only one who knows me as Mary Dare."

Once again, Jesse felt the sick spinning sensation of being sucked under by a wave. "You lied about your name."

"It seemed prudent at the time. Dare is my mum's maiden name. My real name is Mary O'Donnell. Mary Dare O'Donnell. I never told Granger about the Dare part."

"And you never told me about the O'Donnell part."

She set her hands on her hips. "I woke up after a ship-wreck to find myself with an angry stranger. Why would I simply tell all? I was running from Granger. Up until the moment I married you, I was running from him. What you might concern yourself with, boyo, is your sister."

"Annabelle?" A chill sped through Jesse. "He was in-excusably indecent to you, but Annabelle is his wife, not his—" He shut his mouth. Too late.

"Not his whore, as I was," Mary finished for him.

"I didn't mean—"

"You did, and you were right." She shivered. "The reason he had such frightening plans for me was that his wife is barren. At first I didn't know he was married, but he told me the truth after we…" She ran her hand down her stomach. "He told me she longed for a baby, that she would raise mine as her own, give it a lovely home and a fine education, all the advantages I could never offer a child."

Jesse wasn't surprised that the line of reasoning had failed to convince Mary. She believed fiercely in the power of love. She considered no one, no matter how wealthy or well-intentioned, was better equipped to love a child than its own mother.

He felt a twinge of sadness for Annabelle. She had been such a sunny, happy-go-lucky child, skipping through the ornate houses in Portland and San Francisco without a care in the world. What was she like now, all these years later?

And what in God's name would she think when she learned her brother had married her husband's lover?

A raw fury, bitter with the taste of futility, engulfed

Jesse. "We can't discuss what could have been or should have been," he said. "We have to discuss what is. The fact is, I married you without knowing who fathered your child."

"I didn't mislead you deliberately." She leaned against the porch rail and rubbed the small of her back.

"Nevertheless—"

"Why must this be such a problem?" she asked, clearly exasperated. "You—" She broke off and tilted her head, as if listening to a faint noise. Her hand kept rubbing the small of her back.

"What's wrong?" he demanded. "Is something wrong?"

She frowned. "Nothing. And you didn't answer my question about Granger. You have a different life here. You haven't seen him in years. Can't you go on like that?"

"No."

"Why not?"

"Because if Granger has become the sort of man you describe—a man who would lie to an indigent woman, dishonor her, then try to take her baby—then he's a danger to my sister."

She swallowed hard. He could see her throat move in the bluish starlight. "You have to go to Portland. To see Annabelle."

"Yes." He hadn't left the cape in twelve years. He would have to make the voyage by boat. *By boat.*

"And you have to tell her the truth about me."

"The truth?" he demanded hotly, rounding on her. The answer thrust itself into his mind, propelled by a dark malevolence that had been born in his heart the moment Emily had died. Without hesitating, without weighing the effect the words would have on Mary, he said, "We'll just explain to Annabelle that we're about to become the par-

ents of Granger's child. It'll be a bit awkward at family
gatherings, wouldn't you say?''

She stumbled as if he had struck her. She clutched her
stomach and kept moving, back down the steps, back into
the yard, back into the night.

''Mary—''

''Stay...away from me.''

He leaped down the stairs toward her. What the hell had
he been thinking? ''Mary—''

She cried out, and in the milky starlight he saw her
stumble and sink to the ground. Racing to her side, he
scooped her up in his arms. She was wet, not with cool
evening dew, but with a heated liquid.

''What the hell—''

''My waters broke,'' she whispered, her face contorted.
''The baby's coming.''

Moving as fast as he could, Jesse brought her to the
birth-and-death room adjacent to the kitchen. Panic boiled
in his veins as he laid her on the bed, then rushed to stoke
the stove beneath a huge kettle of water.

Of all the times for Palina and Magnus to be away. Jesse
was alone with a laboring woman, and he had no idea how
to bring a baby into the world.

Especially since the woman was his wife. His Mary.

Working with feverish speed, he fetched a clean nightgown and a pile of blankets. She lay unmoving on the
bed. Her eyes were wide open and her face was flushed.

''Dear God,'' she said between her teeth, ''I wish Mum
were here.'' She brought her knees up, clenching her teeth.
Jesse found himself holding his breath as she grappled
with the pain.

After an eternity of agony, it passed, and she looked up
at him. ''Can you help me get into the nightgown?''

He didn't know if he could stand to see her in this state,

ripe to bursting and about to give birth to Granger's child. But he had no choice. She gave him no choice.

"Here." He knelt beside the bed. His hands were clumsy as he fumbled with buttons and laces. The dress...what a time to remember the last time Emily had worn this dress....

"I have no idea what a lady wears to a baseball game, Em," he said in exasperation. *"You'll look fine no matter what you wear."*

"Is it anything at all like tennis?" she asked with a pretty pout. *"If so, then I can wear my tennis—"*

"It's not like tennis, Em." He laughed, filled with warmth for her amusing ways. *"Wear that nice blue dress with all the pleats in the back."*

"You just like that one because it shows off my bosom."

The blue fabric tore as he pulled it off Mary. He flung the dress away, flinging away the memories along with it. Somehow, he managed to get the flannel nightgown on Mary and to light several lamps around the room. Then he strode for the door.

"Where...are you going?" she asked in a thin, strange voice.

"To town. To fetch Dr. MacEwan."

"And leave me alone?"

"I'll tell Erik to stay with you. The beacon will have to do without watching tonight."

"Erik? Bless the boy, he's got a heart of gold but not a lick of sense. All this—" she cradled her huge stomach with her arms "—is bound to frighten him. Can't he go for the doctor?"

"He'd get lost in the woods." Jesse lifted his mackintosh from a hook behind the door. "I'll be back as soon as I can."

"You're taking one of the horses."

"Yes."

"It would be quicker to take the pilot boat."

Jesse froze in the act of shoving an arm into the cloak. Years-old dread thudded in his gut. "I'll take the horse."

"You'll be gone two hours at least," she said. "Jesse, please don't go."

He didn't want to hear the pleading in her voice, but he couldn't ignore it. "I have to."

"You don't. You could stay with me. You could help me bring this baby."

"I don't know the first thing about bringing babies."

"Neither do I."

"See? You need Fiona—"

"I need *you.*"

He jammed his hat down on his head. "Look, every minute we argue about this is a minute lost." He grabbed a lantern from the kitchen and turned away.

"Jesse." Her voice called to him, faint and sweet.

He stopped. He didn't want to turn and look at her, to see the pallor on her cheeks or the fear in her eyes. But he made himself do it. She was his wife. He had pledged an oath to her.

For better or worse.

He turned. The sight of her tore at his heart. She was pressed against an untidy bank of pillows, the quilt drawn up to her chin. The fragility that always haunted her beautiful face had never been more apparent as she gazed at him with beseeching eyes.

"Yes?" he asked.

"I'm afraid."

When she said the words, he felt as if everything had been drained out of him. He had no resistance to the stark honest need in her voice, in her face. He had no argument for the truth she admitted. He had no choice.

He set down the lamp. "I'll stay."

Eighteen

Jesse was afraid. During the breathless respites between the blinding twists of agony, Mary could see that. She made her eyes focus on him, because she didn't know where else to look. And what she saw on his face was fear.

There was so much to fear. That she would perish and leave him with a baby he hadn't made, didn't want. That the baby would die, and with it, her heart. Or that they would both survive and be his family, whether he wanted them or not.

The only solution likely to suit Jesse Morgan, she decided, was for both her and the baby to die. Then he could retreat again into his world of grief and loneliness, never to emerge again.

But he didn't want her to die. She knew that by the way he gripped her hand through the pains. By the way he whispered things—nothing and everything—in her ear.

As the night wore on, the periods of respite, when the pain ebbed, grew less and less frequent. Eventually, the lulls ceased altogether. Taut bands of agony shoved her deeper and deeper into darkness. As she slipped in and out of fitful awareness, she kept telling herself that she had

come here for a reason. Not to die. Not to bring more grief
to Jesse Morgan. But to give him life. As she was trying
with all her might to give life to the baby.

But trying wasn't enough, and hope darkened to despair.
"Why...is it...taking so long?" she gasped. "Oh sweet
Jesus, I want my mum..." Though barely able to draw a
breath, she lapsed into disjointed prayers. Shadows blan-
keted her and blurred at the edges, then grew light, un-
dulating and lurching. She lost all sense of who and where
she was. She heard Jesse's voice; it sounded as if he was
calling down a well, the words swirling and echoing, then
dispersing to nothing.

She knew what he wanted, to call her back, to urge her
to fight, but she couldn't. She was so weak, so hopeless
now, with no sense of resolve, no sense of herself, only
an overwhelming fatigue. She just wanted to let go, let go,
let go....

And then, like a pinpoint in a velvet void, she saw first
a flicker, then a sparkle, then a sustained bright light shining small, but starting to glow around the edges. And the
image threw her into another time, another place....

*Timbers groaning in protest. Men shouting. The whine
and thud of pumps. Feet scrabbling along a crazily slanting deck. Barrels and crates being jettisoned. And chill
water all around her, slipping over her, crawling along
her scalp and holding her under, pressing at her chest.*

She had seen that same patch of darkness, had felt the
same drifting sense of nothingness. Until she remembered
the baby. Resolve came to her on an upsurge, a fountain
inside her, and she grasped at some floating object—anything—and surfaced, gasping.

And there was the light. The beacon. A sweep of silver
across an endless glistening field of black.

Again. She saw it again. Felt the pull of its life force.
Just as she had before, she went toward the light, not quite

knowing what it was, just knowing that she had to reach it. She had to.

Did he know? Did he know he was her salvation? And did it matter to him? She felt his hands gripping hers, and his voice rumbled deeply. She thought she could make out the words: "Try, Mary. Please. You have to try. Please."

The "please" rang in her head. Jesse Morgan never said please. He must be desperate.

She blinked, dragging herself out of the strange visions of light. Despite her pain, she was eager to see this new Jesse, this man who held her so tenderly and said "please" as if he meant it. Slowly, so slowly, his face came into focus. Ah, that face, so noble and filled with suffering. So incredibly dear to her.

She held him in her gaze, but she couldn't speak. A fresh pain swept through her like a forest fire, and in the wake of the fire came an utterly overwhelming urge to birth the child. To bear down, not even allowing herself to breathe until she brought forth this baby.

She heard a low sound and realized it was her own voice, forced between her clenched teeth. She felt a sick pounding in her ears. Felt her face flush a heated crimson, felt every sinew in her body tighten.

"Mary, oh Christ, Mary..." Jesse moved to the foot of the bed.

She wanted to call him back, to let him know she needed to feel his hands on her shoulders, her brow, but she found it impossible to speak. Low, wordless sounds kept escaping her. She drew her knees up and strained with all her might, always looking at Jesse, her eyes pleading with him, as if he held the power to grant her release.

In the lampglow, the harsh lines of his face stood out stark and pale with fear. "I think...I see the head," he said in amazement. "Wait—oh shit—I can't see it any-more..."

She could make no sense of his words. She knew only the awful pressure and the all-consuming need to bear down, harder and harder, no need to breathe or think or feel or—

"Mary! It's—God, it's here, it's—"

The pressure lifted like a puff of smoke going up, dispersing, disappearing into a blue sky. She felt nothing for a moment; she was detached from her body, from sensation. And then, in the blink of an eye, she fell back into herself, sobbing with all her might, reaching out with her hands, reaching for the small, pasty, red-streaked creature, gathering up the bundle along with yards of blankets, holding and hugging the precious gift to her breast and sobbing, still sobbing, shuddering with the power and the ecstasy of what she had just done.

Jesse leaned against the blue cabinet and shut his eyes. He trembled, feeling drained and exhilarated all at once. He was reminded of the moments after a bold sea rescue, only this was more intense, more overwhelming. He'd just witnessed a miracle. He was part of that miracle.

Mary's tattered sobs filled the room along with the musky, bloody scent of birth and—incredibly—the faint calls of crows and the Jonssons' rooster, signaling the dawn.

Mary had labored all night. Her baby had been born.

And *he* had delivered the baby. Christ Almighty. He'd delivered her baby. Behind his squeezed-shut eyes, he saw it again, saw the tiny, streaked crown of the head. In a strange and unexpected way, it was as devastating as seeing the face of God. The face of an angel.

"Jesse! Help!"

He fell to his knees beside the bed. "What? What is it?"

"The...ah..." She gritted her teeth and her face red

dened as it had in those last few moments before the baby. "The afterbirth," she said between her teeth. "And you have to cut the cord."

"Cut the—" Terrible images flowed out from a dark place in his mind. Knives, scissors, sharp things—

"The cord, Jesse. You tie it off and cut it. Surely you've seen it done with animals."

"Yes, but—"

"Well?"

He found twine and a sharp knife. Some thinking part of him must have anticipated this moment, for the objects lay close at hand on the wall shelf. He didn't even remember getting them ready last night. Feeling hopelessly awkward and utterly terrified, he stood over her, looking down at the bundle she held. "I guess I'm ready."

She nodded wearily. He had no idea how it was possible, but she looked beautiful. Her hair lay in disarray; dark circles bruised the flesh under her eyes. But a glow, a triumph, seemed to emanate from her. He saw joy so intense that it shone like the risen sun from her eyes.

He wanted to touch her, to gather her into his arms and tell her how lovely she looked, how proud he was of her. But he couldn't do that. Something was wrong, something neither of them wanted to see or acknowledge....

His hand shook as he pulled back the folds of the blanket. Streaked with blood and fluids, the blanket would need cleaning right away. Absurdly, he made note of that. Then he saw the tiny stained head and the elfin chest and the cord, whitish blue and twisted.

He reached down with the twine and froze.

The child wasn't moving.

"Mary, I think—" His throat felt dry, as if he had swallowed sand. "The baby. Is it all right?"

"What could possibly be wrong?"

"Mary." Everything inside him crumbled to ashes. He

thought he had known darkness before, thought he had known grief, but nothing in his experience had prepared him for this depthless agony.

How ironic that he had found it at last, found the one thing that hurt more than his own grief. It was Mary's. Her sadness would hurt more.

"Mary," he said again. He gently touched her brow, smoothing back a stray lock of hair. "There's no movement. No sound. No breathing."

"Damn you!" she burst out. "How dare you say it?" She flung her head from side to side on the pillow. "Damn you, Jesse Morgan. Damn you, damn you, damn you!"

He could see the madness grip her. He had no idea what to do. Instinct alone drove him to take the bundle from her arms, to snatch it away so she wouldn't have to face her loss.

She nearly came out of the bed. "Give me my baby!"

"No. Mary, it's best if—" Jesse went stiff in every muscle. He felt it. A flutter. A shifting. His body responded before his mind. This subtle twist was a movement he recognized. At night these past few weeks, he had felt it when Mary curled herself close to him in sleep. It was the movement of the baby.

A thin little cry, like the mewing of a kitten, emerged from the blankets.

As hot and sharp as needles, tears formed in Jesse's eyes, then disappeared before they were even born. "The baby's all right, Mary." Relief almost staggered him, but he managed to lower himself gently and settle the infant in her arms. "Now, let's take care of that cord."

Tears streamed unchecked down her face. "Ah, Jesse," she said, "I'm so happy. So very, very hap—" She gasped. "Jesus Christ on a flaming crutch!"

He dropped the ball of twine. Coldness seized his chest. "What? What is it now?"

"Is it a boy or a girl?" she demanded.

He swore between his teeth. "How should I know?"

"You delivered it, my dear Captain Morgan."

"I wasn't paying attention to that, for chrissakes."

She began to laugh weakly, at the same time pulling aside the blankets. "A boy," she said, the joy and triumph he had seen earlier suffusing her face anew. "We have a son."

Jesse plowed a hand through his hair. He knew he should be exhausted, but he couldn't rest. Like a biddy hen, he rushed around the room, exchanging the soiled bedclothes for clean ones, bringing Mary water to wash and a fresh nightshirt and a stack of diapers she had spent the last several weeks hemming. She and the baby stayed in a cocoon of blankets, alternately napping or just resting as she gazed with mute adoration into the small one's face. A time or two, she held the baby to her breast, but Jesse wouldn't let himself watch or think or feel.

Not yet. Not now. It was too soon.

As the day wore on, he tried to sort through his feelings. He was pleased for Mary. Relieved that she and the baby were well and comfortable. But as for the child, he could summon nothing beyond that initial relief. He was not its father. He hadn't the first idea what to do with a baby.

He stole a glance at Mary and saw that the two of them were napping again. She lay curled around the baby, and only his tiny head was visible. Jesse felt a jolt of recognition. Uncannily, hauntingly, the child looked very much as Mary had when he'd pulled her from the sea. The same otherworldly, beautiful face. The same dark red squiggles of hair plastered against fair skin. The same bluish eyelids, delicately webbed with tiny veins.

"I didn't rescue you," he muttered under his breath, and walked out of the room. He stayed away for a long time, until he heard Mary call his name. Then he brought her a cup of milk and some toasted bread.

She smiled her thanks and ate with good appetite while the baby slept on, as deeply and unknowingly as Mary herself had slept those first days after being rescued.

"I've thought of a name," she said.

He didn't reply. He stared at the puncheon floor, noting the grain of the old wood as if it were a matter of great importance.

"David," she went on. "David Dare Morgan. Do you like it?"

"What's not to like?" He balanced her cup on the empty plate and stood up.

"I chose David because of its Biblical meaning. The parish priest once read the story to me, a long time ago. David was very important."

"You mean King David."

"David, the son of Jesse."

He nearly dropped the dishes, but managed to turn toward the door. "He's not mine."

"Oh, for heaven's sake. He bears your name. You brought him into the world. In your arms he took his first breath. What else can he be but your son?"

"Granger's."

"Granger doesn't know of him. He doesn't ever have to know." Jesse didn't want to hurt her, but he couldn't lie, either. "You know I'll take care of you and the boy. Keep both of you safe and sheltered and fed. But don't expect too much from me."

"Why not?"

"Because I don't have anything to give you."

He expected her to burst into tears. Instead, she smiled knowingly. "Jesse Morgan, you've given me life. Hope. A home and your name and the respect of a community.

And now you've given life to my son. Our son. You call that nothing?"

"I call it duty. I took an oath—"

"Damn the oath. You didn't do any of this because of some oath you took. You did it because you need to love again—"

"You're looking for something that isn't there, that'll never be there. Now, get some rest. I've got work to do."

"What's that you have there?" Granger asked, striding into the west parlor.

Annabelle nearly jumped out of her skin. Her small fist closed around a pale yellow sheet of paper. "Granger, dear, you startled me," she said, flushing.

He leaned over her fireside wing chair. She could feel his stare focusing on her clenched fist. "Fairchild said a telegraph came."

Drat the butler. Couldn't he keep a single thing to himself? "Oh!" she said, pretending she'd just remembered it. "I've had a most unexpected message from my brother."

"From Jesse?" Lean and catlike, Granger walked around to the front of the chair and held out his hand. "Let's see it."

Lord, but she wanted to defy him. To fling the crumpled page into the crackling fire and refuse to tell him what it said. As usual, she obeyed, holding out her hand to him, giving him the wad of paper. In truth, she didn't need the telegraph, for she'd already committed it to memory:

Apologies for being such a poor correspondent STOP
If you have the slightest need of me then wire back
on the instant STOP Jesse Kane Morgan STOP

Granger finished reading. "The slightest need of him? What the hell does he mean by that?"

It meant Jesse had guessed. Somehow he knew what Annabelle's life had become, and he wanted to help.

She looked into her husband's face and said, "I haven't the slightest idea, dear."

Granger tossed the page into the fire. "Do you intend to reply?"

"It would seem the courteous thing to do."

He walked back behind her chair, gripped her shoulders, the bite of his strong fingers searing the warning into her muscles. "Don't trouble yourself with it, darling. The man's insane, and has been for years. I'll take care of the reply."

Annabelle sat perfectly still, knowing his grip would not slacken until she conceded. "I'm sure you will," she said softly. "Thank you, dear."

In the middle of the second night after the birth, Jesse awoke to the sound of wailing. He jumped out of bed and stuffed his legs into his jeans, not stopping to fasten them as he hurled himself down the stairs.

The sound was eerie, like a cat caught in a trap. He felt its vibrations in his marrow. Fumbling, he lit a lamp and went into the birth-and-death room. He had told Mary it was best for her to stay down here rather than trying to climb the stairs so soon after giving birth.

She'd seen right through him, but she hadn't argued.

He lifted the lamp to see what was the matter. She lay helplessly on her side, the baby next to her squirming and straining, his mouth wide-open and emitting a terrible feline wail.

"What's the matter?" He drew a hand down his face, trying to adjust to the rude awakening. His cheeks felt bristly, and he couldn't remember the last time he'd shaved.

"He's hungry." Mary raised her voice above the howl. How could such a tiny creature raise such a racket?

Hoping his patience would last, Jesse set the lamp on a shelf. "Then I guess you should feed him."

"I...can't." Her voice sounded thick with unshed tears.

He didn't understand. He hadn't allowed himself to look too closely, but he'd seen her hold the child to her breast several times. "You've been doing it—"

"Something happened," she said. "I just suddenly filled up, and now I'm too...*full.*"

"Jesus Christ." He didn't want to think about this, didn't want to have to involve himself in something as intimate and elemental as a mother nursing her newborn. But her misery penetrated his heart. He found himself bending over the bed, reaching for the squirming, squealing bundle.

As he picked up the baby, the back of his hand brushed her breast. The sensation shocked him. Her flesh felt feverish and hard as a rock. Her size had ballooned beyond all imagining.

"Jesus Christ," he said again, covering his amazement with anger. He straightened up and held the baby, but it was awkward because the infant was squirming so. With surprising strength, the little mite arched his back and hollered. That sound. It was surely the sound that accompanied the devil's chariot to hell.

"He can't...latch on," Mary said, sobbing openly now. "And it hurts. It hurts...."

Jesse jiggled the baby a little. This made him stop crying for a moment. "Can I get you anything?"

She lay on her side and sobbed.

Swearing under his breath, Jesse stalked over to the washbasin. He had thought he could keep his distance from this little intruder. He had thought Mary—a natural mother if there ever was one—would handle everything, provide everything the baby needed. Yes, that had been the plan. Jesse would provide for her, and she'd provide for the child.

It wasn't working like that. Already, chaos reigned. The baby wasn't letting him keep his distance.

Because her skin had felt so hot, he dipped a clean towel in the basin. Mindful of the baby, he wrung it out and brought the towel to Mary. "Here. Hold this against you."

Sniffling, she pressed the damp fabric to her chest and closed her eyes. How weary she looked, her face wan, the normally cheerful set of her mouth drawn down. A lock of hair strayed across her cheek and nose. With one finger, Jesse reached down and smoothed it back.

The baby made an angry sound, and Jesse could tell he was gathering strength for another howl. He stood quickly. "Just rest a while," he said, and strode out of the room.

He paced up and down in the darkened house, growing more resentful by the minute. He hadn't asked for this, any of this. Not for Mary, and certainly not for the child. He had no idea how long he paced, feeling as if he held a live coal in his hands, expecting it to burn him any moment. But at length he heard a sleepy voice calling his name.

He went back to the room where Mary lay. He saw a subtle difference in her. She looked less tense. Her shoulders were relaxed, and she was smiling once again.

Her gown and the bedding beneath her were soaked. "I think I can feed him now."

He didn't question her, but helped her out of bed and into a dry gown. A sweet, damp odor pervaded the air as she sat on a cushioned chair. Milk.

With relief, Jesse handed her the baby and busied himself putting dry bedclothes on the bed. He didn't look at

Mary; the wet, smacking sounds of the baby's greedy mouth told him that the crisis was over.

For now.

The gifts started to arrive almost immediately. Several times a day, Mary caught herself weeping with happiness and exhaustion. Everyone was so good to her, so complimentary of the baby and so thoughtful in those compliments.

"He's the very image of you, Mary," Hestia declared. "I believe that hair will come in as red as your own. Jesse must be so proud."

Mary smiled, thankful for Hestia's choice of words. No one mentioned that Jesse hadn't fathered little Davy. No one likened the sweet lad to anyone but his mother.

An ambassador from Swann House, Hestia brought an array of gifts—handmade quilts and rattles and teethers and toys, little jackets and sweaters and booties and caps. Fiona joined the women, hallooing with a special joy as she bounded across the yard. "I hear you mistook the lightkeeper for a midwife," she said with a braying laugh.

"Faith, and didn't I just?" Mary said, as she gazed down at the baby. This morning she had bathed him; he smelled sweeter than anything she could imagine.

"Look…at…you." Fiona reverently picked up the baby, now clad in a white flannel gown and tiny socks knitted by Hestia's ailing boarder, Rheingold. "Just look at you," Fiona repeated. "Oh, dear God in heaven, is there anything finer in the world than a newborn babe?"

Mary's heart rose to her throat as Hestia and Fiona cooed and fussed over the baby. Was it a woman's lot, then, to fall instantly and completely smitten with a new baby? These ladies adored Davy with uncritical and unstinting love. Mary wanted—oh, she *wanted*—that to be true for Jesse, too, but all she could remember was the coldness in his eyes, the bleakness in his face when he had said, "He's not mine."

Naively, she'd thought her joy at bringing Davy into the world would rub off on Jesse. But it seemed to have the opposite effect. He was more withdrawn and silent than ever.

How could she break through that fear? How could she change his mind? She had no idea, but she knew she must. They were meant to be together. She had come to him through an act of destiny, and to disregard that was a sacrilege.

"How are you feeling?" Fiona asked, breaking in on her thoughts.

"Well," Mary said, "I eat like a horse, feed the baby like a cow, and the rest of the time I just sleep along with little Davy."

"Excellent. That's as it should be." Fiona seated herself in the wicker chair Jesse had dragged into the room for visitors. With gentle, assured hands she opened Davy's gown and subjected him to a thorough and professional examination. "He couldn't be more perfect. Now, the eating and sleeping aside, is all well here?"

"Of course. Why wouldn't it be?" Mary was appalled to feel tears spring to her eyes.

"Oh, dear Lord," Hestia said. "I was the same way when my babies came. Filled with elation one moment, and all weepy the next."

"And your husband?" Mary asked in low, rasping tones. "Did Captain Swann stay clear of you and the baby for days and days?"

Fiona eyed Mary keenly. "Give him time. Everything has changed for him so quickly. He'll come round." She buttoned up the baby's gown. "Won't he, little man? Won't your papa come to adore you to bits?"

Her singsong voice coaxed a smile out of Mary. It was

sweet, seeing the matter-of-fact Dr. MacEwan let down her professional reserve, charmed by little Davy. Hestia busied herself putting away the gifts, all homemade by loving hands.

"I am so blessed in my friends," Mary said, and the tears came again, but she laughed through them. In the company of women, she felt surrounded by the essence of her mother's love. Even though Mum was no longer here, Mary felt her presence in the way Hestia smoothed her hands over the knitted lamb's-wool blanket, saw it in the joyous crinkles in the corners of Fiona's eyes.

Do you see us, Mum? Mary asked silently. *Your grandson is going to be fine. We're all going to be fine.*

And so she believed, especially when Magnus and Palina returned from Astoria and came bursting into the house, chattering away in Icelandic, then both of them breaking down and crying when they saw the new baby.

"It's crowded in here and it's getting late," Fiona announced over Magnus's gruff sobs.

"Yes, yes," Hestia said briskly. "There's so much to do with all the little ones in the house these days. I'm teaching the Clune children to read."

Mary savored the sparkle of delight in the widow's eyes as she bade them goodbye. Since opening her home to those less fortunate, Hestia had lost the pinched look that had haunted her. Now she looked serene and full of purpose. People needed each other. It was such a simple idea. Why was it so hard for Jesse to grasp?

Proud as new grandparents, Palina and Magnus cradled Davy between them and murmured lovingly to the baby. Mary waited without saying anything. Such moments were to be cherished in silence, with no words interfering. Perhaps it was a trick of the afternoon light, or perhaps it was pure magic; a glow surrounded the three of them as if they were a church painting.

The love in the faces of the older people was so apparent that Mary found herself once again on the verge of tears. *I have a family,* she thought. All her blood relations had died in Ireland, and here she was halfway around the world, and she had found a new family.

The moment passed, and never once did Davy awaken. Mary took him from Palina. "He fits just so in the crook of my arm. I can't even remember what I used to do with myself before he was born."

"This is the happiest event we've had at the station," Palina declared. "How proud Jesse must be."

Mary ducked her head. But not quickly enough.

"There is a problem, eh?" Magnus thumped his knee. "I have but one fist left. Pray it is enough to wallop some sense into his thick head."

"No—"

"Wait—"

Both Mary and Palina spoke at the same time. They looked at each other and laughed.

"Let him be for now," Palina said, then added something in Icelandic. "You were not so very charming immediately after the birth of Erik."

Magnus affected a scowl, but he bent and kissed his wife's brow before leaving the room.

"Now," Palina said. "Tell me."

Mary smoothed her hand over the downy fuzz on the baby's head. "I had to be stronger and braver than I ever thought was possible. And just like the last time, it was Jesse who got me through it."

"Just like the last time?"

"When I was drowning. It felt the same."

Palina smiled broadly. "Yes. Yes. Jesse helped you through it. That is as it should be. I am not surprised."

"But he's different now that the baby's here," Mary confessed with a catch in her throat. "More like the way he was when I first got here. He wants to be alone, wants nothing to do with me or with Davy. I think he wishes we had never happened to him.''

"If you ask him, that is what he will say." Palina rose and knotted her shawl with deft hands. "But look at me. I am an old woman. A busybody. I stare at people and I see them as they truly are. I see things that are invisible to others.''

"I don't doubt it, Palina. I never have."

"When I look at you and Jesse together, I see the love happening.''

A strange chill spread through Mary, prickling her scalp. She felt it in her gut—the starkness of the blunt statement. "What do you mean?''

"Exactly that. You do not see it, because you are too busy feeling it and pretending it's easy. Jesse is too busy feeling it and fighting it. But I see the way he looks at you when you're not aware of his gaze. I see the way you care for him. And so when you think he wants you gone, it is not that. He is simply afraid to lose you.''

Jesse found that if he tried hard enough, he could avoid thinking about Mary and the baby for whole minutes at a time. So long as she slept with the infant downstairs, so long as he stretched his duties at the lighthouse as much as possible, he could pretend nothing had changed.

He left the beacon and went down to the sheltered cove below Scarborough Hill, where the trees thinned and gave way to fields of ferns rolling down to the water's edge. He hadn't checked on the pilot boat in the nine days since the baby's birth. According to the telegraph from Annabelle, she was well and busy, looking forward to their parents' return from the Continent after Christmas. Apparently, Granger had limited his misuse to Mary.

Jesse felt a shameful wave of relief that he wouldn't

have to go to see his sister, after all. The very thought of setting sail struck him cold.

As always, he sensed a waiting silence down by the water. Abel Sky had once told him the hill was a hallowed retreat of the Chinooks. In the time before the white man had come, the natives brought their chieftains here for canoe burials.

A light wind rippled off the water and sang through a pair of white hawthorne trees. The sound had a whispery quality to it as if the old chieftains' ghosts were stirring. Shaking off the fanciful notion, Jesse went to the boat and found it, as always, in perfect repair. He cared for it with the same devotion he cared for the horses. But unlike the horses, this never left the shore. Its hull and fixtures gleaming, the craft waited for a moment that would never come, not so long as Jesse was the lightkeeper.

He spent a while clearing away dried leaves that had blown into the cockpit, but inevitably, the time came for him to go back to the house. He stood in the boat for a moment, feeling a roar of frustration build in his chest. It was ridiculous. He was torn between a boat he feared to sail and a home he feared to enter.

Swearing aloud, he returned to the house. He stomped up the stairs and crossed the porch, banging the door behind him.

Mary sat by the hearth in the rocking chair Magnus had made for her as a gift. She wore a dress Palina had sewed from blue cloth, and the firelight cast a warm glow over her. The dress was unbuttoned in the front, and she held the infant to her breast.

When he stepped into the room, she raised her face to him. Her mouth was curved in a soft, beautiful smile. This was the first time he'd actually seen her nurse the baby. He wasn't prepared for the tenderness it stirred in him.

"Uh, I'd better get more wood for the fire," he said, taking a step back toward the door.

"There's plenty of wood."

"Then I'll see to the horses."

"Erik fed them not an hour ago."

"Sometimes he forgets—"

"He never forgets." She kept staring at him.

He tried with all his might to wrench his gaze from her breast. The skin was like cream, the baby's mouth a rosebud fastened around the nipple. The image branded Jesse, scorched him, made him burn with unthinkable lust.

He took another step toward the door.

"Jesse, don't leave," she said. "I made chicken soup for supper and Palina brought another loaf of rye bread."

"Call me when it's ready."

Her expression never wavered. "It's ready."

"Call me when you're ready."

With a glint of defiance in her eyes and a deliberate, unhurried motion of her finger, she detached the baby from her breast. Jesse couldn't help seeing it all vividly. The glistening hungry mouth. The engorged nipple with a tiny teardrop of rich milk clinging to it. Then it was gone as Mary fastened her dress.

Before he knew what was happening, she handed him the bundled baby. "Here. He's practically asleep. You put him to bed and I'll set out supper."

Jesse stood in the middle of the room with the baby in his big, clumsy hands. The infant felt as light as an autumn leaf, and as fragile. A fairy or maybe an angel, not a flesh-and-blood human being. He was too small, too delicate, too perfect to be real.

He smelled of milk and warmth and Mary, and the fragrance alone nearly melted Jesse to the floor. He steeled himself with a reminder—this was Granger's son. Granger's bastard. Jesse would always be a distant, reluctant uncle to this child.

But Mary was his wife.

Mary had named the child David. David, son of Jesse.

He went to the room where Mary and the baby napped during the day and slept during the night. Feeling awkward, he set down the swaddled form.

"Put him on his side," Mary called from the kitchen. "And put the pillows and bolsters around him so he doesn't fall."

In just a few short days, the room had been transformed. A milky, powdery smell hung in the air, and everywhere there were baby clothes and diapers, a rattle carved of driftwood and a conch shell decked in feathers, a gift from Abel Sky.

Jesse glanced one last time at the sleeping baby and wished he hadn't. How tiny he looked, adrift in the middle of the bed. Like a bit of flotsam lost at sea.

Nineteen

~~~⊸∽⊙∾⊶~~~

"People have been warning me about the winters here."
Mary lifted her face to the crystal-blue November sky.
"They kept saying we wouldn't see the sun until next
March."

Jesse slapped the reins on the rump of the horse as the
road leveled out to the main street of Ilwaco, and gave his
usual disinterested grunt.

"The weather suits me just fine." She inhaled deeply.
How she loved the crisp cool air of a seaport—the briny
smell of nets hung to dry from tall posts at the dock ends,
and the scent of tar wafting from the shipyard.

Davy made a small squeak of bewilderment as Jesse
drew the buggy to a halt. Mary smiled down at the baby.
At six weeks of age, he was alert, and this morning, he
had gifted his mother with the inexpressibly precious favor
of his first real smile.

"Watch a moment. Maybe he'll smile again," she said,
putting her hand on Jesse's arm.

Out of politeness, he stared at Davy for a few seconds.
"I don't think he's going to do it."

"He did it this morning. I saw it with my own eyes.

Didn't you, *a gradh*," she cooed. "Didn't you, my treasure?"

Davy blinked up at her. His eyes had begun to lighten in color. She suspected they would be blue.

Granger Clapp had blue eyes.

She slammed the door on that thought and waited while Jesse tied up the buggy and helped her down. A sense of excitement stirred inside her. This was her first visit to town since having the baby, and she was anxious to show him off.

The people of Ilwaco didn't disappoint her. In the mercantile, where they went to buy new haycock covers, Abner and Mrs. Cobb made an appropriate fuss, and the little Cobbs gathered around, begging for turns to sit in the big wing chair behind the counter and hold the baby.

At her surgery, Fiona pronounced Davy fat and flawless.

Bert Palais, at the paper, slapped his vested chest, pushed back his visor, and declared that he wanted to write a nice announcement.

"I'd rather you didn't," Jesse said tersely.

Bert blinked. Mary blushed. "My husband's always been a private man," she said.

"I'll say." Judson Espy, the harbormaster, pushed into the newspaper office. "Well, now, look at this." He grinned hugely at the baby. "A little woodchopper of your very own, Jesse."

"Woodchopper," Jesse muttered.

"Aren't you a woodchopper, aren't you, aren't you?" Judson said in a ridiculous voice, his grin broadening from ear to ear.

Davy made another squeaking sound. Mary feared he would start to wail, but instead he grinned right back.

And they were all there to see it.

"I haven't heard this much fuss since Donati's comet passed over," Jesse said.

Mary tried to tell herself it wasn't important that he didn't share her joy in a milestone like Davy's first smile. She tried to tell herself Palina was right, that Jesse loved her and the baby in his own distant, awkward way. But as she watched him go about his business, in his normal terse, dignified fashion, she felt the cold shadows of doubt creep over her.

At midday they called at Hestia's house. Mary sought the privacy of a second-story lounging room to change Davy and feed him. As she was sitting in an upholstered chair beside a potted palm, feeling the rhythmic tug of Davy's mouth drawing nourishment from her body, she felt a wave of inexpressible sadness.

Against her will, she thought of Granger Jones. No, Granger Clapp was his real name. Jones was how he was known to doormen and stupid Irish girls. She remembered the day he'd revealed his plans for the baby. He'd never doubted it would be a boy—and he'd been right. He told Mary the lad would have a beautiful nursery crammed with toys, nannies dancing attendance on him, the finest schools in the land, a career of importance at the shipping company. At first she'd thought she would be part of those plans. How silly her assumption seemed now.

Granger had wanted the baby. Only the baby. To him, Mary was simply a broodmare. But now, thinking of the way Jesse ignored the poor lad, she wondered if he might not be better off with a father who wanted a son more than anything else in the world.

Her heart recoiled from the very idea, and she dragged her thoughts back into the present. She studied the paisley pattern in the carpet and the fleur-de-lis shapes of the leaded glass in the upper part of the window. The beveled glass cast rainbows across the wall, glittering with the richness of illusory color. But it was all a trick of the light.

When the sun went behind a cloud, the colors disappeared and the world returned to drabness.

Fiona swore it wasn't so, but Palina insisted the mother's mood affected the nutritional value of her milk. Mary cradled Davy's small body against hers and thought how blessed she was to be safe and healthy.

But she still slept in the downstairs room.

The light tread of a footstep on the stair startled Mary. A woman in a tattered wool bonnet and a threadbare coat appeared on the landing.

"Hello," Mary said.

The woman gasped and shrank back against the white wooden rail. She dropped one shoulder and flinched, and her bonnet fell askew.

"I didn't mean to give you a fright." Mary modestly drew her shawl, covering the baby. "I'm Mary Morgan."

Pressing herself against the rail, the woman came down a few steps. Her hands shook as she replaced the bonnet, but she wasn't quick enough; Mary saw the angry shadow of a bruise on her cheek.

"Pleased to meet you," the woman whispered, then hastened past. Wondering who she was, Mary finished feeding the baby and returned to the salon, where Jesse waited. He looked out of place in Hestia's house, his size incongruous on the fringed fainting couch, a dainty teacup perched on his knee.

"...and a woman's vote counts for just as much when it comes to domestic matters, that's my opinion, if you really want to know," Hestia was saying with a self-important sniff. "I intend to tell the territorial governor about it myself, even if I have to ride pillion all the way to Olympia." The moment she saw Mary, Hestia's tone changed to doting. "Oh, my dear sweet baby, there you are."

"You're all in a dither." Mary settled the baby in Hestia's plump, reaching arms. "What is this all about?"

"Some unpleasantness I was just discussing with your husband. I sent the sheriff after some riffraff and he did nothing, said there was no law against a man minding his own affairs. I wanted that scoundrel ridden out of town on a rail—"

"Who?"

"A logger. Goes about getting drunk and beating innocent citizens, but the sheriff wouldn't arrest him for it."

"Why ever not?" Mary felt a rise of indignation.

"Because the victim was his wife, can you imagine?" Hestia said.

Mary remembered the woman with the bruised face. She felt a flash of outrage, then leaned over and hugged Hestia. "She's staying here, isn't she?"

"Livvie Haglund is *living* here. She won't go back to that lout. I simply won't allow it."

"Ollie Haglund hasn't tried to see her?" Jesse asked.

Hestia's florid cheeks paled a shade. "Actually, yes. I— he gave us a bit of a fright, but Fiona happened to be here, and she ran him off with Captain Swann's whaling harpoon. I worry, though. What if that horrid man comes back? He's the size of an ox, and twice as ornery."

Jesse rose from the fringed couch and set down his cup. "Ollie won't be back." He strode from the room. There was a swish and a thud as he opened and shut the door behind him.

Mary stared after him. "He's going after that Haglund fellow."

"I suspect he is." Hestia smiled with grim satisfaction.

"What do you suppose Jesse will do?"

"Dear Mary, I don't think we want to know."

Jesse's knuckles were split and raw, and wearing gloves chafed them, so he drove home with his hands exposed to the freezing November air. When he came in from putting up the buggy, he could feel Mary's eyes on his hands.

"I'd best go wash up," he said.

"Supper's on. Abel Sky brought us a salmon."

As he stood at the washstand with his hands plunged into the cold water, he thought how amazing it was, having a beautiful woman putting supper on the table. Having someone to talk to, someone to listen to. Someone to worry about and laugh with and fuss over.

He squeezed his eyes shut and sluiced water down his face and neck, then scrubbed himself mercilessly with a towel. Scowling, he clumped down the stairs and took his place at the dinner table.

"Davy's sleeping like the dead," said Mary. "The outing must've tired him today."

Jesse didn't reply. He never knew what to say when she spoke of the baby.

She eyed his torn knuckles as he ate. "Whatever it was you did," she said, "I'm sure Hestia and Mrs. Haglund are grateful."

"It's bad business for Hestia to be giving sanctuary to women like Livvie Haglund."

"Is it then?" Mary asked with a flash of her old temper. "And what would you have her do, stay with her brute of a husband until he does something permanent to her?"

"Of course not," he said. "But if Hestia starts taking in women fleeing their husbands, the husbands are bound to get in an uproar over it. I can't run them all off."

"No one asked you to." She stabbed at a bit of roasted salmon. "But there should be a place a woman can go and know she's safe." She looked him in the eye. "Don't you think so?"

He said nothing.

"Sometimes being safe is the dearest wish of a woman's heart."

"Uh-huh."

"Word is bound to get out that Swann House is safe for women like Livvie Haglund."

"Uh-huh." Jesse looked out the window at the swaying tops of the towering trees. He knew what Mary was doing, and he wondered if she was doing it on purpose. She was drawing him into the life and the heart of the community. For years he had lived at its fringes, a distant, dignified presence, acknowledged but never included.

In just a few short months, she had induced him to celebrate the centennial, help establish a community at Swann House, run off an abusive husband. It had all happened without consulting him. Without seeking his approval. It had simply happened.

He finished his supper and Mary started washing up. "Let me," he said gruffly, nudging her aside. "You go sit a while in the keeping room."

Instinctively, he was quiet, not banging the dishes or sloshing the wash water as he poured it into the sink. In ways he could not begin to count, the baby had changed his life.

Despite his efforts to be quiet, a little mewling cry came from the room off the kitchen.

"Would you get him for me?" Mary asked.

She was always doing that. Finding excuses for him to pick up the little tyke, to smell him and handle him and build up such a fierce yearning it was almost unbearable.

"My hands are wet," he said.

She rose from the settle and slipped into the bedroom. He could hear a soft murmuring as she picked up the baby, fed and changed him. Every moment she was in there, he imagined the sight he would never get used to, could never get enough of—Mary with her breast bared, suckling the baby.

He stalked out onto the porch and started taking deep gulps of cold air. It was a blustery night, but clear. Magnus was on watch, and the beacon swung its arc in long, regular blinks.

There were things Jesse didn't remember about falling in love. With Emily, he had been too young, too naive, to feel the depths he felt now. To feel the pain and the ecstasy meld and become one. To feel a yearning that cut as sharp as a knife.

Perhaps he had never felt that for Emily. Things were simpler with her. They came from the same world. He'd been a promising young man, she a well-bred lady from a good family. There had been no challenge, no obstacle. Just the love, which soared like a bird for a few short years, then crashed into the sea.

It was happening again, but differently this time. He was a different man. A man who knew what it was to love and lose. And there was nothing simple in the way he felt about Mary. Nothing easy about the situation they were in. She wanted him to be a father to the child of his rival. She thought he had it in him to do that.

She wanted him to be stronger and nobler than he could ever be. She expected it. She believed in him. He tried to show her that he was a bitter, selfish man undeserving of her faith, but again and again she tried.

When the wind freshened and chilled him through to his bones, he went back inside. Mary was on the settle, holding the baby. Jesse built up the fire in the hearth, put on his spectacles, then opened the book he was reading—a depressing French novel that was all the rage. The evenings when he wasn't on watch, like tonight, were the worst. He didn't quite know what to do with himself. Usually he read for a while, until Mary bade him good-night and took the baby off to bed in the downstairs room.

"Jesse?" she said.

"Yes?"

"I'd like to ask a favor of you." She cleared her throat and waited until he turned and looked at her. Then she went on. "I wonder if you could be teaching me to read."

She never ceased to startle him.

"To read."

"I'd like to learn. Is it very hard?"

"I've never taught anyone to read before. Why do you need to know right now?"

"I just want to start." She propped her feet up on a wooden stool and laid the baby on her thighs so that he was staring up at her. The look on the lad's face made Jesse want to touch the baby. He didn't, of course.

"Right now?" he asked. "This minute?"

"There's no reason to delay." She looked down at the solemn face of the baby. "I want to read stories to Davy one day."

Jesse experienced a rush of guilt. She didn't believe he would ever read to the lad. And she was right. He, who'd had nothing but books for his companions the past twelve years, was not willing to share his one passion with the child. It didn't matter right now, when the lad was so little, but it would matter soon, before Jesse knew it.

"I can tell him stories, of course," Mary said. "I remember all the tales Mum used to tell. But I want to read him new ones. Will you help me?"

He knew he would hate himself for doing it, but he went to the long wall shelf and took down an old, well-thumbed volume. The smell of musty pages and ink wafted upward as he opened it and sat beside Mary.

"This was a favorite of mine when I was a youngster." He flipped to the endpapers. "'Happy Christmas to Jesse,

from your grandparents, the Morgans,'" he read from the
inscription. "I was four years old when they gave it to
me."

"Was it, then? And what's it about?"

"A collection of stories. The best one is this—'A Tale
of Peril in the Cave.'"

"Would you read it to me?"

"Now?"

"Aye, now."

Jesse pushed his spectacles up the bridge of his nose
and began to read. He had the oddest sensation, as if this
moment had happened before. And it had, in a way. He
vividly remembered his father coming into the nursery
when he was a lad, sitting by the bed and reading from
the book. That was probably why Jesse loved it so. Not
because the stories were particularly good, but because he
associated the book with the sweetest memories of his
childhood.

And now he was sharing them with Mary and the baby.
The moment felt right, even though he knew it was wrong.
He didn't know how long he read, but he glanced out of
the corner of his eye at the baby and saw that the lad had
drifted off to sleep.

A ridiculous sense of accomplishment rose in Jesse,
then redoubled as he felt Mary's head droop onto his
shoulder. He sat still, savoring the moment. He inhaled the
scent of her hair and the milky odor of the baby and the
soapy smell of the blankets.

And he felt something rare and strange inside him.

Happiness.

A denial leaped in his mind. He was not supposed to
feel happiness. But he did. He did. The feeling panicked
him. He set aside the book and gently took the baby from
Mary. "Come, my loves," he whispered. "To bed with
you."

She mumbled softly as he took her hand and led her off to bed in the downstairs room. Before he could stop himself, he bent and brushed his lips over her brow, then did the same to the baby.

It was the kiss that undid his soul. He fled from the room and headed for the sanctuary of his own, taking the stairs two at a time, yanking the door shut behind him. There was no candle; he had not stopped to get one. Only the watery bluish light from the autumn moon and the stars filled the emptiness.

He gripped the bedpost and breathed deeply for a long time, trying to turn back into himself. Into the cold stranger he had trained himself to be. But it was getting harder and harder.

He nearly jumped out of his skin when he heard the door latch click. Mary stood there, the baby in one arm and her other hand holding a flickering candle. She wore a nightgown. Her feet were bare, her hair loose and flowing.

"Is something the matter?" Jesse asked.

"Yes."

"What? Are you sick, or—"

"Nothing like that." She raised her beautiful, supplicating eyes to him. "We don't want to sleep downstairs anymore. We want to come back to your bed, Jesse."

Her words slashed at him. The panic returned in waves. "The bed's too damned small," he objected.

Her face fell. "No, it isn't."

"I could hurt the little one, roll on top of him."

"That's ridiculous." She glared at him. He glared back. Then her shoulders sagged. "You really mean that, don't you? You don't want us."

He said nothing. If he tried to explain, he'd only hurt her more.

Her long red hair whirling, she turned, marched to the

door and went down the steps. He heard her footsteps stomp all the way into her room and the squeak of bed-ropes as she settled into the bed.

Jesse let out a long breath he didn't know he had been holding. He had to ask himself—did it hurt more to love someone, or to force himself not to love her?

And was there anything in the world more painful than hurting Mary?

She should just leave him. She shouldn't stay and let him torment her. Fool woman. She wanted things from him he couldn't give. She made him want to be so much better than he was. And that led to nothing but frustration.

Yet when he awoke the next day with a bold plan in his head, he shrugged off his doubts.

Twenty

~~~

Mary banged around the house like a madwoman, scrubbing and polishing, chopping vegetables for a stew, making fresh bread and punishing the dough with her fists. When that wasn't enough, she bundled Davy up and brought him outside with her while she worked in the garden. She laid him in the wheelbarrow and complained to him loudly while she dug in the dormant beds and cast away weeds.

"He's got some nerve, he does, banishing us to the downstairs bedroom," she fumed. "And disappearing at dawn without even a by-your-leave. Honestly, my lad, your da has got a lot to learn about being a da."

What she refused to say aloud was that she ached for Jesse. She ached to feel his arms around her, his lips on her skin. She wanted him inside her, and she didn't know if she would ever be that close to him again.

"The lout," she said. "By the hand and arm on me, I'll give him what for, see if I don't."

She worked furiously, neatening the beds and getting them ready for winter. The larkspur had yielded seed enough to make a glorious return in the spring. She pruned the roses and covered them with a blanket of wood chips.

A flock of birds passed overhead, going south to warmer climes.

There was such a sense here of the circle of life, a rhythm as regular as a heartbeat. How happy she could be in this place, if only Jesse would let down the wall he had put up.

He called himself selfish, yet he had opened his home to a stranger. He called himself a coward, yet he rode unhesitatingly into the waves to rescue drowning men. He called himself a hermit, yet he drove Ollie Haglund out of town for hitting his wife. Jesse Morgan was a bundle of contradictions, a hero who swore he was no hero, a man who swore he would never love, falling in love not just with his wife, but with another man's child.

She knew it was happening. And Jesse knew it, too. That was why he'd been so prickly lately. But her patience wouldn't last much longer.

She heard the rasp of a saw and a lot of pounding coming from the barn. She burned to know what he was about, sawing and pounding, not coming out to have lunch or even to say good day to her. Pride kept her from going down and checking on him.

When the sun began to set, she took Davy inside for a bath. He loved his bath, and he smiled all the time now, cooing with delight when she soaped his plump, silky body in the kitchen sink. She heard Jesse come in, but she refused to turn and look at him. It was up to him to make amends.

"I'll just be finishing here," she said tersely. "There's fresh bread and stew, if you're hungry. I believe Davy and I will go to bed early tonight."

Jesse didn't answer.

She heard a soft thud but resisted turning. Lifting Davy out of the water, she laid him on the sideboard and gently dried and powdered him, savoring his soft body and his ready smiles, the way his legs peddled the air as she pinned his diaper and put him in a fresh gown.

Finally, when he was warm and dry and cuddled contentedly against her chest, she turned to Jesse. He stood by the kitchen table, looking solemn and infuriatingly handsome. On the table sat the most extraordinary thing she had ever beheld.

"It's a cradle," Jesse said awkwardly.

"Oh, my, yes." Filled with wonder, she went to the table. It was made of fine-grained wood and shaped like a little boat, the rockers smoothed and sanded to perfection, the headboard carved with scrollwork.

"It's for the lad," Jesse added.

She couldn't suppress a smile. "Yes."

Inside, her soul exulted. This was his first gift to Davy. She traced her finger in the carved inscription. "Is this his name, then?"

"Yes. David Dare Morgan."

His name. Jesse had carved his full name into the cradle. "And he's to sleep here."

"I would hope so. The thing was a lot of trouble to make."

"We are a lot of trouble, aren't we?"

The corner of his mouth flickered upward. "Uh-huh."

"I never promised we wouldn't be."

The other corner of his mouth slid upward. "I guess I don't mind so much."

"Are you sure it's all right?" Jesse whispered after the baby had been put down for the night in the cradle. He gritted his teeth for a moment, trying not to feel the torment she stirred in him. He hadn't even touched her yet. They stood in his bedroom—*their* bedroom—facing each other and feeling somehow more awkward than they had the first time.

Christ. Wanting her was making him crazy. "I mean," he said, fumbling his words, "you're not going to be hurt by—"

"What hurts is the waiting." She took his hand and guided it downward, over her stomach.

His nerve endings leaped like flames. This was the first time he had touched her intimately since she'd had the baby. How tiny she had become. Tiny here, at least. He skimmed both hands upward, over the incredibly generous swells of her breasts.

She was more lush and ripe now than she had been pregnant. There was a new, faint sweetness in her smell— milk and the baby's skin and the subtle musk of blood and life, the scents that had overwhelmed him the night of the birth.

He watched his own hands in fascination. They were the hands of a stranger—the hands of a bridegroom—as they worked independently of his mind or will. One by one the little pearlized buttons down the front of her dress gave way beneath his fingers. He parted the chemise beneath like a veil, exposing the satiny globes of her breasts, so full, so incredibly full. And at the tip of one of them was a tiny moist gleam of milk. Jesse found the vision so erotic that he pulled in his breath with a hiss and squeezed his eyes shut, trying to keep from attacking her right then and there.

When he opened his eyes, he was astounded to see that she was crying. Huge silent tears rolled down both cheeks, giving her the look of a weeping angel, heartsore for all eternity.

"What?" he asked tautly. "What is it? Did I hur—"

"No." She clutched her chemise back together and gripped it, white-knuckled. The tears never stopped as she spoke. "I feel so huge and such a mess. All I want is to be unsullied for you, as a bride should be. We never go to have that moment, Jesse. That first time, free of the past. Ah, how I wish I could come to you, all fresh and new and clean. You must think—"

He pressed his fingers to her lips, now wet with tears. "Don't tell me what I think," he said, pressing her against the bedroom wall and lifting her hands away so that her chemise gaped open again. Frustration built inside him. "Goddammit, don't tell me what I think."

"But I can see it in your eyes. Why couldn't I have met you first?"

"If you hadn't met Granger first, you would never have ended up here."

"I know, but listen—"

"No, *you* listen. I'm not sure who decided that a man expects—wants, dreams of, whatever—an untouched virgin bride in order to be satisfied. Why any man would prefer a shrinking, untried girl to a woman who knows the heat of pleasure, a woman whose body bears the evidence of passion, is beyond me. There aren't words to say what it's like, standing here with the lamp burning low and your breasts bare—" He had to stop to catch his breath. He wasn't accustomed to giving long speeches. Particularly on the subject of a woman's breasts. Particularly when all he wanted was to take her to his bed.

"You mean I don't disgust you, looking like this?" she asked in a small voice.

"Disgust me?" he repeated incredulously. "Is that what you think?"

"A moment ago, when you looked at me and then closed your eyes, I thought you might be wishing things could be different. That I was pure. That I was all yours."

"I won't lie. I do wish things were different. Part of me does wish I'd been the first man to touch you. To kiss you. To hold you and put my babe in your belly. No doubt you've wished the same about me."

"But instead we came together so...damaged, the two of us."

"Yes. Damaged." The truth tasted bitter in his mouth. "But when we're together, it's better. We're whole and new. I didn't close my eyes because I was disgusted. I did it because I've never in my life seen a sight as beautiful as you look to me now, and I wanted to savor that."

"Jesse—"

"I've never wanted a woman like I want you." As he spoke, he peeled her dress and chemise down over her shoulders, letting the clothing drop to the floor. Then he removed her pantalettes and stockings and carried her to the bed, drawing back the coverlet and setting her down. He hurried to get out of his clothes.

She lifted her arms toward him. "Come to me, Jesse. We've waited too long."

"Then," he said with a wicked gleam in his eye, "we can wait just a little longer."

"No, oh, God—"

"Just a little longer," he repeated, bending over her, his tongue tracing a slow, damp path down the side of her neck, lingering at her pulse, then going lower. She was as evocative as the sea itself, surrounding his senses, filling him with such overwhelming beauty and power that for a moment he felt disoriented, a dreamer shaken awake to find a reality more colorful and more wondrous by far than anything he could imagine. The sweetness of milk was there, and then the taste of Mary herself, which he had tried so hard to forget, tried in vain to forget.

She cried out softly as his mouth and hands made love to her. He could feel her fingers clutching his shoulders, his back, and it felt good to know she wanted this as much as he did.

"Now, Jesse, now," she said, so quietly he almost didn't hear. "We've waited long enough."

Only the knowledge that before this night was out, they would do this again—and perhaps again after that—made him comply. He touched her gently, and his hand trembled a little when he remembered, just for a flash, the baby. He remembered the night of terror and ecstasy and confusion followed by the long, bleak loneliness of separation.

But with her breathy sighs in his ears, he returned to the present, to the belief that something good and strong had happened between them, that this could work. The silky texture of her, all moist with wanting him, caught him up in a grip of unbearable need. Nearly trembling with the effort to be gentle, he braced himself above her and eased into her, waiting for her to rise up to meet him and join with him.

Ah, there. The warmth. The closeness. The intimacy that was so deep he had no sense of himself and of her separately, but of the two of them together, completion. The blackness in his soul was fading. He could feel it like the sun burning away the shadows, bringing light and heat to a place that had known only darkness and ice for years.

With an exultant cry, edged by pain and ecstasy, he poured into her, surrounded her, covered her, a cocoon. Though he had made love to her in the past, this time there was a sense of fulfillment he had not felt before.

"Jesse, Jesse," she whispered, her voice lilting in his ear. Just that and no more. His name. "Jesse." Yet in her voice he heard a world of meaning.

The night passed slowly, for he made love to her again, then cradled her while she slept. But he didn't sleep. He couldn't sleep. He was overwhelmed by what had happened between them, by the changes that were taking place with each moment. He still resisted the pull of her, still knew that loving her was dangerous, but he accepted in some distant part of himself that she had won. She had made him want to love her.

As the pale gray of dawn washed the sky with a hint of light, a small sound came from the room below. The noise was so quiet he was certain Mary would never hear it, but she sprang awake.

"That'll be our son," she said, a sleepy smile on her face.

The tiny sound crescendoed to a wail of anger.

"Just like his father, he is. All bluster and temper, but soothed easily enough." She leaned down and placed a warm kiss on his mouth, then gathered the top quilt around her and hurried on light feet to feed the baby.

Just like his father, he is.

Jesse slammed a fist into the empty pillow beside him.

On watch at the lighthouse that night, Jesse couldn't stop thinking about Mary. Asleep in the bed they shared once again. He wanted to be with her, wanted it with a sharp craving that pierced him like a physical pain.

What had he gotten himself into? Where was his armor?

She was making him depend on her. Making him count on her love. He didn't know if he could stand to do that. But a part of him no longer cared. Recklessly he longed to open his heart to this fragile woman with her iron will.

Restless, he climbed up to the beacon house and stared out at the sea and the sky. A cutting chill shot through his wool jacket, howling up under the eaves.

But there was a shattering clarity to the night. Not a single cloud softened the edges of the cool white slice of moon. In distant, icy beauty the stars glared down at him and down at the waves biting the shoreline.

It lingered, that sense of futility he carried with him. He lived at the edge of a force he couldn't overcome. The sea ruled him. At its whim, it had taken away all he held dear. And at its whim, it had given something back to him. Mary and David.

But for how long?

After a time he went back inside. He turned up the lamp and took out the logbook. He opened it to the first entry dictated by Mary, the one she had insisted on telling in her own words. He had laughed with her that night.

There was not another woman in the world who could make him laugh.

After that, she had dictated other entries. He reread them like an old man visiting the memories of his youth, feeling wistful yet a little distant. Mary had taken it upon herself to describe a geoduck clam—"and a great terrible tube of raw flesh it was!"—and to give her version of the rescue of the Russian fishermen—"Sure and the Great Almighty Himself would agree that it's a horrid dangerous thing... But the fearless lightkeeper had no thought for his own safety as he battled for the lives of the poor Russians..."

A puffin was "a little waddling elf of a thing" and sea lions were "selkies—I know it by their eyes. I can see the human souls inside them." As he read over the words she had dictated, he caught himself smiling. No one he'd ever met saw the world in quite the way that Mary did. Her quirky, off-center view of things was both unique and charming. She saw colors and visions with the untrained and uncritical eye of a true believer. She believed in magic and destiny and love, believed strongly enough for both of them.

And she had the power to make him believe.

In the log, he came to his own record of the birth of Mary's child: "30 September 1876, five o'clock of the morning. Mrs. Mary Dare Morgan was delivered safely of a son."

What a wealth of emotion he had managed to conceal behind the terse entry.

"Yoo-hoo!" Mary's voice called up the stairway, followed by the familiar *bong* of oversize boots climbing the iron stairs.

He jumped up from the worktable. Dread clutched at his chest. She had not been here in weeks. Was there some emergency? Something with the baby? The thought caused the back of his neck to prickle. He hurled himself down the stairs, meeting her as she was coming up. One look at her face took the edge off his fear. She was smiling brightly and looking particularly appealing in a caped mackintosh and wide-brimmed hat.

"What's the matter?" he asked.

"Nothing serious." She opened the overcoat and held out a swaddled bundle. "I've got to go down to the Jonssons'. Palina isn't feeling well." Before he could reply, she thrust the bundle into his hands. He caught a glimpse of Davy's downy hair and dark blue eyes, open wide.

"Mind the lad for me while I go. Erik said she's just a wee bit under the weather, but we don't want Davy catching anything from her, do we?"

"Can't you wait until morning?"

"She's ill. I'll not make her wait." Without further ado, Mary turned and clumped down the stairs.

"Damn it, I can't watch the child and the station at the same—"

"He'll be no trouble at all," she called, her voice echoing up through the lighthouse. "I've just fed and changed him."

"But—"

"He'll be good as Burren gold from County Clare."

"I don't know how—"

"Goodbye!" The lower door shut behind her.

Jesse stood unmoving on the iron stairs. He stared down at the baby in his arms. The baby stared back.

"Christ on a crutch," he muttered under his breath, borrowing one of Mary's expressions. "What the hell am I going to do with you?"

The baby blinked slowly. It was as if he were a fairy child, pale as the moon, his face as perfect as the heart of a rose.

In spite of himself, Jesse felt a smile tugging at his mouth. The baby's mouth moved, too, but he didn't smile. He screwed up his tiny, perfect face and let loose with a huge howl of sheer misery.

The sound of the baby crying was hardly new to Jesse, but this was the first time Mary wasn't close at hand to comfort and silence him. Jesse was alone, the lad was crying, and he didn't know the first thing to do about it.

His every instinct urged him to flee the lighthouse, to go after Mary and insist that she keep Davy with her. But the sight of the beacon's track swinging past reminded him of his duty. He had to stay and tend the light.

Frustrated and furious, he stomped to the gear room and gave the equipment a turn. It was awkward, working with the screaming baby in one arm while he cranked the gears with the other, but somehow he managed.

Then he went up to the mezzanine. The hollow interior of the tower magnified Davy's cries until they reverberated like thunder in Jesse's head. He couldn't escape it. He couldn't run away. He had to stay and weather the storm.

"Come on there, young sailor," he said gruffly. "That's enough of that." Mary spoke to the baby constantly. The sound of her voice usually soothed him. "No more crying now, little one," Jesse said.

The child stopped crying and stared at him. A single tear fought its way clear of a round blue eye. Jesse began to hope the storm was over.

Davy took a deep breath. Then he loosed a fresh yowl, longer and stronger than the previous ones.

"I scared you, didn't I?" While panic set his heart to

knocking in his chest, he tried walking in a circle, pacing the periphery of the small room. "You're not used to my deep voice, are you?" He felt more desperate and foolish with each passing moment. "Calm down now, there's a lad. Calm down."

The baby cried harder, stiffening his tiny spine and braying out his misery. Jesse had thought he'd known what it was to feel powerless. But before this moment, he hadn't known anything. In a strange way, this was worse than the sea, because the howling baby posed more than a physical threat. Davy's misery threatened Jesse's heart.

He had to be logical, to think rationally. He set the baby on the table, cradling the small head in his hand. He gently unwrapped the blanket, trying to see if a stray pin or hook might be bothering the child. But no, the diaper was dry, the pins fastened neatly and cushioned so they didn't touch the delicate skin. It struck Jesse how perfectly formed this child was, even with limbs flailing while he squalled as if the very demons of hell were haunting him.

Jesse wrapped him up again, making a sloppy job of winding the pale yellow blanket. Mary made it look so simple, maneuvering the child and the blanket as easily as kneading dough. Perhaps children were like horses—they understood instinctively if the person handling them was inept.

What else? Jesse asked himself. She said she'd just fed him, so the problem couldn't be hunger. A small brazier kept the room warm, so the lad couldn't be cold.

The moments that followed were the longest of Jesse' life. He knew no more helpless feeling than this, than being alone in a room with a crying baby who wouldn't stop no matter what. This was one problem he couldn't turn his back on, couldn't walk away from. Davy was totally dependent on him. The baby couldn't be talked to, reasoned with, ignored. He—and his bawling—just *were*.

Damn her, Jesse thought. Damn her for leaving him alone with the child. What if an emergency came up? What if someone needed rescuing? She didn't seem to realize the chance she was taking—with the baby, with Jesse, with other people's lives.

She knew he couldn't look after a child all by himself. Was this her idea of a joke? Or a test of some sort? If she thought throwing him together with the baby and then abandoning him was a way to get him to care about Davy, she was dead wrong. If anything, he knew now, more than ever, that he was never meant to be a father, especially to a child he hadn't sired.

He scowled at the living proof he held in both hands, at arm's length. Davy's face was growing redder and redder. Mary had told him that infants' tears, like the tears of the elderly, were sparse and only appeared in a time of extreme distress.

"Looks as though I've brought you to a moment of extreme distress," Jesse said.

The baby inhaled with a frightening whoop, then cried louder. His little body shook from head to toe. Jesse drew his shoulders up to his ears. There was no sound in creation quite so disconcerting as a baby crying. "Stop," he said, knowing his words would have no effect. "Just stop. Please. Goddammit, I don't know what to do."

A few years back, Dr. MacEwan had treated an infant for severe bruises to the head. Fiona hadn't actually come out and said it, but she had implied the baby had been injured by its father attempting to silence his cries.

Jesse despised himself for even thinking about the incident. The crying was making him crazy, but not crazy enough to hurt a defenseless infant.

Singing. Sometimes Mary sang to the boy and it quieted him. But Jesse didn't know any songs.

Pacing, holding Davy beneath the arms while the boy's

pedaling legs dangled free, Jesse looked at the squalling face. He racked his brain. Surely he knew a song, one song, one—

"Ah. Here's a ditty for you. From my days at university," he said. "Although some might say my singing is a form of abuse." Jesse sang with gusto, off-key, raising his voice above the baby's wails:

> "Grass widows and princes, a warning I sing
> Of the sad wicked doings of David the King
> With Bathsheba, wife of poor Major Uriah
> Who was bathing one day, when the king
> chanced to spy her...."

The baby fell still. His little head wobbled on his neck and his eyes gaped wide. His mouth formed a small, red "O" of surprise. Jesse couldn't tell whether the child was staring at him in horror or in happiness, so he stopped singing.

Immediately, the infant started wailing again.

Immediately, Jesse began to sing again:

> "What man could resist such an awful
> temptation?
> He forgot he was King of the sanctified
> nation..."

He did a little dance step from side to side as he sang. The baby quieted and stared. His head kept wobbling. Probably not good for an infant to have its head wobbling like that, Jesse reasoned.

Jesse brought the baby into the crook of his arm. But the lad didn't seem to like lying back and looking up at the ceiling. So Jesse moved him against his chest. To stop the wobbling of the head, he cupped it in his hand and pressed it with hesitant gentleness to him.

How fragile the child felt. Jesse had a flash of memory of himself as a boy, holding a kitten in joy and wonder. The baby seemed that small to him, that delicate.

And blessedly, blessedly quiet.

Jesse sang a sea chanty more softly, then finally let his voice trail off to a tuneless hum. The baby didn't seem to mind. He stayed quiet but alert, his cheek pressed to Jesse's chest and his little hands clutching at the fabric of his shirt.

"But I have to wonder," Jesse said in a ridiculous, sing-song voice, "how your mother expects me to go about my duties with my hands full of you."

Experimentally, he tried putting the baby down on his quilt on the floor. An ominous squawk warned him that abandoning Davy now would be a big mistake.

"All right, all right," Jesse said through his teeth. "So you don't want me to put you down." He recalled seeing Mary moving deftly through the kitchen and garden with Davy in one arm, working with the other. It must be a special skill of women. Yet it was time to tend the oil reservoir, so he took the baby with him.

Still using that light-toned voice that the boy liked, Jesse narrated every action. "You see, I have to check the level of the oil in the reservoir, and then it's a matter of seeing that the gears are turned..." Though he worked with leaden slowness, he managed to get everything done. "Let's check the gauges," he suggested to the boy. "This one measures pressure and that one is an anemometer. Although I can see with my eyes the way the wind's coming in." He carefully climbed the slanting ladder to the beacon room.

The baby's eyes rounded at the sight of the big rotating lens. "Looks like a giant cut diamond, doesn't it?" Jesse remarked. "If you study it from a certain angle, you can see rainbows in the crystal."

Jesse shocked himself by wanting, just for a moment, to see the boy grow big enough to see the rainbows in the crystals.

"It happens when the sun goes down, too. When it's just sitting above the horizon line, the prisms catch the light." He paused and looked down, studying the baby in the bleached light spilling from the beacon. Davy was as beautiful as his mother, though in a totally different way.

What would he be like as he grew up? Jesse caught himself wondering. Would he be blithe and optimistic like Mary, taking the world's problems by the tail and forging through life with a song on his lips? Or would something happen to the lad, a disaster that would steal all the life out of him and make him defensive and dark and fearful?

More than anything, Jesse wanted to protect Davy from such a fate. Horatio Morgan had probably wanted the same thing for Jesse. He had probably, one day long ago, cradled a baby boy to his chest and wished the very moon for him.

Jesse thought about his father with unexpected fondness. Perhaps Mary was right in saying he'd left too soon after Emily's death. He should have stayed, should have faced his grief, shared it with the people who loved him. Instead, he'd turned his back on them, hurt them all by his neglect.

"Come on then," he said to Davy as if the infant had a choice. "You can help me fill out the log for the night." He eased himself down the narrow ladder and took a seat at the desk, turning the baby so the lad could see the lamp and the desk. "And no long, dramatic recitations like your mother makes," Jesse cautioned. "One dramatist in the family is enough."

The baby made a little buzz of discontent. Hurriedl

Jesse drew a picture of a face with big round eyes and a smiling mouth. The baby stared. Then Jesse drew a fish and a horse. The drawings were crude, but they seemed to distract Davy.

Later, Jesse entered in the log the temperature and the conditions. He sat back, staring at the terse line of words across the page. He stared for a long time. The rhythmic *thunk* of the rotating beacon harmonized with the incessant low roar of the sea below the promontory.

He felt a difference in the baby. The little head wobbled, then collapsed softly against his chest. At first he was alarmed, but the elfin fists were still clutched into his shirt and he realized the lad had fallen asleep.

Amazement, distrust, then a dawning joy filled him.

There was nothing so triumphant as getting a squalling infant to sleep, he decided, yawning. It was exhausting business, having a little one to worry about every moment.

He gazed at the words in the log until the ink blurred. He felt the gentle rise and fall of the baby's breathing, felt the child's warmth like embers from heaven.

And then he knew the reason for his blurry vision. Tears seared his eyes, rained down his face. Deep, silent sobs racked him. His throat felt knotted with desire for all that could never be his.

The breakdown was so complete that he expected to see shattered pieces of himself strewn across the floor. Every wish, every desire, every happiness he had denied himself for twelve years suddenly dangled in his sight. But out of his reach. He just didn't have the capacity to love Mary the way she needed to be loved. To take her child into his heart and make him his own.

For a long time, he sat weeping in silence, while the baby held against his chest slept on.

"Why can't you be mine?" he said through gritted teeth. "Goddammit, why the hell can't you be mine?"

Twenty-One

~~⟐⟐⟐~~

Mary stood at the bottom of the iron helix of stairs in the lighthouse, her head cocked. She heard the moan of the wind wending through the cliffs. She heard the ceaseless beating of the sea against the shore, and the swift whistle of a breeze up the grillwork steps to the beacon. But no human sounds.

Perhaps Jesse had ended his watch early and gone back to the house. No, that wasn't like him. Not even taking care of a baby could make him change his ways when it came to his duties at the lighthouse. Unless—

Dread clutched at her. Perhaps something had happened with Davy. *God, no, please no*...denials raced through her mind as she hurried up the stairs. Only with Jesse would she trust the life of her child—because it was the one thing Jesse did best. Protected people. Helpless women, defenseless children. He might not realize that it made him special, but it was true. He could be counted on to protect people.

Or die trying.

By the time she reached the top of the stairs, she was prepared for any disaster. Anything except for the sight that greeted her. She stopped in the doorway, breathing hard, one hand clutching at the frame. She stared at the scene before her as if it were a painting hanging in a gallery.

The rising sun slanted in through the small portals. The lens rotated rhythmically, still lit for the night. The room glowed with the colors of the dawn. On the table, papers lay scattered in un-Jesse-like disarray. Crude drawings of a horse, a seagull and a sailing ship decorated the papers. On another sheet was a life-size face with a garish smile.

At the writing desk, the candle had burned to a stub, guttered, and died. Atop the logbook were a pair of large stockinged feet, crossed at the ankles. Her gaze traveled along the length of Jesse's legs. The chair leaned against the wall so that he could stretch out full length.

Snuggled against his chest was Davy, sleeping peacefully, his little face pale and perfect in the soft dawn light. How tiny he looked with Jesse's hands around him. And Jesse...

She dared a step closer. The early light was kind to him, softening the harshness of his bold features, suffusing his face with a restful look. Her dark angel; she had thought of him like that from the start.

Then something caught her eye. A faint mark on his cheek. The salty ghost of a dried tear.

Her breath caught. Something last night had made Jesse Morgan weep. The very idea caused her stomach to knot. She had wanted him to learn to weep, to let go, to let out the things that poisoned him from the inside. But now that it had happened, would he hate her?

"Dear Lord," she said, looking at her son. "What in heaven's name have you done to your da?"

Jesse awakened. His first instinctive reaction was to cradle the baby more firmly against him.

"It's all right," Mary said quickly. "I'll just take him, then." She reached for the baby.

Jesse glanced down at the incline of his chest. "Let the lad sleep. He's peaceful like this."

"Are you certain?"

"Uh-huh." He yawned and blinked at the light. "Is Palina all right?"

"She'll be fine. It's a touch of the grippe. Are you sure—"

"I'm sure." He drew his hand down over his bristled cheeks. "Quit fussing over us like a mother hen. He'll wake when he wakes, and I'll bring him down to the house."

She took a step back, then another, then another. She felt as if she had met a stranger. But this was Jesse. Jesse who roared at her and kept to himself and ignored the baby.

"I'll start breakfast, then," she said at last.

"You do that."

"I'll do that." She turned and walked quietly down the stairs. She wanted to whoop for joy, to grab the center post of the staircase and swing around it, letting her feet fly out from under her. There was no feeling, she thought as she sprinted down the path to the house, quite so sweet as hope.

"If you could have one thing you wished for," Grange Clapp asked his wife, "what would it be?"

Startled, Annabelle put aside her petit point. "I'm afraid you've caught me off guard. I haven't an answer for that." She watched his eyes closely. If a storm was coming, she would see it first in his eyes. She had learned that long ago.

But he merely smiled and leaned back in his wing chair, lifting his after-dinner port to his lips. "Just say the first thing that comes to mind."

She swallowed. He had been quieter than usual lately

almost amiable. Almost exactly like the dapper man she'd fallen in love with. She didn't want to say the wrong thing. "What could I possibly wish for? I have everything I want—a fine husband, a lovely home, friends—"

"Ah, and those friends. You don't see as much of them as you used to."

"They're busy with their children, and—"

"And you have no child," he reminded her.

His voice was light, teasing. It slashed at her like a knife. She snatched up her petit point, stabbed the needle into the fabric.

"I can give you one," he said. "I can give you a child."

Tears blurred her eyes. "But we've tried for so many years."

"A baby," he said. "There's a baby…he needs a home. I thought—"

"Granger!" She stood up, the needlework falling from her lap. "Do you mean we'll finally adopt a child?" She had been begging to do so for years, but he had resisted, insisting that raising a child sired by strangers was unnatural.

"Yes, but the circumstances are quite…unusual." He fixed her with the masterful glare that had governed her behavior since their wedding night. "I shall need your full cooperation."

"Of course, Granger." *A baby. A baby.* Her heart exalted. "What must I do?"

"I wish I knew what this was about," Jesse grumbled as he drew the buggy to a halt at the harbormaster's office in Ilwaco.

"All Judson would say when he came to the station," Mary repeated, probably for the fourth time, "is that you're to come immediately. He didn't know you and Magnus were off hunting, and he said he couldn't wait."

Jesse frowned as he hitched the horses. It wasn't like Judson to be mysterious. But when Jesse went around to help Mary and the baby down, his frown disappeared. A month had passed since the endless night he'd spent with Davy in the lighthouse. In that month, Jesse had learned and grown more than he had ever thought possible.

He bent and placed a soft kiss on Mary's mouth.

"What's that for, boyo?"

"Do I need a reason?"

She laughed. "It's nice to come to town. We haven't been in an age."

"I don't like coming to town."

"You'll learn to like it."

He shook his head, slipping his arm around her. "This could work—the three of us," he said awkwardly.

"Haven't I always said so?"

"As long as the world keeps its distance," he cautioned her.

"You can't keep the world at a distance."

"I've done so for almost thirteen years."

"But not any longer. You have a wife and a son." Her gaze swept the town, with its busy harbor and pastel-painted houses along the quiet streets. "We belong in the world."

"We belong where we live best. Alone. At the lighthouse station." He stepped onto the boardwalk and guided her with his hand under her elbow. He couldn't tell her he feared what might happen if he suddenly became a fixture about town. He couldn't tell her about the shadow haunting his days, no matter how hard he tried to disregard it. Davy was the son of his sister's husband.

What a miracle it was, to love Granger's child.

On the walkway outside the harbormaster's office, Jesse

paused. He wasn't sure what made him stop and turn to Mary, to stare at her while she stood holding the baby, but he found himself closing the distance between them.

"Jesse?" she asked, looking up at him.

It was the look that touched his heart. It always did. From the first moment she had gazed at him, he had seen his own destiny in her eyes. He brought his hand to her cheek, cupping it while his thumb skimmed the rise of her cheekbone and the fullness of her lower lip. He bent and kissed her brow, then the top of Davy's head.

Extraordinary things had been happening to him since she had come into his life. But in the past month, since he had made his peace with Davy that night in the lighthouse, everything had moved faster and intensified. And fallen into place.

He had stopped seeing his life as a penance to be served. Mary and Davy showed him it was a banquet of pleasures as well as pain, and the pleasure was savored more acutely because of the pain. Love was difficult; he had always known that, but he was no longer afraid of it. Because with Mary the agony was sweet. And never beyond his endurance.

"What are you doing?" she asked. "You're looking at me so strangely."

"Such a lot of things to say," he mused, noticing everything about her, the scattering of freckles across her nose, the flecks of gold in her eyes, glinting in the cold December sunshine. "And I can't tell you a one of them. I'm not a man of many words."

She lifted her hand to cover his, then brought his fingers to her lips. "Let's go inside and see what it is Judson needs on this fine day."

They stepped inside the office, a large, rectangular room with navigational charts on the walls and the smell of ink in the air. In all of his wildest imaginings, Jesse never could have guessed who he would find waiting for him in the harbormaster's office.

He stopped and froze, and felt Mary do the same beside him. His blood ran cold; then heat suffused his face and his chest began to ache. He studied the lone figure by the window.

She managed to look forlorn, somehow, as she gazed out at the shipping lanes and the loading docks closer in. The harsh winter light outlined a perfect brow and a flawless cheek, an attractive turned-up nose and a fall of yellow curls cascading from a fancy bonnet.

He finally found his voice. "Annabelle?"

She turned, the brim of a velvet bonnet shading her face. "Hello, Jesse."

"What are you doing here? Where's Granger?"

"I came alone. I had to see you."

"You got my wire, then."

"Yes, thank you, Jesse."

"Your reply said everything was fine."

"That's...what it said." In the slight pause between her words, she peered inquisitively at Mary.

And Mary, because she was Mary, grinned with delight. "You're Annabelle, then. Jesse's told me about you. Showed me your picture."

Annabelle smiled a little. The sight of that smile nearly knocked the wind out of Jesse, for suddenly she was a little girl again, shy Annabelle, smiling her secret smile, her eyes shining with all the desperate, elaborate dreams of a young girl.

Except there was sadness in her eyes now.

"Then you have me at a disadvantage," she said.

"I am Mary. Jesse's wife. And this is Davy, our son."

Annabelle didn't know it yet, Jesse realized, but she was looking at her husband's bastard. She took a step toward Mary. "I'd always hoped you would marry again, Jesse," she said. "And the baby." She caught her breath at the sight of Davy, dozing snug in Mary's arms. "He is beautiful. The most beautiful thing I've ever seen."

Jesse saw with shock and dread that she was weeping. Tears poured down her face. Mary seemed to sense the awkwardness of the situation. "I'll be taking the baby off to see Hestia," she said briskly. "You know they always love to make a fuss over him."

Jesse nodded without looking at her. His gaze stayed riveted on Annabelle. "We'll see you at Swann House," he said.

He heard the office door open and close. Still he stared at his sister. "Something's wrong," he said. Apprehension squeezed his chest. "Have you heard from Mother or Father? Is it bad news?"

"No, quite the opposite. They're enjoying Europe immensely." She fumbled in her reticule and took out a handkerchief. "It's about Granger." She drew in a deep breath. "But I don't know you anymore, Jesse. I shouldn't have come—"

"I was your brother long before Granger ever laid eyes on you. Damn it, Annabelle, what is going on?"

A bittersweet smile curved her mouth. "I've always known I could trust you. Each time I had a problem, you were there to help me. You never snitched when I misbehaved. You always took the blame for my pranks. No wonder I'm here. I can trust you with anything. You'd never betray me."

My wife had your husband's baby.

He studied his sister. How different she was. Grownup, when he'd always pictured her as a coltish twelve-year-old with skinned knees and burrs in her hair.

Now she was a lady, slim and elegant, draped in velvet and lace. She stared down at her kid-gloved hands. Her fingers trembled; then she clasped them together tightly.

"I understand that you abandoned your interest in the company, but I didn't know who else to turn to."

"About what?"

"About a matter I recently discovered." She swallowed audibly. "I was in Granger's study, looking for a pen, when I came across a ledger book. I didn't think anything of it—he always said I had no head for business. But a devilish urge made me look."

"No head for business?" Jesse snorted. "You? Even when you were six years old, you used to charge me interest when I borrowed from your pin money. At finishing school, you devised a plan to fund an expedition to the Sandwich Islands."

"Granger didn't know about any of that."

Jesse wondered how a husband could be so unaware of his wife's true nature. "What did you see in the ledger book?"

"I only had to glance at the figures to realize what they were." There was a catch in her throat. "Granger's been stealing company funds for years."

Jesse tried to feel angry. He had helped to build the company, to turn it into the major shipping concern. But it all seemed so remote now. So pointless.

"So confront him," he said simply. "Or I'll do it for you, if you like. Tell him to make amends, make things square with the board of directors."

She bit her lip. "I don't think I'm ready to do that yet."

"What's he done with the money?"

"He's converted it into paper bills. I found a coffer in the attic. He's just...hoarding it, Jesse. I have no idea why."

To steal another woman's child? To start a new life?

"We'll have to have it out with him," Jesse said grimly.

She turned away, ducking her head. "He's gone. Disappeared. And the money is gone." Her hands got busy again, fingers twining into the tasseled strap of her reticule. "At first, I thought I could go on for quite a while like that. Alone. Telling people he was away on business." Her voice took on an eerie, lilting quality. "But then the duns started coming. The bill collectors."

She leaned on the back of a chair, looking for a moment like an old woman. "All his debts are coming due, and there's nothing to pay them with. I've sold most of my jewelry. Let go of the servants. But still the collectors come." She sighed heavily. "Still they come."

"Where is he? Do you have any idea?"

She shook her head. "San Francisco, probably, but I've no idea where. I do know one thing. He led a double life."

"What?" Jesse braced himself.

"He kept women and had friends I didn't know about and—oh, God!" Pressing her knuckles to her mouth, she began to sob raggedly.

He felt a squeezing sensation in his chest. The past had caught up with him. He understood now that he couldn't live apart, as if the rest of the world didn't matter.

Annabelle raised her drenched eyes to him. "I used to feel sorry for you, living here all alone. But now you have Mary and a son of your own, and you have infinitely more than I do."

"Anna," he said, using his childhood name for her. "Can it be as bad as all that?"

She laughed bitterly. "I, with my friends and connections, my lovely home and my gowns. Where are my friends now? They deserted me when I could no longer hide my circumstances." She shook with grief. "I came here expecting to find you paralyzed with loneliness and regrets. Instead you have a lovely wife. A perfect son. How blessed you are, Jesse. How very, very blessed."

Mary watched nervously from the parlor window of Hestia's house as Annabelle and Jesse came up the walk.

Even from a distance, one could see the family resemblance. They were both tall and incredibly well-favored, with strong features and tender mouths and glacial eyes.

Mary noted a few subtle differences. Annabelle was fair-haired, while Jesse's hair was a rich brown. Her bearing, too, was unlike her brother's. Jesse moved like a man comfortable inside himself. He had an innate grace honed by the practice drills he did as a sea rescuer.

There was a strange quality about Annabelle. For all her beauty and regal bearing, there was something furtive about her. It was elusive, like the gardenia fragrance Annabelle wore. Perhaps Mary's mind was playing tricks on her, but she didn't trust the flatness of Annabelle's gaze or the slight dip her shoulder made when Jesse turned toward her to reach for the front gate.

Had he told her? Had he told his sister about the baby's father?

Her throat closed in panic. But when she opened the door with a smile fixed on her face, she felt a measure of relief. He gave a tiny shake of his head.

Not yet.

She noted the tension in Jesse, too, and it alarmed her. That distance. That coldness.

"Such a pleasure to meet you at last," Hestia said, wreathed in smiles, coming up behind her. Socially, this was a coup for her, and she was clearly reveling in the chance to play hostess to the famous Mrs. Clapp of Portland. "I've read so much about you in the society pages. All your good works in the city. You're a very great lady."

"Thank you," Annabelle said.

"This all must seem terribly provincial to you—ah!" Hestia's face lit up. "Here's Livvie with some tea."

Livvie Haglund smiled and greeted Annabelle. Shy as

always, she blushed, then removed herself after setting down the tray.

"Your servant—"

"She's not a servant," Hestia said. "She lives here. We have quite a unique situation at Swann House."

"What happened to the poor woman's eye?"

Hestia flushed and looked away. "An old injury. She had some trouble with her hus—" She caught herself and flushed deeper.

"She can no longer see out of that eye," Mary said quickly. "But she manages quite well."

Annabelle had the most extraordinary reaction. She went pale as marble, still as a statue. Aye, that's what she was, a marble statue, cold and emotionless. And then incredulous. "Her husband beat her? Injured her?"

"We don't usually talk about it to strangers," Hestia said. "But you're a most special guest, Mrs. Clapp. Some women come to Swann House to escape their brutal husbands."

"Is she...safe here?" Annabelle asked.

"Yes, indeed. We are quite proud of Swann House. Would you care to take a tour? Perhaps you'll think about becoming a patron..."

As the two ladies stepped out of the parlor, Mary released a long breath she didn't know she had been holding. She turned to Jesse, but her mind was on Davy, who was in the kitchen being spoiled by Mrs. Clune. "Tell me," she said. "What did she say about Granger?"

"There's trouble. Her husband has stolen a great deal of money and disappeared."

Mary took a moment to digest this. Turbulent emotions stormed through her. Fear. Apprehension. Disbelief. Relief. And perversely, a tiny twinge of regret. She had loved Granger once. For all the wrong reasons, she had loved and clung to him.

"Does this mean he's gone? For good?" she asked cautiously. "Surely it does. Only a fool would stay near at hand once his thieving has been found out. He's probably far away by now."

"You can never go far enough," Jesse said.

His words sent a gust of wind through her heart. "What do you mean? What—"

"My sister is coming to the lighthouse to stay for a while," he said.

"We have to tell her, don't we?" Mary asked. "We have to tell her about the baby."

Hestia wouldn't hear of Annabelle going to the lighthouse station. Not when the keeper's house had such limited accommodations and her own home had a lovely guest room, all made up and just waiting for company.

Jesse had to admit she was right, and Annabelle looked relieved to be staying in town. They said goodbye in the front garden of Swann House. It was late afternoon, and a chill had crept in along with a roll of clouds from the west.

Jesse stepped back and watched his sister and his wife, the baby in Annabelle's arms. They looked lovely together, Mary's red hair and high coloring a vivid contrast to Annabelle's fashionable pallor. In another life, in another world, they might have been friends.

Annabelle lifted Davy high over her head and laughed when the baby gurgled and smiled. Yet through her laughter, she was weeping, her voice broken as she gave the infant back to Mary. "He is so perfect," she said. "I can't have children of my own."

Mary didn't try to commiserate or deny it. She hugged Annabelle and let her hold the baby a few moments longer. Then, on the way home, she told Jesse what she was thinking.

"I had the baby your sister should have had."

* * *

That night, she came to him in the lighthouse. "I took the baby to stay at Palina's," she said softly. "He's such a good sleeper now. He won't wake until morning."

Jesse nodded. Did Mary know he often stood looking down into Davy's cradle, watching him sleep?

That afternoon, the world had turned on Jesse, darkening his heart to hope. He knew why. He had forgotten that he was responsible for Emily's death. He had forgotten that he was meant to finish out his life sentence alone. He never should have thought he could have what his soul ached for, a family to love.

Mary stood looking at him with her heart in her eyes. She was wearing her nightgown and robe. Her hair hung loose, cascading in a ruby red fall over her shoulders.

"We're going to tell her," she said.

"Yes. We're already agreed on that."

And then what?

She crossed the tiny room and took his face in both her hands, gazing down at him. "You're pulling away from me. I can feel it."

"I can't be what you want me to be," he said, trying to ignore the coolness of her hands, the scent of her—flowers and milk and springtime. Ripeness. Fullness. Vibrancy. *Life*.

"Ah, you're so much more, if only you'd see it. Let yourself look at me. See yourself in my eyes. You have more honor and caring in you than a thousand men, and you don't even know it."

Before he could respond, she put one leg on either side of him and sat in his lap, straddling him. The old swivel chair groaned under the added weight—or was it he who groaned?

He was surrounded by her, the softness of her hips on

his knees, the softness of her hair brushing his face as she
bent her head to his, the softness of her lips brushing his
mouth lightly, tentatively, then insistently. No one but
Mary had ever touched him like this. No one but Mary
knew the tortured doubts in his soul and offered an answer.

He flared to life beneath her, erect and hotly uncomfortable, his mouth hungry. With a harsh growl, he braided
his fingers into her hair and crushed her lips to his. Their
mouths mated, sharing the moist warmth of passion, and
heat blazed from the very center of him, from the place
that had known only blackness for so long. She was his
beacon in the darkness, yet he knew his shadows were
surrounding her, swallowing her. Didn't she sense that?
Wasn't she afraid?

She moved her hips a little—but it only took a little.
His questing hands slipped downward, parting the robe
and the nightgown, cupping her round, heavy breasts. He
couldn't stop himself, couldn't stop the burning need to
bend his head, to taste her there, just there, and when he
did, bolts of light illuminated his heart. Mary sighed and
dropped her head back, making a little noise in her throat
as she gave herself up to sensation. She was so honest in
that way, never trying to hold in her own passion.

His hand skimmed over her belly; it was taut and flat
again, as if the baby had never been. His fingers touched
her lightly until her sighs escalated to small, urgent gasps.
There was a craving in him that raged beyond simple love-
making. The constant rhythm of the beacon and the boom
of the sea echoed the swish of blood in his ears. He cupped
her against him and lifted her, then pressed her back on
the worktable, parting her gown all the way so that she
was exposed, naked, vulnerable.

"Jesse?" she whispered, her voice trembling in fascination.

"Hush. Just let me…" He bent over her, kissing her

long and softly while his hands and fingers cherished her, found the shape and texture of her...there...he trailed his mouth down, parted her, tasted her. The sea and the musk of womanhood filled his senses. He loved the sounds of shock and passion she made, loved the way she writhed and strained toward him. He went on and on, even when she begged him to stop. On and on, until his body was shaking with the demand for release. He stripped off his jeans and she opened his shirt, then he kissed her mouth, sharing the taste of her, the dark sweetness of passion. At the same moment, he joined himself with her and she cried out, clasping her legs around him and whispering his name urgently.

He wanted to take his time with her, but she was insistent, rising to meet him and moving until he took up her rhythm and was lost. He felt himself being pulled into a void where there was nothing but pure sensation. No thought. No emotion. Nothing to complicate the glory of the moment. It was shattering, completely overwhelming. He collapsed on her, his skin covered in sweat, his breathing ragged. The sensations subsided, leaving him drained.

After what seemed like a long time, Mary stirred beneath him. "Jesse?"

"Mmm."

"I love you, Jess—"

"Not now. Don't say it now."

"But I have to. For heaven's sake, if I can't say it now, then when can I?"

"When I can say it back."

She turned her head away, and he removed himself from her.

Slowly. Gently. Reluctantly. His body wanted to stay, to love her. His heart and his conscience held him back. He put on his jeans but not his shirt while Mary sat up on the table, looping the tie of her robe around her. He took one look at the tears on her cheeks and sat in the chair, planting his elbows on his knees and burying his hands in his hair.

It was futile. Futile to try to love this woman, to try to fill her heart with all the things she needed. He lifted his gaze to hers, forced himself to see the tears she shed. "All I can ever do for you," he said, "is hurt you."

"That's not true. You've made me happier than I ever thought it possible to be. But you just don't trust things to go well. You expect disaster around every corner."

He thought of Annabelle. Did Granger know she was here? "And I'm right," he said. "I'll do my best to protect you and Davy. But God knows if that's enough."

"Don't be so cynical. Of course you'll protect us."

"I'm only a man. Not a hero."

She nibbled her lip. Brushed a tear from her cheek "Davy's mine. I'll never give him up. Not to anyone Annabelle has no claim on him. None."

"She doesn't." Jesse took a deep breath. "But she has a claim on me. She's my sister. The baby's very existence is a slap in the face to her, because she can never have children."

"Are you saying you have to choose between loyalty to Annabelle and loyalty to Davy and me?"

"Are you saying you'll ask me to make that choice?"

"She's an intelligent woman, Jesse. When we tell her the whole story, she'll understand."

"You don't know my sister."

"Nor do you. You've been apart for years."

He said no more, and Mary realized it was futile t argue. As she walked to the Jonssons' house to get the baby, she realized that with Jesse, nothing would ever b simple. Or painless. He was infuriating in that way. Didn he understand how desperately they needed each other? Not just her, not just Jesse or Davy, but all three of them.

But he was right this time—there would be no easy solution.

Twenty-Two

Twenty-Two

Troubled, Mary held Davy in one arm and pushed open the door with the other. The moment she stepped inside the house, she frowned, cocking her head. She smelled flowers. Gardenias.

"Annabelle?" She hurried across the room to the settle, where Jesse's sister waited. "What a lovely surprise," Mary said, flushing bright crimson. How disheveled she must look, with her hair mussed by the wind. And by Jesse's loving. "I'm so delighted you've come to visit."

Deep in the shadows of her velvet bonnet, Annabelle smiled. A small, tight smile. "The house is charming," she said. "Where is my brother?"

"He was on watch at the lighthouse." Untimely remembrances of the previous night came back to Mary. The things he had done with his hands and mouth, the things he had made her feel, were so powerful she grew weak thinking about it. "Sometimes he does a few chores before coming back here."

Annabelle's long-lashed gaze swept Mary from head to toe and lingered on the baby. "Chores. I see."

"Can I take your wrap?" Mary asked awkwardly.

Annabelle touched her fur storm collar with a gloved hand. "No, thank you. I'm quite comfortable."

Mary settled Davy in his cradle. She'd fed him at Palina's, not wanting to make him wait, and now he was sated and groggy, ready for his morning nap. "I'll put water on for tea and then get dressed." After stoking the kitchen stove, she started up the stairs.

"How is Davy?" Annabelle asked, bending over the cradle.

Mary had no idea why she had such a cold reaction to Annabelle. "Fit as a fiddle. He's a good little lad." She hastened up to the bedroom, frowning. Every moment she kept the truth from Annabelle, the tension heightened. She hoped Jesse would return soon.

She brushed out the skirts of her warmest dress—a tea gown of sapphire cashmere from Emily's storage chest. Jesse had given it to her recently, and the darkness had not come over him as it usually did when something reminded him of Emily. She combed and braided her hair, then hurried downstairs.

Annabelle sat at the table. Her cape of fine seal plush glistened in the morning light. Mary wouldn't let herself get exasperated. Annabelle was born and raised a lady; she wouldn't know the first thing about brewing a pot of tea or adding a log to the fire.

"There now," Mary said cheerily, fixing the tea herself and bringing it to the table. "This will keep us warm."

Annabelle lifted her teacup. Mary was amazed to see her hand trembling almost uncontrollably, sloshing hot tea down the front of her cape.

"Are you all right, dear?" Mary asked, hurrying to the sideboard for a towel. She leaned down to dab at the wet spot.

Annabelle gasped as if Mary's touch hurt her.

Mary jumped back. "I'm sorry. Did it scald you?"

"No." Annabelle's normally light, girlish-sounding voice had a razor's edge. "I have a bruise there, that's all. An old bruise." Like a child suddenly reminded of her manners, she smiled cordially and took a dainty sip of her tea. Yet there was nothing childlike in the icy depths of her eyes when she said, "I had to be punished. I kept making a muddle of things."

"Annabelle, dear, I don't understand. Punished? By whom? And for what? You didn't make a muddle of anything," Mary assured her. *Hurry home, Jesse.* "Nothing that's happened is your fault—"

"Oh, for heaven's sake," Annabelle said, "I'm always at fault." Moving mechanically, without seeming to realize what she was doing, Annabelle began to spoon sugar into her tea. One, two, three spoonfuls. "But I always learn my lesson. How foolish of me to run away from Portland." Three more spoonfuls. The tea would be undrinkable. "My place is at home. My place is with Granger."

"But you said he was cheating the company. That he'd absconded with a stolen fortune. Of course you had to turn to your brother." Mary took the teacup from Annabelle and set it aside.

Annabelle stared at the cup. Then at the bowl of sugar. Then at Mary, with cold, dead eyes. "Granger told me what you did," she said. "He told me you had his baby. He was going to give it to me. He was going to let it be mine."

Mary's blood chilled even as tears heated in her eyes. "Oh, Annabelle," she whispered. "I'm so very, very sorry. Jesse and I wanted to tell you together—"

"The baby is supposed to be mine," Annabelle said flatly. Though her voice lacked all expression, Mary knew it concealed a world of longing and pain.

"I know how desperately you must want a child," sh

said. "But Davy is mine. He belongs to me. And to Jesse."

"You had Granger's baby. It was supposed to be mine," Annabelle said stubbornly.

"Please listen. What I did with Gra—with your husband—was wrong. Very, very wrong. The fact that I didn't know he was married is no excuse. I should have been strong instead of giving in to loneliness, to a weakness of the flesh. But the baby belongs to those who brought him into the world, those who love him best," she said, trying to stay calm. "Davy is my son. Mine and Jesse's."

"That's where you're wrong," said a deep male voice.

Mary stood so abruptly that her chair fell backward, hitting the floor with a loud crack. She saw him, saw Granger, handsome and ruddy and strong-looking. Saw the determination in his eyes. Saw the adoring desperation in Annabelle's face as Granger crossed the room and stood behind his wife, resting his hands on her shoulders.

The gesture might have been solicitous, but Mary saw his fingers bite hard. And suddenly she understood everything. All the things she had observed in Annabelle earlier came back to her—the slyness, the flinching, the shifts in mood from giddiness to despair.

Granger mistreated her. Mary understood that clearly now. Perhaps he wasn't as obvious about it as Ollie Haglund had been, getting drunk and belting his wife, but it was just as severe.

Annabelle lifted a shaking, gloved hand and covered Granger's. She was still his creature.

Oh, God in heaven, where was Jesse? Mary managed to remain calm as the question swirled through her. But perhaps, she thought hurriedly, it was best Jesse wasn't here. When he learned of Annabelle's suffering, what he had done to Ollie Haglund was mild compared to what he would do to Granger Clapp.

"Where is he?" Granger demanded. "Where is my son?"

Mary rushed over to the cradle and picked up the sleeping baby, blankets and all. "He's not your son," she said, feeling a surge of fierce defiance. She took a surreptitious step backward, into the keeping room. She had to get to the door. She had to ring the fog bell, signaling an emergency.

"You have no right to him," she spoke calmly. "I never belonged to you. My son will never belong to you."

"There is no point in arguing," he said. "I always get my way."

She remembered how she used to look forward to his visits. How she used to crave his kisses and, when he spoke, hang on his every word. Now she felt sick. Why hadn't she seen what he was?

"We'll sort everything out once we're away," Granger continued.

"Away," Mary whispered. "Where—"

"I didn't tell her," Annabelle said, her voice a high squeak.

Granger didn't appear to be listening. With long, purposeful strides, he crossed the room. "Come then, ladies. Time to go."

Mary panicked. She seized the closest weapon at hand—the perfect glass globe on the mantel. In a flash, she remembered the day Jesse had given it to her. He had been gruff, ungracious, yet oddly endearing in his quest to bring her something the sea hadn't damaged.

I'm sorry, Jesse.

She hurled the glass float at Granger's head. It hit him a glancing blow, making a sickeningly loud sound. Shattering glass exploded in the air. He sank to the floor, a rivulet of blood snaking down his temple.

Annabelle sobbed. "Oh, my God! You've killed him!"

Mary headed for the door. The bell. She had to reach the bell.

Just as she rushed across the porch, a shadow overcame her and blocked her way. It was Granger, bleeding and furious. He lifted his fist. "Now. It's time we got under way, ladies."

Jesse sat in the cockpit of the pilot boat, scowling at the letter from the lighthouse commission. The annual inspection was almost upon him, and he'd been busy all day. He had finished the caulking and rerigged the sails. He'd oiled the pulleys that let the boat out into the estuary, repacked the bearings of the tiller and checked the fuel in the pilot lights.

He knew why he'd been driven to do this today. All morning, he'd wrestled with his conscience, finally bringing himself to a decision. Things had to be done. Had to be said.

I love you, Mary.

Four words. How stupid he'd been to resist saying them for so long.

Knowing Mary, she had already guessed that she'd stolen his heart. The moment she had awakened in his house, flinging a pitcher at his head, she had captivated him. No, before that. Before she had even opened her eyes. It was just as Palina had said all those months ago. She was his destiny. Who was he to argue with a force as powerful as the sea itself?

He loved Davy, too, with a fierceness he hadn't been prepared for. Mary had taught him that being a father wasn't a matter of blood, but one of love.

Jesse glanced at the sky and swore when he realized the sun was about to set. The days of winter were short, the sun sinking before four o'clock. He'd let the entire day slip by, and it was his turn at watch tonight. He hastened up the hill and fired up the beacon for the night, gave the gears a turn and clattered back downstairs.

There was just enough time to go to the house and tell Mary what he'd been too thickheaded to say before. Maybe she'd come with him to the lighthouse again. Just remembering what they'd done last night heated his blood.

He climbed the bluff to the house, surprised to find himself running. He did that a lot lately. He was always in a hurry to see Mary and the baby.

The moment the house came into view, he felt a subtle but undeniable difference in the atmosphere. A heaviness, reminiscent of the lull before a storm, hung in the air. Something was wrong. No smoke wafted from the chimney. No cooking smells spiced the air. No lamp shone in the window.

Puzzled, he wondered if she might have stayed at the Jonssons'. She must be more angry than he'd feared.

All I can ever do is hurt you. He couldn't believe he'd said that—was it only this morning?

He'd make it up to her. He would tell her he loved her. He would say that he always had, always would. Together they'd go to Annabelle and tell her about the baby. And then they'd go on from there.

He stepped inside the house just to check. The scent of gardenia hung in the air. Had Annabelle been here? Something crunched beneath his boots. Frowning, he looked down. Broken glass. Aqua-colored. The glass fishing float.

Maybe he'd finally pushed Mary too hard. Maybe she'd left him at last. Did she hate him so much, then? Hate him enough to destroy the only gift he'd ever given her?

Heartsick, he hurried to the barn, mounted D'Artagnan bareback, and raced down the hill to the Jonssons'. His lantern made crazy streaks of light in the night woods. A freshening wind tore at the treetops. The storm was coming in earnest now.

While he waited in the Jonssons' yard, Palina came out on the porch. "Jesse?" She raised her voice over the howl of the wind. "Is something wrong? Where is Mary?"

A strange, unpleasant buzzing started in Jesse's ears, sounding like a swarm of angry bees. "I thought she was here with you."

"She came for the baby in the morning, but no one's seen her since."

The buzzing sound crescendoed. He thought of the broken glass. Annabelle's perfume. Something was wrong. Something was terribly, terribly wrong.

A drumbeat of hooves sounded. Jesse turned to see a lamp bobbing swiftly through the darkness. Digging in his heels, he urged the gelding across the yard to see who was coming.

It was Judson Espy, the harbormaster. By the time Jesse reached him, the rain had started. It slashed through the sky, riding the high wind, cutting like knives. Judson was shouting something; Jesse only heard the last of it.

"...didn't authorize the tug to take him out, but he went anyway. Must've bribed the tugboat skipper. He should be crossing the bar any time now."

"Who?" Jesse demanded.

"Some fancy city fellow."

The past was happening all over again. Once again, Jesse had failed someone he loved. He should have foreseen that Granger would come. He should have protected Mary.

Dread rolled over him as Judson pushed a scrawled letter into his hands. Granger and Annabelle had gone to sea with Mary and Davy.

Only Granger didn't call him Davy. He called him "my son."

A hole opened in Jesse, and everything drained out of him. Everything except the rage. The hate must have showed on his face, for Judson looked worried. "Now, we'll just make a plan here, and find a way to stop—"

Jesse didn't wait to hear the rest. Slamming his heels into D'Artagnan's sides, he drove the horse through the rain, up to the top of the bluff where the lighthouse stood.

The gelding was excited; all the horses grew agitated during storms. They weren't fearful. Jesse had trained the fear out of them. Rather, they welcomed the sense of danger pumping through them. He used to feel the same way. But that was before Mary. Before he had learned to care.

Taking the stairs three at a time, he entered the beacon house. Grabbing his spyglass and shoving open the iron-and-glass door, he went out to the pulpit. The wind screamed through the iron pilings and the grillwork of the catwalk. The surf boomed so hard that Jesse tasted salt spray on his lips. Rain lashed at him, slanting sideways.

Cupping his hand over the end of the glass, he lifted it to his eye. He spied Granger's ship. It was the schooner *Trident*, appropriated from the Shoalwater Bay Company. The boat was only a quarter mile out, but it might as well have been in another world. He could see the *Trident*, but there was no way to get to it.

Unless...

Unless he went after her. Jesse recoiled from the thought. But God! Mary. He had to save her. The pilot boat was down at the bottom of the bluff. In this wind, it could make good progress.

The paralyzing fear spread over him. He couldn't do it, couldn't sail into the churning waters, couldn't let himself be swallowed by the storm.... Yet in the wake of the terror came the knowledge that he had to face that fear, do battle with it, take away its power over him.

Common sense jabbed at him. The schooner had too much of a head start. Even at its fastest, the pilot boat couldn't overtake it.

Unless...

The outrageous idea streaked like a lightning bolt through Jesse. He stood on the catwalk in the rain, hearing the thump of the rotating lens and the roar of the storm, and deep in his gut, he knew what he had to do.

He was the lightkeeper of Cape Disappointment. He controlled the light, which in turn controlled the heading of the ship. According to his signals, the ship would be guided through the channel and safely out to sea.

Unless the schooner lost its way. Just as Emily's ship had lost its way....

"We're so sorry, Mr. Morgan," the old lightkeeper had said. *"My assistant was in charge that night. He got to drinking with some Portland swell and he let the light go out. Just let it go out."*

Jesse felt a sick echo of his rage that night so long ago. The echo grew until it became a scream inside his head. Because now he realized who that Portland swell was—Granger Clapp.

That fury had propelled Jesse to have the lightkeeper dismissed. He'd never discovered the identity of the Portland man—until tonight. He had made a promise never to let the light go out. No ship in sight of his beacon would ever suffer the fate Emily's had, running aground and breaking up because the lightkeeper had been careless.

It wasn't with carelessness that Jesse made his decision. It was with cold calculation.

He knew what he was risking. But he also knew what he was capable of. He knew what the past years had taught him. Years of watching ships go in and out, years of knowing precisely how the crossing was made. He knew where the shoals were and where the channel let out.

He had to do it. He had to.

For a moment, he stood in the lashing rain and the howling wind, stunned by the magnitude of his decision.

He went inside and looked at the rotating lens, the layers and layers of crystal that had held him prisoner for so long, just as they held the glowing lamp inside their cold facets. Then, with his hand as steady as solid rock, he reached in and extinguished the light.

Twenty-Three

In a stateroom of the schooner *Trident*, Mary and Annabelle clasped each other tightly while merciless swells heaved the ship up and down. Davy alone took the adventure in stride, asleep on a bunk in his swaddle of blankets.

"I'm sorry," Annabelle kept saying. "I'm sorry."

"Hush," Mary commanded her. "I know what Granger is capable of making a woman do. I don't blame you, and neither will Jesse."

But as the storm tore at the schooner, she wondered if they would ever see him again. The four-man crew did their best as the *Trident* bucked through the waves, but their shouts up and down the decks had grown ragged with desperation.

"I was mad to listen to him." Annabelle grimaced as the boat listed. The brass fixtures in the stateroom rattled. "He made it sound so perfectly reasonable. He said we would claim the child because he is the father. That we'd bring you along until the baby's weaned, and then just send you away."

Or more likely do away with me, Mary thought, but she didn't say it aloud.

"I wanted a baby so badly that I didn't think about what it would mean to rip an infant from his mother's arms."

"And his father's," Mary said. "Jesse—and no one else—is Davy's father."

A wave rammed into the ship, upending a small table and a wooden chest. Mary looked at the baby, but he slept on, lulled by the motion of the ship. Annabelle cried out and clutched at Mary as the contents of the chest spilled across the stateroom. Bundles of paper money littered the floor. Something metallic and shiny skittered along the deck.

Annabelle picked it up. "A gun."

Mary recognized the Smith and Wesson with its pearl stock. She had felt the deadly chill of the revolver's blued barrel held to her temple the night Granger had told her she could never leave him.

Somewhere outside, emergency bells started to clang. Fearing a fire or worse, Mary struggled to the door. On the midships deck, the skipper was screaming at Granger.

"Sir, the light at Cape Disappointment went out!"

Mary crushed her hand to her mouth to stifle a gasp. Jesse would never, ever let the beacon go out.

"Carry on without it, then," Granger bellowed.

"But sir, it's impossible. We've got no point of reference to guide us across the bar. We'll run up on the shoals for sure."

Mary yanked the door shut. There was no point in telling Annabelle; she was on the verge of hysteria already. Mary closed her eyes to pray, but all she could think of was Jesse. Perhaps she should have listened to him more closely. He was always trying to tell her to get her head out of the stars and realize that life was a struggle, that sometimes it takes more than a glib tongue and a sense of humor to get by. Maybe if she'd believed that, she wouldn't have been such easy prey for Granger.

"You were right, my love," she whispered. "But I learned it too late."

Seconds later, Granger barged into the room. "Your fool of a husband is playing games with me," he said.

She looked him in the eye, just as she had the night before she had fled San Francisco. "You're a dead man," she said.

His hand snaked out and wound into her hair. "Then I'll take you to hell with me."

The windproof lamp in the prow of the pilot boat flickered. Hauling back on the tiller, Jesse aimed the small craft out to sea. He had made this voyage a hundred times—but only in his dreams.

The reality was more fearsome by far, because he never could have dreamed what was at stake. The fear inside him was a greater monster than the swells that rose around him like mountains of glass.

Terror threatened to suck him down, hold him under. But he couldn't let it win. Mary was out there, lost on the shoals.

It was the most terrifying voyage of his life, but for Mary and the baby he would risk everything. Cloaked in his sou'wester hat and oilskins, he let out sail and battled his way toward the treacherous north-bank shoals. Between lifts of the enormous swells, he was able to glimpse the lights of the *Trident*.

The schooner was embedded at the keel. Even through the bellow of the storm, Jesse could hear her timbers groaning. Soon she would begin to come apart. The wind veered, and an ebb tide ran. Breakers enveloped the *Trident,* staving in a cutter. With every wave, the vessel lifted, its twin masts reaching up like the arms of a drowning man.

The moments seemed endless as he swept toward the

schooner. And then, once he had it in his sights, time seemed to pass too quickly. He had mere seconds to take out the line with the grappling hooks, to toss it across the churning water. Half a dozen times, he tossed the hook and missed. Once he nearly lost himself when a wave reared up and slapped him flat into the hull of the pilot boat.

Finally, the hook caught and held. Gritting his teeth, Jesse reeled himself toward the schooner.

"Mr. Clapp," someone on deck shouted. "We have company!"

Granger flashed Mary a look of contempt and strode out of the stateroom. Annabelle lay collapsed on the small bunk, sobbing hopelessly.

Mary gathered up the baby, making a sling of his blankets and tying him against her. Her hands shook, and her breathing came fast. The terror darted through her, stabbing, cold as ice. Awkwardly, she stumbled out on deck. She preferred to take her chances with the storm rather than with Granger.

Salt spray stung her face the moment she stepped outside. She tucked the blanket more securely around Davy Everywhere she looked, the ship had sprung leaks. Waves smashed the bulwarks and flooded the spar deck, swamping everyone knee deep in water. The sole ship's boat lay hull up on the deck, a sharp iron bar sticking through the splintered wood.

"Sweet Jesus," she said, clinging to a thick rope. Instinct made her look in the direction of the lighthouse, but the beacon had gone out. Where in God's name was Jesse

The crewmen and Granger had gathered at the starboard rail. After a moment, Mary saw why. A pilot boat had found them.

She felt the first inkling of hope, then astonishment a

the pilot, a big man in oilskins and a wide-brimmed sou'wester, boarded the schooner.

"Man the pulleys," the pilot shouted.

He didn't have to speak more than once. The crewmen fitted a pulley onto the line. One by one, they started sliding down the rope to the pilot boat.

Mary darted back into the stateroom. "Annabelle!" she called. "A boat's come to rescue us! Come quickly!"

Annabelle lurched across the room. Still shielding the baby from the storm, Mary helped her through the door. By the time they got out to the deck, all of the crew had evacuated the *Trident*. Only Granger and the newcomer remained.

But instead of manning the pulleys, they were locked in deadly battle. The pilot's hat had blown free. Long hair blew wildly around his face.

"Jesse!" Mary screamed his name. Shock and disbelief and terror exploded inside her. Jesse, who had vowed never to go to sea again, had come for her.

But the hatred of these two men was bigger than the storm itself. Ignoring the gales of wind and the bruising waves, they fought each other, fists flying and feet kicking out.

"Dear heaven," Mary said, keeping hold of Annabelle's hand. "They'll get us all killed." With her head down into the wind, she struggled toward them. The baby, startled at last to wakefulness, began to cry. "Jesse!" Mary called again.

He looked at her. It was just a brief glance, barely more than a blink, but Granger pounced on the moment, shoving Jesse back against the rail. He jerked something from the cuff of his boot and raised his arm.

The large blade of a knife flickered dully in the gathering night.

Even as she launched herself toward Jesse, she knew

she wouldn't reach him in time. The seconds froze and melded into a single instant of horror. She saw the blade arc downward. Its tip was aimed for Jesse's exposed neck.

An explosion split open the world, as if lightning had struck or a cannon had been fired. At the same moment, Mary saw Granger's body jerk and lift off the deck, yanked by the force of some large, invisible hand. Then she saw a dark splotch blossom on his chest. She saw him die even before he staggered, then fell backward over the ship's rail.

Trembling with amazement, she slowly turned. Annabelle stood slumped against a stanchion, clutching the Smith and Wesson in both hands.

The feeble light of a watery dawn cracked the horizon, illuminating the beach in somber gray tones. Magnus and Judson had mobilized everyone with the horses and surf runners. The rescuers surged from the shore to meet the pilot boat, crammed full of the weary survivors.

And one fatality.

The body of Granger Clapp lay astern, covered by rain-pelted canvas.

Fiona and Hestia, hardy as sea dogs in their mackintoshes and boots, swooped down on Annabelle and hurried away with her. Jesse knew they would take her to Swan House. He hoped she would heal there.

As she was walking away, Annabelle turned, the misty dawn light stark upon her thin face, the dying breeze plucking at her lashing strands of hair. She locked eyes with Jesse, lifted a trembling hand to her heart, then to her lips. He recognized the look of someone who had faced her deadliest demons and survived. He knew that, this night, he had done the same.

"She'll be all right," Mary said, holding the baby i

her arms and pressing herself to Jesse's side as if to assure herself that he was real.

"Yes," Jesse agreed, bringing his hand up to cradle her cheek. "She'll be all right."

"And us?" Mary whispered. "Will we?"

"I hope so." His voice cracked, and he stopped speaking for a moment to press his lips against her salt-laden hair. "If you'll forgive me," he added.

She leaned back a little to look up into his face. Her fingers lightly traced his cheekbone where Granger's fist had bruised it, then his lower lip, split and beginning to swell. "A man doesn't ask forgiveness from a person whose life he's saved—twice," she said. "You risked so much. I can't believe you took to the sea—at night, in a storm—just to find us."

"To have you in my life is worth any risk." Despite the physical exhaustion seeping through him, he felt alive as never before. He had taken control of the one thing that was crippling him—his fear of losing loved ones to the sea. He had fought that battle and won it.

"Mary." He spoke the words that had formed in his heart long ago, the words that wouldn't go away no matter how hard he fought them. He'd come to the end of a long journey—a journey of the soul that had taken him twelve years was finally over. "The more I draw from the well our love has created, the more I find a source of strength that I never knew was there."

A flock of seagulls wheeled overhead, their plaintive cries signaling the passing of the storm. A tear slipped from the corner of Mary's eye. "Ah, Jesse, I've never heard you speak so. Like a poet, you are. I l—"

"It's my turn," he said, pressing a finger to her lips. "My turn to say it. I love you, Mary."

She nodded, laughter mingling with her tears. "I know. Haven't I always known it?"

"Always," he admitted, bringing his arm around her and leading her up the winding path to the bluff. "Let's take our son home."

Epilogue

Washington State
1889

On Sunday, something washed up on shore.

The morning had dawned like all the others—a chill haze with the feeble sun behind it, iron-colored swells gathering muscle far offshore, then hurling themselves against the huddled sharp rocks of Cape Disappointment.

All this young Davy Morgan saw from the catwalk high on the lighthouse, where he had gone to extinguish the sperm-oil lamp and start the daily chore of trimming wicks and cleaning lenses.

And to see, once again, the rainbows that would form in the crystals when the sun broke through the haze. His father had taught him that when he was very small—taught him to see the rainbows.

But it caught him, the sight down on the strand.

He wasn't certain what made him pause, turn, stare. He often gazed at the gray-bearded waves slapping the fine brown sand or exploding against the rocks. He often thought what a wonder it was to live here, where the earth and the sea met.

Amma Palina told him stories of strange creatures and treacherous adventures. Aunt Annabelle liked to read stories, too. She'd even started a lending library in town, and she taught reading and writing to the little ones who lived at Swann House.

Davy believed every one of the legends and tales. Believed with his whole heart. On this day he sensed the tingle *Amma*'s stories always gave him. He felt a disturbance in the air, like the breath of an invisible stranger on the back of his neck. One moment he was getting out his linseed oil and polishing cloths; the next he was standing in the bitter wind. Watching.

He would never quite understand what made him go to the iron rail, hold tight with one hand and lean over the edge to look past the jut of land, beyond the square-jawed cliffs, down onto the storm-swept beach.

A mass of seaweed. Strands of golden-brown kelp shrouding an elongated shape. For all he knew it could be no more than a tangle of weeds or perhaps a dead seal, an old one whose whiskers had whitened and whose teeth had dulled.

As Davy stood staring down at the shape on the beach, he felt...something. A sudden knife-twist of...what?

Inevitability. Destiny, his mother would call it.

Though there was no one about to see him at this early hour, Davy straightened the brim of his cap. It was part of the livery of the Klipsan Beach Rescue Squad, organized by his father the year Davy was born.

Davy rang the fog bell to alert everyone, then clattered down the stairs. He followed the path to the beach, filling his lungs with salt air and watching the sun break through the morning clouds.

He slowed his steps as he approached the heap of seaweed. It was rounded at one end—the shape of a human head. For a moment, his hackles rose, and he felt a shiver of apprehension. The sea was not always kind. In his twelve years of growing up here, he had learned that much.

He edged toward the rank-smelling jumble, touched it with a booted toe. At the same moment, he heard voices. His father's deep boom and his mother's lilting chatter, followed by the bright laughter of Shannon and Malcolm. Monte Cristo, the family dog, barked and ran circles around his family.

Davy sank to his knees and started digging through the heavy weeds. If there was something awful here, he wanted to hide it from his younger sister and brother.

The strands of kelp were spongy and cold to the touch. Clinging thick and stubborn to—

To what?

He encountered a thick web of rope, all woven together. A net of some sort, attached to—

To what?

Working feverishly now, he dug at the rounded head-shape, finding the object hard and cold, wrapped in the rope webbing. He pulled hard, and the rotted hemp fell away to reveal something extraordinary.

It was a perfectly round glass ball. Intrigued, he took it down into the surf, kneeling, barely feeling the chill of the water through his trousers. Using sand and seawater, he washed the slime from the glass until it shone a bright, clear aqua.

His father had once described a Japanese fishing float to Davy, but he'd never actually seen one. The fact that he'd found something so rare and perfect filled him with pride. Grinning, he stood up and turned to greet his family. As they approached, Davy felt a funny surge of thickness in his throat. A surge of love.

They looked so fine to him just then, with the rising sun behind them. Mum looked as pretty as a girl with her laughing eyes and smiling mouth. Little Shannon, running toward Davy on chubby legs, had hair as red as Davy's own. Malcolm, who was tall for his age and much too serious, was the image of Papa, with long dark hair and eyes the color of Davy's favorite bird feather.

And Papa...well, he was just *Papa*. Full of laughter and high-flown ideas and private thoughts he would only share with Mum. Every once in a while, he'd get a faraway look in his eyes, and Davy would sense a sadness in him. But then he would come back to them, laughing, his huge arms reaching out to draw Davy into a hug.

They were reaching now, those brawny arms that had held Davy through nightmares and the croup and a spill from one of the horses. "What did you find there, son?" Papa asked.

Davy's grin grew even wider as he held out the treasure. The morning sun shot brilliant light through the globe of glass.

Mum gasped. "Jesse, look what he's found!"

Papa put his arm around her. For a second, he got that distant look in his eyes. Then he kissed the top of her head and held her close.

"Here, you can hold it," Davy said, handing his father the globe. Davy was ready to turn his attention to Monte Cristo, who was in a frenzy for a game of fetch. As he picked up a piece of driftwood and flung it into the surf for the dog, Davy glanced back at his parents. He had no idea why a glass globe from the sea would make his mother cry, but she was weeping, pressing her face into Papa's chest.

Even so, Davy could see her lips starting to smile, could hear her sobs turning to laughter. It was always that way with them, he thought, picking up another piece of driftwood. They always found some reason for joy. Always.

Afterword

Today it is hard to appreciate the treachery of the Columbia bar as it was in the nineteenth century. Thanks to man-made jetties, the location of the old bar, which caused more than five hundred shipwrecks, can only be identified by slight ripples and channel markers.

The use of horses in sea rescue is based on fact. Prior to the establishment of an organized rescue service, stallions were trained to swim through the breakers, letting shipwreck victims cling to their tails. As many as six people at a time could be hauled to shore in this manner.

The renowned lifesaving crew, fictionalized in this novel, was actually organized by lightkeeper Joel Munson in 1877. The initial lifesaving station at the mouth of the Columbia was erected at Fort Canby in 1878. Their motto was, "You have to go out, but no one says you have to come in."

If you're very lucky and very persistent, you can still find antique glass floats along the storm-swept beaches around Cape Disappointment.

Turn the page for an excerpt from

THE DRIFTER

by

Susan Wiggs

coming in June 1998
only from

One

⌘

Whidbey Island, Washington
1893

"Don't scream, or I'll shoot," warned a low-pitched, masculine voice.

Leah Mundy jerked awake, blinking frantically at the night shadows in her bedroom. She found herself looking down the barrel of a gun.

Sheer panic jolted her to full alert.

"I'm not going to scream," she said, dry-mouthed. Lightning flickered, glancing off the dull blue finish of a Colt's barrel. "Please don't hurt me." Her voice broke but didn't waver. In her line of work, she had learned to control fear.

"Lady, that's up to you. Just do as you're told, and nobody'll get hurt."

Do as you're told. Leah Mundy certainly had practice at *that.* "Who are you," she asked, "and what do you want?"

"Who I am is the man holding this gun. What I want is Dr. Mundy. Sign outside says he lives here."

She squinted into the shadows. Thunder pulsed in the

distance, echoing the thud of her heart. Beyond the gun, she couldn't make out anything but a dark shape. *Oh God oh God oh God*... Waves of terror washed away all clear thought. She heard herself blurt, "Dr. Mundy does live here."

"Well, go get him."

"I can't do that."

"Why not?"

She swallowed, trying to collect her wits, failing miserably. "He's dead. He died three months ago."

"Sign says Dr. Mundy lives here." Fury roughened the insistent voice.

"The sign's right." Rain hissed on the windowpanes. A loud male snore drifted down the hall, and she glanced toward the noise. *Think think think.* Maybe she could alert one of the boarders.

The gun barrel jabbed at her shoulder, and she changed her mind.

"For chrissakes, woman, I don't have time for guessing games—"

"I'm Dr. Mundy."

"What?"

"Dr. Leah Mundy. My father was also a doctor. We were in practice together. But now there's just me."

"Just you."

"Yes."

"And you're a doctor."

"I am."

The large shape shifted impatiently. She caught the scents of rain and brine on him. Rain and brine from the sea and something else...desperation.

"You'll have to do, then. Get your things, woman. You're coming with me."

She jerked the covers up under her chin. "I beg your pardon."

"You'll be begging for your sorry life if you don't g
a move on."

The threat in his voice lashed out like a whip. She didn't
argue. Spending three years with her father back in Dead-
wood, South Dakota had taught her to respect a threat
issued by a man holding a gun.

But she'd never learned to respect the man himself.

"Turn your back while I get dressed," she said.

"That's pretty lame, even for a lady doctor," he muttered. "I'm not fool enough to turn my back."

"A man who bullies unarmed people is always a fool,"
she snapped.

"Funny thing about bullies," he said calmly, using the
nose of the Colt to ease the quilt down her body. "They
pretty much always manage to get what they want. Now,
move."

She yanked off the covers and shoved her feet into the
sturdy boots she wore when making her calls. Island
weather was wet in the springtime, and she'd never been
one to stand on high fashion. Then she wrapped herself in
a robe, tugging the tie snugly around her waist.

She tried to pretend this was an ordinary call on an
ordinary night. Tried not to think about the fact that she
had been jolted out of a sound sleep by a man with a gun.
Damn him. How dare he?

"Are you ill?" she asked the gunman.

"Hell, no, I'm not sick," he said. "It's…for someone
else." Another thing she'd learned about bullies—they almost always acted out of fear.

"I'll need to stop in the surgery, get some things."

"Where's the surgery?"

"Downstairs, adjacent to the kitchen." She pushed open
the door, daring to flash one look down the hall. Mr. Battle
Davis was a light sleeper, but despite his name, he
wouldn't know the first thing to do about an armed in-

...der. Adam Armstrong, the newcomer, probably would, ...ut for all she knew, he could be in league with the gunman. Aunt Leafy would only dissolve into hysterics, and Perpetua had her young son to consider. As for Mr. Jasper Pomfrit, he'd likely grab his ancient rifle and join her abductor.

The gunman jabbed the Colt into her ribs. "Lady, don't go doing anything foolish."

Leah let go of the urge to rouse the household. She couldn't do it. Couldn't put any of them at risk.

"You may call me Dr. Mundy," she said over her shoulder. Her hand slipped down the banister as she made her way to the foyer. The man wore a long, cloaked duster that billowed out as he descended, sprinkling rainwater on the carpet runner.

"You're not a lady?" he whispered, his mouth far too close to her ear. His voice had a curious raw edge to it.

"Not to you."

She led the way along a hall to the dark surgery. In the immaculate suite which occupied the south wing of the house, she lit a lamp. Her hands shook as she fumbled with a match, and her anger renewed itself. As the blue-white flame hissed to life, she turned to study her captor. She noted a fringe of wet hair the color of straw, lean cheeks chapped by the wind and stubbled by a few days' growth of beard. A wide, unsmiling mouth. He pulled down his dripping hat brim before she could see his eyes.

"What sort of ailment will I be treating?" she asked.

"Hell, I don't know. You claim you're the doctor."

Leah told herself she should be hardened to doubt and derision by now. But some things she never got used to. Like someone—even a dangerous man hiding behind a gun—thinking gender had anything at all to do with the ability to heal people.

"What are the symptoms?" she asked.

While he hesitated, she lifted the flap of her brow
leather medical bag, checking the contents. Capped vial.
of feverfew, quinine, digitalis, carbolic acid for cleaning...goose grease to soothe any number of ills. Instruments for extracting teeth and cleaning suppurating
wounds. A clinical thermometer and stethoscope sterilized
in bichloride of mercury, and a hypodermic needle for
injecting medicines into the bloodstream.

"The symptoms?" she prompted.

"I guess...fever. Stomach cramps. Babbling and such.
Wheezing and coughing, too."

"Coughing blood?" Leah asked sharply.

"Nope. No blood."

It could be any number of things, including the dreaded
scourge, diphtheria. Leah tucked in some vials of muriate
of ammonia, then took her oiled canvas slicker from a
hook on the back of the door. "I'm ready," she said.
"And I might add that forcing me at gunpoint isn't necessary. It's my calling to heal people. If you want to put
that away, I'll still come."

He didn't put the gun away. Instead, he pushed the flap
of his duster back to reveal a second gun. The holster—
darkened with grease for quicker drawing—was strapped
to a lean, denim-clad hip. Clearly he was a man unused
to being given what he asked for. He jerked the barrel
toward the back door, motioning her to go ahead of him.

They passed through the waiting room of the surgery
and stepped out into the night. She could feel him behind
her, his height and breadth intimidating, uncompromising.

"Is it far?" she asked, indicating the coach house, a
black hulk in the sodden gloom. "Will we need the
buggy?"

"No," he said. "We're going to the harbor."

A seafaring man, then. A pirate? Whidbey Island saw
its share of pirates plying the waters of Puget Sound and

p into Canada. But this man, with an arsenal of weapons concealed under his long caped coat, had the look of an outlaw, not a pirate.

He was a stranger, yet he needed her. The oath she had taken compelled her to go. What a peculiar life she led. In the back of her mind, her father's voice taunted her: *Leah Jane Mundy, why couldn't you have settled down and married like a normal woman?*

The rain drummed relentlessly on her hood. Her booted foot splashed into a puddle and stuck briefly in the sucking mud. She looked back at the boardinghouse. The tradesman's shingle hanging above the front porch flapped in the wind. In the dark, the white lettering was barely legible, but the stranger had found it: Dr. Mundy, Physician. Rooms to Let.

"Get a move on, woman," the gunman ordered.

The gaslight in the surgery window flickered. There was nothing beyond the lampglow but blackness. No one in sight but the stranger holding the gun on her, pushing it into her back to make her hurry.

Just who the devil was this man?

Rising Star, Texas
1893

"He called himself Jack Tower," said the sheriff, taking off a pair of ill-fitting spectacles. "'Course, there's a good possibility it's an alias."

"Uh-huh." Joel Santana stroked his hand down his cheek, the skin like shoe leather beneath his callused palm. Damn. He'd been looking forward to hanging up his gun belt and spurs, and now this. Many was the evening he'd spent thinking about a parcel of green land, maybe a flock of sheep, and a good woman with broad hips and a broader smile....

He crossed one aching leg over the other and absently whirled a spur with his finger. "And you say the fugitive took off six weeks ago?"

Sheriff Reams laid his spectacles atop the hand-drawn map on the desk. "Six weeks Saturday."

"Why'd you wait to call me in?" Joel held up a hand. "Never mind, I know the answer. You and your deputies had the situation under control. This is the first time your posse ever let one get away, am I right?"

"As a matter of fact, Marshal Santana, it's true."

"Uh-huh." It always was. They always waited until a criminal had hightailed it across state lines and the trail had grown cold; then they called in a U.S. marshal. "I guess we'd better get down to it, then. You say this man—this Jack Tower—murdered the mayor of Rising Star."

"That's right."

"And did he?"

Reams narrowed his eyes. "Damn right he did. Probably wasn't the first. He had a hard look about him. A mean look, like he didn't have a friend in the world and didn't care to make any. You need to bring that boy back and hang him high."

"Hanging folks is not my job, Sheriff." Joel lumbered to his feet, fancying he could hear his joints creak in protest. Too many years on horseback had ruined his knees.

"What in blazes do you mean?"

Joel pressed his palms flat on the desk and glared at the map. The shape of Texas formed a mutated star, its panhandle borders so artificial—yet so critical when it came to enforcing the law. "I bring in fugitives, and I'll bring in this Tower fellow. But his guilt or innocence isn't up to us. It's up to a judge and jury. Don't you forget that."

"I won't."

But he would have, Santana knew. Likely if Jack Tower

...adn't fled, he'd have been strung up on a high limb and left for the buzzards to fight over.

"So what've you got?"

The sheriff lifted the map, revealing an ink-drawn illustration of a man with cropped, spiky hair, a beard and mustache. The drawing had indeed captured the mean look.

"This here's your man. He didn't leave much behind. Just a tin of Underhill Fancy Shred Tobacco and half of a broken shirt button." Reams handed them over.

"Oh—" Reams laid a tintype photograph in front of Joel "—and this here's the woman he fled with. Her name's Caroline. Caroline Willis."

"She's my...wife."

Leah heard a heartbeat of hesitation in her abductor's grainy voice before the word *wife*. It wasn't her place to question, but to heal.

Still, she couldn't help wondering why the simple statement hadn't come easily to the stranger's lips. It had been Leah's unfortunate lot to attend the deaths of more than a few women while the husband stood nearby, wringing his hands. There weren't many things more wrenching than the sight of a man who knew he was about to lose his wife. He always looked baffled, numb, helpless.

She glanced over her shoulder at the gunman. Even in the uncertain light of a ship's binnacle lamp, he didn't appear helpless. Not in the least. At the harbor, he'd forced her into a dinghy. With the gun in his lap and his fists curled around the oars, he had rowed like a madman. It took him only moments to bring her out to a long schooner moored about a quarter mile offshore.

She'd shivered and climbed the rest of the way down the ladder, into the belly of the boat.

It was the leakiest, most unseaworthy schooner she had

ever seen. The twin masts creaked in the whipping wind, threatening to break off at any moment. The smell of damp rope, mildewed sailcloth and rotting timber pervaded the air of the once-grand aft stateroom.

The mainmast was footed right in the middle of the stateroom. Its stepping, where it was fastened to the floor, looked as if it would crumble. The wooden column was anchored in place with old rope rather than trenails, as if someone had repaired it in haste.

The stranger's wife lay in a recessed alcove bunk on freshly laundered muslin sheets, her head centered on a plump goose-down pillow, her eyes closed and her face pale. Suddenly Leah no longer saw the boat or the faded opulence of the stateroom. All her fear and anger fled. She focused her attention on the patient. Without looking at the man, she motioned for him to bring a lamp. She heard the rasp of a Lucifer and a sibilant hiss as he lit one and brought it forward.

"Hold it steady," she commanded. "What's her name?"

Another hesitation. Then, "Carrie," came the gruff reply.

Observation. It was the most basic tenet of healing. *First, do no harm.* Generations of doctors had violated that, poking and leeching and bleeding and cupping until a patient either died or got better out of sheer exasperation. Thank heaven it was more common practice these days for well-trained doctors to stand back, to observe and ask questions.

And so she observed. The woman called Carrie appeared almost childlike in repose. The dainty bones in her face and hands pushed starkly against translucent flesh. Nordic blond hair formed a halo around her small face. Her dry lips were tucked together in a thin line. Frail, defenseless and startlingly beautiful, she slept without seeming even to breathe.

And she looked as if she was on the verge of dying.

Leah unbuckled her slicker, shrugged it off and held it out behind her. When the stranger didn't take it immediately, she gave the garment a slight shake. It was plucked from her hand grudgingly, she thought. She refused to let her attention stray from the patient.

"Carrie?" she said softly. "My name is Dr. Mundy. I've come to help you."

No response.

Leah pressed the back of her hand to Carrie's cheek. Fever, but not enough of a temperature to raise a flush on the too-pale skin. She would have no need for the clinical thermometer.

Gently, Leah lifted one eyelid. The iris glinted a lovely shade of blue, vivid as painted china. The pupil contracted properly when the lamplight struck it.

"Carrie?" Leah said her name again while stroking a thin hand. "Can you hear me?"

Again, no response. The skin felt dry, lacking resilience. A sign of dehydration.

"When was she last awake?" Leah asked the man.

"Not sure. Maybe this afternoon. She was out of her head, though. Didn't make a lick of sense." The shadow shifted as he leaned closer. "What is it? Will she be all right?"

Tension thrummed in his voice.

"I'll do my best to figure out what's wrong with her. When did she last have something to eat or drink?"

"Gave her some tea with honey this morning. She heaved it up, wouldn't take anything else. Except—" He broke off, drew in a breath.

"Except what?"

"She asked for her tonic. She needs her tonic."

Leah groped in her bag for the stethoscope. "What sort of tonic would that be?"

"Some elixir in a bottle."

Elixir. Snake oil, most likely. It had been her father's stock-in-trade for years. Leah herself was not that sort of doctor. She found her stethoscope. "I'll want to analyze that tonic."

She adjusted the ear tips and looped the binaurals around her neck. Working quickly, she parted Carrie's nightgown at the neckline. Again, she was struck by the freshly laundered cleanliness of the garment and bed-clothes. It seemed incongruous for an outlaw's lady. A gunman who did laundry?

Pressing the flat of the diaphragm to Carrie's chest, Leah held her breath and listened. The heart rate was ele-vated. The lungs sounded only slightly congested. Leah moved the chest piece here and there, listening intently to each quadrant. It was difficult to hear. Storm-driven waves slapped at the ship's hull, and a constant flow of water trickled somewhere below.

She palpated the areas around the neck and armpits, seeking signs of infection. Then she moved her hands down the abdomen, stopping when she felt a small, telltale hardness.

"Well?" the stranger said. "What's wrong?"

Leah removed the ear tips of the stethoscope, letting the instrument drape like a necklace. "When were you plan-ning to tell me?" she demanded.

"Tell you what?" He spread his arms, looking genu-inely baffled. It was probably all an act, though, Leah thought.

"That your wife is pregnant."

His jaw dropped. He seemed to deflate a little, sagging against the wall of the hull. "Pregnant."

Leah tilted her head to one side. "Surely you knew."

"I..." He drew his hand down his face. "Nope. Didn't know."

"I estimate that she's a good three months along."

"Three months."

Ordinarily Leah loved to be the bearer of this sort of news. She always got a vicarious thrill from the joy and wonder in a young husband's eyes. Such moments made her own life seem less sterile and lonely—if only for a while.

She stared at the stranger and saw no joy or wonder in him. His face had turned stony and grim. He certainly didn't act like a man who had just learned he was going to be a father.

"So that's the only thing wrong with her," he said at last.

"It's not 'wrong' for your wife to be pregnant."

For a moment he looked as if he might contradict her. "I meant, so that's the only thing ailing her."

"Hardly."

"What?" he asked harshly. "What's wrong?"

"What's wrong is that your boat is on the verge of sinking." She glanced pointedly at the loose, creaking base of the mast. The worm-eaten wood thrust up through the deck. The strain of movement had made big gaps in the caulking where the rain seeped through and ran down the length of the mast. The ropes holding the post in place strained with a whining sound.

"This is no place for a patient. We've got to move her." Leah coiled the stethoscope and tucked it back into her bag. "As soon as it stops raining, bring her to the house and we'll put her to bed—"

"I guess you didn't understand," the man said in an infuriating drawl.

She scowled at him. "Understand what?"

He stuck his thumb in his gunbelt and drummed his

fingers on the row of bullets stuck in the leather loops. "You're coming with us."

A chill seized her, though she took care to hide her alarm. So that was why he'd abducted her at gunpoint. This outlaw meant to pluck her right out of her own life and thrust her into his. "Just like that," she said coldly, "without even a by-your-leave?"

"I never ask leave to do anything. Remember that."

By the time Leah had finished neatening her bag, she had worked herself into a fine fury.

With a quick movement that had him going for his gun, she shot to her feet. The old boat creaked ominously.

"No, *you* don't understand, sir," Leah said. "I have no intention of going anywhere with you, especially on this leaky hulk. I'll treat your wife after you bring her to the boardinghouse where she can enjoy a proper recovery."

Leah tried not to flinch as he trained the gun on her.

"She'll recover just fine right here, with you tending her," he said.

Leah glared at the too-familiar blued barrel, the callused finger curling intimately around the trigger. "Don't think for a minute that you can intimidate me. I won't allow it. I absolutely won't. Is that clear?"

His lazy gaze strayed over her and focused on her hands, clutching the bag in white-knuckled terror. "Clear as a day in Denver, ma'am."

She hated the mocking edge in his voice. "Sir, if you hope to give your wife a decent chance to heal, you'll let me go, and after the rain you'll bring her to the house where I can treat her."

"You call yourself a doctor, so how come you can only doctor people in your fancy house?"

Fancy? She almost laughed bitterly at that. Where had he been living that he'd consider the boardinghouse fancy?

"I refuse to debate this with you," she informed him.

"Fine. I'm not fond of debating, either."

"Good. Then—"

"Just get busy with Carrie and I'll be in the cockpit, making ready to weigh anchor."

Red fury swam before her eyes, obliterating everything, even the hated gun barrel. "You will not," she said. Her voice was low, controlled, yet he seemed to respond to her quiet rage. He frowned slightly, his hand relaxed on the gun and he regarded her with mild surprise.

"Lady, for someone at the wrong end of a gun, you sure have a mouth on you."

"Sir," Leah went on, "you cannot simply pluck me from my home and sweep me away with you."

She leaned against the mast stepping for support. Her gaze followed the fraying rope across the heading of the room; the line exited through a portal and was tied somewhere above.

"Don't lean on that," the outlaw ordered. "It could bring the aft mast down."

He stepped forward, and for the first time, she got a good look at his eyes. They were a cold blue-gray, the color of his gun barrel, and his gaze was piercing, as if he saw more of her than she cared for him to see. Leah experienced an odd sensation—like fate tumbling them along, throwing them together with an inevitability she didn't understand.

No. She would not surrender to this man.

"That is precisely why you cannot force me to come with you," she stated, moving away from the mast stepping. "This ship is unseaworthy. Honestly, what sort of sailor are you, to be out in this tub of—"

"Shut up." In one long-legged stride, he came to her and pressed the chilly round eye of the gun to her temple. "Just...shut up. Look, after Carrie's better, we'll put you on a ship back to the island." He added under his breath, "And good riddance."

The touch of the gun horrified her, but she refused to show it. "I will not go with you," she stated. Clearly this man had no appreciation for how determined she could be. He'd never outlast her. "I have too many responsibilities in Coupeville. Two of my patients are expecting babies any day. I'm treating a boy who was kicked in the head by a horse. I can't possibly come along on a whim as your wife's private physician."

"Right." He removed the barrel from her temple.

She brightened and took a step toward the door. "I'm glad you decided to see reas—"

"Yeah. Reason. I know." He gave her shoulder a shove, thrusting her back into the room. "Now, get busy, woman, or I'll make sure you don't *ever* see your patients again."

He stepped out into the companionway. Leah heard a bolt being thrust home as he locked her in the stateroom with his wife.

From the cockpit of the creaking schooner, Jackson T. Underhill looked up at the sky. A white gash of lightning cleaved the darkness into eerie shards. The thunder roaring in its wake shouted a warning from the very throat of heaven. It was crazy to be out in this weather, crazy to sail in night so deep he could barely get a heading.

But Jackson had never been much for heeding warnings, heavenly or otherwise. He jammed his pistol back into its greased holster, fastened the clips of his duster and cowled when the wind tore at the backside of the coat, separating the flaps. The garment was made for riding astride a horse, not sailing a ship. But everything had happened in such a hurry, everything had changed so quickly, that the last thing on his mind had been fashion.

Bracing himself against the wind, he cranked in the anchor. As he lofted the mainsail, the mildewed canvas luffing in protest, he heard indignant thumps and muffled shouts from the stateroom below.

Add kidnapping to his list of crimes. That, at least, was a first for him.

Yet when a healthy puff of wind filled the sails, he felt a measure of relief. The unplanned stop at Whidbey Island hadn't been so costly, after all. He had a doctor for Carrie, and no one was the wiser. The doctor wasn't at all what he'd expected, but he'd have to put up with her.

A lady doctor. Who would have thought it? He'd never even known such a thing could be possible.

Leah Mundy was a prickly female, all pinch-faced and lemon-lipped with disapproval, and there wasn't a thing to like about her.

But Jackson did like her. He'd never admit it, of course, and would never find occasion to, but he admired her spirit. Instead of getting all womanish and hysterical when he'd come for her, she'd taken it like a man—better than most men he knew.

He felt a twinge of guilt when he thought of the patient she wouldn't see tomorrow, or the next day, perhaps even the day after that. But he needed her. God, Carrie needed her.

Pregnant. Carrie was pregnant. The thought seethed inside Jackson, too enormous for him to grasp right now, so he thrust it aside, tried to forget.

Dr. Mundy would help Carrie. She would heal Carrie. She had to.

Jackson pictured her bending over to examine her patient. That's when the doctor had changed, shed her ornery mantle. He'd seen something special in her manner—a sort of gentle competence that inspired faith in him.

It had been a long time since Jackson T. Underhill had put his faith in anyone.

Yet Dr. Leah Mundy inspired it. Did she know that? Did she know he was already thinking of her as an angel of mercy?

He'd thank her, maybe even apologize as soon as they got under way. It was the least he could do for a woman he'd ripped from a warm, dry bed and dragged along on an adventure not of her choosing. The least he could do for a woman he intended to take to Canada, then abandon.

He'd barely gotten moving when he heard a strange *thunk*, then an ominous grinding sound. The whine of a rope through a wooden pulley seared his ears. With a sick lurch of his gut, he glanced up to see the topmast swaying against the dark sky.

He let go of the helmsman's wheel and dived for the rope. It disappeared, snakelike, through a porthole in the hull a split second before he reached it.

"Shit!" Jackson said, then held his breath. Maybe the mast would stay put. Maybe—

A terrible wrenching sound shattered the night. Like a giant tree, the aft mast came crashing down, barely missing Jackson as he flattened himself into the gully of the cockpit.

His curses roared with the thunder. Dr. Leah Mundy, his angel of mercy, his divine savior, had just brought down the mast of his ship.

Take 3 of "The Best of the Best™" Novels FREE

Plus get a FREE surprise gift!

Special Limited-time Offer

Mail to The Best of the Best™

3010 Walden Avenue
P.O. Box 1867
Buffalo, N.Y. 14240-1867

YES! Please send me 3 free novels and my free surprise gift. Then send me 3 of "The Best of the Best™" novels each month. I'll receive the best books by the world's hottest romance authors. Bill me at the low price of $3.99 each plus 25¢ delivery per book and applicable sales tax, if any.* That's the complete price and a savings of over 20% off the cover prices—quite a bargain! I understand that accepting the books and gift places me under no obligation ever to buy any books. I can always return a shipment and cancel at any time. Even if I never buy another book, the 3 free books and the surprise gift are mine to keep forever.

183 BPA A4V9

Name	(PLEASE PRINT)	
Address	Apt. No.	
City	State	Zip

This offer is limited to one order per household and not valid to current subscribers.
*Terms and prices are subject to change without notice. Sales tax applicable in N.Y. All orders subject to approval.

UB08-197

©1996 MIRA BOOK

The SECRETS WITHIN

The most unforgettable Australian saga since
Colleen McCullough's *The Thorn Birds*

Eleanor—with invincible strength and ruthless
determination she built Australia's Hunter Valley
vineyards into an empire.

Tamara—the unloved child of ambition, a catalyst
in a plan to destroy her own mother.

Rory—driven by shattered illusions and desires, he
becomes a willing conspirator.

Louise—married to Rory, she will bargain with the
devil for a chance at ultimate power.

Irene—dark and deadly, she turns fanatical dreams
into reality.

Now Eleanor is dying, and in one final, vengeful
act she wages a war on a battlefield she created—
and with a family she was driven to control....

EMMA DARCY

Available in October 1997 at your
favorite retail outlet.

She was innocent…of everything but love

PRESUMED GUILTY

Someone was sleeping in Miranda Wood's bed. But he wasn't really sleeping—he was dead. There was no one who would believe she hadn't murdered her former lover, least of all the dead man's brother. But Chase Tremain couldn't help but fall for her—even when it was clear that someone wanted to keep them apart…forever.

TESS GERRITSEN

Available October 1997 at your favorite retail outlet.

Indiscreet

Camilla Ferrand wants everyone, especially her dying grandfather, to stop worrying about her. So she tells them that she is engaged to be married. But with no future husband in sight, it's going to be difficult to keep up the pretense. Then she meets the very handsome and mysterious Benedict Ellsworth who generously offers to accompany Camilla to her family's estate—as her most devoted fiancé.

But at what cost does this *generosity* come?

From the bestselling author of *Impulse*

CANDACE CAMP

Available in November 1997
at your favorite retail outlet.

"Candace Camp also writes for Silhouette® as Kristen James